# Payton
# Hidden Away

Jonathan Korbecki

Published 2016 by Jonathan Korbecki

Inquiries should be directed to https://www.facebook.com/jonathan.korbecki

ISBN-13: 978-0692678107

For everyone who believed I could.
Dedicated to everyone else.

# Payton
# Hidden Away

## *Atlanta, Georgia. This morning.*

They say you never forget your first love, but sayings like that are born of convenience. Clichés and puns and motivational blurbs on Facebook walls are timely and thoughtful and funny for a day. They might earn a number of 'likes' and result in a few Retweets, but they fall apart when needed most the way memories fail with inconvenient precision.

"Kristine Lambert," she repeats. "Kristie."

The name sounds familiar, like finding something lost years ago but was never missed until accidently stumbled across while looking for something else. Mentally, I start spinning through my rolodex, my contact list, my clients, colleagues and co-workers while trying to match a face with the name. I'm an accountant because I remember patterns in numbers, yet I'm struggling to conjure up a clear memory of who she is even though on some level I remember loving her the way every teenage boy loves a teenage girl.

Kristine Lambert. My high school sweetheart. My first love. The one I swore I'd never forget. I hear her voice over the tiny speaker of my iPhone, and I can place it in context with her name, but it's been so long that I can't remember her face.

"How did you get this number?" I ask.

There's a long pause. Long enough to make me wonder whether or not there's anyone on the other end. I even consider hanging up except I can still hear something. Breathing maybe. And the longer I listen, the more uncomfortable I feel, squirming in my chair, fidgeting nervously. Memories lurk at the fringes, coming back in fragments. A smile. A wink. The sound of a laugh. A taste of her raspberry drink on my tongue.

"Tony," she whispers. "I need your help."

"Today's not a good day," I say quickly." I've got vendors coming in next week, and I've got wall-to-wall meetings that I haven't even started preparing for. It's a—"

"I can't do this on my own," she interrupts. "These last few days have been…" She pauses. "I found something."

"You found something? How did you find this number?"

"Tony…"

"It's been what, eighteen, nineteen years, and suddenly you call me out of the blue to say you need my help? I can't just drop everything."

"I don't think she just disappeared," Kristie says. "And I think I have proof."

This is not the way I wanted to start my day. Whatever happened and whoever I was back then isn't me now. I'm just a guy in his late thirties who looks like a guy in his early forties. Through premeditated acts of introversion, I've managed to blend in with the rest of those carefully perched at the center of society's bell curve. I have an office, a desk, a brass nameplate, a plastic cactus and a window seat overlooking our inglorious parking lot, but nobody seated on either side of these paper-thin walls knows who I am or what I do.

"What are you talking about?" I ask. "Proof of what?"

"Tony," she says, and this time there's a crack in her voice. "I think she was murdered."

# One

After hanging up, I sit behind my Herman Miller desk in my Haworth chair for several minutes. I'm trying to remember what happened more than half my life ago, and I'm finding that it actually hurts to drag out what I'd intentionally put away. It took years to forget my past, and I was so successful in doing so that I'm not sure I could find the house I grew up in even if I went looking for it. I don't remember the street number. I don't even remember the street name. All I have is a vague recollection that my leaving Payton County had something to do with the disappearance of...someone.

I stare at the clock on my desk. It's one of those novelty items you earn as a reward for ten years of servitude. It's got a brass plate with brass hands set floating in a clear glass blob, and it's telling me I've been sitting in silence for nearly fifteen minutes. Frustrated, I take a swipe at the clock, miss badly and manage to push a stack of papers from my desk instead.

Papers go fluttering.

Burying my face in my hands, I draw a breath, careful to fill my lungs, careful to exhale slowly. Opening my eyes, I look around the empty office. It looks ridiculous with the plastic cactus in the corner and my window seat overlooking our inglorious parking lot.

*I need you.*

I turned my back on her all those years ago, so it should be that much easier to look away again now. Whoever Kristie has become is not the girl I left behind, so any emotional attachment we ever had is long gone. I don't owe her anything, and even if I did, I don't remember what. Yet there *is* a sense of guilt. Whatever it was that happened must have been bad. Really bad.

I close my eyes to think, clamping my jaw shut, trying to rewind two decades while attempting to remember something—anything—that would clue me in as to why I would have—

And then it happens.

A flash. It's so brief that had I not been concentrating, I would have missed it altogether, but at the back of my subconscious, behind a lifetime of snapshots that include a fatherless childhood, a mismatched wedding, a miscarriage and a divorce, there's a shadow in the corner of my memory banks, and in that corner I see a smiling face. A big, dumb smiling face with one tooth cracked in half. It's the face of a man-child, a little boy trapped in a man's body, and though that big smile covers the landscape of his flushed cheeks, his eyes are dull, almost as if he sees nothing.

Then it's gone.

My eyes flutter open, jarring me back to reality and my empty office with papers scattered on the floor, the sound of a car alarm drifting in from outside and a phone ringing from the other side of the thin walls.

I don't remember a lot about what happened or who was involved, but I remember that face, I remember that smile, and I remember being afraid. I also remember my best friend, and Kristie, and that summer—that magical, beautiful, horrible summer. I know I left for the wrong reasons, and I know there was something I could have done or something I *should* have done, but I don't remember what. None of it adds up to a complete memory, but it does reaffirm one thought, and that is that I need to go home.

Logging off the PC, I pack a few things, fitting them into my laptop bag. I restack the papers on my desk, put away the pens and pencils, turn out the desk lamp and stand. I take one last look around to see if I've left anything before—

"Going somewhere?" Phil asks. Phillip Beltran. My boss.

"Yes," I murmur while slipping my laptop into the bag. I zip it shut before wrapping it over my shoulder.

Phillip is blocking my exit, his impressive business paunch hanging over his belt and causing the buttons on his neatly pressed navy blue shirt to stretch to their limit. "Going where?"

"I don't have time to explain," I answer. "I need a hiatus. A few days."

"A few days? You can't take a few days. A few days is competitive suicide in our business. I need you here. Next week's critical, and we have a lot of prep work between now and then."

"I should be back by then."

Phillip remains rooted in the doorway. "What's this about?"

"It's personal." I pause knowing an explanation so vague won't be enough. Sighing, I lean against the desk while trying to figure out the best way to summarize something I barely remember into a single sentence. "Look, I just got a call from a childhood friend. Someone died that we both knew, and she asked me to come home."

"Home?"

"Where I grew up."

Phillip shrugs. "I thought you said you grew up here?"

"I went to school here. I'll call you from the road."

"You're driving?"

"Flying." I grab my bag and brush past him. "It's a figure of speech, Phil."

"Are you okay?"

"I'm fine." I'm not, but I pretend that I am. If I were actually okay, I'd be filling a glass halfway full all the way to the brim, I'd be demonstrating moral fiber in the

8

context of core values, and I'd be talking a lot of bullshit. Lying isn't easy, and I know this because nobody gets good at anything without years of practice.

"Tony…"

"I'll see you on Monday," I say, punching the down arrow. I'm trembling as I wait for the elevator. One floor after another, the numbers light up. I can hear the gears grinding, the pulleys squeaking, and the elevator car climbing. Eventually, the doors will open, and then?

And then this is where we'll start, picking up where we left off two decades earlier when I fled town. Memories in fragments, conveniently imprecise, mashed together as expressionless faces in a blurred class photo. But there's also that stupid smile and that cracked front tooth, there's Kristie sobbing while looking at me with hatred in her eyes, and there's someone else who looks just like her hiding in a place I swore I'd never go. The bell goes 'ding,' the elevator doors open and then.

## Part II

When I woke up this morning, things were good. Not great. There's always room for something better, but I felt moderately optimistic right up until she called. At 10:21, I was Tony Abbott, master of my own universe. I had a good job, a decent apartment, a mediocre outlook and a relatively okay life. Now, at 10:52, everything I've made myself into has been undone.

The sun makes me squint as I step from the revolving doors. The over-ambitious entrance to InteGREAT Inc. boasts a waterfall and a brick walkway lined with greenery leading right up to its front door. It's like a stranger luring a kid with candy. InteGREAT Inc. is the windowless van parked near the school, Phillip Beltran is the suspicious looking guy selling ice cream at recess, and I'm the sucker lured by the promise of the great American dream.

I make my way across the lot, but my car isn't where I remember parking it just two hours ago. Baffled, I look around, but all the cars look the same. Same color, similar make and a style like any other. I have to hold my key ring over my head and walk around like an idiot while repeatedly pushing the panic button until the lights of my Camry finally light up. It's not until I close the door and shut out the sounds to lock in the silence that I allow myself a moment to acknowledge even a hint of the fear I'm feeling.

It's real. It's happening. I'm going back.

I start the engine, back out of the parking space, pull forward and drive toward the exit. Robotically, I stop and look both ways. There's no traffic, but I feel compelled to wait a moment anyway just to see what's coming around the next corner. I'm an accountant because I remember patterns in numbers, yet for some reason I'm thinking in fractions that don't add up, like a hanging chad—something of a misnomer that I can't seem to get out of my head. I don't even remember what it means. I keep coming back to the number 44, and I can't figure why, but something tells me it has something to do with the fourth row, fourth seat in some little baseball park hidden away in the armpit of America.

## *Part III*

My apartment doesn't feel quite like my home anymore. All of my things are in their proper places, but they don't feel like mine either. It feels like an exhibit with a chain barrier and one of those signs reading '*Do not touch.*' I bought each stick of furniture, each book and each framed picture as a means to define myself as an individual, but now as I look around, nothing I own seems to reflect who I am. I feel like an intruder in another man's life, poking through dresser drawers, closets and medicine cabinets as I pack my suitcase. Opening the blinds, sunlight streams in, revealing a space that feels packaged for someone else.

I step out onto the balcony. The sounds of the city hang like a cloud just below me. Honking horns of all shapes and sizes, faint laughter, faint shouting, people spilling into the streets like dominoes. Smells of diesel, asphalt and hamburgers. I can't remember why I moved to Atlanta in the first place. All I know now is that I don't belong here, though I don't know that I belong there either. I feel like an orphan stranded somewhere in between.

*Tony, I think she was murdered.*

I haven't talked to Kristie since I left home. I haven't even thought about her. Well, maybe in the beginning, but just like any friends you move away from, those thoughts become less frequent until they're no longer thoughts. They're black and white prints from a life left behind. I remember her being pretty, but at that age, all girls are pretty. We were just kids messing around, jacked up on teenage hormones. Who really knows anything at that age?

There are other memories too. Things like an ice cream stand, a rusty bike, a hammock, Payton Hill—that place teenagers go to make out. And things like that big, goofy smile boasting a row of chocolate-stained teeth, one of which was cracked in half during a fight while defending—

*Yo, Triple A…*

I smile without meaning to. Triple A. I'd forgotten my own nickname, and I'd forgotten who'd given it to me. Ritchie took shortcuts, and since baseball was his whole world, and since my first, middle and last name all started with 'A,' and since he didn't like multi-syllable words, Anthony Alexander Abbott became Triple A. Together, we owned that town. We would—

Ritchie.

Ritchie Hudson.

My best friend.

I'd forgotten all about him. Him and his ways. Him and his transient little world where the term 'couth' did not apply. Nor did manners. He couldn't understand the meaning of either any more than he could discriminate between the two. He was just a big oaf, rudely stumbling his way through life, as innocent as the bug that smacks the windshield and splatters, the wipers smearing its remains.

*Yo, Triple A,* the distant call repeats from the back of my mind, this time with more urgency. I lean over the railing, looking down. The city is down there; millions of people, millions of cars, millions of miles of pavement, but when I look up, I don't see anything that resembles the city life I've become adjusted to. There's only a grassy slope held upright by trees swaying gently in the breeze, and there's a chubby kid trudging up the hill toward me, that big, dumb smile on his face. "What you doin'?" he asks.

"What?" I ask, unaware that I've spoken aloud.

"I gotta show you somethin'."

"It can wait."

Ritchie eyes me a moment before shaking his head. "Not really. You'll wanna see this."

"It can wait."

Ritchie narrows his eyes. "Look, there's something I *gotta* show you. It's *important.*" He slaps me on the arm. "Let's go."

I blink my eyes, the general sounds of the city drifting up at me. There is no hill, no trees, no grass. There's just another gray building like mine not fifty feet away, an old man across the way leaning against his railing while smoking a cigarette and staring at me.

"I'm going," I whisper, turning my back and returning to my apartment to finish packing. I'm tossing in all kinds of crap. Underwear, socks, jeans, shirts, shampoo, shaving cream, toothbrush, toothpaste, mouthwash, deodorant and all the things I don't really need but I have enough room for. I even pack Viagra. It's past its expiration date, which reminds me of how long it's been since I was last laid, but it's also the only medicine I have in my medicine cabinet. I don't even have aspirin, a thought that reaffirms my own judgmental perception of where I stand amidst society's reliance upon pharmaceutical propaganda.

My hands are trembling as I zip the suitcase shut, and it's a sad commentary that my entire life apparently fits somewhat comfortably into a single suitcase. Standing in the open doorway with the lights out, my shadow stretches into the lonely apartment, though it's not like I'm feeling nostalgic. I haven't been happy here since I moved in, but now that I'm leaving, all those 'things' I spent so much time picking out—the couch, the recliner, the TV, the bookcase, the end table—they all look like an argument intended to keep me from changing my mind.

Locking the door behind me, I push the keys into my pocket, grab my rolling suitcase by the plastic handle and make my way along the hall to the elevator.

11

## Part IV

I hate airports.

The long lines, the uncomfortable seats, the vending machines, the food wrapped in plastic, the impatient people, the prices, the magazines, the carpeting, the escalators and the robotic voice coming from the ceiling asking me over and over for my attention please.

I hate flying.

The seats that smell like a smoldering vacuum cleaner, the upright tray tables, the seatbacks, the air vents recycling stuffy air, the SkyMall magazines, the in-flight passenger announcements, the feeling like I'm going to puke the moment the wheels leave the tarmac, the little bastard sitting behind me, the gorgeous flight attendant that waits on the couple one seat ahead of me and the male flight attendant who asks if I'd prefer soda or juice.

I hate rental cars.

The pretentious smile at the front desk, the paperwork that comes folded in a glossy pocketbook with a picture of a family laughing on the front, and my bill tucked inside, the new car smell that's been baking all day under the hot sun, the controls for the windshield wipers and blinkers which are on the wrong side of the steering wheel, the radio and all of it's digital choices, the air conditioning and it's—

Actually, the car is pretty nice. I'm just grumpy.

## Part V

Kristine Lambert. She had a middle name, but I'll be damned if I remember what it is. I probably wouldn't have remembered her *last* name if she hadn't told me. It's odd, but the harder I try to remember my past, the fuzzier it all feels. I've heard of things like memory repression and amnesia, but I never really believed in it. Not until now.

It's eighty miles from the airport to Payton County—an hour and some change by car—so I have plenty of time to get frustrated while trying to remember the inconsequential details of my childhood. It's still hard to wrap my head around the idea that just this morning I woke up in Atlanta, and only a few hours later I'm in Michigan driving toward a place I call 'home.' It doesn't sound like home, but maybe that's okay. Atlanta doesn't feel like home either.

"Kristine Lambert," I say aloud. "Kristine Lambert. Kristie."

She's a skeleton in my closet. Kind of like my ex-wife. They're both chapters in my life that have ended. The difference between the two is I don't remember why I left Kristie. I remember with great clarity the reasons why I left my marriage. I remember how Heather and I fought, I remember how nothing I did was what ever good enough, I remember how our inability to conceive was my fault, how the miscarriage was also somehow my fault, and I remember feeling free the day our divorce was finalized.

Thump-thump, thump-thump.

One thing I *do* remember is Michigan highways. Cracks in the pavement beneath the tires will sing you to sleep until potholes jar you awake again. The slogan "Pure Michigan" does not apply to its roads.

Thump-thump, thump-thump.

The radio offers no relief. There's nothing but country or Christian music out here. I try scanning the dial but find nothing to my liking, so I switch the radio off and return my concentration to the road that seems to stretch into forever.

Exit 110 is coming up fast. I'm exhausted, and I almost disregard the sign entirely when something at the back of my mind triggers a memory. None of the landscape looks familiar, but there's something about that sign...

*Exit 110*
*Route 89*
*1/4 Mile*

Route 89 was the fastest way out of town, and since every kid fantasized about leaving, we looked at the two-lane highway stretching into oblivion like the Yellow Brick Road. We said Route 89 led all the way to the edge of the Earth and beyond, and it must have, because anyone who took Route 89 never came back.

That means I'm close.

Yanking the wheel, I swerve off the interstate and follow the exit inland, merging onto a two-lane highway that feels hidden from the rest of the world. The trees get taller, hovering overhead like cheerleaders waving pompons as they welcome me onto the playing field. The hairs on my arms stand up. Without even checking my odometer, I instinctively know I'm only five miles from town. It looks familiar. I don't think I would have remembered it had I not seen it, but now that I'm here, it all looks vaguely familiar. I can't remember things as explicit as street names, but still, these markers...these trees...that house...

I crank my neck as I pass an old farmhouse on my left. It's battered and neglected, having been abandoned for decades, yet it's still standing. So is the barn. I remember that place. The old Johnson farm—Payton's last outpost. I hung out there a hundred times as a kid. They say it's haunted, and I smile as I zip past, crest a tall hill and head into town. As I draw closer, I recognize the landmarks right down to the trailer park on my right. The trailers are exactly the same, just a bit worse for wear.

A sign on my left reads *Payton County Welcomes You*, but I don't feel all that welcome. People will see me. They'll either recognize me or they won't. Either way,

13

they'll stare. This isn't exactly a town designed for tourism. There's only one hotel, and the 'vacancy' sign is always lit.

5:48 p.m.

There's my elementary school on the left, and there's Jimmy Taylor's house where we lit a firecracker and accidently burned the garage down. They still haven't rebuilt, and the old charred ruins are overgrown with weeds.

There's Janet's house. Janet something or other. The house is in desperate need of paint or siding, but it looks like somebody still lives there. I wonder it's her parents or someone else—maybe even Janet. We were eleven when she flashed me. She hadn't fully developed yet, but boobs are boobs even to an eleven year old kid. She wouldn't let Ritchie near her no matter how much he begged, but she asked me if I'd like to touch them. They didn't feel like I'd imagined after years of silently rubbing one out from within the sanctity of my bedroom where I kept the door closed and my eyes shut while my mom watched TV from the other side of the wall.

And there's John Fisher's house. He was only nineteen when he got hit by a drunk driver and killed. We were only nine, so nineteen seemed like a lifetime away. All that changed when I saw the skid-marks and the blood on the road. I watched with gaping wonder while they took photographs, a tennis shoe still connected to a foot sticking out from under the tarp.

On the other side of the street is Old Man Jacob's house. The sailboat he half-buried as some kind of weird lawn ornament is still there too. Nobody really understood why he did it, but then again, no one really understood Old Man Jacob either. There isn't a lake within fifty miles of Payton, so why he owned a sailboat to begin with seemed to baffle everyone. Ritchie had sex with Jill White inside that boat while Mr. Jacob mowed the lawn around them, utterly oblivious. Ritchie said it was the best sex he ever had, but I think he was just trying for attention. Ritchie didn't love Jill. He only ever loved one girl.

Today, the boat looks terrible. The mast fell over years ago, and the windows are broken out. Mud has ingrained itself into the fiberglass and moss has taken root. The roof of Old Man Jacob's house has fallen in too, and the door is hanging wide open. The place is abandoned, and my guess is the bank was unable to sell the dump after he died.

And there it is; the old high school, though it's not quite like I remember. It looks tired, as if it survived a war. Incredibly, however, it appears as though it did survive since the old marquee sign out front is welcoming back students for the fall semester set to begin in just under four weeks.

The baseball stadium is on my right, and I'm astounded by how small it seems. The bleachers can't hold thousands of people the way I remember them, and the outfield is mostly brown grass. It's odd how the memory works. When I was a kid, that place was larger than life. Today, it just looks like a high school baseball park in desperate need of some attention.

I haven't thought of these people or these places in years, and if I weren't here today, I never would have thought of them again. Even so, I can feel an eerie sense of wonderment as I drive through town. There's the old gas-station, but it's been remodeled into a bright green and yellow BP. There's the former Pic 'n' Pac grocery mart, but now it's called Apples 'n' Oranges. I suppose this is progress, though you'd never know it judging by the lack of cars in the parking lot. And Gerry's Auto Sales across the street is boarded up. It doesn't look like Gerry has sold any cars there for years.

There's Rachel Roberts pushing a stroller for two while a little girl walks beside her. I can't believe I remembered her name just like that. She's put on sixty pounds or more since high-school, and she looks tired and sunburned, but it's clearly her. I'd recognize her fire-red hair anywhere. She was a popular cheerleader while I was nothing more than a name in the yearbook, yet I had a gargantuan crush on her right up until I started dating Kristie.

And there's the Payton Inn, owned by Jim and Sherry Loren. They were always nice folks, though I once told Sherry a knock-knock joke that she never did get, and I think she held it against me for embarrassing her. All the high school kids liked the Lorens because they'd rent rooms by the hour and wouldn't ask any questions. It's not like they approved of teenage fornication, but owning a hotel in a town that doesn't need one isn't exactly a gold mine. They needed the money. Nobody visits Payton on purpose, so the only customers they could count on were horny teenagers. Prom night was their biggest night of the year. All the parents knew what was going on, but nobody said anything because they had done the same thing when they were the same age. It was a Payton tradition. Half of the children born out of wedlock were conceived in one of those 26 rooms.

The Payton Inn is now a Days Inn. The difference is the sign. The fountain isn't working, but it never really worked right anyway, so I guess that's not much of a surprise. Sadly, the pine trees the Lorens had planted and nurtured from saplings are now dead, just skeletons poking at the sky. The neon light that always reads 'vacancy' now only reads 'ancy,' and even those letters are blinking on and off as though they are moments away from burning out for good.

Pulling into the parking lot, I hit another pothole and realize the nostalgic dream of Payton County has ended. Shutting of the engine, I climb out. The parking lot is empty, but the smells, the humidity, and the sounds of my hometown are exactly the same as I remember them as a kid even though the overall feeling has changed. Everything is quieter, slower, emptier and weedier. Shrugging off my disappointment, I walk under the enormous overhang that was once used for curbside pickup. There just isn't enough traffic to necessitate anything quite so fancy, and as if to validate my assumptions, the hotel shuttle is parked out front, but its front tire is flat, and looks to have been so for some time.

Discouraged by the notion that my own cynicism has tainted the perception I have of my hometown, I step forward, pointedly reminding myself that all things change over time, age forgets no one, and I should expect less while doing more. It's then that I feel something crunch under my shoe. Lifting my foot, what remains of a cockroach sticks to the underside of my Sketchers, its wiggling legs not yet aware that the body they're attached to has died.

## *Part VI*

There is no bell as I enter the hotel, but the door squeaks as though it's straight out of a horror movie where the bellhop is some dead guy with birds eating his face. The girl at the front desk looks up and snaps her gum. She's just a kid. "Help you?" she asks as she sets down the Vogue magazine she's reading.

"I wasn't sure you were open," I answer with a half smile.

She just snaps her gum. "We're always open."

It was clearly a joke that she clearly didn't understand.

"I need a room."

She frowns and starts typing on her computer. "Just you?"

"Me, myself and I."

She looks up, chews with boredom, and looks back down. "Smoking or non-smoking?"

"Non."

"One night?"

I frown. "I'm not really sure. Does it matter?" I look around. "I mean...does it matter?"

"For my computer."

I shrug. "It'll probably be a few days. How about through Sunday?"

She stops chewing and looks up. "On purpose?"

I frown.

She snaps her gum again, rolls her eyes, and starts typing.

The silence is awful, and I feel compelled to fill it. "I used to live here."

"I'm sorry."

I chuckle. "You love your job, don't you?"

"More than life itself." She types some things into the computer that looks straight out of the 90s, clicks her mouse, and chews on her lip. "Cash or credit?"

I hand over the plastic followed by more typing. Finally she sends something to a dot matrix printer. I haven't seen a dot matrix printer since high school, yet there it is, sliding back and forth, chirping and hissing as it tediously prints one line after another. She tears the page off, circles the 'X' next to 'Customer Signature' and slides it across the worn countertop.

I sign.

She hands me a key. Not a keycard. An actual brass key. "Room 16," she says. "All the way at the end. Past the ice machine." She sniffs, wiping her nose on her wrist. "The maid comes at ten, so if you don't want her in your room, hang the sign on the knob."

I take the key and I'm about to turn when I wonder aloud, "am I the only customer here?"

She'd already picked up her magazine again. She doesn't even look at me. "No."

"No?"

"There's another."

I look around at the dilapidated interior before bending down and picking up my bag. "Love what you've done with the place."

This time she does smile, but it's an ironic smile ebbed with little humor. "Enjoy your stay."

I nod with a smirk and walk out. I park the rental outside 16 and unload. The room smells like carpet shampoo, so I open the drapes and prop the door open to let fresh air in. Then I switch on the AC, which grunts and groans before finally leveling off and spewing cool air into the tiny room. I flop down on the bed, kick off my shoes and wiggle my toes inside my sweaty socks. The cool air feels good, and as I lay sprawled across the bed, I figure things could be worse. I haven't been back home in so long that maybe this isn't such a bad thing. I'm actually somewhat curious about seeing Kristine again. After all, she was my first. Suddenly curious, I scrounge around until I find a phonebook tucked in the bedside drawer. Sure enough, she's listed under 'Lambert,' which means she's not married. The number is local, indicating she moved from Lawton to this side of the crick. I recognize the street name she's listed on, but I don't remember where it is.

The open door seems to be inviting me outside, and as I stare beyond the interior of this tired room into the world out there, I begin to wonder what lies beyond, what's changed, and what's still the same. I put my shoes back on, pocket the key, lock the door and hesitate.

Home.

I could drive, but I'd rather walk. Besides, my legs need stretching, and it feels good to walk the same sidewalks I walked as a kid. After awhile I even start to feel better despite the clouds rolling in overhead. The air is saturated with moisture. It was always humid here in the summertime, but that was part of the charm. Freeze in the winter, sweat in the summer. It's all so familiar, and it's all good. Small-town good. The people, the smells, the lawns, the shops, the houses. I remember all of it. The cracks in the sidewalk, the cracks in the roads—my town. It's not beautiful or even quaint. It's a dump that should be bulldozed, but it's still my home.

And me? I am the epitome of Payton County. They say no one leaves; no one gets out. But I did, and now I'm back, reaffirming all those hand-painted signs that hang in the spotless windows of eccentric tourist shops proclaiming '*Home Is Where The Heart Is*.' If Atlanta isn't 'me,' then maybe Payton is. I've got savings. I could sell all

17

my stuff I left back there and start over here. I could blend in quite easily, perching myself on that bell-curve, getting wrinkled and going gray until everything I forgot either comes back or I ultimately disappear.

# Two

## *Yesterday*

"Tony? You comin'?" He has to holler to get his voice to carry. I look up, squinting against the glare of the noonday sun before waving him off and returning my attention to the clear brook beside me. Sunlight reflects off the water as though from a mirror. Ritchie is about a hundred paces up the path from the other side of the stream, hands on hips, his pale face snow white against the bright sunlight. He's my best friend, but this is one of those moments that I'd rather he'd do me the courtesy of using his indoor voice so I can enjoy the simple solitude of the gurgling stream.

"Tony?"

I ignore him, running my fingers through the chilly water, the sun warming my shoulders. When I look closer at the liquid glass rolling lazily past, I can see the minnows hovering in space. They're still—as if waiting, appearing almost hypnotized, moving only slightly now and then to dodge a twig or something flowing downstream. They're frozen in time without much on their little zombie-like minds, and in many ways I envy them. Nothing is simpler than black on white.

"Yo, Triple A," Ritchie calls, clumsily retracing his steps.

I really don't feel like talking much. Four beers under the hot sun will do just about anyone in, and now that I've had an hour to revel in the artificial buzz that's beginning to morph into a headache, I'm feeling somewhat introspective and not terribly social. But Ritchie is trying to drag me back to reality by poking at my mounting headache with nagging persistence, and I can't help but wonder if my melancholy has something to do with Kristie Lambert.

"What's goin' on?" Ritchie asks from the other side of the stream. "You comin' or what?"

"I don't feel like it anymore," I answer, just wanting to sit.

Ritchie stops and frowns. "Why?"

"You go on ahead," I say. "I'll catch up."

"When?"

"When I feel like it."

Ritchie looks at me like I'm nuts. "Come on, you know better than to make me cross that log more'n once, but I'll do it if I have to."

"What's the big deal? Just go on without me."

"If you don't get on your feet pronto, I can assure you I will *not* be a happy camper."

"Go," I insist, shooing him away.

"I can't go by myself."

"Why not?"

"Because." When I don't say anything else, Ritchie frowns, puts his hands on his hips and spits. "I wasn't invited."

"My point exactly."

"Don't make me beg, man. And what's the matter with you? There's gonna be girls there."

"You'll be fine."

"The hell I will. You know that's not my forty."

"Forte," I correct.

"Number one," he continues, undeterred. "Kristie'll be there, and if she's there, her sister'll be there, which means you gotta be there to take my back. Number two, both the towns of Lawton and Payton is gonna be there except for you if you chicken out, and number three, I'm your best friend, and best friends help their buddies out."

I just sit there.

"I need your help."

"I got a headache from those beers you made me drink," I grumble.

"It was two beers."

"Four."

"Four beers. Big deal."

I clamp my mouth closed, glaring.

"Come on, bro," Ritchie begs. "I can't go without you."

Sighing audibly, I shake my head, groan and stand. Carefully wiping the grass from the backside of my jeans, I make my way toward the rotted log that serves as a makeshift bridge over the water. "I'm not your bro."

"I'm the closest thing you're ever gonna have to one."

"That's still not all that close," I mumble.

I stare at the log stretched across the stream. Unless you're willing to take off your shoes and roll up your jeans, the only way to cross the Old Beaver is a three-million year old tree that fell across it forever ago. There's a town-wide bet on when the termites will win the war and collapse Beaver Crossing as we've come to know it.

"Come on," Ritchie coaxes.

The Old Beaver serves as the dividing line between the towns of Payton and Lawton, and since neither Ritchie nor I come from money, it's our only way to cross without walking the ten blistering miles around.

I hesitantly test the log with my foot. Ritchie made it across, and he's a lot heavier than me, so the odds are in my favor that it'll hold. Using my arms to balance, I take a timid step forward, one foot in front of the other.

"You're such a pussy," Ritchie complains. "Grow a pair."

"You are more than welcome to go on by yourself if you're in such a hurry," I answer. "My balance sucks." Ritchie throws a small pebble at me, and I waver—nearly falling in. "Cut it out!" I shout. "You do that again, and I'll kick your butt."

Ritchie smiles. "In your dreams."

Another step forward. The water running underfoot is deep. Four feet or more. A slip here, and I might as well call it a night and go home rather than show up at a party smelling like the Beaver. Another pebble hits me, this time in the face. Ritchie is laughing as I waver and nearly take a cold plunge.

"I swear…"

Ritchie giggles as he hurls another pebble my way. It zings past my face, making me incensed, but before I can get too mad, he turns around, drops his pants to shows me the dark side of his moon.

Sometimes I wonder why I hang out with him at all. Then again, Ritchie is Ritchie. For better or worse. I can't stand hypocrisy, and neither can he. He's about as genuine as a person can get. What you see is what you get, and while I was right when I said he wasn't my brother, he was just as right when he said he was the closest thing to one I'd ever have.

I step off the other side of Beaver Crossing and shove him with the underside of my shoe even while he's still hunched over and giggling with his pants down and his hairy butt waving in the sunlight. He stumbles forward and falls face first into the weeds. Pulling his pants up, he's less than amused as he gets to his feet. "Now I got dirt all over me."

"You really think a little dirt will make much of a difference?"

"I can't let Joanne see me like this."

"Good," I mutter, looking back across the stream toward Payton. "Can we go home now?"

He frantically wipes at the dirt on his knees. "What's it gonna take to get her to like me?" He continues swatting at his pant leg. "It's like she sees me and goes the other way."

"Maybe if you sneak up on her, put a bag over her head and suffocate her," I suggest, turning toward Lawton which is visible in the distance, though the heat of the afternoon makes it look like it's wavering under water. I begin trudging along the game trail toward town.

"It's 'cause I'm ugly, isn't it?"

"Jesus, Rich, you're not ugly, and it's not my decision. Joanne likes you as a friend. Just be happy she's okay with you hanging around. Who knows what might happen down the road."

"Why you always gotta be so vulgar?" he snaps.

"What's that supposed to mean?"

"You know how I feel about you taking His name in vain."

I shake my head. "I don't get you. You have the filthiest mouth in town, yet you get your panties in a wad anytime anyone says anything."

"It's just that there's a difference. There are good bad words and bad bad words. My dad taught me."

"You hate your dad."

"That don't make him wrong."

This is the hard part of being friends with a guy like Ritchie. Most people think he's the life of the party, and a lot of the time he is, but all they see is a big teddy bear. And while I love him like a brother, taking care of myself is hard enough without having to drag him around as my sidekick. It's like he can't have fun unless I'm there, yet one tiny little slip—a bit a blasphemy—and he goes ballistic.

"Sorry," I mutter. "Won't happen again."

Ritchie looks at me as though he might kill me before shrugging, turning his back and slumbering toward Lawton. "Come on. We're gonna be late."

I follow but from a distance. I've upset him. "Sorry, man."

"I said forget it."

I catch up. "Seriously, are we cool?"

He hesitates before turning. The sun is behind him, the shadows hiding his face. He stands there for a second, his face hard. Then he lurches out and socks me in the arm. Which hurts. I'm rubbing the pain out when he breaks into a grin and slaps me on the shoulder. And that's how friends are, I guess. Argue, fight, whatever. All it takes is a moment to pull everything together, and we're suddenly best buds again, sharing secrets and talking shit. Except we're not talking. We're walking side by side with him lost in thought, and for Ritchie Hudson, that is no small feat. He's not a big fan of thinking. He'd rather react. Like the time he stole a car because it seemed like 'fun,' or the time he lit a tree on fire because he was mad at the neighbors for blowing all the fall leaves back into the Hudson's front yard. Ritchie exudes drama, but he doesn't fully understand it. It's just the way he operates.

"What are you thinking?" I ask.

"Nothin'."

"You're thinking something."

"I ain't."

"Come on. What is it?"

"Stop it. You're antagonisticking me."

I shake my head. "Antagonizing, stupid."

He shoves me, and I go sprawling, nearly doing a face plant. I bust up laughing, but he just frowns. He was right, though. I was antagonizing him. I know darn well he's thinking about Joanne—Kristie's twin sister. Both are blond bombshells with blue-eyes, a perfect rack and legs that go all the way up. They epitomize the all-American girl, and I'm the luckiest guy in the world to be dating Kristie. She could have had anyone, and for some reason she picked me. Richie hasn't been as lucky. He thinks the world of Jo, but she feels indifferent toward him.

Joanne is unique. She's as pretty as her sister, but different in a million and a half ways. Legally, she's deaf which has made her the butt of everyone's joke since grade school. Now that she's 'sprouted,' guys want to think she's just like her sister even though all they see is the clumsy little girl with no depth perception who used to run into trees and flagpoles on the playground. She was finally fitted with a headband a few years ago called a 'bone conducting hearing aid,' and while her hearing is far from perfect, she can at least participate in conversations now. She never learned to read lips very well, she still slurs her words when she talks, and sometimes you need to repeat yourself, but I think she's awesome. She's a total dork that doesn't take crap from anyone. And she's smart too. The problem is, Ritchie doesn't like her because she's pretty or smart. Ritchie seems to like her because she's the only girl in two towns who doesn't give a shit about baseball.

And that's the other thing. Ritchie's the starting pitcher for the Payton Pirates, and he's good. As in amazingly good. His ERA this year is .63, which is insane at any level, but what makes it even more impressive is that his outfield is terrible. He's practically doing it all by himself. It's either strike them out at the plate or keep the ball on the infield. He's already smashed every record in the entire state. Every girl knows him, and most of them like him, but because Joanne doesn't, she's become the only girl he'll 'settle' for.

"Just try being a little less you," I suggest.

"What's that supposed to mean?"

"You know exactly what it means."

He frowns. "I don't get it. What's so wrong with me?"

"Nothing's wrong with you. Just relax."

I guess that's why we're best friends. I'm the brains. Ritchie's the brawn. Ritchie relies upon me to make sense of the world, women and everything else the way I rely upon him to sort out the more obvious decisions such as how to not get my ass kicked when I say the wrong thing to the wrong person.

"You're around her more'n me," Ritchie says as we make our way through the tall grass of the field. "Does she ever say anything?"

"I don't want to talk about it anymore. Beside, I think she's seeing someone."

Ritchie stops and turns—a sour expression on his face. It's an expression I know well, and secretly fear. When he looks at you like that, he means business. "Who?"

I shrug. "I have no idea. It's not like I hang out with him. I'm just saying."

"I knew it." He shakes his head. "I mean, I didn't know it, but I *knew* it."

"It's not like she's engaged or anything," I say in a casual attempt to undo what my stupid mouth has already done.

Now he's upset. Lawton is less than a half-mile away. We'll be there in under ten minutes just as the sun is setting, and Ritchie, the big lug, is lumbering ahead, head down, his slouch emphasizing his disappointment.

23

"Relax, Rich. It'll all work out."

"Doubtful."

Ritchie has his share of problems, but when it comes to girls, he's as innocent as a spring rain. I love him for who he is—his excitement over the dumb stuff, his seriousness over baseball, his disregard for authority, his color blindness as it pertains to race, his ability to shrug off pressure, his adoration for women, his misperception for how things really work, and his sometimes impish, sometimes simple take on life. And I guess that's why I sometimes also fear him. For the same reasons. Ritchie is Ritchie. For better or worse.

## Part II

"Hey sweetie." Her face peels back in one of those adorable smiles I can't seem to get enough of. Her arms are opened to me, and she's all dolled up—a bit of eye-shadow and lipstick, her hair slightly curled, and a miniskirt that reminds me why boys chase girls.

I close my arms around her and draw her close as I bury my face in her hair so I can relish the scent of her shampoo. My hands slowly caress her back, and I'll admit that I'm slightly aroused at the feel of the bra-strap under her shirt.

"Are you wearing cologne?" she asks as she pulls away, her eyes gleaming.

"My secret weapon."

She smiles and leans up on her tip-toes, inhaling and smiling. I swear there is nothing like being a teenager. It's the best feeling in the world. She kisses me on the lips, and I can taste the remnants of a raspberry drink on her tongue. She settles back flat on her feet and rests her head against my chest, squeezing me. "I missed you," she says quietly.

I smile and tell her that I missed her more, but my mind has drifted. I do have a secret, but it's not my cologne. It's something she needs to know, but I can't say it here. Not now. Not like this. When I tell her, she'll act excited, but she'll be crushed. I'll see it in her eyes no matter how she smiles or what she says. She'll be crushed, and seeing that hurt in her eyes will crush me.

"You okay?" she asks,

"Are you two done?" Ritchie interrupts, smacking me on the back of the head as he enters the house. "Where's the beer?"

Kristie stares—her eyes searching mine.

"I'm fine," I say, exaggerating a smile.

"I'm on the hunt," Ritchie calls from inside.

"I'm good," I repeat.

"Yeah?" she asks.

"Where's Joanne?" I whisper, looking around.

"Upstairs, I think. Why?"

"Might want to keep her up there."

"Are you changing the subject?"

"No. I'm worried about Ritchie."

She snickers. "Relax. He's a teddy bear."

"That's what I keep hearing."

"Hey," she says, drawing my attention to her pretty eyes. "Focus on me." She points at her chest. "Boobs. Remember?"

Boobs.

Girls aren't stupid. They know exactly what we're thinking. I don't know if I'm in love or not, but if I'm not, I'm awfully close. And if I'm awfully close, then I'm awfully turned on. And if I'm awfully turned on, then there's this uncomfortable and somewhat difficult 'issue' I need to hide brewing slightly below my belt.

"Yo, Triple A," Ritchie interrupts, grinning. "Beer's gettin' cold."

"I thought that's the point," I answer sarcastically.

"Well, yeah…I mean…"

"Haven't you got anywhere else to be?" I snap. "Like, I don't know, stalking someone?"

Ritchie's face goes dark. "Kiss my grits, buttface. Maybe I'll stalk you."

"Whatever gets you off."

He frowns, but he must have gotten the point, because he turns his back and wanders back into the living room.

"That was kind of harsh," Kristie whispers.

"He'll be fine."

She smiles, her hand brushing the bulge in my pants. "What's this?"

Blushing, I push her hand away, turn away with embarrassment and enter the house. She follows me in, wrapping her arms around me from behind. A few of Kristie's friends are seated around the living room. There are six chairs and ten girls. Ritchie is sitting in one of those chairs facing the couch. He's sitting rigidly, his legs restless. I can't say that I don't know what it feels like to be nervous like he is, but as far as I'm concerned, he's on his own. If I say anything, it'll only make things worse, particularly for me.

I take my place beside Kristie on the couch. She leans over and whispers in my ear that she loves me. It's awkward, but I think she likes that it's awkward. In fact, I think she's reveling in the awkwardness while doing whatever she can to make me feel even more awkward. I do my best to take my own advice and relax.

The conversations taking place around the Lambert's living room are what I would expect on an afternoon like this—bad jokes, little giggles, a few bored looks. It's a group of acquaintances pretending to be friends without realizing that being friends isn't something you really need to work at. But it's still good and calm and relaxing right up until the moment that *she* appears.

Joanne.

Ritchie was relatively quiet before, but now he sits straight up, his fingers digging into the edges of the armrests he's clinging to. His face goes beet-red as he clumsily tries to steal glances while trying not to get caught, but Joanne knows it. So does everyone else. The other girls are covering their mouths to keep from giggling while Ritchie squirms. He's my best friend, and the fact that they're toying with his mind is starting to irritate me. Ritchie's a good guy. He just wants what every other guy our age wants; he wants to be someone's hero.

Joanne wanders to the center of the room where the keg is perched on the coffee table. She begins filling a paper cup while slowly tracing her upper lip with the tip her tongue. Ritchie just sits there fidgeting nervously. Staring.

Bless his big ol' dumb heart.

She finishes pouring her drink and looks over as she straightens. It's her way of remaining the object of his affection as well as the centerpiece of the entire room. And she certainly has our attention. Everyone's looking. Me, Ritchie, the other guys—even the other girls. She's proving that she can be every bit as sexy as her sister, and as long as she doesn't speak, no one can tell the difference.

"My sister's a tramp," Kristie murmurs.

"She's just having fun," I return. I feel bad for my friend, and I feel bad for Jo. Yet in a way I'm relieved. I've always been a bit jealous of the way Ritchie can own an entire stadium filled with screaming fans—the way he can tip his hat just slightly, and the place goes bonkers. He grins that stupid grin, and kids, adults, and old farts alike roar until they're hoarse. He doesn't have the same power here. Here it's different. Here, that power is hers.

Kristie says something, and I nod even though I don't hear a word she says. I just smile like a trooper and play along. My mind continues to wander, drifting to that ugly subject I'd rather avoid.

"Something's wrong," Kristie says.

"What do you mean?"

"With you."

I sigh. "We're back on this again?"

"Why, is something bothering you?"

"Nothing's bothering me," I say. "I told you, I'm fine."

"You're not fine. You're totally disconnected. You're sitting here, but you might as well be a million miles away."

"What's with the third degree?"

"Nothing. I'm not…I'm not accusing."

"Well, I'm right here."

"You sure?"

I nod. I'm sure. Or pretty sure anyway. Or maybe I'm not sure. I still haven't figured out a way to break the news that in two weeks I'll be moving out. I'll be hopping on a jet and moving halfway across the country. The University of Georgia said yes, and that's a pretty big deal. No one in my family has ever graduated from anywhere, so it's pretty important that I do. It's also a long way away, and she's not going to understand. Hell, I'm not even sure I do. I know it's a great opportunity, and I need to take it because it's there for the taking, but I'm eighteen years old, and what do eighteen year olds know about great opportunities? What do kids my age know about anything? All I know for certain is I have a beautiful girlfriend, the best of friends and a comfy little life here in Payton, yet I'm two weeks away from turning my back on all of it.

I guess that means I'm not okay. I'm a mess, but I can also bullshit with the best of them, so I do, and she buys it, and no one else notices, because they're watching Joanne toy with Ritchie, and Ritchie's dying one beautiful moment at a time.

# Three

## *Today*

Payton County. 6:41 pm. The sun will be up for some time yet. It's the middle of July, and in Michigan, that means it'll still be light after ten. Here the summers never end. Here, the sunset is a reminder that the morning is only a few hours away.

Walking the streets of my hometown, I feel like an outsider. Everything feels the same, yet so much has changed. Payton is dying. Maybe it's already dead, but nobody got the memo. A few of them look my way, and I think they're staring because I'm in a town that never has visitors. People don't stop in Payton to vacation, and they rarely stop for gas. The town is out of the way, and given the fact that I'm walking instead of merely driving through indicates that I'm here on purpose.

"Help you?" an old man asks after shutting off his lawn mower, adjusting his cap and hitching his belt. He steps gingerly over his freshly cut grass, which bears a close resemblance to whacked weeds.

"Just out for a walk," I answer.

The old man tips his hat again. "You know someone here?"

I nod.

"Maybe I can steer you in the right direction. I know pretty much everyone."

"Thanks, but I'm not lost."

He doesn't look convinced.

"Just out for a walk," I repeat.

"Uh huh." The old man steps back, hitches his belt again and looks around while running his tongue under his lower lip—back and forth, back and forth. Any neighborly cheer he'd been pawning is lost in his dull eyes. He looks frail enough to tip over in a stiff breeze, but he's determined to stand up straight in order to show me how much he distrusts me. There isn't much life left behind those eyes. They're dull pits, hollow and black, staring directly into my soul.

Rather than waiting for him to step aside, I walk around him. It means stepping off the sidewalk and on the grass, but the creepiness of our conversation has compelled me to ignore neighborly etiquette. "Have a good one," I mutter as I walk past.

"I remember you as a good kid," the old man calls. "You were more polite back then."

I turn. "Excuse me?"

"Before you skipped town," he mutters, but he's already shuffling his way back across the scraggly lawn. I should recognize him, and it's the fact that I don't that upsets me. Rather than calling back, I turn away to find a heavyset woman walking toward me. Her face is fixed in a frown.

"Tony?" she calls. "What you doin' back here?" She stops a few feet from me, tilting her head before a slow smile breaks across her face. She opens her arms, the heavy fat wiggling back and forth. I offer a timid smile, but I make no move. "You don't recognize me, huh?" she asks, her smile only growing wider as if she's the world's best-kept secret.

I smile. "I'm sorry."

"Nobody thought we'd see you again."

"Well, here I am."

"Holly," she says as if that makes perfect sense. "Holly Andrews."

Holly Andrews. The little girl down the street who had a big time crush on me when I was ten and she was six. My god, she looks ten years older than me. Weight aside, her hair has thinned and grayed. The bags under her eyes that used to make her look like she was forever smiling have turned into gray tea-bags that look like melting wax, and she's got a very unattractive scar that makes the right side of her lip droop. I guess that's what life in Payton does to you.

"I see you tryin' to work through it," she says with a smile.

"It's been a long time."

"Some get lucky." She shrugs. "Some don't."

"How have you been?" I ask, not all that interested.

"Five kids." She holds up five fingers on the left hand to emphasize. "Three husbands." Three fingers on the right.

"Well, they say three's a charm."

"There's nothing charming about it. The third one only stuck around long enough to charm me out of my retirement savings." She giggles. And snorts. "I'm on to unlucky number four."

"Congratulations."

"It's so good to see you," she says with a grin, re-opening her arms. It bothers me that these people recognize me. I don't recognize them, which gives them the advantage, leaving me vulnerable. And the longer I'm here in this depression-saturated town, the more I just want to leave.

"You too," I lie.

"Wanna come in for a drink?" she asks, motioning toward her house. "I just made up a fresh batch of punch for the kids. There's plenty to go around."

I shake my head. "I'd love to, but I'm meeting someone. I just thought I'd go for a quick walk. See the town."

She smiles and settles back. "There's not much to see." She giggles, waving a chubby hand. "Anyway, I wasn't insinuating nothin'."

"I wasn't suggesting that you were."

"Married?"

I lift a ring-less left-hand and wiggle my fingers. "Divorced."

"Bummer."

"I'll stop by before I leave."

"Yeah?" Her tone carries a hint of doubt.

"Sure."

"You mean like the last time?"

"Meaning what?"

"Meaning when you left town all those years ago, there was that whole…thing."

That thing. First the third degree from the old man, and now her. I can see her eyes reading mine. She's prying, digging in with her talons, but I refuse to give her the satisfaction of cornering me on a subject that's none of her business.

"Forget it," she says, a false smile spreading across her lips. "Can't blame me from bein' curious."

"The Welcome Wagon around here could use a tune up," I grumble.

"Payton's still a small town. There's not a lot to talk about. Someone like you shows up, it's bound to stir the hornet's nest." she grins. "I meant it though. Stop by if you can. No strings attached. It's been twenty years since all that, so no guilt trips, I promise."

"I'll stop by." I turn my back on her and this town.

This town.

This town has turned into that place you see on TV when someone local snaps. As they lead the perp away in shackles, everyone will say what a nice guy he was, and what a great place this town is, and they'll say it to the camera while wearing a bathrobe or a wife-beater. They'll say it without shame, and they'll say it from right here, right smack-dab in the middle of a rash that can't be itched. I'd leave except I came for a reason, and that reason has nothing to do with these people. In a way, it doesn't even have anything to do with this place. I decide to work my way back to the hotel. I don't want to appear as though I'm trying to flee, but I don't want to socialize either. It's been a long day, and I'm not mentally prepared for this. Not the town, not these people—not any of it.

My phone rings, and the caller ID says 'Restricted.' I answer anyway.

"Tony?" she asks.

I wouldn't have been able to place her voice this morning, but now that I've had a chance to process, everything sweet and sorrow in what was once the perfect girl is recognizable even over a bad connection.

"What did you decide?" Kristie asks. "Are you coming? Can you come?"

"I'm out for a walk."

Silence.

"$32^{nd}$ looks like hell," I say. "The whole town does."

"$32^{nd}$?" she asks. "$32^{nd}$ Street? Here in Payton?"

"I just flew in, and now my arms are killing me."

Silence. I at least expected a courtesy giggle…

"Where are you?" she asks.

"32$^{nd}$ and Main."

"Why didn't you call me?"

"You never gave me your number."

A pause. It's like I can hear her thinking on the other end. She analyzes everything, and I guess that's partly why we didn't make it.

"I can't believe it," she says softly. "You're actually here."

"In the flesh."

"How about dinner?"

I draw a breath, standing stupidly in the middle of a sidewalk while sprinklers twist and spin all around me. "I'm at the Days Inn."

"Of course you are," she replies. "It's the only hotel in town. What room? I'll pick you up."

"I have a car."

"So do I."

"Sixteen."

"I'll be there in ten minutes."

"I won't," I reply. "Like I said, I'm out for a walk. This town is unbelievable. What the hell happened here?"

"What do you mean?"

"You know exactly what I mean. What happened here? The people are zombies, the businesses are boarded up. What's going on?"

Pause. "It's still the same old Payton."

"No," I reply. "It isn't. Nothing's the same."

"You okay?"

I shake my head, but take my time answering as I look around again. "I'm not sure."

"So, when should I meet you?"

I look around, my phone pressed against my ear. I do a quick calculation. "Give me a half hour."

"I'll be there."

I hang up, turn the corner, and start back toward the hotel. There are kids playing in the street, but they hold up their hockey game to watch me pass. Everyone's curious. Everyone's staring. Even the kids. I'm a stranger in a town where everyone knows everyone else.

This walk was a bad idea.

"Hey guys," I say as I pass. None of them answer. They just stare, so I keep walking. Eventually they go back to their game, and eventually I stop looking back. I consider jogging the rest of the way back to the hotel just to get out of the spotlight, but if I run, the whole town will see, and then they'll wonder even more. I keep my

31

pace brisk while keeping my posture casual—head bowed, hands buried deep in my pockets as I head home.

Home.

Home, at this point, doesn't apply. I don't have a home. 'Home' isn't here, and it isn't back in Atlanta. Home is where the heart is, but at this point, I don't know where my heart is either.

The sun is orange fireball in the sky, slowly looming larger as the afternoon ages. The hotel parking lot remains hot, the tar-filled cracks lifting like gum from the bottoms of my shoes. I don't know what I'm doing back in this dilapidated little town, and I have no idea what to expect tonight, tomorrow or three days from now, but one thing is certain as I turn the key and open the door, and that is I'll need a shower before Kristie shows.

## Part II

A knock at the door. Staring at my reflection, I figure I look okay, but mentally, I'd rather close the drapes, pull the chain and watch some mindless TV. It's been a long day, but resting will have to wait, because she's here, and just like when we were kids, she's nothing if not prompt. Thirty minutes on the nose.

Crossing the room, I'm prepared for anything. I vaguely remember the girl I dated, though my recent run-ins with Rachel Roberts and Holly Andrews isn't far from my mind. As I open the door, I'm prepared for the best while bracing for the worst. I guess, in a way, I'm selfish enough to hope Kristie's let herself go so I won't feel so bad that I abandoned her here.

But she hasn't, so I do.

I'm standing in my open doorway—tongue-tied. There she is, and she hasn't aged a day. I'd recognize those baby-blues from a half mile away the same way I'd recognize that hesitant smile. There might be a couple of thin laugh lines and a hint of gray mixed in with the blond, but she still looks young, and she still looks fresh. In fact, she looks just like I remember her; perfect.

"Hey," she says sweetly.

"I...uh..." I pause, wondering what to say next. Across the parking lot, the gum-smacking girl that checked me in at the front counter is outside leaning against the wall. She's either smoking a cigarette or a joint. And she's staring. At me.

Kristie follows my gaze before turning back. "She's a little young."

I frown and turn away, walking back into my room. Kristie follows, looking around as though the condition of the room is going to reveal something about me. And maybe it does. The room is in shambles; clothes on the bed, draped over the chair, wet towels and wash cloths on the floor of the bathroom, all my personal things stacked on the back of the toilet.

"I hadn't exactly prepared for guests," I say, my voice trailing off.

"It's a hotel room."

"I was trying to conjure repressed memories by recreating the ambience of my childhood bedroom." No response. Nothing. Not even a smile. "Nobody ever gets my jokes."

Now she smiles. "That's because I'm hungry."

"I'll drive."

"You remember where you're going?"

"Even if I didn't, it's a small town." I grab my wallet and keys from the nightstand before corralling her back toward the door where I lock up and lead her across the parking lot to the rental. "There are only so many streets to choose from."

"One day this place is going to surprise you."

"Oh, believe me, I'm surprised."

She climbs in and pulls her door shut. I already know where I'm taking her even before I take the wheel. Our favorite hangout was always Dune's. We'd go there in the evenings and camp out on the deck, the lights along the railing, the stars shooting across the heavens like out of a movie.

"So, can I ask where you're taking me?" Kristie asks.

I just shrug. No sense in ruining the surprise.

"It's not there anymore," she murmurs, turning away to gaze out her window.

"You don't even know where I'm going."

"Yes, I do."

"You're just—"

"Dune's." She turns to me. "It's gone."

"Where'd it go?"

"Burned down. Something like six years ago. They said it was arson, but nobody could ever prove anything. I think it was Mr. and Mrs. Jenkins. They skipped town after they collected the insurance. They never even considered rebuilding."

This information is timely enough, but I'm already irritated as I come upon the hole in the world where Dune's used to be. It looks like the city never even bothered to clean up the mess. The charcoaled and rotted out remains still stand, weeds and fledgling trees growing where I used to dine as a kid.

"Typical…" I say.

Kristie just stares straight ahead.

I pull into the overgrown parking lot before turning around. "Now where?"

"We passed a Burger King."

"Burger King? Really?"

"There's Cherries off Lincoln."

"Neither of us are dressed for Cherries."

"It's a small town, Tony. Our options are somewhat limited."

"I'm not arguing." I shake my head as I drive slowly along the street. "I'm just saying."

33

She sits quietly for a second before tugging on the door handle.

"What are you doing?" I ask frantically. "We're moving!"

"I suddenly don't feel so good. Can you pull over?"

"I'm in the middle of the street."

"Then hurry it up."

Reacting quickly, I pull to the side of the road. She struggles with her seatbelt, finally gets it off, kicks open the door and leans over, straining against her seatbelt while vomiting all over the street.

I cringe. "You okay?"

"Can we go?" she asks, pulling the door shut.

"Should I take you home?"

"I'm fine."

"Are you pregnant?"

"Jesus. No, I am not pregnant. I'm nervous."

"About what?"

"Can we just go?"

"We're going."

"I don't feel us moving."

"We're moving," I answer, stomping on the gas. "Here we go."

She fishes through her purse and settles on a Tic Tac before offering me one. Then she crosses her legs and resumes her quiet stare out the passenger-side window.

"I'm taking you home," I say softly.

"I told you, I'm just nervous."

"What in the world is there to be nervous about?"

"A reaction from you like that one."

"So, this is my fault?"

She rests her forehead against the glass, her breath white fog. "Twenty years and you haven't changed at all."

I shake my head, equally frustrated. "Maybe that's the problem. I haven't changed, but everything else has."

She doesn't answer, but I recognize the cold silence she's placed between us. It's always been her way of putting me down. It's how she makes it clear that she's right, and I'm wrong. Guilty by attrition. Or was it proximity?

"Pull in here," she says suddenly, unbuckling her belt while pointing at a restaurant coming up on the right.

I frown. "O'Riordan's?"

"They have good steaks."

"Is it new?"

"Compared to what?"

"Compared to I don't recognize it."

"They were here before you left."

"I don't remember it."

34

"Blame it on old age."

The parking lot's mostly empty, so parking is convenient. She climbs out, and I catch the wiggle of her perfect butt as she strolls toward the entrance. Then she turns and brushes the hair out of her eyes. "You comin'?"

I pull the keys from the ignition and step from the car. I consider locking up, but this is Payton County, not New York City. I follow her up on the sidewalk and toward the front door where a merry bell announces our entrance, and a jukebox sings hello.

# Four

## *Yesterday*

"**D**o you love me, Tony?" she asks, grinning up at me with those baby blues. Her head is my lap, her Geography textbook in hers, but she hasn't looked at it in probably ten minutes or more. "Anthony." She giggles. "Anthony Alexander Abbott."

I'm perched up against an old oak tree while highlighting what I hope are pertinent pieces of info I'll need for my science final. "Of course I do," I answer without even looking up. At this point, I say 'yes' out of habit. I mean, she asks me like every five minutes. It's probably love, but I'm seventeen years old. What the hell do I know about love?

She sits up and tosses her hair until it cascades over her shoulder and seductively hides half of her face. She smiles. "Triple A."

"What?"

"Nothing. I'm just saying."

"Saying what?" I'm totally engrossed in highlighting the shit out of this book.

"Your name. Triple A. It sounds like the name of someone famous," she sighs dreamily. "Like a rock star."

She never calls me Triple A. Only when she's mad. So I look over. She looks so pretty like that. Perfect skin, perfect hair, perfect teeth. I may or may not be in love, but I'm certainly in lust. She leans in. Her lips are soft, her tongue warm. Her hand finds the bulge in my pants and gives it a slight squeeze. Embarrassed, I roll away and stand—turning my back.

"What's the matter?"

"Nothing," I say.

"What are you so embarrassed about? That's the way things are supposed to work, you know." I can hear her stand. Then she does that thing she does where she wraps her arms around me from behind and rests her head against my back. "Besides, I like it," she murmurs. "I like knowing it's because of me."

Now I'm even more uncomfortable. It's not the same for girls. Girls can tell if a guy is turned on, but it's not as easy the other way around, and I hate knowing that she can tell and I can't. "Don't be mad," she says, starting to sway—holding on from behind while encouraging me to sway with her. There's no music, but we don't really need any. She loves to dance. She's always moving to something, and I swear I'll never get tired of watching her move. Of course, I can't actually see her since she's holding onto me from behind, so I turn back to face her, and she greets me with an incredibly white smile, her eyes twinkling. Leaning on her tip-toes, she kisses me, and all is right with the world.

So much for homework.

She rests her head against my chest and slows things down. "I hate that you're leaving," she whispers, and here comes the guilt trip.

"It's not permanent. I'll be back for Christmas."

"But Georgia?"

"What's wrong with Georgia?"

"It's so far away…"

Now she's running her hand under my shirt, and while the sensation is foreign, I like the feel of her cool fingers against my skin. Still, I'm leery someone will walk up at any moment and berate us for being lewd in public, and I squirm uncomfortably, looking around.

"What's wrong?" she asks.

"What if someone…"

But she's getting braver. She's moved her hand lower, now caressing the outside of the front of my jeans. "It's okay," she whispers.

Every teenage kid dreams of losing his virginity, and I'm no exception, but seriously? Out in the middle of a public park? This place is totally exposed. Sure, it's up on a hill and set back from the main path, but it's also a small town. Everybody knows everything about everyone else.

"It's okay," she repeats.

Of course it's okay. It's amazing. I've never been so excited in my whole life. But I'm also terrified. She's holding me with her eyes to make sure I won't bolt while using her hand to encourage me. I'm not sure how far she's prepared to go, but I can tell she's getting into it. Her chest is rising and falling as she breathes, and my worries of getting caught are slipping away. At this point I think I'm more worried that it might actually happen, right up until—

"Yo, Triple A!" comes a distant call. Immediately, I break from my trance. Ritchie is trudging up the hill toward us. "What you doin', man?"

My erection shrivels like a deflated balloon, and Kristie backs off, disappointment evident in her eyes.

"Are you guys dancing or somethin'?" Ritchie gasps as he makes the steep climb. "I been looking all over for you."

"I've been hiding from you," I say, my tone rigid.

Ritchie is panting by the time he reaches my side. "Too much…" he tries and shakes his head as he leans his hands on his knees. "That is one big ass hill." Finally, he straightens and slaps me sharply on the back. "What are you two doin' way up here?"

37

"I'm spending time with my *girlfriend*," I say.

Ritchie looks at Kristie then me before breaking into a grin. "Cool."

I bite my tongue, reminding myself to remain calm. "And?"

"And what?" he pants.

"And why are you here?"

"I gotta show you somethin'."

"It can wait."

Ritchie eyes me a moment and then Kristie before shaking his head. "Not really. You'll wanna see this."

"It can wait."

Ritchie narrows his eyes at Kristie before turning on me. "Look, there's something I *gotta* show you. It's *important*." He slaps me on the arm again. "Let's go."

"Jesus, Ritchie, I'm kind of in the middle of something."

He just stands there, hands at his sides, sweat stains under his arms, his chest heaving. "I swear I'm gonna knock you flat if you keep talkin' blasphemy like that."

"Then stop pissing me off."

He shakes his head, exhales and lifts his yes. "Let's go."

"I'm not going anywhere."

"You gotta see this. I'm tellin' you."

"I'm not—"

"Go ahead," Kristie interrupts. She looks me in the eye and offers a tiny nod. "Go with your friend. I don't want you two fighting."

"We're not fighting."

"Go. It's okay."

"See?" Ritchie says, the light returning to his eyes. Apparently he's caught his second wind, and something has him unusually excited. "Even the old ball and chain wants to get rid of you."

"Give me a minute," I answer.

"We ain't got a minute, bro. This is a limited time offer. We gotta go. Now."

"Then at least give me a second," I snap.

Ritchie frowns, but nods. "Make it quick." He turns his back and starts shuffling back down the hill.

Kristie looks up at me with those baby-blues. "I'm not mad," she says. "I promise."

"I'm sorry," I say. "Ritchie is Ritchie."

"For better or for worse."

I smile. "Right."

"To be continued?"

I kiss her, savoring the leftover minty goodness of the Tic Tacs she's been sneaking all afternoon. "I'll see you tonight," I promise, kissing her forehead.

She shakes her head. "My parents will be home. I'll call you." She smiles. "It'll be late. Probably after ten."

"I'll miss you."

She giggles. "You better."

One more quick kiss, and I scoop my books, shove them into my backpack, and trot down the hill to catch up with my friend, spilling the ball cap he's wearing as I pass by. He swings carelessly. "Dumb ass," he murmurs as he retrieves the hat. Together we race toward the sunset, seemingly on a collision course with nothing.

## Part II

Even though I graciously agreed to give up what might have been the most important day of my young life, Ritchie is pouting as we make our way out of the park, and to make sure I know it, he's wearing a scowl while refusing to look at me.

"Where are we going?" I ask. "What's so important?"

No answer.

"You just made me walk away from my girlfriend, and I did it for you, so you'd better open that pie hole of yours and tell me why."

The Ritchie Hudson silent treatment continues.

"Ritchie, if you're planning on pouting like a little bitch, I swear to God I'm leaving you here."

He frowns. "Sorry."

"No you're not. If you were sorry, you would have clued in to the fact that she and I were at the top of the hill and away from prying eyes for a reason."

"Sorry."

"You're not sorry."

"I sorta am."

"Where are we going?"

He opens up into a wide grin. "To make all your dreams come true."

"My dreams were on the verge of coming true, stupid."

"I mean, like your other dreams."

"What are you talking about?"

"Trust me." He rips my book-bag from my hands and tosses it into the ditch. "Now we're even."

"You're such a…" I climb into the ditch to retrieve it. "Now everything's wet. My books, my notes—everything."

"Quit yer cryin'. You're acing all your classes anyway."

"Finals are in two weeks, asshole. I need those notes."

"What difference does it make? You already got accepted. In two more weeks you're all the way gone. A new zip code, a new city, a new life. You're leaving us all behind anyway. You might as well skip finals and leave town now."

"Is that what this is about?"

39

"Is that what what is about?"

"What did I ask you like ten minutes ago? Where. Are. We. Going?"

"The one place that might convince you to stay."

"It's not like I'm leaving forever."

"Yeah, well once you see this, you might stick around. This is, like, the most amazing thing ever."

"What is?"

"I seen Sharon on my way past, and she was sunbathing. Nude."

"Sharon who?" I ask. "Sharon Daniels?"

"No, Sharon fucking Stone. How many Sharons do you know?"

"What do I care if she's sunbathing nude?" I ask. "Ritchie, I've got a girlfriend, and if you hadn't noticed, I was already on second base when you so rudely interrupted."

"Kristie's cute," Ritchie says. "I'll give her that. She's cute, but she ain't no Sharon Daniels."

"And it's not like you can just *accidentally* walk by her backyard," I argue. "What were you doing, peeping through her fence?"

"There wasn't nothin' accidental about it. And it's not like she was hiding. She's just making it easy. I think she likes it. Hell, if I had a body like that, I would."

"You've got a body like a Mr. Potato Head. I'm going back."

I even turn away, but Ritchie grabs me by the arm. "You're not going nowhere. This is a life-changing moment. Trust me."

"This is pathetic. Seriously, you should be embarrassed," I answer, but I follow anyway.

For the record, Sharon is over twenty one. Four years may not sound like a lot, but to an eighteen year old kid, it's the difference between 'girlfriend' material and 'untouchable' hotness. Her dad is a salesman who's always traveling, and her mom is a flight attendant who's also largely absent. Sharon never went to college, so until she sorts through the long list of potential husbands begging for her attention, she's staying at home on her parents' dime. She's an only child, spoiled from birth and starved for attention, and to her benefit, she has the kind of body that warrants attention, so she puts it on display, advertising to the highest bidder.

Ritchie leads me along an abandoned train track that runs up behind Sharon's fenced in backyard. It's one of those wooden fences where the slats are four inches wide with only a half-inch gap in between. The fence is old and weathered, the planks gray and shriveled from brutal summers under the hot sun. I feel like a thief stealing my way into someone's private life. The afternoon is dry, the bugs out in force and the ground under our feet crunchy and loud enough to give us away.

"Are you sure about this?" I ask.

"I will be if you'd keep it down," Ritchie hisses. "Come on." He leads along the wooden privacy fence that guards the Daniels back yard. I'm getting nervous. If we get caught…

Ritchie stops beside a knothole, crouches over and peers through. Standing, he looks at me with a big teddy-bear grin and nods. "Take a look."

I crouch down and peer through the hole, and sure enough, there's Sharon Daniels lying on her back on a floating mattress in the middle of their swimming pool wearing nothing more than her birthday suit. Her breasts are soft round mounds on her chest, her nipples a dark pink. Her legs are long, tanned and toned from hours upon hours of jogging. Her stomach is as flat as the sea after a storm. And right there, as if her legs are runways leading all the way to Heaven, there is a patch of brown curly hair at the center of every teenage boy's universe. This is the first woman I've seen naked in real life. It's so much more amazing than Playboy or some still life photograph. This is a girl every guy in town has probably jerked off to at one point or another.

"Lemme see," Ritchie whispers, and I back off a step so he can look. He shakes his head, licks his lips and sighs quietly. "Unbelievable."

"This is wrong," I say. "I mean, we're spying on her."

"It's right," Ritchie replies as he stands. Sweat is running in beads from his forehead. "It's right in so many ways."

"Maybe we should go."

"Maybe we should stay, and maybe you should be a little quieter so we don't get caught." He bends down again, closes one eye and peers thought the knothole with the other. His mouth curls into a smile. "That body was *made* to be seen."

"Come on. Let's go."

"Just take one more look," he says, backing away. "One more look, and if you still wanna go, we'll go."

"You are such a pervert."

"Oh, and you're not? You're just playin' it cool 'cuz you got a girl, and you want to act all non-challent."

"Nonchalant, dumb ass."

"That's what I said."

"I'm not looking."

"Look."

"I'm not looking."

"Look, or I'll yell so loud the whole neighborhood will know you're here."

"You're such a—"

Ritchie fills his lungs, puffing out his chest, ready to unleash a howl that will not only alert Sharon to our position but everyone else within a fifty mile radius.

"Fine," I hiss. I shake my head and turn back to the fence. Crouching down, I peer through the hole. By this time, she's slipped off her inflatable raft and is swimming toward the ladder. Her movements are graceful—sleek. The angel on one shoulder is telling me to look away, while the devil on the other is insisting nobody gets hurt. Besides, the devil argues, Ritchie's probably right. She *wants* to be seen.

Sharon climbs out of the pool and turns to face the sun, giving me a perfect view of her bare backside while she squeezes water from her hair. Of course, she has

41

absolutely no idea that I'm peering through her fence or that I'm even here, enjoying her body in all of its glorious—

She turns suddenly, as if she's heard something, and looks directly at the knothole I'm peering through. *Directly* at the knothole. We even lock eyes for a second before she looks away. Maybe she didn't see me. Even so, my heart is now thundering in my chest, but I keep watching as she prances slowly across the grass and sits on the porch swing only a few feet away. She's sitting on the swing, buck naked, kicking her feet out as she swings back and forth. She knows I'm here. She has to. How couldn't she? She's just swinging away, her wet hair dancing against her bare skin.

"Oh my god," I mouth silently.

"Lemme see!" Ritchie hisses.

I raise a finger to my lips and point at the knothole before drawing a finger across my throat. Ritchie urgently points at himself then the hole. I back off so he can look, and immediately his eyes widen with amazement, his mouth dropping open. I have to admit, watching his expression is almost as entertaining as watching Sharon.

"Dude," he whispers.

"I know."

"Dude."

"We should go."

"Kiss my grits, you got a girlfriend," he whispers back. "I got calluses."

"You're going to get caught."

"Find your own peephole."

"That's not the…" I'm frustrated. "That's not my point."

He just waves me off.

I flip him off before walking the fence until I find another peephole. This one's not as big, and the angle isn't as good. I can see a bare leg and a white thigh, but that's about it. Even so, god sure knew what he was doing when he made Sharon Daniels. She swings a few more moments before getting out of the swing. She watching something, and I think it's a butterfly. Or maybe just a bug. No, it has to be a butterfly, because she's following it, and why wouldn't she? It's perfectly natural for naked girls to frolic after butterflies for no particular reason…

She's walking my way, allowing me a full view of incredibly nude body. Sharon stops only a few feet away and leans over to smell a flower on the butterfly bush the Daniels's's have planted beside the birdbath.

The stupid bushes are blocking my view.

Sharon stands, a butterfly perched on her forefinger, and she's facing me, but her eyes are locked on the winged caterpillar. She looks amazing. Perfect. This is the most amazing moment of my entire life. It's the—

She looks up and locks eyes with mine, and it's like there is no fence. Or a peephole for that matter. It's like I'm standing naked in front of her instead of the other way around. My blood freezes, my heart stops and my knees cramp. Then she winks. She actually winks. It's only a tiny gesture as if not to give herself away to

Ritchie, but it's definitely a wink. She knows I'm here. But instead of freaking out or getting mad or flirting or waving, she just stands there looking at me while allowing me to look at her. She holds that pose for what feels like forever before she turns and prances toward the house. She pulls open the slider, steps inside and disappears. I stand back, barely able to breathe. I can die now. I can die a happy man having lived a full life. I just walked on the moon.

Ritchie approaches and slaps me on the back while shaking his head in disbelief. "Can you believe what just happened?"

"You're forgiven," I answer.

Ritchie runs his fingers through his curly black hair. "Damn right I am."

Damn right. Damn right he's forgiven, damn right he's my best friend, damn right Payton is my hometown, Sharon is our angel and Kristie is my princess. Teenagers can spend entire summers killing time doing dumb stuff like this. The sun never sets, the leaves never fall, and youth lasts forever. We're rebels with a one-track mind. We're lost when it comes to logic. Beer, girls and friends. That's what it's all about.

"Come on," Ritchie says. "We need to celebrate."

Damn right we do.

## Part III

"Where we goin'?" I ask, following my friend back along the rusty old tracks.

"I got beers."

"And I gotta study. And since my books are ruined, thanks to you, I have to start all over."

"You are such a baby," Ritchie snaps. "I ain't got better than a C-minus on any tests yet this year, and here we are, both on the verge of graduating at the same exact time. Imagine that."

I can't imagine that, but I also can't argue with that, and I can't help but grin as I follow my best friend back to his place. We sneak into the basement where Ritchie unveils a stash of bad beer he's got hidden under his dad's workbench. He tosses me one, and we start drinking while playing video games on mute as his parents shuffle around upstairs. I've known Ritchie since we were eight, but I've only met his parents a couple of times. Ritchie doesn't bring me here. He doesn't bring anyone here. He doesn't often talk about his parents, and on the rare occasions that he does, he doesn't have a lot of nice things to say.

His mom is sheepish—all painted smiles. She's the kind of woman who makes the best of a bad situation. And even when she knows things are bad, she'll turn the other cheek and ask that the rest of us do too.

43

Ritchie's dad is different story. He's tough. I don't think he likes kids. I'm not even sure he likes his own son. He definitely doesn't like me. He doesn't even pretend to. Ritchie and I met back when we were kids as I was getting pummeled by two other guys. Ritchie took my back and changed the game. His dad knows this, which means—in his eyes—I'm weak, and he doesn't tolerate weakness. He was a Marine, and now he's a truck driver, and to him, I'm just the neighborhood 'wimp' who can't take care of himself.

From down here in the basement, we can't actually hear what they're saying up there, but we can hear enough to know they're arguing, and as the beer settles in, I'm starting to feel all giggly, and it's hard to keep quiet.

"Keep it down," Ritchie hisses. "My dad catches us down here, and he'll whoop both our asses."

"I though you said your dad was your hero?"

"My dad's an asshole, and if he catches us down here drinking his beer, he'll kill us both."

"He won't kill us."

"Actually, he might."

"Then why are we here?"

Ritchie grins. "'Cuz sometimes it feels good to be bad."

"I'm leaving," I say, setting the controller down.

"You're staying. Just keep it down."

"You've told me things about your dad, and I don't think I need to see it up close."

"Just be quiet, and we'll be fine. He never comes down here."

"What if this time he does?"

"Just be quiet!" Ritchie hisses. He shakes his head as he returns his attention to the game. I sit motionless, not sure what to do. Ritchie looks over. "You gonna play or not?"

"Not sure."

"Just 'cuz he's up there don't mean we can't have fun down here."

I smile and reengage. What a day. What a perfect day. First Kristie, then Sharon and now Ritchie. My girl, my fantasy and my best friend. Not even Hollywood could script something like this. When you're seventeen, the world is limitless—even in a shithole, going-nowhere town like Payton.

"You don't wanna leave," Ritchie mumbles, tearing me from my moment of self-actualization and returning me to his basement and this lousy couch that has to be at least fifty years old. The fibers feel like they're attaching themselves to my butt.

"What?" I ask.

"Leave," Ritchie responds while keeping his mind and his eye on the game. He's contorting his face and moving his arms around as he manages the controls as if the added animation will make all the difference in the world. "When we graduate."

"This again?" I look at him a moment before coarsely returning my attention to the game. "I told you, it's not like I won't be back."

"For what, Christmas?" he shakes his head. "Don't give me that. You ain't comin' back."

"I'm coming back. This is still my home."

"Then why even go? I mean, why go off to college if this is where you want to be? You don't need a fancy degree to be successful here."

"I'm coming back to visit. I never said anything about staying."

He frowns, shaking his head. "I'm just—" Then suddenly, his face contorts, and he grimaces, closing his left eye and turning his head. He slaps at the right side of his skull before shaking it off.

"You okay?" I ask.

"Fine."

"You don't look fine."

"I get headaches."

"What kind of headaches?"

"Headaches."

"Yeah, but still."

"It's cool."

"It's not cool."

"I take aspirin."

"And that works?"

"What do you care?"

I shake my head. "God, Rich, grow up, will you? I have a chance to actually do something with my life. Why can't you be supportive? As my friend?"

"But this is home. You even said it yourself. This is home. This is where we're supposed to raise our families. Here you don't gotta worry about things like money. You don't need a fancy degree to live the dream."

"But there's a whole world out there."

"Yeah, but this is home. Here I'm somebody."

"I'm not talking about you."

"I'm the best pitcher in five counties."

"Ten."

"I *can't* leave."

"No one says you have to."

"But I don't wanna stay if you're not gonna be here."

"Look, even if I go, you're still my brother. I'll drag your hairy ass with me." I shower the enemy with digital bullets, bringing dire consequences to my opponents who 'oof' and 'grr' in digital death.

"Yeah, you say that now."

"I don't get you. You're not stupid. So, take some courses at the community college over in Lawton. Get your grades up, and come with me."

"I wouldn't shit in that town."

"That's a colorful image."

45

"My future's plain as ice. I'm—"

"Rice."

"Huh?"

"Plain as rice."

"My point is, I'm gonna work for Taylor Collision all my life, and that's just the way it is. They're already prepping me for when Jeff retires, and I already do 60% of the runs as it is."

"You should be thinking about applying for baseball scholarships. Any school in the nation would be stupid not to look at your numbers."

He considers for a second before again shaking his head. "I can't do it out there. This is my town. These are my fans. Here I'm somebody."

"I don't get it. You can—"

"No, *you* don't get it." His eyes are welling. "You're not even…" He turns back to the TV.

"What?"

"Nothin'."

"I'm not even what?"

"You're always saying I'm not stupid, but I am." He slams the controller on the couch cushion beside him, the words 'Game Over' flashing on the screen. "They tested my brain, man, and those tests say that I'm three points above being legally retarded. That means I'm smart enough to know I'm stupid. Payton is all I'm capable of. I'm not a big league pitcher. I can barely drive a tow truck. But it's enough to afford a little house and a coupla kids, and people will still want to buy me a beer even when I'm old and fat because at one time, a long time ago, I was pretty good at throwing a baseball."

"You're not retarded," I repeat. "If you were retarded, we would have nothing in common and we wouldn't be friends, but we do, and we are. We've been best friends our whole lives. Besides, those tests are rigged. I scored low too."

"Whatever."

"The hell with the tests. You're not stupid. Don't let them get to you. You're tougher than that. And you're the best pitcher anyone around here's ever seen. Stop whining like a pussy, get off your ass and *make* them pay attention. Jesus, Rich, let them *see* you."

He pouts.

"You know what I mean," I grumble. "My vulgar, blasphemous language aside."

"I just don't want to lose my best friend."

"You're not losing your best friend." This is weird. My great day has suddenly turned into something sour. I've never seen Ritchie like this before. He doesn't lean on anyone—especially like this. He sounds weak, and I don't know how to support him.

"You're movin' to another state," He murmurs.

"Yes, I'm moving to another state. For a little while. I've been working my ass off these last twelve years so I'd have the opportunity to move to another state. UGA opened their arms to me, so I'm flying south."

Ritchie looks depressed.

"Look," I say, knowing any explanation I give won't explain a thing. Not to him. "I want a lucrative future. I want something more than Payton County. Payton is nice. Payton's like a...like a..." I struggle to come up with a proper analogy. "Payton's like an Oreo cookie. An Oreo cookie is nice and good and all that, but if you had to choose between an Oreo cookie and a whole cake, an entire cake with the works—white frosting and chocolate chips and all that, which would you choose?"

Ritchie sits quietly.

"You'd pick the cake," I say.

"I might not."

"Trust me, you'd pick the cake."

Ritchie says nothing. He just stares at the TV.

"Payton doesn't have much," I try. "It's a population nothing, prospects zero small town out in the middle of nowhere."

"Can't you at least stay through the summer?"

"I can't. I already accepted that job at the university bookstore."

"But you already got a job here."

"The university pays more, Rich, and the job starts in June. If I work through the summer, my first semester is already paid for."

"But school won't be over yet."

"For us seniors it will be."

"The baseball season won't be over yet."

I bite my tongue, considering my words carefully. "And I'm sorry about that. I mean it. I'd love to be able to hang around long enough to see you finish out the season, but I can't. But if we make the state championship, I'll come back and watch you pitch. I promise."

"Don't make no promises you can't keep," he murmurs. "*Bro*."

"Don't guilt-trip me."

"I ain't doin' nothin' of the sort."

"Are we going to play or argue like little old women?"

"We're playing," he grumbles.

"Good, then let's play."

"Fine," he snaps, picking up his controller and turning his attention back to the TV. This is such an odd conversation, and not a pleasant one either. He nods, and I feel like I'm looking out for a little brother. Not that I have a little brother, which just amplifies the weirdness especially when it's usually Ritchie looking out for me. Ritchie thinks for a moment, his eyes distant even though fixed on the screen across the room. Finally, he swigs from his beer, burps and nods. "Are we playin' or what?" he snaps.

47

"We're playing."

"Well, you got the thing," he argues. "Press 'play.'"

I smile as I turn back to the screen and resume action. The battlefield livens and we are tossed back into the action, our guns blazing as we shower our opponents with bullets. Digital blood smacks the screen and we are amazed by how far graphics have come in only a few years.

"Wow," he whispers, this glow all around him—an innocence, and for me, it's a revelation. Not the game or the beer or even Sharon Daniels. But Ritchie. Underneath his tough-guy persona there's a little boy who's terrified of everything; school, work, life, girls—the whole world. Even me. He's afraid of growing up, despite how much he hates his parents and the shackles they hold him back with. No disrespect to God or anything, but Jesus Christ, that's a lot to deal with at that age.

# Five

"Nothing works out the way you want it to," she says, sifting through her salad while still chewing. Lifting her eyes, she holds her fork upright, a bit of chicken perched upon the prongs. She wags the fork at me as if to make a point. "I learned that lesson at the tender age of twenty-one."

"Are you being sarcastic?"

"No." She snags the bite of chicken from her fork and begins to chew. "It's a fact." Then she shakes her head. "No, not a fact. It's a fairytale."

"What is?"

"All of it. All that crap they cram down your throat when you're a kid about growing up to be whatever you want to be. It's a fairytale. It's like blowing on the white feathers of a dandelion. They tell you to make a wish, but it's an illusion, and pretty soon all you've got is weeds."

"So, what happened?" I ask. "When you were twenty-one?"

She lifts her eyes and studies me a moment before returning her attention to her salad. "That was the year my dad was injured in an accident."

"At the plant?"

She nods. "It's also the year I got pregnant and gave birth to a still-born baby boy." She looks at me, and I can see the fatigue in her eyes. "I named him Anthony."

"I'm...sorry." I don't know that I am, but it's awkward as hell.

"I think I cursed God about a hundred times that year. Maybe more."

There's a blob of chewy meat in my mouth that I can't bring myself to swallow, and I'm looking across the table at a girl who apparently named her dead kid after me. I don't know who her son's father was, and I don't really care to. I didn't even need to know that she had been pregnant. Ironically, my eyes drift to her left hand. There is no ring.

She smiles, lifts her hand and wiggles her ring finger for a better view. "Jeff Taylor," she says.

"Jeff Taylor?" I'm stunned. "The guy whose dad owns Taylor Collision?"

"Owned," she answers. "Past tense. Jeff ran it into the ground. If you ever want to see the face of ADHD, well, there you go."

"What did you see in him?"

"I was young and lonely," she says, washing her meal down with a sip of ice water. "He was sweet." Her glance is accusing. "And he was *around*."

Guilt trip.

"Anyway," she continues, her eyes returning to her meal. "He's out of the picture." She chews for a moment before looking up again, catching me staring.

"It's none of my business," I mumble.

"You're acting like it is." When I don't answer, she continues. "Anyway, by the looks of things, you're doing just fine."

"By the looks of what things?"

"Where do you live now?"

"Atlanta."

"Can't be cheap to live in Atlanta."

"I do all right."

"Got a nice apartment?"

I smile. "I have an average apartment."

She matches my smile. "Suits you."

"Nothing suits me."

"An apartment does. You can just pick up and go at a moment's notice."

Guilt trip #2. I'm not taking the bait. I didn't fly across the country just to be reprimanded for a decision I made half a lifetime ago. I don't remember everything that happened, but I know enough to know that it wasn't all my fault. "Why did you stay?" I ask. "Here, I mean?"

"You mean *after* she disappeared?" She pauses, looking at me hard enough to make me feel uncomfortable. "Why'd I stay?" she asks. "Why'd you come back?"

I hear her ask the question, but I don't answer. I'm barely listening. My mind has drifted, because the words '*after she disappeared*' are lodged like a kidney stone in my mind, chiseling at my memory, and suddenly I know why she called.

"You okay?" she asks.

I forgot. I completely forgot. I mean, I remember Joanne, but I forgot that she went missing. There was that whole thing—a missing persons—but I wasn't even here. I was down in Georgia getting ready for fall semester while they were organizing huge search parties up here. They traipsed through fields and looked in abandoned buildings for weeks. Joanne Lambert made front page news from June until December. My mom gave me all the updates when I called on the weekends, but—

They never found anything.

"Tony?" she asks.

"Yeah?"

"You okay?"

"No, I'm not okay. I don't remember."

"You don't remember? Which part?"

"Any of it. All of it. I forgot." I shake my head. "I forgot about her."

"About Jo?"

"How do you forget something like that?"

She sits back, clearly angry. "You *forgot*?"

I shrug.

"Are you for real? You *forgot*?"

"What, you think I'm lying? You think I'm *happy* about this? I have this big blank spot that I can't reconcile, and it's eating up half my fucking childhood. I can't remember anything. When you called this morning, I couldn't even remember what you looked like."

She stares at me from across the table, a table which might as well be the Grand Canyon given the distance between us. I *do* remember, but only fragments of that lost summer. I remember that Joanne left without saying anything to anyone, and nobody knew why. But I also remember that by that time I was already gone.

"She disappeared the same day you left," Kristie says softly.

I stare at her, realizing that if what she just said is true, then maybe this is a trap. After all, if Jo and I really did both leave on the same day, then despite my inability to conjure memories into a contiguous timeline of events, the timing does seem a bit suspicious. Kristie might be setting me up.

"I left for school," I say defensively, my voice sounding anything but confident. "It had been in the works for weeks."

"Did she go with you?"

"What's that supposed to mean?"

"I don't know. I'm just asking."

"I have no idea where Joanne went," I say, looking her in the eye. "I wasn't here."

"You swear it?"

"What difference does it make? I don't remember."

She exhales and folds her arms, about to say something then stopping. There's some more glaring before she gets over it, leans forward and starts picking at her meal again, her eyes on her plate. "Fine. I believe you."

"Your support is overwhelming."

"I had to ask."

I shake my head.

"You asked me why I stayed," she says, chewing. "We all did. My mom and dad. And me. I guess we were waiting."

"For Joanne?"

"No, for fucking Santa Claus."

I toss a fry at my catsup before plucking the crumpled napkin from my lap, wiping the grease from my fingertips. "Sorry."

"Jesus Christ, Tony, wake up."

"I'm trying."

"Then try harder."

"I'm trying," I repeat, my tone soft.

Kristie leans her elbows on the table and runs her fingers through her hair. "It's been a nightmare that just won't end. A twenty-year nightmare. I mean, after we got the letter, we kind of thought maybe she'd come back. Then when Dad got hurt, I couldn't just leave Mom here all by herself to take care of him."

I take a sip of water to cool my throat. "What letter?"

She picks at a fry. "Joanne's letter."

"She sent you a letter?"

Kristie looks up. "You didn't hear about that?"

I continue to stare.

She pushes her bangs behind an ear but doesn't look up. "She sent us a letter."

"When?"

"You really don't know?"

"Jesus Christ, Kris, no, I didn't know."

She shrugs. "We got it something like a year after she left."

"If she sent you a letter, then what makes you think she was murdered?"

Tears well in Kristie's eyes, but she smiles as if to hide them. "Forget it. It's complicated." This is a strange comment, and I think this might actually be the first time she's ever lied to me. "How's your mom?" she asks suddenly, dabbing her eyes.

"You're changing the subject."

"I've gotten good at that." She chuckles. "Years of practice."

I study her for a long moment. I can tell she's not going to talk about it. She's going to do things like ask me about my mom even though she doesn't really care, and I'm going to things like answer in order to keep this pointless conversation going. "She's doing good," I answer. "She's living in Chicago with her sister. She moved over that way a long time ago."

"I know."

"You know?"

"Everyone knows. When someone moves out of this town, it makes front page news for, like, three weeks."

I chuckle. "Yeah, I guess so. Anyway, her sister's husband passed away, so Mom moved in. They share rent."

"You still see each other?"

"Holidays and family reunions. Things like that."

"Are you still close?"

I shrug. "It's complicated."

"Touché."

"If the shoe fits."

"If you can't beat 'em, join 'em."

"What goes around, comes around."

"You can say that again."

"That again." I smile.

She grins while shaking her head, once more playing with a wayward bang that refuses to be tucked behind one of those cute little ears. "That was one of the things I always liked about you." She takes a sip of water, careful as she sets the glass back down. "You loved your mom. You took care of her."

"She and I have had a unique relationship ever since Dad died. I was pretty young, and I don't remember a lot, but even then I remember us having good and bad days." I smile. "But she's still my mom."

"Sounds comfy."

I wag a finger at her. "Don't start, Kristine."

She wrinkles her nose. "God, you know how I hate that name." She takes a bite and smiles as she chews, but I know her. I know how her mind works. She's thinking about how she's going to tell me why I'm really here. "So, when I called you," she says, swallowing before taking another sip, "why'd you come back? I mean, if you don't remember anything, and since there's no one left here..."

Guilt Trip #3.

"Except..." she says, awkwardly.

"For you," I say, filling in the gap.

"For Ritchie," she suggests.

I go rigid.

"Hmmm." She smiles. "Touchy subject?"

"Sort of. We haven't spoken since I left either. Things didn't really end well between us."

"So, you *do* remember?"

"Enough."

"Of what?"

I smile, but there's nothing funny about it. I do remember something. A number painted on an aluminum bleacher. The kind you'd see in a stadium. The numbers are blue, the paint worn, but there it is, just like a tattoo that won't wash off. The number 44.

"You were best friends," she continues. "How do you just...do that to your best friend?"

"You were my best friend, and I did it to you, didn't I?"

She leans back, wiping her mouth. "Yeah, I guess you did."

I set my fork down. "I'm sorry." I look at her and realize I might be the world's biggest turd for leaving her all alone to fend for herself for the past twenty years. I'm out of things to say. The waitress comes by, and yes, everything is fine, but she tops off our nearly untouched glasses of water anyway.

"What am I doing here?" I ask once we're alone again. "You called me, asked me to fly halfway across the country, and whether it's guilt or amnesia or God knows what, here I am."

53

She gingerly picks up her and picks up her purse, which she places on her lap—under the table and out of view—before leaning forward. "I found something." Her voice is barely a whisper.

"That's what you said on the phone."

"Remember the old Johnson farm?"

Suddenly my steak has lost its appeal, quivering on my white plate in a pool of red blood mixing with A1 sauce. Yes, I remember the old farm. I passed it on the way into town, and I reflected on it then, but now that she's bringing it up, I'm wondering what it has to do with anything. "Sure," I answer, and sure, I remember. Sure, I remember that Ritchie and I used to shoot bottles out there to kill lazy afternoons. Sometimes we'd even get lucky enough to have a rabbit or squirrel serve as a moving target. And now that I think about it, sure, I think...I think...

"Tony?"

Route 89. That was the way out of town. Route 89 led all the way to the edge of the Earth and beyond. You didn't take Route 89 unless you never planned on coming back. To us kids, the farm marked the final outpost, or as we called it, the point of no return.

"I was over that way the other day," she says quietly.

"I passed it on my way in," I say, chewing again, but this lump of meat isn't going anywhere. "I was surprised to see it still standing."

"That place always gave me the creeps," she says. "I remember as a kid thinking the Devil lived there. Its peacefulness was like bait. It *lured* us in."

"Then why'd you stop?" I interrupt, washing the bit of meat down my throat with a gulp of water. I keep my tone light, the conversation casual. Not that I feel either light or casual. Everyone knows you don't just wind up at the old Johnson Farm and keep the conversation casual. Twenty years ago the driveway and yard was littered with rotted boards and hundreds upon hundreds of broken bottles from the numerous teenage excursions of tempted bravery bent on drunken dares. Even if you're wearing steel-toe boots, you don't just wind up 'over that way' unless there's a reason to.

"My car broke down," she says. "I had to walk back."

"But your car's working fine today?"

"It was an easy fix. They said it was just a loose thingamajig."

"Is that a technical term?"

She smiles.

"What were you doing out on Route 89?" I ask. "You weren't trying to leave town, weren't you?"

She smiles again. "No. Well, yes, but no—not permanently. I visit my friend Natalie over in Lansing once a year. Remember Natalie Biggs?"

"Sure."

"She lives there now. She comes home for Christmas. I go there in the summer. It's kind of became a thing."

"The way things often do," I say with good humor.

She throws a French fry at me. "I'm being serious."

I chuckle. "Sorry. Go on."

"There's no cellular service out there, so I was stuck walking. And it was raining, so I stopped to wait it out in the barn."

"And?"

"And…you."

I frown.

"We have history out there, and I'm not embarrassed to talk about it." She's blushing, so I know she *is* embarrassed if only a little. "I mean, do you ever think about me?"

"Sure," though she should know better, and maybe so should I. If I can't remember details from that summer, then why would she believe that I remember anything about her? Somewhere along the line I made a choice to forget as much as I could, and I would have never returned had it not been for her phone call.

"You remember how all the kids used to say that place was haunted?"

I nod. "Ritchie used to drag me out there. We'd go out there when there wasn't anything else to do. I guess he was bound and determined to prove to the world how unafraid of ghosts he was."

The humor has drained from her face, and I realize the time for telling jokes has passed. She tilts her glass and takes more than just a sip. Her eyes are misty when she looks up. "When I was out there yesterday I sat down on one of those old bales of hay. The lighting wasn't all that good, but I could still see. Sort of. The barn doors were open, and it was around midday, so I could still see all the stuff the Johnson's left behind." She smiles. "Nobody's touched any of it. Even after all these years. It's like an antique store, but eerily devoid of life, you know?"

I shrug. "I haven't been there in years."

"Well, it was still light enough to read all that graffiti you and Ritchie spray-painted on the walls."

I shake my head. "That was Ritchie's idea."

She smiles. "Even the part that reads AAA plus KL?"

Now it's my turn to blush.

Her smile begins to wane, and her attention drifts. I might as well be sitting alone.

"How is everything?" the waitress asks. Again. She's like a fly that won't shoo.

"Fine," I return, though my tone isn't terribly friendly. The waitress nods with a half-smile before turning away.

"Then I saw it," Kristie whispers, leaning forward. She pushes the bangs from her eyes. "It was in the corner, next to an old bale of hay and mostly buried. I wouldn't have even seen it except for just a bit of color poking through the dirt. And you know how Joanne is. She likes bright colors."

I can feel my pulse racing.

Kristie leans back and reaches into the purse on her lap. She pulls out what looks like a rotted piece of orange cloth wrapped over a horseshoe-shaped wire. Dirt has

55

ruined the original vibrant color, and moths or mice or something had chewed a lot of the cloth away leaving only bits, but despite the poor condition, even I recognize what Kristie's holding.

"Jesus," I whisper, leaning back. I've suddenly lost all interest in my meal. And Kristie's face is already stained with tears.

"She was wearing this the day she disappeared." Kristie whispers. "She only had two of them, and the white one was still in her room. That means she was wearing this that day." She draws a breath. "She wouldn't have taken it off. Not on purpose."

"It's okay," I say, but I know it's not. I take the cloth-wrapped wire from her hand to examine it. It was Joanne's hearing headband. In better days, it didn't look much different than the kind of headbands girls wore in their hair to keep the long bangs out of their eyes. It looks different now, but just the sight of it dredges a slew of memories I had long buried. Joanne's disappearance destroyed this town.

I was in Georgia by then, but the cops tracked me down anyway. They asked all kinds of questions I didn't have answers to. They asked me about Kristie. Then they asked me about Joanne, but I didn't know anything. I told them the truth. I was at UGA on scholarship, and I'd taken a job at the bookstore. I invited them to check the records. Everything checked out, and they eventually left me alone.

It's terrifying not being able to remember. I remember bits and pieces of the day I left, which is more than I remembered just yesterday, but at best, what I do recall is broken fragments that don't add up to a whole story. I remember being scared, but I don't remember why. I remember wanting things to go back to the way they had been, and I remember knowing they couldn't. It was over. All of it. It was over between Ritchie and me, and it was over between Kristie and me. When I left, I knew I'd never be back. I'd never come home. It wasn't a vow. I just knew I'd never be back because of what had happened, and I vaguely remember passing the old Johnson Farm on the way out of town. Once the farm was behind me, so was Payton. I was on a Greyhound bus, and everything I owned was packed tightly in a single suitcase beside me—kind of like the one I brought with me when I flew in earlier today.

Funny how things revolve in circles.

"If she was wearing this the day she allegedly hitchhiked out of town," Kristie murmurs, "then why was it in the corner of that barn?"

I look down at my meal. Just a few more bites of tender meat sitting in red and black sauce, wiggling—almost alive. "It doesn't mean she was murdered," I murmur.

"Oh come on, Tony, she never came home. She never called. We never heard from her."

"What about the letter?"

She shakes her head. "I'm not talking about the letter. I'm talking about her. She never showed up. She never picked up the phone. She and I were close. We're identical twins. Twins have a unique bond even close brothers and sisters don't share. They *can't* share."

"Were you two fighting? When she left, I mean."

"Sure, she and I fought. We fought a lot. Sisters fight."

"Did you fight the day she disappeared?"

Kristie leans back. "What do you think? You were there."

"I don't remember."

"That's a cop out."

"It's not. I honestly don't remember."

"Come on, do you honestly expect me to believe that?"

"There are all these flashes," I say demonstratively. "Images. Like photographs. Bits and pieces. But they're not whole scenes, just snapshots."

Kristie shakes her head. "I called you this morning because you were there—the day she disappeared. You two were close."

I just shake my head. "I don't remember being close…"

"Well, regardless of what you choose to or choose *not* to remember," Kristie murmurs. "*I* still love her. By now we would have heard something. More than just some stupid letter. I would have *felt* something."

"So you think she's dead because you don't *feel* anything?"

"No." Kristie shakes her head. "I think she's dead because I found this." She waves the wire in my face, her eyes tearing up. "For almost twenty years we've buried our heads in the sand and accepted the lunatic premise that she just hitchhiked her way into the sunset—that she'd hooked up with the wrong guy or something. It was that letter that kept us from considering that maybe she never even left town. Nobody looked around to see if she might still be here."

"So, what's it got to do with me?" I ask.

"Because you were there. That afternoon. You were *there*."

I'm sitting in a stupid restaurant booth, and she's asking me to re-engage old memories and feelings that I'm not sure I even remember. She's asking me to return to something I intentionally left behind. Joanne wasn't part of my family, and Kristie isn't either. They were a fantasy I've made a point to forget. I'm frustrated, agitated to the point of just throwing my hands up and tossing in the towel.

"Forget it," she murmurs, picking at her napkin.

"We got a few days to figure this out," I offer. "I don't have to be back to the office until Monday, so let's think."

She looks at me like she knows something I don't. "You're not going back." She doesn't just say it as a conversation piece. She says it matter-of-factly, as if it's already been carved in stone.

"Actually, I am. I've got a plane ticket that flies out on Monday, and I'm leaving or I lose my job," I say. "If you want to play Nancy Drew and dredge up old memories, then we can do that for a few days, but don't—"

"Is this some kind of game to you?" Kristie asks, her eyes welling.

"I was just—"

"Fuck you!" she shrieks. She grabs the headband from me, shoves it in her purse, stands and storms from the restaurant. If I wasn't emotionally involved before, I am

57

now. So are the other restaurant patrons who are staring at me, cheeks bulging with un-chewed food. Some of the faces are familiar, and I can tell they suddenly recognize me too. A sea of frowns judge me, and I'm suddenly the schmuck everyone remembers me as. I drop thirty bucks on the table and stand to leave even though I'm still hungry.

This just keeps getting better and better.

## Part II

Now that I've officially offended the one person I'd hoped not to offend, maybe I won't have to stay in Payton through the weekend after all. This has been about the worst ending to a lousy day that I can imagine, and I'm feeling about as low as a slug that just ran face first into a brick wall.

I drive straight back to the hotel, lock the car and then lock myself in the room before setting the alarm for six a.m. By six thirty I plan on being on Route 89 heading out of town toward the airport. This was a bad idea. The whole trip.

A hot shower and some cold ice water later, and I'm spread out on my bed watching *Jeopardy*. I'm not getting any of the answers right, and I'm feeling terribly uncomfortable as I squirm on top of the scratchy bedcovers. I don't belong here. I'm tempted to call her, but I don't have her number, and even if I did, there's nothing to say. She's right. I'm wrong. This town is messed up.

There's a knock at my door. Sitting up, I look down at the way I'm dressed—or rather that the way I'm undressed. Pasty white skin, flabby gut, unclipped toenails. I didn't even bother to comb my hair after showering, and now I'm sitting in nothing but boxers. Scrambling, I pull on a pair of jeans and push my arms through the sleeves of one of my button-down shirts.

"Coming," I call as I finger-comb my hair while crossing the room to the front door. I unto the deadbolt, turn the handle and open the door to her, a smile on my face.

Only, it's not her.

And the stupid smile smeared across my stupid face quickly melts.

He's put on some weight, and he's lost a lot of hair. His face is creased with lines of age and wear. He looks fifty-five years old, yet I know he's only two weeks older than me. His appearance is as intimidating as his body odor, and I'm surprised to realize that I'm more shocked by his appearance than I am by the fact that he's standing in the doorway with a scowl of sheer hatred directed at me.

"Ritchie," I say softly, trying to smile while realizing I don't have it in me.

"What are you doin' back here?"

"Good to see you too," I say, quietly thankful that my voice is not yet shaking.

58

"I told you not to come back," he grumbles, and his voice is deeper than I remember. He is a brute of a man, tattoos on both arms—a roll of fat hanging out from under his T-shirt.

"It's been a long time, Rich. This is my home too."

"The hell it is," he grumbles, and he is not placating me. "This is my fuckin' town." He shakes his head. "Not yours."

I'll admit that my reappearance in Payton may have been unwarranted, but I'll be damned if Ritchie Hudson is going to tell me that this is *his* town. This is my town too.

"Ritchie, it's been a helluva long day." I thumb over my shoulder into my room. "You want a—"

I am in the process of offering him a beer when a fist comes out of nowhere and strikes me squarely across the jaw. There's a white flash, a burst of pain, and that's how my day ends.

# Six

## *Yesterday*

"You okay?" she asks.

Payton Hill grants a perfect bird's eye view of the city. Technically, it's outside the town limits, but the name was adapted and it stuck. We're sitting up on Payton Hill under the boiling sun, which is this big fiery death ball dangling in the sky as though it's about to melt mankind. It's only May, yet this is the hottest spring I can remember. It feels more like August, and I don't do well when it's this hot. Even so, a teenager couldn't ask for a better backdrop, and he couldn't ask for a better set up. I'm with my girl and she smells great, feels great and looks great. Her bare arms, neck and face are milky white, the shadows doing their thing to make her more 'angel' than 'human.'     My motivation rests somewhere in the vicinity of getting laid. She's not Sharon Daniels, but Sharon is more like a cartoon—the one where the cartoon boy-dog sees the cartoon girl-dog and jumps up, tongue out, eyes bulging, tail waging. Kristie isn't Sharon Daniels, but she's beautiful and gorgeous and willing and much too good for me. I love her legs—caramel glazed and glistening under the light, and I love the way her eyes twinkle with unfettered adoration for me. I love the way her hair smells, and I love about a million other things about her. It takes practice to remind myself that she is not a goddess, yet after years of staring at women clad in underwear in Sears catalogues, my mind has imagined a hundred times over what the real thing must feel like. Her tongue, her fingers, her breath, her hair, her toes, her belly-button, her taste. Everything about her is feminine and so much different than my lanky, hairy, smelly body that I can't help but wonder what she sees in me.

"Tony?" she asks.

"Yeah?"

"You okay?"

"Fine. Why?"

I'm on my back, one leg up, my hands behind my head. She's on her stomach, her chin on her hands, her hands on my chest. "You're quiet again."

"I'm fine."

"What are you thinking about?"

"Us."

She rolls over onto her stomach and rests her chin on her folded hands upon my chest while looking me in the eye. "What about us?"

"Just us. This and that. You know."

"No, I don't know. Are you thinking about us as a couple or as two people? Or are you wondering how much longer you have to lie here before you can go play with your friends?"

"I don't *play* with my friends."

"You know what I mean."

"And I'm not..." I trail off, suddenly flustered. This is so typical. My mom does this sort of thing all the time. She analyzes everything I say before twisting it around and using her own brand of word-trickery to tell me what my problem is even before I've had a chance to figure out if I even have a problem. "I didn't mean it that way."

Kristie rolls away onto her back. "Forget it. I don't want to fight."

"I didn't realize we were fighting."

"You're ignoring me again."

"I'm not ignoring you. If I were ignoring you, I wouldn't be here with you."

"You're only here in body. Mentally, you're somewhere else. Probably Georgia."

I bite my tongue. "That's totally unfair. I was enjoying what I thought was the perfect afternoon my girlfriend."

"Now you're placating me."

"What does that even mean?"

"I think it means you're lying to me."

"You don't even know?'

"Joanne said it."

"In what context."

"I don't know. Why?"

"Well, find out what it means before you start using it on people who might take offense."

"I told you, I don't want to fight."

"We're not fighting."

"It feels like we're fighting."

"Only because you're using words that you don't understand."

"Or you."

"Or me."

She's quiet. She even closes her eyes as if in deep thought. "Fine. You want me to say it? I'll say it. I don't think you love me." She shakes her head. "There, I said it."

"Did I miss something?"

"If you loved me, you wouldn't be moving away."

"But I'm moving away *for* you."

"You're moving...you're doing this for *me*?"

"Yes."

"So, you're moving away and leaving me behind as some kind of *favor*?"

"Well, it's not exactly like—"

"God, you're a narcissist."

"Good word. Did you learn that today?"

"Fuck you."

I bite my tongue. I shouldn't have said that. I baited the hook and she took it hook, line and sinker. "I'm sorry."

"You don't love me."

"You think this is easy for me? Leaving you behind? You think I haven't thought about cashing in my chips and settling on Payton-is-the-best-I-can-do? I want *more*. I want more for you, and I want more for *us*. I'm not...placating you."

She's about to say something, but my using that word against her shuts her up. And now she's angry.

"I promise I'm not," I continue. "And I didn't use that word just to piss you off. I mean it. I love you." I do, in fact, love the hell out of her, and it's killing me to hear her talking to me like this, especially when I've been thinking about what I've been thinking about. My heart is thundering in my chest, a question I've been toiling over for the last three weeks repeating itself like a broken record in my mind. Now just doesn't seem like the right time. Then again, she's pissed, so what better time to pop the ultimate question than when everyone hates everyone?

"You're just saying what you think I want to hear," she says. "You're just—"

"What if I were to ask you to marry me?"

"Don't start. I'm not in the mood."

"I'm serious, Kristine."

She looks up. "You're serious? You're *seriously* asking me to marry you?"

"What if I am?"

"Because you love me or because you're afraid of losing me?"

Oh my God, really? A guy can't ask a simple yes/no question without having it twisted into a fuckin' pretzel. I just asked the girl to marry me, yet she's still not happy. Dating is a big, giant crap bag. Even after you think you've found the right girl and all that awkward stuff is supposed to be behind you, it's not. You still can't win. It's a perpetual chessboard. It's not about the right question or the wrong answer. It has to be some combination of what-ifs and that's-that scenarios that guys don't understand because girls dream up demented scenarios while reading *Cosmo* and eating granola bars at pajama parties.

"I'm hungry," she decides. "Where are we going?"

"What?"

"I'm too hungry to talk about it."

"You're too hungry to talk about marriage?"

"I'm too young to talk about marriage," she says, jumping up. "I'm too hungry to argue." She extends her hand. "Come on. I'm buying."

"You're not paying. It's not like I'm destitute. I can afford a meal for my girlfriend."

62

"You don't get paid till Friday."

"I've got a few bucks."

She keeps tugging on my hand. "On your feet, you chauvinist pig. You always buy. Today's my treat. I'm in the mood for chili."

"Who eats chili in the middle of summer?"

"I do. Dune's has the best."

I shake my head, take her hand and lead her toward Payton proper feeling pretty confused. I just popped the question, and she just blew me off. Actually, she just threw my inappropriately timed question right back in my inappropriate face leaving me feeling like a wet puppy. I don't even feel like we're dating anymore as we walk down the hill hand in hand. I feel like I'm in a movie playing the boyfriend even when I know the girl whose hand I'm holding is only agreeing to do so because she's getting paid to do so.

The sidewalks lead us into town, the crosswalk our threshold. The streetlights and neon signs aren't exactly Las Vegas, but it's a small town and looks like one. We cross the street, and like a gentleman, I open the door for her. There's a sign by the front counter reading '*Please Wait to be Seated*,' and there's a friendly looking hostess that appears to be devoid of 'friendly.' She smiles, but it's not real. It's one of those smiles that's only worth minimum wage.

"Name?" the hostess asks.

"Peters," I reply with a straight face. "Harry."

That's my teenage jocularity coming out. I don't know why I'm trying to be funny. I don't feel funny. I feel hollow. I feel like I swallowed a bloody booger, that acidic taste, that gurgling nausea in the pit of my stomach. Maybe humor is a defense mechanism. Who knows? Ask my shrink.

"Harry Peters?" she repeats. She raises a razor-sharp eyebrow. "Harry Peters?"

"I'm very sensitive about my name." I can't seem to let it go.

"Funny," she says humorlessly. "Mr. Abbott."

And now I'm pissed, and I feel myself getting defensive without really wanting too. She just called me Mr. Abbott, but only my dad ever went by Mr. Abbott, and he's dead, and this minimum wage whore should have some goddamn respect before getting lippy with her customers. After all, I'm paying her salary with my 10% tip.

Kristie giggles.

The hostess snaps her gum, eyes dull. "A table or a booth or by the window?"

"A booth will be fine."

She grabs two menus. "Right this way."

Kristie is eyeing me suspiciously. "I doubt she meant anything by it, Mr. Cranky Pants," she whispers, acutely aware that our friendly hostess has hit a nerve. We take our seats, planted smack dab in the middle of the spotlight. We have napkins, silverware and empty glasses.

"You're wandering," Kristie says.

"I'm right here," I promise.

Our waitress appears with two ice-waters, a pad of paper and a Bic pen. Her nametag reads KATHRYIN, and she's eyeing me defensively as though I'm a smarmy comment away from lunging at her. Maybe I am.

"I like the phonetic spelling," I say with a smile.

"Excuse me?"

"Your nametag. The misspelling. Kathryin. With an 'i.'" When she doesn't blink, I add, "after the 'y'."

She looks at the nametag, an effort that requires her to scrunch all three chins into three tiny rolls. "Is there something funny about my name?" she demands, looking up. "Harry Peters?"

"No ma'am," I say. "I meant to say that it's a lovely name."

"You ready to order?"

No, I'm not ready to order. I'm ready to punch her in the face, but the French dip is on special, and Kristie is eyeing me with that look of hers.

"We'll need a minute," I return.

Kathryin with an 'i' after the 'y' smiles without meaning it. "Sure."

"What's the matter with you?" Kristie hisses after our waitress walks away.

"I can expect spit in whatever I order."

"This was supposed to be fun."

"I'm having a blast."

She leans back, eyeing me—studying me. "Is it me? Is it what I said?"

"No. It's not what you said."

"Is it because you're leaving?"

"It's not because I'm leaving. There's nothing wrong. I'm fine. Really."

"Is it your dad?"

I look up sharply. I don't mean to. It's more like a defense mechanism. You knock your funny bone and you kick. I just kicked.

"It's your dad." She takes a sip from her water. "Why don't you ever talk about him?"

"It's not my dad. I don't even remember my dad."

"Come on, you were fine when we walked in, cracking jokes and stuff. Yet, she called you 'Mr. Abbott,' and you clammed up."

"I wasn't fine. I was pissed off."

"At me?"

"No." I shake my head. "Can we not…I'm fine."

"Why are you so mopey?"

"I'm not mopey. I'm misunderstood."

"Like an artist?"

"Exactly like an artist."

She frowns "Sometimes I feel like I hardly know you. I've never even seen the inside of your house."

"It's not my house. It's my mom's house. Besides, you're not missing anything."

"And I've never met your mother. You've hung out with my family, like, how many times? Twenty? Thirty?"

"Are you keeping count?"

"I'm being serious."

"You'll meet her."

"Don't you love her?"

I shrug. "Yeah. I do. She's my mom."

"Then what's the problem?"

"There is no problem. You'll meet her."

"When?"

"Whenever."

Kathryn is eyeing us from the opposite side of the room. She knows we're too young to drink, so perhaps we're too young to tip. Apparently, we're already on her short-list, and we haven't even ordered yet.

I look over the top of my menu at Kristie and watch her quietly. Her hair is slightly out of place, and her skin slightly pink from the sun. Her eyes are darting back and forth as she reads through her choices, and she looks so pretty. She looks up suddenly and catches me staring.

"What?"

I say nothing. I just look. And look. And look. She smiles slightly—unable to hold it back—the twinkle returning to her eyes, the edges of her perfect lips turning upward. Neither of us say anything, but neither of us need to. Enough is said just with our eyes, and I know her well enough to read her smiles. This is one of those good moments where we click instead of clack, where I'm growing into a man and her a woman. We're realizing that we are an 'item' and this is love. She's prepped to say something. Something romantic, something—

"You are such a pervert," she whispers with a smile.

"Ready to order?" Our personal Jesus has returned with a vengeance, breaking us from our trance, and this time she's not taking 'no' for an answer.

"I think we're going to need another minute," I say, and Kathryn with an 'i' after the 'y' sighs audibly before haughtily turning her back and waddling away. Kristie just covers her mouth, giggling quietly.


## Part II

"I can't believe they invited us over," Ritchie says as he combs his hair for the umpteenth time. The more he combs it, the more ridiculous he looks, and I suspect he knows this, which is why he's keeps starting over.

"*They* didn't invite *us* anywhere," I mutter. "Kristie invited *me*."

"She said I could come too."

"That's because you asked if you could come. What's she supposed to say, no?" I look at my friend making a mess of himself as he buttons his shirt which, of course, he's buttoning all wrong.

"Joanne's gonna be there," he murmurs.

"I'm sure she's counting the minutes."

Ritchie looks at me with a hurt expression. "Why do you always gotta talk down to me? I'm supposed to be your best friend. You're supposed to have my back."

"I got your back. I just don't want you getting your hopes up."

Finally realizing he's buttoned his shirt in the wrong order, Ritchie starts over. His big clumsy fingers are shaking. He is really nervous. I know he has a crush on the poor girl, but she's never reciprocated, and it's too bad, because other than being a big dummy, he's a decent enough guy.

"Hurry up," I say, heading out the front door. Standing in the sunshine, I'm reminded that summer in Payton is like an old vinyl record. Everything turns, but nothing seems to change. It all just stays the same. Skip, skip, skip.

The screen door opens behind me, the smell of cologne ruining the fresh air. As usual, he's overdone it. "I think I used too much," he says as he contorts his face while trying to look at the collar of his shirt. "I spilled a bit."

"A bit? Like what, half a gallon? Jesus, Ritchie."

He frowns, biting his tongue. "Come on, man. What did we talk about?"

I roll my eyes. "You're right, I'm sorry. Me and my mouth. Won't happen again."

"You always gotta be so vulgar."

"What do you want me to say?"

"Nothin'. Don't say nothin'. When you get the urge, just don't say nothin'. I hate it when you talk like that. It's not you."

"I won't do it again."

"You're gonna do it again."

"I won't do it again."

"You're gonna do it again."

"Then yell at me when I do."

He shakes his head before pointing towards Lawton. "Let's go." And just like that, we're straight out of a Mark Twain adventure, once again two buddies making our way through the dry grass toward the Old Beaver. The afternoon is waning, the sun the hottest it's been all day and the color of the sky somewhere between yellow and orange. It's a July heat hot enough to make me sweat, so it must be awful for Ritchie who sweats year round and a half-gallon of cologne might actually play in his favor.

## *Part III*

We cross the Beaver and follow the path toward Lawton. Ritchie is going on about baseball, which is a welcomed relief considering I expected him to ramble on about Joanne the entire time, but today it's all about the Tigers and what a lousy season they're having. Truth be told, I haven't been paying much attention. It's early yet, but according to Ritchie, their season is already over.

"I can't do it," Ritchie says. "Not in the Bigs, I mean."

"Of course you can. You're just scared."

"I ain't scared of nothin'. It's not like that."

"It's exactly like that."

"I'm being prodigal."

"*Practical*, ya dumb ass, and that's still the wrong word."

"I pitch for the Pirates. Nobody I faced is pro material."

"Yet you'll never know for sure until you try out."

He slumps. "I don't wanna try out. I don't want to move away. I wanna stay here."

On his behalf, I'd gone as far as digging up contact info for a few talent scouts in the Detroit area, but Ritchie refuses to call. Whenever I bring it up, he gets angry or changes the subject. It's like he doesn't want to hear about his 'potential.' He wants to pretend he's stupid and worthless and stuck here, and because he's worthless and stupid and stuck here, we might as well make the best of a bad situation. He's got the talent, but he doesn't have the grades, and scouts don't come to Payton. Not on purpose anyway. He's the best pitcher I've ever seen—on TV or in real life, but if nobody knows, then it's just wasted talent.

The sounds of Lawton are closer now, and soon we're walking along the familiar streets and sidewalks. The older trees hang like umbrellas overhead, shading us from the merciless sun and allowing Ritchie to dry out by the time we reach the steps of the Lambert's front porch. As usual, Ritchie hangs back and fidgets while trying to decide the perfect pose for when the door opens.

Kristie greets me with a wide smile, a big hug and kiss before inviting us in. Ritchie is quiet as a mouse as he sits in the same chair he always sits in while looking nervous. It's quiet other than the whisper of bugs drifting in from the outside and Ritchie's fingers drumming the arms of the chair. Suddenly, there's the sound of someone bounding down the steps. Joanne dances her way down the staircase before dancing through the living room and right into the kitchen. Her eyes are closed, and she has headphones on cranked so loud that even from across the room I can make out the song she's listening to. That's the only way she can hear anything, but despite the tiny crackle coming from her headphones, I can almost hear Ritchie's jaw hit the floor. Joanne is wearing a white tank-top, red panties and nothing else. There's some white, a bit of red and a whole lot of skin. I have to admit that even I'm impressed. I'm dating Kristie, and the two have the exact same build, so it shouldn't be a big deal, but it is, because it's like I just saw my girlfriend scamper obliviously through the living room in her underwear. Only it's not my girlfriend. It's *her.*

Kristie turns my jaw, redirecting my attention back to hers. "Don't get any ideas, mister."

I don't say anything. Not because I have nothing to say, but because I can't say it. Not without expecting some serious backlash.

"Apparently, she doesn't know you're here yet."

"Can she hear what she's listening to?"

"*Legally* deaf," Kristie emphasizes. "Not *totally* deaf."

"Yeah, well, you should probably talk to her before Ritchie freaks out even more than he already is." I nod Ritchie's way, and sure enough, he's squirming, his mouth slightly open, fresh sweat stains appearing under his arms, his hands locked so tightly to the armrests that his knuckles have turned white.

"He looks like he's going to pop," she giggles.

"This isn't funny. I'm being totally serious."

She frowns. "I'll be right back." She crawls off me before leaning in to whisper into my ear. "P.S. I look even better in the same outfit." She kisses my cheek before heading for the kitchen.

This leaves me with a dilemma growing in my pants that is going to be very difficult to hide in about ten seconds. I shift uncomfortably while trying to find a sitting position that looks natural. Kristie re-emerges from the kitchen and trots up the steps. Coming back down with Joanne's shorts and headband, she disappears back into the kitchen.

"Figures," Ritchie mutters. "I thought Jo did it on purpose."

"We've talked about this," I say, still trying to find a natural looking position on this stupid-ass couch. "Play it cool."

He nods, but he's sweating. He looks at me, then the kitchen door, then me, then the kitchen door. Poor guy. I feel lust and love and hate and anger and things like that, but something tells me Ritchie feels those same things on a whole different level. He looks terrible, fidgeting and sweating, eyes darting, fingers nervous, feet tapping.

"Relax, Rich," I whisper.

He nods, wiping the sweat from his brow, exhaling, breathing in and exhaling again. Slowly, he lifts his eyes to the kitchen again, and this time he holds on, waiting. I can almost hear his telltale heart even though he's quiet as a mouse. When the two girls finally emerge, Joanne's face is red with embarrassment, but instantly the two girls bust up laughing, and I can't help but smile. I don't think Ritchie fully understands what's so funny. He just bites his lip, his eyes devouring Joanne.

"Hey," Joanne says, her tongue thick. I always thought her muddled accent was kind of annoying, but seeing her like this, totally cool and confident with what just happened, I have to admit, she's bad ass. And good for her.

"So, what's on tonight's agenda," Kristie asks as she sits down and wraps her arm around me.

I shrug. "I was thinking maybe a bonfire out by the Beaver."

"That would be fun," Joanne says. "I'll call Lindsey and Mary."

Ritchie sits still, his fingers still locked around the ends of the armrests.

"How about you, Ritchie?" Kristie asks. "Bonfire? No bonfire? Yay or nay?"

"Good," he nods.

Jo giggles.

Kristie leans over and whispers in my ear. "He wore too much cologne again." Her breathing in my ear isn't helping with my little 'problem' downstairs, so I sit up, shifting again.

"You okay?" Kristie asks.

"Ritchie says he's going to pitch for the Tiger's one day," I say in a desperate attempt to divert attention from me.

"I never said that," he replies, turning red. "I said I'm not good enough."

"Whatever," I say, waving him off. "No one can hit your junk." I even throw in a Bostonian accent. "Fer-gedda-bou-dit."

"You're exaggerating."

"When you're a Cy Young winner, I want you to remember us little people."

"Kiss my grits, Triple A-hole," Ritchie mutters. He's playing it cool while trying to hide stolen glances.

Jo knows what's going on. Hell, she's reveling in it. She loves the attention. It's got to be a major ego boost, and to be fawned over by the biggest name in sports this side of Det roit has to mean something. She's trying not to smile, but I can tell she's covering up, and I'll bet Kristie can tell too.

"Tony's right," Joanne says finally. She doesn't dare lift her eyes. "I've seen you pitch. You're good. Real good."

Ritchie shakes his head. "My grades are shit, and I only got two weeks left. It's over." He even looks like a wet puppy. He's breathing heavy, he's sweating, and I can only imagine the terror he's experiencing inside. All those emotions crammed into that frumpy frame. For a big guy, he looks curiously innocent.

"I do pretty good in math," Joanne says.

Ritchie nods. "Everyone does pretty good in math. Except me."

"That's not what I meant, ya big dummy."

In the past, it's only ever been me with the guts to call him anything other than 'Ritchie' or 'Rich.' However, at the sound of her saying 'dummy' in that weird, distorted accent of hers, everyone stops. Everything stops. Even the clock on the wall stops. All eyes turn to Joanne. She's sitting there on the arm of the sofa, one bare knee up, blond hair cascading over her thin shoulders. She looks like a Pepsi commercial.

"And if you're willing to put in the time," she continues, "I suppose I could *also* help you with your English." She even emphasizes 'also' in case he still isn't catching on.

Ritchie sits there, mouth open, eyes wide.

69

"Though when you sign your first pro contract, I expect some kind of kickback," Joanne finishes.

Ritchie is, for the second time in under ten minutes, on the verge of exploding. His face is turning purple, his eyes bulging. To be honest, I don't think he's even—

"Breathe, Rich," I say.

Kristie's hand has migrated to my stomach, and I'm starting to get nervous. If her hand continues to wander south, she'll realize something is literally 'up,' and if I stand, my secret will be revealed.

"I only got two weeks," Ritchie murmurs.

"Then that means we'd better hustle."

Ritchie trembles.

"We do this," Joanne says. "We go all the way. No half-assing it." In her broken tongue, it sounds more like '*No hav azzing it*,' but still…

"All the way?" Ritchie asks.

Kristie buries her face against my chest to suppress her laughter.

"All the way," Joanne continues, and suddenly Ritchie's in the best mood ever.

The phone rings. Joanne gets up and crosses the living room to the end table beside Ritchie's chair. She picks up, but my attention isn't on her. It's on Kristie. Her hand has gone lower, and I try (unsuccessfully) to shift into a position that will flatten things out, but it's too late. Her hand stops, and she lifts her head from my shoulder, a curious look in her eye. Gently, she applies a bit of pressure while a smile spreads over her lips. This time I can't run away like I did back in the park. I was uncomfortable up on the hill when it was just the two of us, but here in Mr. and Mrs. Lambert's living room, while in the company of both Ritchie and Joanne, it's ten times worse. Here I feel exposed.

She kisses my neck before resting her head on my shoulder. To her, everything's cool. We're a couple of kids playing grownups. We are the envy of everyone else. We're past all that 'what if' bullshit. We're officially going steady, which means we're in love, which means I have no reason to be afraid. Which also makes it that much harder to walk away.

"They're not home right now," Joanne says into the phone. "Besides, my dad likes to cut the grass himself. He has a riding mower and *loves* working the stick."

Ritchie is paralyzed, Joanne is teasing him, Kristie is teasing me and I'm dying. Ritchie was right. Two weeks from now, and I'm all the way gone. These moments that feel like Tom Sawyer meets Holden Caulfield meets Hermie Raucher are the best of times, and in a way, also the worst of times. Being a teenager sucks. Not because we're naïve, which we're not, and not because we're invincible, which are, but because we think in mirrors. Everything's backwards. Everything's new and exciting, and all of it is eternal. If I live a hundred years, I swear to God I'll never forget this day.

# Seven

## Today

I wake up on the floor of my hotel room. The front door is wide open. The moon has risen, and the stars are out. The heat of the day is gone, having been replaced with a cool breeze. Ants are eating me alive, crawling over my exposed legs and taking mini bites of tender flesh as though I've already died. I get to my feet, brush the ants off and shut the door before drawing the chain and locking the deadbolt. Turning around, I survey the room. "Ritchie?" I call out, but my room does not answer. I check the closet and the bathroom and under the bed just to be sure, but my 'friend' is nowhere to be seen.

The light in the bathroom is flickering as I lean forward over the sink for a better look. The reflection staring back is unenviable. I haven't aged well. Haunted eyes and sunken cheeks aside, I look older than I am. I scoop water into my palms, gargle and spit before rinsing away the dried blood while hoping that by noon it won't matter anymore. It'll just be a bruise, a memory lying just beneath the surface. It'll be one of those bruises you can't see but it aches anyway. It'll linger for days until I stop thumbing it just to see if it still hurts.

Ritchie doesn't want me here. That much is obvious, but I never expected him to cold-cock me without so much as a 'hello.' And now that Kristie and I have had our first argument, I get the feeling she's not all that crazy about the 'new and improved' Tony Abbott either. I'm not wanted, so I'm not staying. I should never have come in the first place.

*Why did you come back?*

That's the question of the day. And I suppose I'll figure out the answer in the morning or tomorrow or maybe the day after that. All I know for now is that I'm exhausted, disappointed, and frightened. I shut out the light and crawl beneath the sandpaper-like sheets on top of a brick-hard mattress. I don't feel safe here the way I should feel what with the door bolted and the windows locked. But it is what it is, and what it is ain't all that great.

## *Part II*

Silence. Not a sound. No neighbors or birds or running toilets or cars passing by. I'm in a bubble, the world around me holding its breath. Sitting up, the only sound is that of the course sheets rubbing together as I slide them aside and swing my legs over the edge of the bed before rubbing life into my eyes.

Thursday.

I should pack my things and go. Just go. Forget the phone call. Forget about Kristie and Joanne. Forget all of it and just go. Payton is dying. Five years from now it'll be dead. Just like in those old spaghetti westerns, there'll be sagebrush whipping through empty streets, windows boarded over.

I button my shirt, buckle my belt and tie my shoes. My suitcase is packed, and in five minutes I'll be on Route 89 on my way back to the airport. Nobody wants me here anyway. I tuck the suitcase into the trunk before slamming it loud enough to announce my intentions to the entire world. One last look around confirms my sour supposition that no one will even notice once I'm gone.

"Dust in the wind," I murmur as I take the wheel, fire up the engine and peel out of the parking lot onto the main drag. No traffic. No cars. No life. It feels like the rest of the world forgot Payton County even exists. As the residents die off or move away, I imagine things will continue to deteriorate until there's nothing left but a fading sign:

*For Sale*
*Payton County*
*A fine collection of memories*
*...and other assorted shit*

The street light turns red, so I slow to a stop. Across the way on the opposite corner, a young boy is playing on his red skateboard. He's practicing 360s, reminding me of when I was that age. I never owned a skateboard, but I remember playing on this corner. Ritchie was always at my side, and the future always looked infinite.

Looking in either direction, there is no traffic, no cars—no shops open for business. The entire town of Payton belongs to me and the boy, and as far as he's concerned, I don't even exist. He's in his own little world while doing his own thing. I envy both his youth and unintended indifference toward everything else.

The light remains red, and it seems to have been so for the last twenty minutes. There are no cars. There's no traffic. It's just me vs. the goddamn light that's been red forever. Growing steadily impatient, I'm stuck waiting for the dumb thing to turn so I can get the hell out of Dodge.

Still red.

I impatiently drum the wheel with my thumbs before looking both ways again. I've been sitting here for at least two minutes, and I'm about to risk driving through when I notice another car approaching from the west, sailing over the hill at a quick clip. The light for oncoming traffic must have finally turned yellow, because I hear the car rev its engine before lurching forward, a plum of blue smoke puffing from the rear exhaust. The front end lifts slightly as the vehicle's speed increases. Out of the corner of my eye I see a flash of red jump into the road. The boy's on the curb, nursing a bloody elbow while his skateboard slows to a stop in the middle of the street. The boy scrambles to his feet, and knowing how boys think, I already know what's coming.

The light for oncoming traffic turns red as mine turns green. I can see the driver of the other car, but he can't see me—or the boy. He's messing with his cell phone and about to plow right through the intersection.

The kid dashes into the road.

I mash the gas-pedal, my rental car loyally leaping forward.

The boy looks up with fear—eyes wide. The driver of the Buick finally reacts, white-knuckling the steering wheel as his tires scream. My Impala rushes into the intersection.

This is going to hurt like a—

The impact is worse than I expected. My head whips to the side, smacking the window. There's a flash of white accompanied by what seems like a delayed resounding thud and the crumpling of metal. My car is shoved sideways despite the ambitious tires that continue to spin. I feel the car lean the way a sailboat leans when it catches a sharp breeze, and I'm sure I'm going over.

Then everything stops. The rental is up on two wheels—leaning sharply to the side, the engine still running. For some reason the tires have stopped trying to turn. The passenger side is crumpled, the seat pointed inward instead of facing forward, the window shattered, and pieces of glass are still falling like rain into my hair and lap.

I'm wedged in, and ironically that's what I'm thinking about instead of wondering whether or not I'm still in one piece. Something warm and sticky is trickling along the right side of my face, so that can't be good. Undoing the seatbelt, I manage to inch myself out of the bucket seat and crawl up and out of the passenger-side window. I know I should stay put until help arrives, but getting out of the car seems like a better idea than just sitting there waiting for the car to catch on fire or something. Besides, I need to know if the boy is okay. I need to be doing something other than sitting and wondering why I intentionally drove into the path of an oncoming car. Somehow, I've managed to strand myself here, and despite the strong taste of blood on my tongue and the pain in my ribs, I'm already wondering if my actions were motivated by something on a subconscious level.

The morning air is still chilly as I pull myself from the car and collapse onto the hood of the Buick. I hear sirens in the distance, the pain starting to grip me like an iron fist. My leg doesn't feel right, and blood is running into my eye.

I peer through the front windshield of the Buick to find the driver slumped over the wheel. Steam is rising around me from the car's ruined engine, and I can hear the stampeding feet of approaching bystanders. Someone is crying, and it sounds like the voice of a child. Suddenly, the town has woken up.

"Mister, are you okay?" a man in boxers and a wife-beater is asking.

"I've been better."

The police are here. Their screaming sirens are making my ears bleed, and their flashers—at least from what I can still see—are beautiful red and green against a light blue backdrop.

"What happened here?"

"I saw the whole thing!" a woman shrieks. "He saved that boy's life!"

"She's right," the man in boxers says. "Jimmy woulda run that kid over."

"Is he okay?" I ask.

"Jesus, he's bleeding bad," an officer says. "Dispatch, we got injuries on the corner of Main and Lincoln. Send an ambulance. 11-41."

"Roger that 11-41. Ambulance is en route."

"How's the kid?" I repeat. Blood is running over my lips and into my mouth. "The boy's fine," the officer says.

"Hey, I recognize him," someone else says.

I lay my head on the hot hood of the Buick and close my eyes. I can feel sleep coming.

"Stay with me," the officer says, shaking me by the shoulder. "Come on. Eyes up here. Focus on me."

But sleep's coming whether he wants it to or not.

"Isn't that Tony Abbott?"

"Come on, son. Eyes on me."

"What the hell's Tony Abbott doing here?"

I'm probably dying. Later today it'll likely be either Kristine or Ritchie who ID's my body. Maybe then they'll feel bad. After all, I didn't have to come back. I did it for them. And this is what I get.


## Part III

I'm not dead. That much I've figured out. I *am* irritable. But that's to be expected. Beyond that, I don't have a handle on much of anything else. The room is empty except for me and this chirpy equipment what with all its blinking lights. I'm lying in the world's most uncomfortable bed and hooked up to what I think is an EKG. I guess white means clean, so this must be a hospital room, but it does make me wonder about perceptions and stereotypes. Do people get better faster just because everything is white? No. So, even hospitals are liars. Hospitals and doctors and nurses and the people around you who are supposed to care. Paint the walls blood red for all I care. Just tell the truth.

"He's awake."

Tilting my head the other way, I find that I'm not alone. Kristie is here with her mother. Mrs. Lambert is dressed nice, but she looks different. She looks old, and she's dressed old. Then again, it's been twenty years, so I guess we're all old.

Kristie reaches across the bed and takes my hand. "Hey."

"Hey," I return.

It's a pretty deep conversation.

"I'm sorry," she whispers, a tear slipping over her cheek. "About last night."

The only thing I remember about last night is getting punched in the face, and that had nothing to do with her. "Me too," I manage. My jaw hurts when I talk.

"You saved that kid," Kristie says as she wipes her eyes. She leans over and kisses me on the tip of my nose. "He's alive because of you." She beams. "You're a hero."

I don't feel like a hero. I feel like a coward.

Kristie pats my hand.

Mrs. Lambert is unsmiling. "How are you feeling?" she asks.

"Like I've been in a car accident."

Kristie giggles, but I expected a giggle. I was at least hoping for a courtesy smile from Mrs. Lambert, but she offers nothing but a stoic glare as if I just killed her favorite cat.

"Well," Mrs. Lambert says, standing. She's put on some weight, and her hair has grayed. She hasn't aged well. "I'll leave you two alone so you can pick up where you left off messing up my daughter's life."

"Oh my god," Kristie gripes. "What did we talk about?"

"Welcome home, Tony."

"The outpouring of support thus far has been overwhelming."

Mrs. Lambert hesitates, the wheels turning in her mind. She looks like she's about to walk away when she suddenly turns. "Where's my daughter?" she demands.

"Mom…" Kristie begs.

"I have no idea," I say.

"You were the last one to see her."

"Was I?"

The air is dry, so dry you can almost hear the static electricity. It's like a crackle, hanging in the air.

"It's too coincidental that you left the same day she disappeared. Did you kill her?"

"Mom!"

"Where'd you bury her?"

"I have no idea where she is," I repeat, matching her glare.

"I hope that's true," she says, an unfriendly smile on her lips. "For your sake."

"Mom…"

Mrs. Lambert scowls at me before sending a warning glance in her daughter's direction and marching away. Kristie sits on the edge of the bed and gently brushes the bangs from my eyes the way she did when we were young. "Sorry about that," she says. "She tends to hold grudges."

75

"She's right to."

The soft tips of her fingers gently brush the stitched cut over my left eye, and I flinch. She withdraws quickly, gritting her teeth, her eyes apologetic. "Sorry."

"Me too," I say. "About yesterday, I mean."

"What are we going to do with you, Anthony Abbott?" She smiles. "Triple A."

I smirk.

"And just where did you think you were you going? Leaving town?"

I shake my head. "Just out for a drive."

"Out for a drive." She shakes her head. "Right."

"The boy's okay?"

"Not a scratch."

"What about the rental? You think they'll be able to buff it out?"

She snorts. "No, you're pretty much stranded."

I nod. "Figures. This whole trip was a bad idea."

She frowns. "So you *were* leaving."

"Nobody wants me here."

She stares at me. "I want you here. I asked you here." She leans over and kisses me on the forehead. "You need rest."

"You're leaving?"

She sits down and scooches the chair closer. "I'm not going anywhere." She crosses her bare legs. I try not to notice, and when I do, I pretend that I don't.

"Still looking," she says with a smile.

"It's hard not to."

"I always liked that." She smiles. "It was different with you. Not like with other guys."

"I hate to burst your bubble, but we're all pretty much the same."

"You were different. It felt different."

I shift uncomfortably.

"So, what happened?" she asks. "Why'd you run?"

"Which time? Twenty years ago or this morning?"

"Twenty years ago."

"Well, first of all, I didn't run. That was the day I was scheduled to leave. I know we talked about it."

"Yeah," she says quietly. "We talked about it."

"I had that job lined up and an apartment on campus waiting for me."

"You never even said goodbye."

"I don't remember that."

"What *do* you remember, Tony?"

"Hardly anything."

"Like amnesia?"

"Like I don't remember. Some of it's coming back. Like when I run into people I knew or see things from my past, but there's this…" I tap my skull before swirling my finger in cuckoo circles. "It's like there's a blank spot."

"That's a terrible answer."

"Well, there you go."

She shakes her head, biting her lower lip before turning on me. "Joanne's dead."

"And you know this how? Because you found that old hearing aid of hers?"

"I know it because I'm her twin sister."

"What about the letter?"

"Fuck the letter. I know it. I *feel* it."

"Then what do you need me for?"

"I need to know how. And I need to know who."

"I don't have any idea. I can't even remember the name of the street I grew up on. I barely—."

"It was a long—"

"I barely remember you."

She stops, leans back, draws a breath.

"I had to think real hard about it when you called me," I whisper. "I couldn't remember your face. I barely remembered who you were. All there is, is some vague…recollection at best—like a picture out of focus. Something happened that summer. I get it. And I know I was here when it happened, but I don't…" I shake my head. "I just don't remember what."

She's rigid. "If you're telling the truth, then you're talking about repressed memories. Yet you said some of it's coming back."

"In bits and pieces."

"Why would you have blocked it?"

"I have no idea."

"Were you involved?"

"I don't know. And neither do you. We don't even know if there was something to be involved in."

She looks upset.

"I'm sorry," I say.

"Yeah, I get it. You're sorry, I'm sorry, we're all very, very sorry."

"I mean it. I never said it, but I'm sorry about your sister."

Kristie smiles, but it's forced. I mourned Joanne, and I moved on. Kristie hasn't. Apparently, no one else in this spook-show town has either. The people here are stuck in a dead zone mourning a girl who disappeared too long ago to remember why.

Kristie is taking her time. "If my sister was murdered, then she was murdered here. Not in some other city or state. It happened *here*, and somebody in this town knows something."

"That's a big 'if.'"

"Which is why I called you."

77

"What possible difference can I make?"

"You knew her as well as anyone, but you haven't been here all these years since. You haven't stood by, the more obvious clues passing right under your nose. You haven't been here searching for that needle in the haystack."

I need a drink. Tea. Water. Anything. My lips are parched.

"I want you to help me," she says. "Help me find my sister."

"Your sister's gone. I don't know what I can even do."

"Just help me."

"If she's alive, then she's not here. And if she's dead, then what difference does it make?"

"It makes a difference because she's my sister. I need to know. I *deserve* to know. Jesus, just...*help* me." Kristie's not backing down. "I'm tired, Tony. I'm tired of waiting, and I'm tired of not knowing. I need some kind of closure so I can sleep at night."

"She's been gone for two decades. Even if you're right, the best possible outcome you can hope for is finding her body."

Kristie looks down, biting her lower lip.

"Are you sure that's what you want?" I ask. "Right now, you can imagine anything you want to. You can imagine she's living in sunny California with her own view of the ocean. You can imagine her happily married with a couple of kids and a growing retirement fund. The moment you find a body, every last bit of hope you've been clinging to disappears."

"I want to find my sister." She sniffs, drawing a deep breath. "Yes, we're twins. You wouldn't...*couldn't* know what that means. I know she's dead. I know it. I let go of *hope* a long time ago, but you have to understand that I can't just let *her* go." She looks up at me. "I need answers."

I close my eyes feeling way in over my head. I'm not sure I can do this—even for her. "I want to see the letter."

"You'll stay then?"

"In case you hadn't noticed, my only ride out of town was totaled this morning."

"Ironically enough, you might be right. They even stopped running the bus route through here years ago."

"Of course they did."

She pats my hand. "They're going to discharge you tonight. I'll take you home."

"I don't have a home."

She shakes her head. "My place."

I frown.

She leans over again, and I'm expecting another kiss on the nose or maybe the forehead, but her soft lips touch mine, and she tastes exactly the same as she did when we were kids with nothing but time on our hands. My heart starts to thud like a sledgehammer, and it's the same feeling—the same exact feeling. She pulls away, and I look up at her.

She knows.

"I won't be far," she whispers. Her eyes dance to the empty glass next to my bed. "You're out of water. I'll let the nurse know."

"Thanks."

She drapes her purse over her shoulder. "Get some rest. I'll be back a little later."

I nod.

"Guess I still got the touch, huh?" She winks.

I offer a weak smile before rolling onto my side and shutting my eyes. I need a few hours to forget about her and this town. And I need a few hours to remember everything else. She finally leaves me to listen to the intercom summoning Dr. So-and-so to report to room such-and-such. After awhile, the sounds of life and death happening around me become comforting. No stress, no worries. Here I'm safe. So long as the robotic voices continue to call out over the intercom.

# Eight

## *Yesterday*

"**B**aseball ain't all that different from life," Ritchie says as he tosses me the ball. He's all worked up again, a bead of sweat threatening to roll from his upper lip into his mouth. He's not even throwing hard.

"What's that?" I ask.

"I said baseball ain't all that different from life. The pitcher in any game is only as good as his defense. Kinda like a man is only as good as his word. It's symboliasiam."

"Symbolism, dummy."

Ritchie frowns, but he's determined to make his point. "The pitcher puts the ball over the plate, and sooner or later, the batter's gonna make contact. From that moment on, the infield or the outfield either makes the pitcher look good or…it don't."

Philosopher Ritchie is about to go off on one of his epic, if not pointless, soliloquies. It's happened before, and the end result is usually pretty disturbing.

"A guy hits a pop-fly, and it's an easy out," he continues. "But if there's no one to catch it, the pitcher looks like a turd 'cause he let a hit drop. Maybe a run scores. Maybe two. Now his ERA's for shit. He threw a good ball, and the batter popped it up, but life let him down."

"That's pretty profound."

"Look at it upside down."

"You mean the other way around?"

"Multiple things can bail your ace out of a bad inning, but if the infield mucks it up, runners score. If the ace jams the guy and your infield has even an inkling of a clue, they turn a double-play. It's a thing of beauty. You set it up by throwing the perfect pitch, but you still need your guys to turn a six, four, three."

"I once saw a game where they turned a one, two, one triple play or something like that." My words just hang on the air. Ritchie stares at me like I have absolutely no conception what baseball is or what it means. "I mean, you know..."

"That's impossible," Ritchie argues.

"It was something like that."

"It was nothing like that."

"How do you know? Were you there?"

"No, I wasn't there. Were you there?"

"No."

"That's because it's impossible."

"Whatever."

"It's hotter than hell out here."

"And you criticize me for my dirty mouth? You've been cussing all day."

"That's one of them good bad words. God lets those slide."

"You know this for certain?"

"I know this for certain. My dad taught me."

"You hate your dad."

"That don't make him wrong."

I smile. "Déjà vu, huh?"

Ritchie frowns. "What?"

"We practically had this same exact conversation just the other day."

"What conversation?"

I shake my head. "Never mind." Frustrated, I hurl the ball back as hard as I can. Ritchie catches it like a pro before lowering the ball to his side, his eyes never leaving mine.

"What was that?" he snaps. "What did you just throw me?"

"What do you mean?"

"Did you just throw heat?"

"No."

"That was heat."

"No it wasn't."

"You want me to start throwing heat?"

"Not especially."

Ritchie rears back and hurls the ball my way. I react defensively, scrunching my face, lifting a leg defensively while holding out my glove. The ball strikes dead center, smacking my palm and sending a bolt of lightning through my body.

"You like that?" he calls. "Feel good?"

"That's it. I'm out. I'm done."

"It's time for ice cream anyhow," Ritchie says.

I shake the pain from my hand while biting my lower lip. I make a slashing sign across my neck. "No can do."

"Why not?"

"I spent my dough on Kristie," I say. "I'm waiting for my next paycheck."

"It's on me."

"Do I look like I take charity? Why is everyone offering to buy for me lately?"

Ritchie approaches, that dumb grin on his face, and slaps me on the back. "I am a man with a plan, my man. There's someone I'd like me to meet."

"Another girl?"

"No, a dude," he answers sarcastically.

81

"I thought you wanted Joanne?"

"I do want Joanne, but Joanne needs to know she has competition. Otherwise, what's her inception to chase me?"

"Incentive."

"Huh?"

"The word you're looking for is 'incentive.' God, you're a moron."

"I'm also sweating my ass off."

"You're always sweating your ass off."

"I want ice cream."

"You always want ice cream."

"And I told you I'm buying."

I pinch my lips, but say nothing.

"I'm buying," Ritchie repeats. "Let's go."

## *Part II*

We head downtown, all the while tossing the ball back and forth. Underhand, overhand, over the road—over the top of passing cars. It's a game. I can't throw like him, but I love baseball the way Ritchie does. We watch the Tigers religiously whenever they're on local channels. We've even made the trek out to Tiger Stadium to catch a double-header. Twice.

Like gangsters, Ritchie and me walk up to the Soft Spot like we own the joint. Ritchie shoves the baseball in his pocket, leans into the service window, takes a toothpick from the dispenser, pinches it between yellow teeth and winks at the girl working the counter. Her name is Rachel Russell. She's in two of my classes, and she's a cutie, no question.

"What's up, sweetheart?" Ritchie asks.

Rachel frowns. "What do you want, Ritchie?"

"A little bit of chocolate, a little bit of vanilla and a little bit of you," he says with a grin.

"Nice." She snaps her bubblegum, her eyes unimpressed.

"Come on, everyone loves Ritchie Hudson. We're in first place 'cuzza me. We're in the running for state title."

"For what, polo?"

He frowns, angrily. "No, not polo. Nobody plays polo. We don't even have a polo team."

"She was kidding," I mumble.

"I don't like baseball," Rachel says defiantly.

"Well, there's your problem."

"I don't have a problem."

82

I have to admit, she's scoring major points in my book with the way she is handling my over-ambitious friend. I never realized she was so witty. Freckles aside, she just jumped two notches higher on 'Tony's Official Hot List.' She's now bordering on I'd-like-to-know-more.

"Yes you do," Ritchie says. "You're too uptight. Pinched too tight to get me and my friend here a cold one on the house. How about a little team spirit?"

"My boss is from Lawton. Technically, you're the enemy."

Ritchie shakes his head. "Now I'm getting upset. Lawton? Those small-town motherfuckers couldn't pitch a campaign."

"Enough," I interrupt. "You said you're treating."

Ritchie bites his tongue, eyes the menu and looks at Rachel. "You're lucky my friend's here. He's the voice of wisdom. He keeps me in line—keeps me calm. It's pretty hard to make him mad, but once that chain's rattled, you'd better look out."

"Ritchie," I warn.

He frowns. "Two soft-swirls, sweetheart. Chocolate."

Rachel smiles…at *me*, and her smile is really quite cute. "$4.77."

There's something about ice-cream on a scalding hot afternoon. It's an early spring, and it's too late to say no. It's also one of those moments I'll remember for the rest of my life. Someday I'll tell my kids how '*back in the day*' we used to buy ice cream while tossing around a baseball instead of playing video games. Of course, by then, Main Street will be six lanes wide, and ice cream shops will be a relic of the past. We'll probably be zipping around on flying scooters and taking college courses on that new thing called the 'internet' with virtual instructors who are made up of ones and zeroes instead of flesh and blood.

"You seein' your girl tonight?" Ritchie asks.

"We saw each other last night."

"You fuck her yet?"

"Jesus Christ, Ritchie. What kind of question is that?"

His face contorts. "Why you gotta be so vulgar? What did we talk about?"

"I'm being vulgar? What did you just ask me?"

"Did you hear me get all blasphemous?" He pouts, one hand in his pocket, the other clutching the melting ice cream cone. "There's a difference in the way you say it. I ain't kiddin'."

"Tell you what, you watch your mouth, and I'll watch mine. How's that?"

"Just don't piss Him off. That's all I ask."

"Then don't talk shit about my girlfriend. That's all *I* ask." I don't stand up to him very often, but this time he crossed the line. Truth be told, Kristie and I did do the *deed*. And I give credit to Joanne, because she knew her sister would never have a moment alone with me so long as Ritchie was hanging around, so she took him aside and gave him his first tutoring lesson. Kristie led me to her room where she quietly shut her door and locked it. I think we were both embarrassed and shy and nervous, because we both knew what was about to happen, yet neither of us really knew how to start things off. I remember wishing I had brought a condom, but I didn't want to look like a schmuck for expecting something I didn't have a right to expect.

Kristie kept herself busy by putting a red T-shirt over her lamp to create a mood—albeit a T-shirt-over-a-lamp mood—before putting on some soft music. It was lousy music, but whatever. Then we both sat down. Then we made eye-contact. Then we looked away, because we were embarrassed. And shy. And nervous. I wanted to be 'the man,' and I wanted her so bad that my heart pounded a million times a minute, yet at the same time, I wanted the 'event' to be like in one those grainy pornos Ritchie's dad recorded and left laying around. I didn't know if I could actually maneuver my body into those positions, but I would give it a go while trying to make it look natural. Carefully, I—

"Tony!" Ritchie shouts, dragging me back to reality. "You listenin' or what?"

I nod, ice-cream running along the cone and over my hand.

"So, what do you think? Should I send her flowers?"

"Who?"

"Joanne."

"What's the big deal with Joanne? There are a hundred other girls just as pretty as her dying to get your attention."

Of course, I already know what the big deal is. Joanne's the one that doesn't want him back. She's allusive and therefore a prize. Then again—

"Because she's like Kristie," he mumbles.

This is not the answer I expected.

"You and Kristie have this perfect 'thing' goin' on," he continues. "That's what I want."

"Are you saying you have a crush on my girlfriend?"

"No." He tosses his ice cream away. "I ain't sayin' that at all."

"You're saying something that's bordering on awfully awkward."

"Forget it. It's too hot for ice-cream. Damn thing's melting everywhere."

"Then what?" I demand.

He looks at me, and it's the sheepish—almost embarrassed Ritchie who's eyeing me. "You're like my big brother," he says. "I look up to you."

"You're older than me."

"I'm trying to be serious for once."

"Then be serious." I have no idea what this has to do with Kristie, but if he starts making moves on my girl, I swear I'll—

"If we're dating sisters, then there's no competition."

I frown. "What competition?"

"I mean…" He kicks a rock. "You're better than me…"

"Ritchie," I try, but I don't even know what to say. Everybody looks up to Ritchie. He's the small-town hero. I'm nobody. I'm just an average guy trying to finish out high-school, get my ducks in a row for college and romance my girl. My life's a disaster due to all those things that make being a teenager so difficult. "Ritchie, there's no competition. You can date anyone you want, and it's cool, man."

"That's not the point."

"Then what is?"

"I'm..."

"What?"

"I can't explain it."

"Well, you'd better try, because I'm starting to freak out."

He bunches up his face. Kind of like Yoda. "I want the all-American dream. I want you and me to have side-by-side backyards. I want us to have matching three-bedroom ranchers. I want to let my dog out the back door at the same time you let your dog out the back door. We'll wave even though we won't have nothin' to say. Then, on Saturday nights, we'll have backyard barbecues. One week I'll barbecue, and you and the missus will bring a dish to pass. The next week we'll trade off. Your wife will look like mine. Your house will look like mine. Your dog will look like mine. We'll be brothers. Forever."

I stand there. "That's a little weird."

He frowns. "If you marry Kristie and I marry Joanne, then they'll wanna be neighbors too. There won't be no argument. There won't be no competition. And you won't go away to college." Ritchie comes from a messed up family, but he's always been innocently naïve, oblivious to reality. He's a brute, just like his dad, but different. "I told you it's stupid," he mutters.

I look down at my sticky fingers. "How did the tutoring session go last night?"

He shakes his head. "Fuck prepositions."

That's my friend, and that's his way. He's right. Life is like baseball. He does it his way. Rules don't apply, not because he's defiant, but because he doesn't understand the politics. He just wants to throw the ball.

"Prepositions aside, how did things go with Joanne?"

Ritchie shrugs. "I don't know."

"She's tutoring you for free. She wouldn't do that for just anyone."

"It's not like it was a date or anything."

I finish my ice cream and toss the baseball back Ritchie's way, knowing the best way to change the subject is to distract him. Ritchie holds onto the ball while looking off to his right. He's staring, straying from the sidewalk as he leans in the direction he's looking. He'd walk right into traffic if I don't grab him by the shirt and yank him back.

"What are you looking at?" I ask.

"Is that Mandy?"

"Mandy who?"

"Ferguson."

"Mandy Ferguson?"

"Yeah, Mandy Ferguson."

I look across the road and across the vacant Walmart parking lot where a woman is arguing with some guys. To be honest, we're so far away I can't really tell, but Ritchie knows his women the way he knows baseball.

"I don't know," I say. "What's it matter? You got a game tonight. Let's go."

"She don't look happy."

"How can you tell? She's like an inch big from here."

"Come on," Ritchie says, darting across the road.

"Ritchie!"

"Come on!"

Groaning, I follow. Mandy is standing by the boarded up entrance to the old Walmart, and there are three guys crowding her. She's arguing, and by the looks of things, they're not happy either. This shouldn't surprise me. Mandy's been a problem since grade school. She's always getting into trouble for something. She's always getting suspended for things like fighting or smoking or getting caught screwing in the bathroom.

Not that any of that matters to my friend. He likes girls, and he likes fighting. All he needs is a reason. He probably hasn't bothered to notice that there's two of us and three of them. We're out-numbered, but Ritchie was never very good with math anyway.

## *Part III*

"Gentlemen," Ritchie says, walking with long strides. "What's up?" He's intimidating as hell, and I envy that in him. If I looked that bad ass, I'd probably go looking to pick fights too.

"Yeah, what's up?" the biggest of the three says as we draw nearer.

They're seniors. I don't know them by name, but I recognize all of them. They're bigger than us. Bigger than me, anyway. Ritchie can probably hold is own, and judging by the way his hands are twitching at his sides, he's ready to throw down.

"None of this concerns you, Hudson," another says.

"You're right, it don't," Ritchie answers. "But it concerns my friend." He thumbs in my direction.

I frown.

Mandy turns to me. We even lock eyes.

"We're just conducting some business," the one guy says.

"Stock market's closed, boys," Ritchie says.

"Good line," I murmur, wishing like hell I could pull stuff like that off the way he does. Ritchie can hardly string together a coherent sentence until he wants to fight. Then suddenly he's Shakespeare. He lowers his head, lifts his eyes until they gleam, his mouth turned downward, fists at his sides. Mandy looks shaken. Some of her eye-shadow is running. She's been crying.

"Just go," the big one says. "Before anyone gets hurt."

"My friend is also offended by your suggestion that he or I might get hurt." Ritchie says.

"Well, your friend is awfully sensitive."

"I didn't actually say anything," I whisper.

"Mandy?" Ritchie asks. "You okay?"

She nods, looking really small, and she's looking directly at me.

"So, what's the problem?" Ritchie asks arrogantly, pacing with wanton energy. "You guys queer for my ass, or are you hanging around here just for the hell of it?"

I know what's coming even before it happens. I'm about to be in my first real fight since I was eight years old, and it's all going to be over a girl I hardly know.

"Mandy," Ritchie beckons, "why don't you come over here and stand by us."

"She owes us money," the one guy interrupts.

"Not today she don't," Ritchie answers.

I shift nervously. Mandy keeps looking my way, and I can't figure why. There's a sound off in the distance—like a drumbeat, and it takes me a moment to realize that it's the sound of my own thundering heart.

"One last time," Ritchie says. "Walk away. Now."

"She owes us money."

"Not today she don't."

The one guy smiles, and that must be Ritchie's cue, because he looks giddy, almost like he's happy. I know what's coming, but before I can define, plan and execute a brilliant intervention, Ritchie has already launched himself at the one that's been daring him to. I'm wide-eyed as I watch my friend pummel the guy underneath him, which is all fine and dandy except now I'm standing in the shadow of two bigger guys who don't seem to like me very much. One of them even has a tattoo of a scorpion on his forearm that looks to be hand-carved.

That's cute.

"I'm just—"

The tattooed one lunges first. I make a weak attempt to defend myself by throwing a fist, but my wrist just slaps his shoulder. Microseconds later, there's a white flash followed by a searing pain in my jaw. Stumbling backward, I see him rushing at me. I get angry. Then I get scared. Then Scorpion-tattoo-guy lifts me up and drives me backward. We crash. Then we wrestle, and I do a lot of losing even though I manage to land a few good punches. Scorpion lands more.

Scorpion's fists are doing a fine job of finding their target, and I'm tasting blood as it drains backward from my nose into my throat, where it slips along the water slide into my stomach. Yet, with a burst of adrenalin, I swing back and connect with what feels like a concrete wall. This buys me a moment. Scorpion-guy stumbles back. I look over at Ritchie, but he's got his hands full, taking on two at once.

87

My nemesis rushes me. I'm convinced that he's more than a senior. He's a trained fighter. These assumptions are based loosely on the volume of sheer pain I'm experience from each blow to the side of my face. Scorpion throws a wicked punch. And then another. And another.

And then the punishment ends.

I open my swollen eyes and see only the blue sky overhead. I don't know where Scorpion-tattoo-guy went, but then I hear groaning. Rolling onto my side, I see Ritchie and Scorpion rolling over and over on the dusty parking lot. It's an equal fight, and an impressive sight to behold. They're both big guys, but what Scorpion hasn't counted on is Ritchie's fast ball. Ritchie lands a good one, and Scorpion winces, gritting bloody teeth. Instantly, Ritchie's back on his feet, but so am I, and I rush in to intervene. I get between them, my hands up, palms out, facing my friend and begging him to back down. But Ritchie's not buying. I'm not even sure he sees me given how intensely he's glaring at the other guys, a string of blood running from his nose along his lip and chin. The other three are shouting, but they're not rushing back in.

"It's over!" I shout.

"I'm gonna kill you!"

"Stop it!" I repeat.

Ritchie's pointing over my shoulder. "I'm gonna kill you, skin you, filet you and fuckin' eat you!"

"Goddamn it, Richie!" I scream.

This stops him in his tracks, his eyes turning sharply on me. He doesn't exactly soften. He just redirects his hatred.

"Snap out of it!" I holler in my toughest growl, shoving him backward.

There's a moment. It doesn't last long. More like a flicker of light, but I think in that instant, Ritchie hates me like he hates them. Then it passes, and he starts pacing, fists balled at his sides, his eyes on the three hooligans.

"It's over," I say, not quite as loud.

"You want more?" the big guy opposite us asks.

"You shut the fuck up!" I snap at him.

"I ain't even gotten started yet," Ritchie hisses.

I wipe a stream of blood from my nose. "That goes for you too, Rich."

Ritchie casts me a dirty look while continuing his madman-like pace—his face red with rage.

I remain rooted where I am, pinned in the middle, careful not to infringe on my friend's personal space. "We gotta get out of here," I manage. "Now."

Ritchie looks at me, then them and then back at me. "I'm not done."

"Yes, you are." I pause. "You got a game in less than an hour. You want to get tossed off the team?"

Ritchie looks around—maybe for a weapon? His mouth is curved downward, his chest heaving. He looks on the verge of a heart-attack. "Let me kill 'em," he grumbles.

People always joke about things like that. People say things like 'you kill me' or 'it kills.' We use words as weapons until the meaning is so watered down that it means nothing at all. But when Ritchie says it, it sounds different. He means it.

"Not today, Ritchie."

"I swear I'm gonna run you over if I have to," he spits, blood running over his lip.

"Do you want to pitch tonight or do you want to go to jail?" I keep my hands up, palms out. "Let it go."

He flexes, the threads of his T-shirt pulled tight. His eyes are bloodshot, pink spittle running from the corners of his mouth. If he decides to rush back in to finish the job, there's nothing I can do to stop him. I'm shaking—terrified. "Don't do it," I warn, freaking out that he's going to go ape-shit.

He lunges, shoving me. Hard. I stumble, trip and roll. Scrambling to my feet, my hands are already up again. Ritchie is baring his teeth, his eyes wolf-life. "Where'd she go?" he growls, looking around.

Suddenly we're all looking for Mandy, but she's nowhere to be found. Smart girl. She must've taken off while we were being meatheads rolling in the dust to defend her honor.

"Goddamn it," Scorpion mutters.

"Watch your mouth," Ritchie snaps.

"Enough," I snap.

Ritchie stops pacing. His chest continues to heave, but his hands are now on his hips, and I can almost see the fight fleeing his body. Suddenly, he turns his back and storms away. I wait for him to stop or turn around or come back or something, but he doesn't. He just storms across the parking lot toward the road. He's growing smaller and smaller—drifting as he goes. After a few moments I realize I'm still standing in the shadows of three bigger guys who would just as soon kick my ass, so I scamper after my friend even though I'm careful to maintain a safe distance. Ritchie's not right yet. Once he is, he'll be a bucket of apologies and a slew of excuses, but until then, it's hands-off. I'm still weak in the knees, my face feels like putty, and my stomach is like Jell-O, and I'm pretty sure I'd soil my pants if Ritchie were to suddenly turn on me, but he doesn't, because the storm has passed. By now, he's thinking about baseball again.

Ritchie turns around, walking backward, waving me forward. "What you doin' hangin' out way back there? Come on, Triple A. It's go-time. We got a game."

The sun is hot, the afternoon late. The hottest time of the day. No breeze and no relief. I'm sweating and bleeding at the same time. I don't know how it happened, but in the course of the past thirty minutes, my life has shifted slightly off its axis. Everything I knew yesterday feels more like someone else's documentary. I'm following my friend not because he's a leader, but because I'm afraid not to.

# Nine

## *Today*

I have absolutely no idea where I am. Nor do I know what day it is. It's probably Saturday, but that's only a guess. The sun is beating against the shades pulled over the windows. There's even a tear that allows the sun to cut a yellow slit through the air leading to the couch I'm lying on. Bits of dust float aimlessly through the thin shaft of light before disappearing into shadow. Over on the coffee table, magazines are fanned out with intentional carelessness, and the carpet underfoot is meticulously vacuumed. Nothing appears out of place. The television sits quietly in the corner, the refrigerator hums from the kitchen, and I can hear the shower running from down the hall. The room smells clean—like Pledge.

Pledge. That's my clue. This is Kristie's place.

Yesterday seems so far off that it's like a dream—or a nightmare, and many of the details still seem so sketchy that maybe I only imagined them. Only my chest hurts, and my face hurts, which means my rental car is totaled, and until Allstate figures out what to do, I'm stuck here. I explore the bumpy contours of my ragged face with my fingers while recounting the events of yesterday's accident.

The shower shuts off, reminding me that there's someone else here. The door opens, allowing a perfume of humid steam into the hallway. She emerges while drying her hair. All she's wearing is a robe, and she looks good as she pads barefoot across the floor.

"Morning," I say from the couch.

"Hey," she responds, disappearing into the kitchen.

I remember the promise I made to her the night before, and I'm starting to think maybe it was a mistake. Nothing good can come from dredging up old memories. Especially memories that were forcibly buried a decade and a half ago. Best case scenario, we find nothing, which will satisfy no one and end nothing. Worst case scenario, we find the bones of a dead girl.

I stumble into the bathroom and squint at the bright light that burns at my swollen eyes. I haven't shaved in 30 hours, and combined with the cuts and bruises, I look a fright. The great thing about getting older is the lack of conviction to care. I wash my face, gargle some water and strip out of my clothes before stepping into the shower. The water feels amazing, cascading over my body and soothing me into submission.

Five minutes go by. Then ten. I just stand there as the water turns cool before turning the handle and shutting the shower off, the water dripping in a constant stream until it slows to a drip, leaving me standing in a pool of water draining in a tiny whirlpool.

I need to get out of here.

Pulling the curtain aside, I step out onto the rug before wiping my hand across the foggy mirror and staring at the frosty image staring back. I pull a towel from the rack and dry off before pulling on the same clothes I've already been wearing for the last two days, shutting out the light and exiting the bathroom.


## *Part II*


"Breakfast is almost ready," Kristie says as I enter the kitchen. She's got the whole nine yards lined up and ready to go as she divides scrambled eggs onto two plates that are already boasting four strips of bacon and a healthy helping of hash browns. I haven't had hash browns since I was a kid. I was expecting coffee, but this is a royal breakfast, a real dining room table and what looks like real flowers sitting in a glass vase at its center.

"Sit," she orders with a smile, so I do. Setting a plate in front of me, she kisses the side of my cheek.

"Thanks," I mumble. "This is amazing, but it's way too much. Seriously, you could've gotten away with some coffee and Lucky Charms."

"I know," she answers with a smile. "But I remember your appetite."

Digging in, I realize I'm hungrier than I thought, and the plate is clean before I'm full. I help myself to the remainder of the hash browns. Without thinking twice, I pause to run the empty skillet under cold water, swishing the water around before setting the skillet in the sink. She didn't ask me to, but we've always worked well as a team. We always did things for the other because they needed doing, not because it was expected. She smiles as I take a seat and bury the hash browns under a layer of catsup.

"Funny how things work out," I say.

She cocks her head. "Have things worked out?"

I shrug. "I mean, us being here, having breakfast together after all these years."

Kristie stands and carries her plate to the sink where she starts dishes while staring beyond the window into the backyard. I'm left to admire her from behind. The way her white robe hangs over her thin frame, the way her feet are buried in big, poofy slippers, the way her wet hair clings in stringy strands to her neck. She's the same girl I remember falling in love with, but now she's a woman I hardly know.

"I want to go over to the old Johnson farm today," she says, her voice soft.

"What for? You already found the headband."

"Which is why I want to go back."

I draw a patient breath. "A hearing aid doesn't mean murder."

"Maybe not, but two decades of silence does." She washes her dishes, stacking them noisily.

I'm glad I've finished breakfast, because I've suddenly lost my appetite. I don't want to go back to that place. I don't remember everything that happened there, but the things I do remember weren't exactly Kodak moments. Not a lot of spring picnics out at the ol' Johnson Farm.

Standing, I cross the kitchen and place my plate on the counter. "If it'll settle your mind, then let's go." I touch her shoulder reassuringly and give a little squeeze.

She reaches up and pats my hand. "Thanks."

There's a robin in her birdfeeder just beyond the window dipping his head and pecking at seed. We stand quietly watching, and for a moment I feel comfortable just being with her. Then I frown, noticing that the fence lining the backyard looks awfully familiar. There used to be a pool here, but it's gone now, though there's still a bit of a depression indicating the hole hadn't been properly filled. "Isn't this where Sharon Daniels used to live?" I ask.

Kristie doesn't look up as she scrubs my plate. "Her parents retired to Florida. I heard she moved to Chicago, but who really knows anymore."

"That's not what I meant."

"Then what did you mean?"

I shake my head. "Nothing." I kiss the top of her head before walking away. "I should swing by the hotel and change my clothes," I say to cover the awkward silence.

"That's fine," she calls after me. "It's on the way." She passes through the living room on her way into the bathroom where she turns on the light and closes the door.

Collecting my things from the end table beside the couch, I head for the front door, step out on the porch and squint into the new morning sunshine. Everything smells familiar, and Payton is as quiet this morning as it was last night. I stand for a moment, asking myself if this feels like home. As much as I want it to, something's off. Frowning, I rock back and forth, testing the wooden planks underfoot. It sags, feeling soft. And beyond the rotting porch, the sidewalk leading to the driveway is cracked and overtaken by weeds. Her lawn is a patchy mess.

"Ready?" she asks, pulling the door shut. But the door doesn't close all the way, and she has to pull hard and hold on before she can insert the key to lock the deadbolt.

"Ready."

She tosses me her keys. "You drive. You know the way."

"I totaled my car yesterday. You sure you want me driving?"

"You totaled your car saving someone's life." She smiles. "I think I can trust you."

I shrug. Fair enough.

# Ten

## *Yesterday*

There's a reason why I don't like going to Ritchie's place. It's not the stench of dried animal urine in the carpet or the flies buzzing around the dirty dishes in the sink or the general dilapidated condition of the home. It's the tension that seems to hover like humidity, permeating the air like a stink that can be rinsed. Even if Mr. Hudson isn't there, that clammy feeling of dread that he could walk through the door at any moment weighs heavily on everyone's mind. There aren't a lot of smiles to go around.

"I think I'll just meet you at the stadium," I say, hesitating at the edge of Ritchie's front lawn. To go any further would be to temp fate. The end of the sidewalk and the start of the grass seems to mark a line better left uncrossed.

"Don't be a buttface. The cockroaches are asleep this time of day." He winks. "Come on. I'll only be a sec."

Reluctantly, I follow, but not before looking for any sign of Mr. Hudson's big rig. The driveway is empty, and the road either way is empty as well. I follow Ritchie up the driveway, through the open garage and into the house.

"Hey, I'm home," Ritchie calls. "Ma?"

"The trash needs to be taken out," she hollers from her perch in the broken recliner in the living room. "They're gonna come in the next half hour, so you'd best get it out now before your father sees it."

"Dad ain't supposed to be home 'til late."

"The garbage man comes early."

He frowns, glaring at me. "Fine," he calls. "Where is it?"

"Right there in the kitchen," she answers. "You're probably tripping over it."

Ironically, Ritchie isn't, but I am. I do my best to sidestep the open bag where two or three flies are hungrily buzzing around the empty tin cans piled near the surface.

"I'll take it out on my way out."

"Don't forget."

"How could I…" he grumbles under his breath before rolling his eyes, shaking his head while beckoning for me to follow him through the kitchen to his bedroom where he strips off his shirt and pulls on his Pirates jersey. "Check it out," he says, nodding toward his bed. "My dad's new Playboy."

"When's he home long enough to read them?"

"He takes 'em with him on the road. Beats off in the parking lot of rest stops."

"Who's this month's playmate?"

"Some broad. Who gives a shit? It's a magazine. You're off banging Kristie while my dad and me are jerking off to Playboy." He shakes his head. "The same copy I might add." He's holding the bottom half of his Pirates uniform in his hands. "I gotta change."

I turn my back. "Does your dad know you look at his mail?"

"'Course he does. He has me hold onto it so Mom don't find out."

"That's cool."

"Is it?"

I shrug. "I dunno. Maybe he's not all bad. At least he trusts you."

"He trusts me like he trusts a politician." I hear the sound of a zipper being zipped. "Let's go get chilidogs first. I'm starved."

I shrug. "Is there time?"

Ritchie doesn't answer.

"It's getting late," I continue. "What time do you need to be at the ballpark?"

Still nothing.

When I turn to look at him, he's got a look of perplexity on his face. His eyes are squinted, lips slightly parted, head cocked as if he's listening for…something.

"You okay?" I ask.

Then I hear it. Some kind of sound coming from the hall outside Ritchie's closed door, but it hasn't yet registered in my mind. It's the look on my friend's face that makes me listen harder. Sure enough, the sound is drawing closer. Footsteps.

"Hide!" Ritchie hisses under his breath.

"What?"

The door bursts open, and I whirl—hands up. Ritchie's father, a beast of a man, lashes out, his big paws striking my chest and pushing me so hard that I'm lifted from my feet. It all happens so quick that I don't even know what's happened until after I'd hit my head on Ritchie's dresser on the way back down.

"Dad, what?" Ritchie shouts.

Mr. Hudson doesn't slow as he barrels into his son and drives him up against the wall. The entire house shutters. Even a towel Ritchie has hanging over his window as a makeshift curtain slumps to the floor.

"You stupid ass!" Hudson shouts. "I told you to cut the grass this week while I was out! Now they're threatenin' to evict us!"

"I cut it!" Ritchie hollers. "On Tuesday! It rained!"

Hudson strikes his son sharply across the face. "And there's an open bag of trash sitting in the middle of the goddamn kitchen floor that you were supposed to take out before they come to pick it up!"

94

"It's cool, Dad. I already talked to Mom about it. It'll be curbside in, like, three minutes."

"They just drove down the street two minutes ago, retard!" He strikes his son again, and this one sounds like more than a slap. It sounds like knuckles against cheekbone. Ritchie doesn't cower, but he also refuses to fight back. Or maybe this *is* his way of fighting back. The big man steps back, panting like a monster, fists clenched as his sides. Ritchie just stands there, his lips pinched tightly, his eyes welling with tears, though not one is allowed to slip.

"When I drive my ass all over this god-forsaken country to put food in your stomach and a roof over your pea-brained head, I expect you to show me some goddamn respect," Mr. Hudson growls. "You do your chores when I tell you to and hang out with your faggot friends after."

As quietly as I can, I try to get myself into a sitting position, but there's papers and trash all over Ritchie's floor. I reach behind my head and gently touch a welt that's also wet and sticky with something warm. Blood.

Mr. Hudson turns on me, his eyes bloodshot red with rage. "Get out of my house, you fuckin' runt. This ain't your home." He steps over my legs on his way toward the door.

"Hey, Dad," Ritchie says softly. His eyes have dried, and now he looks angry.

Mr. Hudson turns back.

There's no humor in Ritchie's black eyes. "You ever touch my friend again, and I'll kill you," he growls.

Mr. Hudson says nothing. I don't know what's scarier—what just happened or the sincerity in my best friend's voice. Less than a half hour ago, Ritchie was saying the exact same thing to those bullies out by Walmart. Now he's saying it to his own dad. And just like before, he means it. But without saying anything in return, Mr. Hudson just walks away, his footfalls drifting away.

Ritchie straightens his jersey and gingerly touches his fingertips to the side of his face. He crosses the room and hovers over me. Extending his hand, he helps me up and pats me on the back. "You were saying?" he asks.

"What?"

"All that stuff about how he trusts me because he lets me hold onto his girly mags."

"Can we go now?"

"How's your head?"

"It hurts."

"Man up. Don't be a girl."

"I'm not a girl." I rub the welt. "But I probably won't be hanging out at your place much more either."

Ritchie looks toward the door. "He used the bad words."

"Is that what you're worried about?"

"I ain't worried."

95

"Can we go now?"

"We're…" Ritchie suddenly winces, pinching one eye shut while reaching up and whacking himself upside of the head.

"Rich?"

He blinks, licks his lips and ushers me toward the door. "We're going," he says. "I'm starved."

"You okay?"

"Fine."

"How are the headaches?"

"Fuck the headaches. I'm hungry."

So I follow him. I don't know why and I barely know how, but I follow. I feel dazed as I follow him down the hall, through the living room where Mr. Hudson glowers at us. We drift through the kitchen and exit out the side door into the garage.

"What about the garbage?" I ask.

"Too late."

"Yeah, but still. Even after all that?"

He stares at me with cow-like eyes for a second before breaking into that big dumb grin of his. "Fuck him. He can kiss my grits."

# Eleven

## *Today*

With my face feeling like putty and my chest feeling like it's been pinched in some sort of enormous vice, I realize that I look as bad as I feel. Every part of me hurts in one way or another, so it's not easy to maneuver my body into the car— my feet on the floor, my knees tucked up under the steering wheel, my butt cupped and my back against the reclined seat. I do so, but not without a number of grunts and groans while contorting my face in what must be a hundred different expressions, most of which are likely unflattering.

"Are you going to make it?" she asks. Her tone is playful though laced with concern.

"The jury's out."

"Maybe this is a bad idea. You want me to drive?"

"I'm already here."

"You sure?"

"I just—"

But she thrusts a piece of paper in my face and holds it there.

"What's this?"

"The letter," she says. "You said you wanted to read it."

"Joanne's letter?"

She nods.

"Jesus." I take the letter from her, unfolding it. The first thing that strikes me is that it's a printout. It's not handwritten. "Typed?"

"I wondered about that too."

"Are you sure it's hers?"

"That's the kind of the point of this discussion."

I frown.

"I blindly believed in that letter since it showed up in our mailbox," Kristie says as she tucks her purse on the floor between her feet. "I've picked over the words so carefully, analyzing it for hidden messages, and it took me a number of years to finally figure out what it was that felt so out of place."

"You mean other than the fact that it was typed."

"She had sloppy handwriting. I used to always pick on her for that. I told her she should be a doctor. The fact that it's typed is noteworthy, yes, but that doesn't mean that it didn't come from her. She could have typed it explicitly because of her poor handwriting."

"What am I looking for?"

"Will you please just read the letter?"

I pull my door shut, cutting the outside sounds, enveloping us inside. "I'm reading it." I'm not thrilled. It's like we're dating again, only without the benefits. Carefully, I unfold the letter, straightening the yellowed page of paper.

> *Dear Mom and, Dad,*
>
> *First of all, I'm okay. I know how surprised you must be to get a letter like this after all this time, but I'm okay, and I'm happy and for now that should be enough.*
>
> *I'm writing because I want you to know that I'm safe, and that I'm not angry with any of you. I didn't leave because I was angry, and I'm not angry now. I left because I needed to. I didn't see any other way out. I just received my fourth rejection from the fourth school I'd had applied to, and I decided that if my dreams were to ever come true I'd have to do more than just daydream. At the time I knew you wouldn't understand, and I didn't want to fight, so I just left. I figured it was easier to apoligize later than ask permission.*
>
> *I'm in California on the coast, south of San Francisco. I don't want to give you the name of the town because I know you'd come looking for me. It's not that I don't want to see you or that I don't love you. I just don't want to go back.*
>
> *Tell Kristie that I'm not mad at her for that day. She'll know what that means. I think I miss her the most and I promise that I'll come back after I've sorted things out and get settled in. I can't wait to vacation down in Payton with you all. Please don't be mad, and please don't worry.*
>
> *I love you all. I'll write again soon.*
>
> *Love,*
> *Joanne*

"It's a nice letter," I say, refolding it. "What makes you think it's bogus?"

"Is that all you see?"

Frowning, I unfold the page and read through the letter again. And again. Then I see it. Or at least I *think* I see it. I look up. "It's just a spelling error," I insist. "And 'apologize' is an easy word to mess up. Even with spell check."

"First of all, no, it isn't an easy word to mess up. Not for her. She was a straight A student. That's not the kind of word she would misspell. Secondly, that's not the only error."

I reread the letter again. Then again. I shrug. "What?"

"Look closer."

I reread the letter again, but I don't see it. I don't even know what I'm looking for.

"There's a comma," Kristie says. "In the salutation, there's a comma between the word 'and' and the word 'Dad.'"

"So."

"So, she also doesn't make grammatical mistakes."

"That's getting a bit nit-picky, don't you think?"

"That's not her only flub. There are missing commas all over the place and there's that line where she says 'I'd had.' She'd never do that. It's not hers. She didn't write it. I stared and stared at this letter for years while waiting for a second letter or a phone call or something. *Anything*. It took me thirteen years to finally figure it out."

"And you've been sitting on it ever since?"

"No. I haven't been sitting on anything. I've be looking."

"And because of a couple of commas, you're convinced she didn't send it?"

"I'm convinced that whoever killed her sent it."

I shrug. "It's a bit of a stretch."

"It's enough to reopen the case."

"There is no case."

"You know what I mean."

I draw a breath. "Look," I say calmly. "I won't even pretend to understand what this is like for you. I don't have any brothers or sisters, and even if I did, it wouldn't be the same as being twins. I *get* it even though I don't *understand* it. I know what this means to you."

"You have no conception of what this means to me."

"Which is why I'm agreeing to go back."

She snatches the letter from my hand and crams it in her purse before drawing the seatbelt across her body. She won't look at me. Her attention is directed straight ahead—straight out the window at the flaking painted brick of the run-down Days Inn. "Then let's go."

"I'm not arguing with you. I'm actually trying to agree."

"Then let's go."

"We're going."

But she doesn't answer. She just folds her arms defiantly across her chest. I don't remember much about her or 'us' or this town, but I am a man, and men have instincts, and if I've learned anything over the course of my time on this earth, combined with the time I've tediously spent attempting to communicate with the opposite sex, it's that I've learned when to fight back and when to shut up. This particular grainy moment is brought to you by the makers of Silence is Golden. So, I turn the key, drop into reverse and check the rearview mirror as I back out of the parking spot. Funny, but as I pull forward, my mouth shut, my mind on fire with thoughts and doubts and any number of things, I feel like I'm on the Titanic, undocking and leaving port. And seriously, if I'm feeling like I'm on the Titanic, then there's an iceberg out there with my name on it, and that's seriously messed up.

## *Part II*

She was right. I know the way. I know the way as well as if I never left. But as I drive through Payton, I probably look like a lost tourist what with the way I'm looking around, craning my neck, doing double-takes. It's probably my unguarded surprise at how much things have changed. If I didn't know better, I'd think it was a different town.

"It's so weird having you back," Kristie says.

"I'm not back."

"We'll see." She's still staring out her window. I don't think she's mad at me, but it's hard to be sure. She was always emotional, and despite the setbacks and disappointments she's clearly lived through, nothing's changed. Either that or things have stayed ironically the same.

I concentrate on the road, on the street names, street signs, business names, vacant lots, and abandoned buildings. All these 'places' feel familiar, yet everything looks as different as me. I've been here for three days, but I still can't get over how far Payton has fallen.

"What happened here?" I ask quietly. "It's like a ghost town."

She's silent and doesn't turn as she leans on her elbow and stares out the passenger-side window.

"You there?" I ask.

She nods.

"Then what happened?"

She shrugs. "People started moving away."

"Why?"

Nothing.

I turn into the parking lot of the Days Inn and pull into an open parking spot in front of room 16.

"Well…" I say, trailing off. "We're here. I'm going to change."

"You want me to come in?"

I stare at her. It's not an advance, or maybe it is. Regardless, my thoughts are wandering—wondering about her motivation "Up to you," I say as I kill the engine and open the door. "It'll be a few minutes."

# Twelve

## *Yesterday*

"What happened to your face?" she asks, waddling toward me. Her thighs are vying for position as they rub together, her feet pointing sideways to support her weight. Kind of reminds me of a duck. The shirt she's wearing is several sizes too small, and her shorts are too short, blue veins running a varicose maze I don't care to see.

"Terrorists," I answer as I open the fridge and pull the milk. Popping the top, I smell inside. It doesn't smell fresh, but it's not sour yet either so I pour a glass.

"That's not funny," she says. "Did you get in a fight?"

"Nobody saw anything. Don't worry about it."

"Who started it?"

"What's it matter? Jesus, Mom, I'm fine. Thanks for asking."

"Enough with the language."

"Don't start. I already get hassled enough by Ritchie."

"Well, he's right, and I still pay the bills around here, so as long as you're living under my roof, enough with the language."

"That's for about another ten days," I mutter under my breath.

"What did you say?"

"Nothing."

"I heard what you said, and if that's the attitude you're planning to take with me, then you might as well move down to Florida now."

"Georgia, Mom. Georgia. Why does everyone think I'm going to Florida?" I sip from the carton and wrinkle my nose. I was wrong. The milk is definitely past its prime. I start pouring out the rest.

"What are you doing?"

"It's stale," I murmur.

"Figures. I thought it tasted kinda funny on my cereal."

"I'll pick up some tonight."

"Should I be worried?"

"About what?"

"What are we talking about?"

"You're worrying again."

"I'm your mother. That's my job."

"Well don't. Makes you look old."

"Thanks. I already get hassled enough by the mirror."

I smile. "Touché. And I didn't mean it like that. You look great."

"I'm not stupid either."

"There's nothing going on. It was a fight. Guys have an insatiable need to prove our male bravado when in the presence of the opposite sex."

"And I suppose you were just an innocent bystander who got caught in the middle?"

"Bad timing."

"Seems awful convenient."

"Trust me, it doesn't feel very convenient." I kiss her on the forehead before turning to the living room. "Stop worrying."

"Where are you going?"

"Homework!" I call over my shoulder.

"I'm worrying!"

I smile, but say nothing as I head for the bathroom where I inspect my reflection. It's bad. My face is swelling, and it'll only get worse as the bruising darkens. My chances of getting laid a second time have been greatly diminished. Frowning, I reach over to turn on the faucet. The water stings, but I force myself to wash off the blood and clean the dirt from the two open cuts. When the blood runs thin and turns from red to pink, I shut off the water and dab my face with the towel.

I miss Kristie.

Maybe after Ritchie's game I'll head over to her place. Her dad doesn't trust me, and her mom isn't exactly 'in my corner,' but so far they seem to tolerate me, so that's a win. Or at least it's not a loss.

I sneak out through the window and drop to the ground. Mom knows I do it, and I know she knows it. I could have gone out the front door, but our silent understanding seems to work better. She has plausible deniability, and we don't fight. If anyone asks, as far as she knows, I'm in my room. Right now she's sitting in the living room and shaking her head. Later she'll close the window in case it rains, but after it gets dark, she'll re-open it a crack so I can sneak back in. I promise to be careful, and she promises not to worry. It's worked this ways for years, and now that I'm going, I worry about her and what she'll do once I'm gone.

"Bye, Mom," I whisper while watching her watch TV through the big picture window where all I can see is the back of her head and her frizzy gray hair. The house is lit up, bright and warm on the inside. It's growing chilly out here, and the sun is orange instead of yellow. Daylight will be replaced with night in under an hour, and I'm already late, so I cast one last look toward home before turning and breaking in a jog toward the ballpark.

I'm sweating again by the time I get there, the game is already underway, and the crowd is already cheering, which means Ritchie is already pitching. As usual, the stands are packed. It's funny, but volleyball, lacrosse and track fail to garner much attention from the locals. They can barely get fifty people to show up on game day. Even Pirate football games sometimes fail to sellout. Pirate Baseball is the big ticket, though it's only when Ritchie's on the mound that the whole town shows up. The bleachers overflow, and the grounds around the park are standing-room only. The feeling is electric. It's like being at a professional ballpark. The loudspeakers blare every time he takes the mound, the fans leaping to their feet and clapping and singing along to *Welcome to the Jungle* by Guns 'n Roses.

I weave my way through the crowd to the stands, the music and the screaming fans deafening around me. It isn't so much Pirate baseball as it's Ritchie Hudson. Makes me wonder why he's as neurotic off the mound as he is. He should be looking at big-time schools that offer baseball programs. He should be laying pipe with every girl in town. Instead, he follows me around like a lost puppy, his head in the clouds over Joanne as if she's the only answer to his every question.

I climb the bleachers to the fourth row, fourth seat. It's the only empty seat in the house, and it's been reserved just for me. 'AAA' has been etched into the aluminum for nearly three years now. 44 is Ritchie's lucky number. He was born on February 13th, which is the 44th day of the year. We were both eight years old when we met, and since there's two of us, eight divided by two is four, and two 4s equal 44. He also wears #44 on the back of his jersey. He didn't even pick the number. It was just given to him, and since he touts fate as the will of God, he's convinced everything happens for a reason. Therefore, he decided the fourth row, fourth seat should be mine. Sort of a good luck charm. Baseball pitchers are, by nature, a bit superstitious, but Ritchie is different. He's an oddball among oddballs, but nobody argues with Ritchie Hudson, and *nobody* makes fun. If he thinks I bring good luck by sitting in the same seat every time he throws, then who's to say otherwise?

"Where were you?" a man asks as I take my seat and begin clapping in tune with the crowd.

"What?" I shout over the noise.

"You're late," he shouts.

"Do I know you?"

"Hudson gave up four runs in the first inning because you weren't here," the man shouts back. "Next time, have some respect."

I look over at the scoreboard and sure enough, the Sailors have a 4-0 lead. I turn back to the field where Ritchie is staring directly at me, that stupid grin of his plastered all over his dumb face. I shrug and point at the scoreboard before shrugging. He just flips me off, which pisses off the ump, and Ritchie gets a warning.

The crowd goes nuts.

*Focus!* I mouth over the music, but Ritchie just keeps grinning like a moron.

The music settles down, but the crowd remains standing as Ritchie goes to work.

"Steeeeeeeeeerike!" the ump shouts, and the energy returns, the crowd going bonkers. Suddenly I know—I just *know*—that even though we're losing, we'll find a way to come back. This game is well in hand.

## Part II

Top of the seventh. The good guys are up 5-4. Ritchie has pitched six full innings, and he's gassed, but the skipper sends him out anyway. They should have tapped the bullpen long ago, but since we can't hit for shit, Coach Dunham apparently feels our best bet is to keep our starter on the mound to protect the one run lead. It's a crucial game. Everyone in the ballpark is well aware of just how crucial it is, and everyone knows that even at his worst, Ritchie is better than any alternative Dunham has in his hip pocket. But Ritchie looks exhausted. His pit-stains have engulfed his entire jersey at this point, turning the entire thing a shade darker. He's lumbering his way out to the mound, cracking his neck and stretching his shoulders by rotating his arms in a circular motion. The crowd is uneasy, murmuring while wondering aloud.

Then Ritchie pulls a Ritchie.

He turns to us and yells something I can't quite make out from here but looks something like "make some fuckin' noise!"

The crowd rises to its feet. I rise with them, and suddenly we're all clapping and cheering like crazed animals, praying for a miracle as he tips his hat before going into his routine. Ritchie gave up four runs on six hits in the one inning I wasn't here. Since then, he's given up goose eggs while fanning twelve and walking only one. This is high school ball. Twelve strikeouts over five innings doesn't just happen by accident.

As Ritchie goes into his warm-up for the seventh and final inning, the music is louder, the crowd louder, the night louder than I've ever heard it before. The stands are actually shaking. I feel a weird sense of anxiety gripping my insides, but I also can't help but marvel at what my friend has accomplished. He's a dud in the classroom. He can't even pass remedial math, but out on the mound he's a god. People are clapping, stomping, graffiti spilling out on the field, the crowd singing along to the music. It's like we just won the Super Bowl, but we haven't even won this meaningless regular-season game.

Yet.

Even from where I'm standing, I can tell Ritchie is gassed. His uniform is soaked, un-tucked and hanging limply over his gut, his eyes bloodshot with fatigue. He's exhaling in wide O's, and he's stretching to buy time. But I also know him well enough to know that this is what he lives for. He'd rather die than let the bullpen take over. He'll throw his back out before he throws in the towel, and as the first batter settles into the box, I wonder if Ritchie's streak will finally break.

Ritchie goes into the wind and hurls.

Thump.

Swing.

"Steeeeeeeeeerike!"

The crowd erupts in chorus, and Ritchie waits for the ball to come back. Catching it on the fly, he turns his back the way he always does, his head lowered. He murmurs to himself, his lips moving ever so slightly as he stares at the ground. Returning to face the plate, he's ready and deals up another swing and a miss. His fastball still looks untouchable. Another windup, another pitch.

"Steeeeeeeeeerike!"

The crowd explodes as the batter tosses his bat in disgust. Ritchie just turns his back, head lowered while his big hand massages the ball. Some kids are lighting sparklers from the bleachers across the way, and they're waving them around. This prompts a reaction from everyone else who owns a lighter, because suddenly there are hundreds, if not thousands, of tiny flames springing up.

Two outs away.

The next batter takes his place at home-plate.

People are shouting themselves hoarse, stomping their feet. I've never heard it this loud before. Ever. The crowd doesn't bother to quiet down even as Ritchie turns back to home plate, reads the signs and settles into his windup. A foul, a ball and a strike later, and the crowd is chanting, clapping, stomping. The world around me is vibrating and shaking. People are waving flags, T-shirts, sparklers, lighters all the while pumping fists and clapping, rolling in waves, the stadium packed. The streets are empty, the homes empty, the stores and shops closed. Payton is closed—shut down. Everyone's here. Everyone.

"Steeeeeeeeeerike!"

The crowd goes nuts, frantic and falling over one another. Two outs.

"Ritchie! Ritchie! Ritchie!" the crowd chants.

One more.

For his part, Ritchie looks focused. He's throwing angry, ignoring the calls being sent in. The game is at home plate. Forget the outfielders, and forget the score. This is between him and the last batter. He's 122 pitches in. He's exhausted, sweating, angry. One hanging slider and we're tied. One well-read fastball, and it's a brand-new game. One slip-up and every fan will go silent. Butts will hit the seats.

But that's only *if*…

Fourteen strikeouts. Fourteen out of the last eighteen batters have gone down on strikes. That's unheard of.

Ritchie's back is to home plate and he's massaging the ball while the batter takes a few warm-up swings. Ritchie turns around, the crowd roars, rising to its feet. We all stand at once, and I can hardly see over the raving wall of raised fists in front of me. Looking around the stadium, I can't help but smile. Everyone is here for him and everyone is here for this moment. We're one out away from an unbelievable come from behind victory—the kind of thing people will recount long after the season ends.

Ritchie rears back and hurls a fastball.

"Steeeeeeeeeerike!"

The crowd is electric. Two more strikes. That's all he needs.

Thump, thump, thump, thump. Shoes, flip-flops and boots stomp the stands, hands clapping, people shouting and shrieking. Ritchie stretches a bit, and I smile, wondering if it's for show—even if just a little bit.

Ritchie faces home plate, spits, adjusts his cap and goes into his wind. He throws a curveball that causes the batter to chase it into the dirt, and the crowd roars with enthusiasm.

Two strikes.

One more. One more and this place is going to implode.

The feeling around me—pumping and vibrating—is surreal. So much energy, so many hopes and so much fear. One bad pitch and this crowd will panic. Never mind the four runs he gave up in the first inning. And never mind the fourteen strikeouts since. It comes down to this. The guy on the loudspeaker is trying to call the game, but you can barely hear him.

Ritchie faces the batter, goes into his wind and rears back. Flashbulbs go off, the sounds around me deafening, and the ball leaves Ritchie's hand. His fastball has been good all night, but this is something else. He found every last ounce of energy, and the ball is in the catcher's glove before either the batter or the umpire have an opportunity to react.

"Holy shit," I whisper in awe.

Around me, the crowd boils over as the umpire calls the final strike. Ritchie just stands there, his arms spread—palms up, a big Ritchie grin is on his face. He suddenly tosses his mitt high in the air. His teammates are rushing the field along with the fans, while I stand rooted. All I can do is shake my head, inspired by my friend's performance. This wasn't just a game. This was a monumental moment in the history of Payton County.

Fireworks explode overhead, lighting the sky. Ritchie is hoisted up on the shoulders of his teammates. He looks my way and tips his hat the way he does when we win. But he looks different. This time he looks like an angel. All that talk of incompetence, all those fears of inadequacy, all that concern of being fat and ugly— it's all forgotten. Out there it's just Ritchie, a big oaf. My best friend.

I'm still clapping, still whooping, still pumping my fist as I stand to leave—fourth row, fourth seat—and make my way toward the stadium exit. The crowd around me is nuts, the world around me all about Ritchie. We're here for him.

But it's different. He's different. He's smiling, but he's not happy. He's empty, and even though this evening is supposed to be about him, it's not. This night is all about *her*. He's acting excited while she's nowhere to be seen. And it's not like he doesn't notice.

I clap anyway.

## Part III

The crowd has spilled onto the field, and it's still so loud that I have to shout. I yell my lungs hoarse, but Ritchie just shakes his head, hands out like he can't hear me.

"I gotta go!" I shout again.

Suddenly, the smile slips from his face. "What do you mean you gotta go? There's nowhere *to* go. This is our night!"

"It's your night, buddy!"

"You gotta stay!"

"Go with your team," I say with a reassuring smile, the crowd pushing me back. "I need to be somewhere."

"But...you're my best friend."

"Brothers in arms, amigo."

I keep getting pushed further and further back, like a boat pulled from the shore. People are crowding him, spraying him with celebratory soda. His uniform is ruined, but he's not thinking about his uniform. He's staring directly at me.

"Fine," he mouths, looking suddenly lost and ignoring the girls grabbing at his shirt. "Fuck you."

I frown.

He waves me off before turning away and allowing the crowd to carry him away.

"If I don't see you tomorrow, I'll see you on Saturday!" I shout over the crowd. "At Greg's party!"

He's not looking anymore. The fans are mobbing him, the mob pushing me back— squeezing me out. I'm suddenly on the outside looking in. Ritchie is drifting away. It's quieter now, but maybe it's because I'm watching instead of participating.

I turn away.

Nobody's trying to leave the ballpark yet except for the few visitors' fans who made the trip in from Muskegon, so it's not hard to get out of the stadium. I walk through the quiet town. Most of the houses are dark, and I imagine almost everyone is still at Pirate Field with the exception of the older folks who have drawn their shades to block out the world.

Eventually the houses thin. Then the paved road gives way to dirt. Then the dirt road gives way to weeds, and I'm all alone in a vast field. I reach Beaver Crossing, tightrope my way across, and finagle my way through the tall grass leading into Lawton. I knock on the Kristie's front door, shifting uneasily as I wait. Mrs. Lambert opens the door and steps back, her nose wrinkling. "You stink."

"It's not me," I say nervously.

"Oh?"

108

"I mean it is me, but it wasn't me. There was a game tonight. Ritchie pitched. I was there, and it was…they were…the fans got rowdy."

"You smell like beer."

I smell my shirt. "I thought it was Pepsi…"

"Hmmm," she answers. "It's also late."

I frown and look at my watch. I have to lean forward into the light in order to see. "It's only…"

"She's messing with you," Kristie calls, approaching from the stairs, grinning.

Mrs. Lambert frowns. "What happened to your face, Anthony?"

"Oh, my god," Kristie says, the smile vanishing. "What happened to your face?"

Apparently, they've noticed my face.

"It doesn't look as bad as it feels," I say before frowning. "Or, the other way around, I mean."

"I got it, Mom," Kristie says.

Mrs. Lambert smiles at her daughter before scowling at me, and suddenly it's a long lost episode of *Leave it to Beaver.* Small town principles combine forces with protective parental boundaries to form Super Mom and her scowl of death.

"What happened?" Kristie asks, pulling the door shut as she steps out onto the porch, her soft fingers exploring the bumps on my face. "Did you get in a fight?"

"Yeah, but it was for a good cause. There were these three guys picking on a girl."

"A girl?"

"Yeah, but we weren't—"

"Which girl? Is she pretty?"

"Huh?"

"Is she pretty?"

"No, I mean…me and Ritchie were—"

"You and Ritchie?" She sighs and backs up. "Well, that figures."

"What's that supposed to mean?"

"It means you don't get into fights," she storms. "Only when your good buddy Ritchie tells you to."

"Ritchie's my friend," I answer.

"I know he's your friend."

I turn my back. "It was Mandy Ferguson. They were—"

"Mandy Ferguson? Jesus, Tony, she's nuts."

"It wasn't like that."

"Then how was it like?"

"It was Ritchie who stepped in. I had to take his back. I had to. It's not like I wanted to fight, but sometimes you do things you don't want to do if it's for a friend. You just do it."

She stares at me. She doesn't shout or yell or bawl, kind of like I half-expect her to. We've apparently reached that point in our relationship where we can accurately judge tone and inflection. Either that or we can't yet we pretend that we can.

"So, what happened to Mandy?" she asks, yet her voice has changed. Her tone is softer.

"She ran off," I answer. "Somewhere in the middle of it."

"It?"

"It was a fight. Guys fight."

"Over girls."

"I told you, it wasn't like that."

"I really wish you'd stop hanging out with him."

"He's my best friend."

"*I'm* your best friend!" she shouts. "Have you fucked him?"

"That's a ridiculous question. You know what I mean."

"Do I? Then are you just fucking me for sport?"

"Do you have to use that word? It's not like that. Mandy was—"

"I'm not talking about Mandy. We're past Mandy. We're on to Ritchie, and Ritchie scares me. I don't like the way he looks at me, and I don't like the way he looks at my sister. Come to think of it, I don't even like the way he looks at you."

I shake my head. "Ritchie's a big teddy bear. You've said it yourself. And he adores you and Joanne. He'd lie down in traffic for the both of you."

Kristie lowers her head, clenches her fists. When she looks up, her face is set. "That's what everyone says, but there's a difference between the way he looks at me and the way you look at me, and I'm telling you, it's creepy."

"It's not what everyone says. It's what you said."

"Not recently."

"But still."

"He's like a little boy. He's totally innocent."

Kristie smiles. "Innocent? How many fights did he get into today?"

There's no arguing with her. She doesn't know Ritchie like I do. I've known him my whole life. Well, at least half of it anyway, and he adores Joanne. Even if his crush is a bit adolescent in nature, it's certainly not just some whimsical Saturday morning cartoon fetish.

"Can you just tell him that my sister's not interested?" she asks, her eyes pleading.

"He knows." I shrug. "It just makes him try harder."

Kristie chuckles before burying her face. "So, what do we do?"

"Nothing. It's fine. He's fine. He's one of the good guys. Trust me, you *want* him on your side. He'll never hurt her, and he'll kill anyone that would. He's like a bodyguard without a W2."

Kristie steps forward and wraps her arms around me, leaning her head against my chest. "He's just so weird."

"He's a goofball."

We stand in the middle of the porch swaying to music that isn't even playing. Her arms are wrapped so tight around me that I swear that I can't tell where I end and she begins.

"What are you thinking?" she asks.

"I don't know."

"You don't know? Of course you know. What are you thinking?"

Everything has to be more than just an answer with her. Everything has to have multiple layers that need to be carefully peeled back so as not to damage the fragile ego that shouldn't be so fragile. And it's not just her. It's women in general. I swear they think differently than we do—reveling in the 'moment' rather than taking time to understand the larger implications. I can't tell her what I'm thinking, because she'll freak out, and then she'll counter with about a billion more nit-picky questions, leaving me to conjure up about a billion bullshit answers. Why can't she just accept the fact that I'm happy when I'm with her? In fact, I am so miserably happy that I just stand there smelling her hair.

Which smells great.

"I'm mad at you," she says.

"What for?"

"I haven't decided yet."

"Well, can we postpone the part where you're trying to figure out why you're mad at me and instead jump to the part where I left the game so I could be with you?"

"Is that supposed to make all this okay?"

"Yes."

She continues to rock with me, her body still pressed up against mine. This would be one of those really sweet moments, except she's decided to make it sexy. Apparently, the time to be angry is over, and the time to be experimental has begun. Her hand has become frisky with a mind of its own.

"Your mother's inside," I murmur nervously.

"But it's too dark to see us out here."

She leads me off the porch into the dewy grass, the moon showing its cheesy face. We are hidden in darkness as she unbuttons my shirt and stands on her toes to reach my lips. She's got my buckle undone, and she's pushing my pants and boxers down. This wasn't exactly what I was expecting. I thought there'd be a bit of me stripping and then a bit of her stripping, but I'm suddenly naked and vulnerable, and she's not. She kisses my lips, my neck, my chest, slowly creeping down my torso to my belly and then...

"I..." I say, shivering. "But what about..."

Being a teenager is the worst.

And the best.

## *Part IV*

I wake up in the Lambert hammock, Kristie at my side. She's still asleep, curled up against me for warmth, her breathing regular and soft. The trees overhead are waving slowly in the morning breeze. Things are a bit on the chilly side, but the air smells clean—like a spring rain. It's the first time I've woken up without a ceiling over my head, and it's one of those moments I know I'll carry with me to the grave. I don't want to forget it. Any of it. Not the smell of the air, not the sound of her breathing, not the feel of the hammock wrapping us together.

Kristie jerks, caught in a dream, and I pull her closer just as the sun breaks over the treetops. As wonderful as everything should seem, I can't help but fear something's wrong. Maybe it's the quiet. The town seems quiet—and not just this morning. There hasn't been any real crime around here for months. Not so much as a convenience store robbery or a teenage arson. With the rest of the world twisting with murder and racism and terrorism all around us, nothing seems to happen in little ol' Payton County. We're overdue. It's as though we've been shielded from the rest of the world. Or maybe we've just been waiting. Or maybe something's been waiting for us.

She jerks again and this time opens her eyes. Yawning, her body shivers as she snuggles up to me. Kissing my neck, she smiles. "Hey," she says.

"Hey."

She yawns, her breath stale, but that's okay. "Did you sleep?"

"For awhile."

"That's it?'"

"For awhile."

She smiles and breathes against my neck, warm breath slinking under my collar.

"Let's just lay here for the rest of our lives," she murmurs.

"We have school today."

"I'm sure we're already late," she answers with another sleepy yawn.

"My algebra final is today. I need at least a B."

"Or what? The University of Georgia changes its mind?"

"No, but still."

"But what?"

"I can't miss it."

She rubs my chest. "Trying to get rid of me?"

"Just sayin'…"

Kristie rolls to the side and tips us out of the hammock. I land awkwardly, and she laughs. Rolling onto her back, she looks up at me with a small smile as I hover over her. Gingerly reaching up, the tips of her fingers brush the bruises on my face. I flinch slightly, pulling back.

"Sorry," she whispers.

I lean in and kiss her quickly. Her breath is stale but still so good that I go back for seconds. I have every intention of stopping at two, but her tongue is warm, and she's giggly and how many more times can I expect to make out with a seventeen year old girl on the front lawn of her parent's house on a Friday morning?

"Stay home," she begs.

"It's one of my finals, Kris. I can't just skip it."

She smiles, but it's a sad smile. "Call in sick."

"Or call in sick."

"Fine. Then go."

"Don't do that."

"I'm not doing anything."

"Now I feel guilty."

She licks her lips, nods and rolls out from under me. She stands, pushing her hair behind her ears. I stand too, and look around. Judging by where the sun is sitting pretty in the sky, I'm already running late.

"You're still planning on the party tomorrow, right?" she asks.

"Of course."

"Good. 'Cause it wouldn't be a party without Triple A."

She only calls me Triple A when she's upset.

"What's going on?" I ask softly, carefully checking my tone.

"Nothing. What time?"

"What time what?"

"What time do you plan on showing up?"

I shrug. "I don't know. Ritchie works until close, so probably not until after eight."

"Ritchie?"

I sigh. "Are we going to start this again?"

She stares at me for a long moment, ugly daggers in her eyes, before shaking her head, turning away and heading up to the house. I consider calling after her, but I've seen that look before, and she's taking those broad, determined steps that indicate she'd rather run face-first into a brick wall than argue with what she calls my 'lunacy." Besides, sometimes a man needs to stand firm in order let her know that she's not always the center of the universe.

I prance my unhappy ass down the driveway and turn toward home. The edge of Lawton stretches out like a runway with Payton all the way on the other side of the field. The sun is rising, and it's going to be a beautiful morning. I walk through the sleepy town that's only beginning to stir and cross into the dewy grass leading back toward the Old Beaver. The morning air smells humid—sticky. Summertime in Michigan has arrived.

Stripping nude beside the Beaver, I toss my clothes into the weeds and stand there free as a bird, swinging in the wind. Then I dip my toe into the stream. And then my foot. And then I step in, shivering as I sink into the cold water that wraps itself around my body and grips me like a glove. I splash around for a few minutes, careful to wash the dried stink from my skin. It's not like it'll be a big secret when I show up for class. All of my books are at home, and I'll be wearing the same clothes I wore yesterday.

113

My hair is a mess and my face looks like ground chuck. The swelling has gone down somewhat, and the bruises never got as bad as I thought they would. It's more of a rugged look. Studying my reflection in the rippling water, I look something like a gangster.

I shake the water from my body the best I can and get dressed before turning toward town. But that good feeling I'd had out in the tall grass disappears as I make my way into Payton. I'm late for school, which isn't unusual, so it's not the end of the world. My algebra final doesn't start for another hour and some change. But as I pull open the doors, my sneakers squeaking, watermarks left with each step, I realize how out of place I feel. Carelessly running my hand through my unkempt hair for the umpteenth time, I stop outside my classroom. Through the window, the students inside look back. Mrs. Lipinski is unimpressed with my disheveled appearance and late arrival. I pull open the door, don a smile, bid the old crow a good morning and make my way through the rows of desks to the back of the room.

But something's different.

Normally I'm just Average-Joe. I'm neither popular nor unpopular. I'm that guy that blends in with the more modest of them, but today they're noticing. Every girl is turning her head and smiling—even blushing. And the guys are frowning. Was it the fight? Did people hear about it? Or is it how I look? Can they tell I'm in love?

"Mr. Abbott," Mrs. Lipinski asks with a sour tone. "Where are your books?"

I smile. "Dog ate 'em."

"A dog?"

"A big Doberman."

There are giggles.

"I had to run for my life," I finish.

More giggles.

"I'm sure you did," Mrs. Lipinski smirks.

I take my seat and smile. The old battleaxe glares. It's a good old fashioned Mexican standoff with twenty other students stuck in between.

"Well," Lipinski remarks, her tone softer. "Look on with Joni then."

Joni is seated right beside me, and she smiles lightly as I scooch my desk toward hers. She points at the page number and taps the textbook, but she's not looking at the book. She's looking at me. Big pretty eyes.

I smile. Damn it feels good to be a gangster.

# Thirteen

## Today

The houses are thinning on either side of the road as we head out of town, and the sun dips behind some fast approaching clouds like an ominous omen as if warning me to get away. Bolt. Run. Go. I wanted so badly for all of this to feel like home. I wanted so badly to remember, but it doesn't, and I don't. And now I'm starting to actually *feel* like a tourist in my own hometown.

"Looks like rain," I say.

Thump-thump. Thump-thump.

Route 89 is even more familiar than Payton, probably because not much has changed. No new businesses have sprung up, and none of the old ones have closed down. I could drive this route blindfolded while following the sound of the cracks beneath the tires.

Thump-thump. Thump-thump.

"Just over this hill," she whispers.

I know it's just over the hill, but if navigating gives her something to do other than nag, then I won't say anything. I already know where I'm going. I saw it on my way in, and sure enough, as we crest the hill heading out, there it is again. The old Johnson farm. It's been close to twenty years, but it looks almost exactly as it did when I left. The roof has collapsed on one corner, and there are trees growing through the porch, but the lawn was overgrown before, and it's overgrown now. That old rusty pickup is still parked in the driveway as if loyally waiting for its owners to climb behind the wheel and fire her up. Not that there's much of a driveway. Poplar trees have taken over everything, springing several feet tall and swaying in the breeze. Even the grass is three feet high.

I pull into what used to be the driveway and roll over the tall grass and small trees, driving as far inland as I can get. We're within twenty feet or so of the rusted out truck when I decide that this is as far as I dare go lest I get stuck, so I put the car in park and kill the engine. Kristie and I sit quietly for a moment before I undo my seatbelt and open the door. Thunder rolls in the distance, the sky overhead growing increasingly dark.

"Let's look in the barn first," Kristie whispers, shutting her door. "Where I found the headband."

The barn has fared far better than the house. It stands coldly against the orange, red and gray backdrop. We traipse through the tall jungle-like grass, which slaps at my arms and legs with snake-like fingers, making me feel caged. I pull open the old door, the rusty wheels squeaking along their track, light bleeding across the dusty floor. Ironically, once inside, I actually feel a bit of relief. There's a quiet harmony in here, secrets playing hide-and-seek. The floor is sandy, and the barn carries that ever-present smell of dry hay. The roof is still relatively intact, so everything inside is mostly dry. Nothing's changed, so it's hard to believe that it's been half my life since I was here last, and I'm oddly aware of how at home I feel, which is a bit unnerving considering how out of place I felt back in Payton.

"Over here," she whispers, motioning me toward the corner. As I draw closer, my attention is drawn to the dull graffiti sprayed on the walls. Had someone asked me about it last week, I would have shrugged it off. I wouldn't have remembered a thing. I'd have dismissed it as 'probably' something I did as a kid, but now, seeing the familiar words splashed over those old wooden boards, I remember it like it happened yesterday. I remember me and Ritchie stealing those cans of spray paint from the local True Value and immortalizing ourselves in the corner of an old barn.

*44*
*The Rejects*
*RH + JL*
*AAA + KLL*

Something's wrong.

"Boys will be boys," Kristie giggles.

I say nothing. I don't even smile. I just stare at that last line.

"What is it?" Kristie asks. "I thought it was sweet."

I shake my head. "I didn't do that."

"What? Which part?"

"The last line. The Triple A plus Kristie Lynn Lambert part." I remember spraying the number '*44*' and '*The Rejects*,' but I don't actually remember the rest. "I didn't add that."

Her smile fades, and she turns back to the wall. She stops as well and reflects. "Then who did?"

I brush past her. "Ask my good buddy the next time you see him." I stop in the corner and kick around some hay and loose dirt. "You found the headband here?"

She approaches me, tucking her hands in her pockets. "Yes."

Crouching down, I start poking in the dirt. Suddenly, I'm a television detective with all the right dialogue and all the right facial expressions, and I'm sporting a poker face worth millions in Vegas, but I see nothing, and what's more, there's nothing to be

116

seen. I use a small twig to cut through the dirt. "The topsoil is loose," I murmur, "but it's solid underneath."

"What's that mean?"

I turn to her. "It means her body isn't here."

Her eyes get misty, and she stands with her hands on her hips. "It's been almost twenty years."

"There haven't been any animals or people in this barn to pack the ground down, but it's hard as rock. Even if she was killed here, and I'm not saying she was, but if she was, her body isn't buried here."

"There's a shovel over there," Kristie whispers.

I stand. "Knock yourself out. She's not here."

Her mouth curls sharply downward, and she lowers her head, covering her eyes with her hand. I hold my tongue. The loss of her sister is not my responsibility, but it's clear that she's still hanging on. "It doesn't mean we can't keep looking," I whisper. "All I'm saying is she's not here. At least not in this spot."

Kristie keeps her face buried in her hands, and it's the same thing all over again. I thought she'd gotten past this stage years ago. The tears, the grief, the condolences. Not sure what else to do, I wrap my arms over her shoulders and pull her to me. "Maybe the headband was just left behind," I try.

She's already shaking her head. "She can't hear without it."

*Can't.*

Not *couldn't.*

Kristie's speaking about her sister as though she's still alive. Joanne's dead. And if she's not dead, then she's gone. And if she's gone, then she's not coming back. The cops did their job. They searched everywhere and interviewed everyone. Either she hitchhiked her way out of town, or she disappeared into the Bermuda Triangle.

Kristie's not satisfied. She frantically begins looking around. Nothing in this barn has shifted in a century or more, but she's a girl on a mission, and she's out to prove me and the rest of the world wrong. She's determined. She's so determined, in fact, that she's risking her life by climbing the rickety wooden ladder leading into the loft.

"I don't know if that's such a good idea," I murmur. "That ladder's more termites than timber by now."

"I have to look." Kristie reaches the loft and disappears. I can hear her shuffling around, and I recognize the futility of her search. Another rumble of thunder overhead causes me to look up. "We should probably go."

No answer.

"See anything?" I call.

"No," comes her distant return.

Of course not. There's nobody up there. Who would be dumb enough to kill another person and then drag the body up a rickety ladder and bury it in the loft of a collapsing barn? But Kristie has to be sure, so I guess I'm stuck here until she's satisfied.

Kristie re-emerges and begins to descend the ladder. "She's not up there."

"You sure?"

Pause. "Yes, and thank you not the sneer."

I pace with hands in pockets. "I didn't mean it like that."

"I want to check the house," Kristie says, hopping off the latter.

"Even though you found the headband in here?"

"Yes." She waits, but I don't bend. I just kind of casually wait. "Is this how you help?" she asks.

"We'll check the house."

The world outside is completely calm as we exit the barn. There's no wind—no breeze. Nothing. The sounds of insects are all around us, but nothing's moving. It's still-life, and it's messing with my head.

"Let's go," I say, leaving through the open barn doors and carefully navigating my back into the tall grass leading toward the house. Kristie follows, and we gingerly step through the grass while watching for snakes. Or glass. Or nails. Once we reach the house, I insist on climbing the stairs first. I test each step, gently applying pressure, half-expecting to fall through. Reaching the top, I usher her forward.

We enter the house together, treading carefully. The place is in terrible condition. Even so, I'm fascinated with the way things were back then and how well the place has held up. It's like a step back in time—better than a museum. Even though two decades have passed, nothing has changed. Nobody's moved anything, despite the hundreds of people that must've come and gone. Everyone has respected the sanctity of what once was, and they've left everything alone. An old couch and coffee table, the rotting magazines, the television. Nobody moved anything. Even the old grandfather's clock is still in the corner where the world stopped at 5:23. The refrigerator and stove are still in the kitchen and glasses remain stacked in the cupboard. The previous owners must have left in a hurry, because two glasses that had been washed years ago are still sitting on an old rag upon the countertop where they had been left to dry. Pictures still cling to the walls and an old pot filled with dirt sits in the center of the kitchen table where I imagine a plant once thrived. Opening the pantry door, the canned goods have been wiped clean, but I guess that's okay. Better than going to waste.

The bathroom is scary. The porcelain toilet broke in half years ago, and there's a black slime growing on pretty much everything. The old shower curtain has some kind of green vine creeping toward the ceiling, and I marvel at how quickly nature takes over.

Kristie heads up the stairs leading to the second floor, and I follow not out of curiosity but rather to make sure she doesn't slip and cut herself on a rusty nail or worse. The house should be condemned. I'm actually a bit surprised that it's still standing.

"They used to sleep up here," she whispers as she steps into the master bedroom. The bed is rotting, but the blankets—rumpled and used—are still on top of the mattress. This is the corner of the house where the roof caved in, so what was once a beautiful space is now rotting away. The dresser has been spilled and clothing is scattered around the room. People used to wear these clothes, and people used to sleep in this bed. The shattered window and the rotting drywall is a reminder that all dreams come to an end.

We leave the room and step gingerly along the hallway toward the next open doorway—a boy's room judging by the broken model airplanes and toys scattered about. Everything is exactly as it was the last time I saw it. It's almost as if it's waiting for a little boy to come back, pick up his coloring book and go to work as though not a day had passed. The dresser is still standing, and upon opening the drawers, clothing is still neatly folded inside. Broken glass litters the floor where the window was broken out. The closet was torn apart—the closet door lying in two pieces upon the floor. Everything else is neat and tidy. I wouldn't have expected this kind of cleanliness. Not from a boy, and certainly not after this many years. It makes me wonder what happened to cause the Johnson's to just up and disappear. There were rumors, of course. One was that Old Man Johnson took his family to the back field and shot them one by one before turning the gun on himself, but nothing was ever found. Nothing. They were just gone. Another theory had them kidnapped by aliens—beamed up into some spaceship before being whisked away and used as experiments.

Kids make up the stupidest stuff.

The last bedroom is where the little girl slept. Her room looks like it might as well have been straightened yesterday. Everything is its place including her dolls and stuffed animals. The curtains are still hanging in rags in front of the window that remains intact. It's like nobody's even set foot in this room since the door was last pulled shut. Even the dust remains undisturbed. The wallpaper is slightly moldy, but the room feels 'safe.' It's as though the spirit of a child is still here.

"She's not in here," Kristie whispers, pulling the door shut. She turns to me and wipes her eyes. "Jo, I mean."

"I'm sorry."

She nods, draws a breath and forces a timid smile. "I want to check the basement."

Whatever makes her happy. Whatever she wants so we can leave. Whatever.

We make our way back down the rickety stairs to the main floor. Kristie pulls open the door leading into the cellar where I can smell the stale, pungent scent even from up here, but we head down anyway. One stair at a time, each step creaking, threatening to give, and even when we reach the bottom, I don't feel any safer. The house could come down at any time. We'd be buried. No one would even bother digging us out, because no one would know we're down here.

Lightning flashes, spreading our shadows across the floor.

"Happy Halloween," I murmur.

She glares at me, apparently in no mood.

119

There's more sand than concrete on the floor. The walls are damp with condensation, and it's not that I'm afraid of spiders, but the big furry monsters down here are enough to make even me squeamish. They're albino white and sitting still as if waiting to spring.

"Well?" she asks.

"Well what?"

"Aren't you leading?"

I bite my tongue. "What exactly are we looking for?"

Her silence is enough to make me regret my question. Stupid, stupid, stupid...

We enter what was a canning room where all the old Ball jars are either broken or filled with some kind of pickled slime. An old wooden door lies at the back of the room, and it's pulled tightly closed. Kristie leans up against me, and I can feel her heart racing. She's scared.

"Seen enough?" I ask.

"She's back there," she whispers. "I can feel it."

"She's not back there. The cops have been all through this place. There's nothing back there."

Kristie shakes her head. "She's back there."

I try to take a step forward, but she pulls me back.

"Do you want to see or not?" I ask.

"No," she replies. "I don't know. It's been so long..."

"Do you want me to look while you wait out here?"

She studies me, draws a deep breath and finally nods.

Biting my tongue while reminding myself that I'm here for her, I step forward only to hear and feel a crunch beneath my shoe. Looking down, I find that I've stepped on a dead mouse. That's for effect, of course. In a grungy place like this, I need to either step on a dead mouse or a live snake because otherwise it's not worth the hype that comes with hunting around a moldy old basement.

I close my fingers around the brass handle, and suddenly I'm Indiana Jones, curious if this door might be booby trapped. For all I know, I'm entering some kind of cursed tomb. I turn my hand, and the knob squeaks poetically. The stiff door gives, yawning open to reveal—

Kristie screams, and I leap back. Closing my eyes I brace for impact but nothing happens. Opening one eye, I look into the room only to see...

                                                                      ...nothing.

Absolutely nothing. Brick and mortar, a few old shelves filled with gunk and garbage and nothing more. Turning angrily, I find her trying to stomp on one of those ugly white spiders dancing around her feet. She finally makes contact, and I hear a pop. She looks up at me and smiles nervously.

"Got it," she says.

"No kidding."

She frowns.

"Anything else you'd like to see?" I ask.

"What's in there?" She tries to peer around me.

I step aside. "Nothing."

"You're sure?"

"Be my guest."

"I don't want to…"

"It's empty."

She steps around me and into the empty room where she looks around. She even scuffs the ground with her shoe, kicking up some dust but not much more.

"Satisfied?" I ask.

She stares at me, exhaling before turning to look around again. Hands on hips, she sweeps the room one more time before turning back. "No…"

"I'm sorry."

"Me too." She looks around, and there are more of those white spiders that seem to be inching closer. "What about that room?" She's pointing into the open doorway of the old coal bin. There's even a small pile of coal, a shovel and a worn, rotting pair of rubber boots.

"See anything?"

She shakes here head. "I hate it down here."

I extend my hand toward the stairs. "Let's go."

Kristie leads the way up the stairs while I admire her shapely behind. I wonder if it's as firm as it was back when we were kids.

"You're looking at my butt," she says. "I can feel it."

"I'm just making sure none of those nasty spiders decided to hitch a ride."

"How thoughtful."

"I'm a thoughtful kind of guy."

"Even after all these years…"

"I'm loyal that way."

"That's not what I meant."

"Your butt is spider-free."

"You're sure?"

"Trust me, I'm looking really close."

We reach the top floor, and she turns on me. "Thank you, Tony."

"I'm just doing my job."

"That's not what I meant." She steps forward, backing me up against the wall. She wraps her arms over my shoulders and pulls me closer. She opens her mouth and touches her lips to mine. I'm defensive until I feel her tongue touching mine. It's weird, and then it's not, and it feels so good to be kissing her again. It feels natural. We kiss like teenagers, her as hungry for me as I am her. When she pulls away, she's blushing.

"What was that for?" I ask.

"Thank you."

"I didn't really do anything. I was just—"

"Stop," she says, pecking me on the lips. "Just stop."

So I do. She looks at me, and I look at her. We do a lot of looking. We're twenty years older than we were then, but it still feels just as fresh, and I'm still just as excited, and she can tell, because she's grinning with that knowing grin that both drives me nuts and turns me on. I take her hand and lead her out the back door onto the porch. The boards creak under our weight, but they hold. The storm is blowing in from the west, the clouds overhead tumbling and fighting for position. The wind has picked up and there's lightning in the distance.

"It's going to be a doozie," she murmurs.

"Want to leave?"

She wavers a moment then shakes her head. "No." She cuddles up to me as the first rain drops fall in big, fat splatters. "I feel better here."

# Fourteen

## Yesterday

Ritchie frowns, that look he sometimes gets in his eye. "What's that even supposed to mean?" he asks. "Try not to be the sore thumb?" He shrugs. "Why would you say that? Why would anyone say that? I'm not a sore thumb. I'm the life of the party. Everyone likes me. They all want me there."

I say nothing.

"Well, don't just stand there like a door knob. What's it mean?"

"Nothing," I say. "Other than it's Greg's party, not yours."

"Greg's an asshole. If he tries anything, I'll kick his butt."

"That's exactly what I'm talking about," I snap. "It's *his* party, Rich. He organized it, and it's his place. And he's not an asshole. He's a good guy."

"Well, if you love him so much, then why dontcha marry him?"

I bite my tongue, refraining from what I really want to say. "All I'm saying is you don't have to be the center of attention all the time."

Ritchie is quiet for a moment. "Bite me."

"Do you really think the fastest way to Joanne's heart is by acting like a moron?"

Ritchie kicks a stone angrily. "But people laugh at my jokes. They think I'm funny."

"They're laughing *at* you."

"The hell you say."

"Just…" I'm overly-demonstrative with my hands again, a bad habit of mine I'm not at all proud of. "Just play it cool. That's all I ask. Play it cool, and everyone will have a good time."

We continue through town, the fat old moon hanging heavy in the sky. I'm dressed nice—casual, though it's apparent to even me that I tried too hard to look casual. Nice shirt, clean jeans, yet the shirt is carelessly un-tucked, and the jeans are meticulously worn. I'm wearing my favorite cologne, and despite my recent battle wounds, I might even pass for a semi-mediocre good-looking guy.

Greg passed me an invite two weeks ago. It was under the table—a nobody-knows-what-nobody-knows kind of thing. Even now I'm not sure he intended for that invite to extend to Ritchie, but if not, he should have known better. Ritchie's my best friend, and he goes where I go.

The idea of a party sounded prodigious, and it's panning out to be a perfect night for a bonfire. There'll be hot girls and cold suds, and that's all fine and everything, but I especially can't wait to see her. Kristie. It's only been two days, but it already feels like an eternity. My head is so wrapped up in seeing her that I momentarily forget that my buddy is by my side. For once he's quiet, and I'm worried that I might have hurt his feelings.

"I hope she's happy to see me," he murmurs.

This makes me feel bad. He should be looking into scholarships and big ten schools, but instead he's wrapped up in her. He can't focus on anything else. It's sad. Sad and innocent all in one. He and I couldn't be more different, yet we couldn't be more the same. We're both meatheads with boobs on the brain.

We walk through the tall grass, stepping high, the dewing grass slapping at our legs. I can hear the laughter from here. People sitting around the campfire and having a good ol' time. The neighbors are probably less than thrilled, but Greg compensates by proactively inviting the whole neighborhood so everyone will feel included and too guilty to complain. Then he invites the cops, just in case anyone does. Of course, the cops never show. They know kids will be drinking, but they did it when they were our age, and their parents did it before them. Besides, there are more important things to do than bust some kids out having fun. Nobody's driving, and everyone walks home, so it's cool just long as someone like Ritchie doesn't fuck it up for the rest of us.

We cross the driveway and make our way into the backyard where there are fifty or more people either seated around a fire or out in the shadows making out. We're fashionably late, and for the first time that I can remember, I am warmly received. Mandy Ferguson is here. She's off by herself, rocking to the music, but she's smiling—at me. It's amazing what one little fight can do for a guy's reputation.

Someone tosses me a beer, and I catch it on the fly. Ritchie gets one too, and he's a wild man as he hops around the fire, shakes his beer, pops the cap and lets the fizz fly. The crowd cheers him on, and he's the man in the spotlight just the way he likes it. My 'play it cool' speech has not had the effect I was hoping for, but so far, everyone seems okay with him being here. I approach Kristie, taking a sip. I sit beside her, lean in and give her a kiss.

"You taste like beer," she giggles.

"I missed you."

"Really?"

"Of course. Why wouldn't I?"

She stares into my eyes, that soft little smile of hers at the corners of her mouth. "I love you."

She said it. She actually said it. I should be freaked out, but I'm not. The weird thing is, it feels nice. What's weirder is I think I love her too. Ritchie is hopping around the fire, stealing the attention of everyone else while I'm here in the shadows with the only person I want to be with.

There's a sound to my right, and I look over to see someone walking past. Her head is bowed, the long hair hiding her face. But I'd know that walk anywhere because it's just like her sister's. Joanne.

"Jo?" Kristie asks.

"Is she okay?" I murmur.

Kristie doesn't answer as she stands and follows her sister.

"Perfect," I murmur disappointedly, mostly to myself.

The sparks dance into the darkening sky. Ritchie has settled down a bit. He's still on his feet, but he's congregating with a small group. Despite the shadows, I can still see him stealing glances toward Joanne who is currently being consoled by her sister. Joanne's crying. Something upset her, though I can't figure what. It's Saturday night, and we're partying. There's nothing to be upset about.

And I hate it when girls cry.

Standing, I down the last of my beer and approach the two sisters. Kristie tries to hold me off, but I didn't come to a party to hang out by myself. Besides, I know them both well enough to arrogantly feel like I might be able to help.

"Everything's good," Kristie says, preempting my question with a vague intervention. Joanne turns away to wipe her eyes so I won't see.

"What's got her upset?" I ask.

"Girl stuff. Can you give us a minute?"

"What's wrong?" I ask Joanne.

Kristie gives me a look, but I downplay it. Joanne turns back and tries to smile. Her eyes are damp as she pushes her long bangs behind her ears.

"She came here alone," Kristie says.

I frown. "So? Half the people here came alone."

Kristie rolls her eyes then cocks her head as if waiting for me to magically connect the dots.

"I mean…" I try, looking around, wondering who we might be able to hook her up with, but the only single guy I see is Ritchie, and that won't work. "It's not like it's end of the world."

"Don't try," Kristie says. "You're a guy."

Joanne looks miserable.

"I'm just thinking…"

"Again, you're a guy," Kristie says. "So, don't *think* either."

This time Joanne grins.

"That's not fair," I insist. "Being a guy doesn't mean I'm automatically stupid."

But Joanne thinks I'm adorable, or at least she thinks I'm adorably dumb, because she's laughing, and laughing is good because it also means she's not crying.

"So, what's the bottom line?" I ask. "She's lonely?"

Any good humor Kristie had disappears, leaving her ugly and angry.

"I didn't mean it like that," I say.

"Then how exactly did you mean it?"

"Joanne," I say, ignoring Kristie. "Take your pick," I say, spreading my arms. "You've got the pick of the litter. Any guy who turns you down is an idiot. You're gorgeous. Own it."

"Hey," Kristie murmurs.

"Well, you're gorgeous too."

An angry glare.

"I'm not implying anything."

"You better not be."

I turn to Joanne. "Pick a guy. Any guy…"

"Any guy?"

"Except for Ritchie…"

Joanne laughs out loud then covers her mouth though she's actually taking a look around, taking stock of her choices. She seems to be cheering up.

"Joanne, honey," Kristie says. "It's a party. Have a good time."

"I need a drink," she says in that awkward slur of hers.

"Let me get her something," I say.

Kristie shakes her head. "I'll get it." She wanders off toward the makeshift bar, disappearing into the shadows.

"You okay?" I ask.

Joanne just hovers, though she does nod.

"Good, because 'okay' is on special. Buy one, get two free."

"So, I owe you big then, huh?"

I nod. "We can work out a payment plan."

"Settle for a hug?" she asks before opening her arms. It's scary how much she looks like Kristie, a thought which makes me hesitate. Then again, it's just a hug. Conceding, I accept her offer, and we embrace like it's no big deal. And at first it isn't. Then it is. The scent of her hair is exactly the same as her sister's. The frame of her body is exactly the same too, and for a fleeting second I wonder if I'd be able to tell the difference. If I can't, then is it love or just lust? This frightening moment gets me thinking about all kinds of screwed up scenarios until I realize she's breathing against my neck, her head on my shoulder, one of those screwed up scenarios suddenly becoming real. Feeling guilty and even more confused, I gently try to pull away, but she tightens her grip and holds on. She doesn't say anything. I don't know if it's the scent of her hair, or maybe the pheromones she's releasing. Or maybe it's because I'm a teenager, and teenagers can't help it. Whatever it is, I want her. I want to kiss her, taste her, feel her—fuck her. I want her, and I have to forcibly break from her and step back.

"Dance with me," she says with a smile, swaying to the music coming from the radio drifting from beyond the fire.

"Maybe I'll just…"

126

"Come on. One dance."

"Kristie will be back in a second."

"I'm not talking about my sister."

"But…"

"One dance."

Sighing, I hold out my arms, and she steps up, a smile on her face. Her eyes are big and blue, her lips full and curious as her hands fold into mine. She presses up against me—crotch to crotch. Glancing toward the fire, I'm afraid I'll see Kristie staring at me with venom in her eyes, but everyone is doing their own thing. Nobody seems to notice anything as we sway just beyond the edge of the firelight.

Well, almost nobody.

Someone's noticing, and that someone is lurking at the edge, eyes trained on me, boring holes directly into my soul.

Ritchie.

He's standing still, all by himself, eyes locked on me, his mouth curved downward in a perpetual frown. The fire dances in his slanted eyes, his hands curled into fists at his side. I don't think he's angry with Joanne. I think it's me.

I pull away from Joanne, ending the dance. "Come on," I say quietly. "Let's find your sister."

## Part II

We're almost back to my place. Ritchie hasn't uttered a single word to me since we left the party. In fact, he hasn't talked to anyone since he saw me with Joanne. He's upset, drifting behind me, eyes zeroed in on my back. That much is obvious, and even if I get the chance to explain, he'd just see it like he wants to.

It was nothing. It was a hug. Two friends hugging it out. Nothing more. Besides, I'm with Kristie, not Joanne. I wasn't doing anything more than trying to console a friend. Of course, this clairvoyant explanation has been worked out only in my mind. I thought for sure he'd confront me once we left Lawton and were out of earshot. Perhaps down by the Beaver. But he stayed quiet, hanging back a few steps the entire trek back into Payton.

My neighborhood is nearly dark. Only a few scattered windows are lit, and it's late—probably three in the morning. I didn't get much time alone with my girl. What was supposed to be a great night wound up a bitter disappointment, and now all I want is to put the evening behind me and get past this 'thing' with Ritchie. I stop at the foot of my driveway knowing I need to say something. Ritchie and I don't fight. We're too close. But not knowing what to say, I settle on ignorance and pretend as though I'm completely unaware that anything is wrong. "Well," I say, faking a yawn. "Goodnight." I turn and make my way up the driveway.

"What you did…" Ritchie says, his voice gruff as it trails after me. I stop. "It ain't right."

"What isn't right?" I ask turning.

"I saw it," he continues. "And I saw you seein' me see it."

"Saw what?"

"You and Joanne." He's not looking away. He's looking right at me. "Was that your way of provin' you can have both at the same time?"

"What are you talking about?'

"That hug."

"A hug?"

"Yeah. When you hugged."

"Is that what you're all bent about?"

"I saw you."

"It was a hug, Rich. That's it."

"Then why you all nervous?"

"I'm not nervous. It was a hug."

"A hug."

"A hug. She was feeling down. And where were you? As usual, you avoided her like the plague."

Ritchie is silent.

"Did you even talk to her tonight?"

He says nothing. He just stares.

"Go home," I say. "Sleep it off. We'll sort it out in the morning."

"You already got her sister," he growls. "You leave Joanne alone."

"You're right. I already got her sister," I snap. "Jo's also my friend, so no, I'm not going to leave her alone." I turn away then turn back. "And for the record, nothing happened. It was a *hug.*"

Ritchie takes a step forward, and I feel my heart seize, but I hold my ground. My best play is to continue pretending this is just a regular conversation between friends. He's not going to punch me, because I'm not angry, and if I'm not angry then it's not a fight.

Ritchie smiles, his stained teeth glinting under the single street lamp. "You think you got what it takes, small time?"

I shake my head. "You're drunk, asshole. Sleep it off."

Ritchie glares at me. I can smell his beer breath and the sweat that's permanently caked into his shirt. He's breathing heavy, probably from the long walk, but maybe because he's still worked up. He chuckles before doing something I never would have predicted. Rather than pounding my face into the concrete like I'm half expecting, he merely turns his back and lumbers away. I'm not sure if this is a good or bad thing. Ritchie's not much of a thinker. He reacts to the moment, and there's no way he's going to just let it go, so that means he's planning something else.

I watch after him for a minute just to be sure he's not coming back before turning up the driveway toward my comfy bed and my big, fluffy pillow. I'm exhausted. The windows are dark, and all I want is to collapse into bed and wake up sometime next year.

I crawl through my bedroom window, careful not to knock anything over or trip on a wayward baseball. I carefully slide the window shut, slip out of my shoes and crawl into bed. I even nearly get away with it.

Nearly.

"That you?" I hear Mom call from far away.

"Go back to sleep, ma," I mumble, burying my face in the pillow.

There's a long pause, and for a moment I think maybe she did go back to sleep. That's when I hear her plodding along the hall. Our house is old, and so is everything in it, so I even hear the doorknob squeak as it turns. A shaft of light cuts across the floor.

"You're in late," she says.

"It was a party. Party's get over late."

"No more fights?"

"No more fights."

"Then what was Ritchie talking about?"

"You heard that?"

Her silhouette shrugs. "The window was open."

"That was nothing."

She's quiet for a moment. "Did you make a move on Joanne?"

"No, I did not make a move on Joanne. I'm with Kristie. The whole thing's a big misunderstanding."

She stands there, her huge frame filling the doorway. "I just don't want to see you and Ritchie fighting. You two mean too much to each other. Don't let some silly little girl fuck it up."

"I got it, ma. Thanks for the graphic image though."

"I'm just worried."

"You're still worrying."

She stands still for a moment. "Goodnight." She pulls the door shut, her footfalls fading along the hall.

"Outta here," I whisper as I collapse into my pillow and stare up at the ceiling. One week. One week and I'm all the way gone. And as if to demonstrate the rebel inside dying to break out, I pound my mattress, tearing off the covers, refusing the tears welling at the corners of my eyes while mouthing over and over, "outta here, outta here, outta here …"

# Fifteen

## *Today*

My hotel window is open. Rain is falling steadily outside. It's the kind of rain I remember as a kid, but nothing seems as familiar as the emptiness in my heart. I'm disappointed in myself. I lied to her, not because I needed to, but because lying is easier than telling the truth. She had it in her head that we'd find her sister's body out at the old Johnson Farm, yet we found nothing, and I let it go. To top it off, I was not vey sympathetic or patient with her. I made up excuses, conjuring up 'that's-how' instead of 'what-ifs.'

I want to go back to Atlanta, but I'm stuck here until Allstate settles my claim. I'd ride the public bus just to get out of the city except there are no buses, and this isn't a city. It's Payton. It's barely even a town, yet I'm stuck here, just like *Hotel California*. Once you're in, you're in for good.

Parting the curtains, I watch the rain. It's coming off the roof in a clear sheet of water, a reminder that no matter how much change there is, things tend to stay the same. I'm stuck here, destined to wait out the storm.

My hair has dried, and I'm wearing fresh clothes, my drenched shirt and jeans draped over the stained chairs in the corner of the room. The television is on in the background, and the cheery sounds of some sitcom I'll never watch is my company. A car drives through the parking lot, its high beams cutting through the rain before pulling into the parking spot next to my room. A couple darts out and disappears from my line of sight, the sound of a slamming door next to mine synchronized nicely with a boom of thunder overhead.

I let the curtains slip shut, and I pace the room, watching TV with my arms crossed, utterly disengaged. My mind is elsewhere—somewhere between here and twenty years ago. At some point after leaving the Johnson farm and before getting dropped off at the hotel, something inside the gray matter of my mind clicked, and memories began trickling in like a slow leak, feeling like a paper cut bleeding out. Things I intentionally forgot, things I unintentionally forgot—*things*. And what I'm suddenly remembering is scaring the hell out me while reminding me why I left in the first place. I feel clammy, dirty and cold, and when there's a knock at my door, I wonder if it's Lucifer himself coming to collect his toll. It's not until I remember that I ordered in that I grab the bills I'd neatly stacked on my nightstand and cross the room.

"Abbott?" the pimply girl asks I open up. She holds up a pizza box stained with grease. "Room sixteen?"

"This is seventeen," I say all smug.

She looks down at the piece of paper she's holding, the rain cutting through the fabric of her shirt and plastering the hair to her forehead. Then she looks at the number hanging on the door. "It says sixteen."

Now I feel bad. "Never mind. It was a joke. A bad one at that."

She frowns, looking like she might cry. "So, this is the right room?"

"Yeah, it's the right room."

She holds out the pizza. "$21.49."

"The guy on the phone said twenty bucks."

"Inflation."

"In the last forty-five minutes?"

She shrugs. "Blame global warming."

I pay for the pizza and throw in a tip. "Have a nice night," I say, shutting the door in her face. Peering through the peephole, I watch her stare at the door a moment before shaking her head and turning away.

Settling on my bed, I open the top and grab a slice of hot pizza, the cheese stretching the way the commercials say it should. The breading is crunchy, but the toppings are soft—the tomato sauce thick as it runs from the edge of the V-shaped slice. Everything about my meal should be perfect, but something's missing.

The television show is going on about some parade, and the cast is making cracks while the audience laughs on cue. My cell-phone rings, and I check the number. Kristie. Wiping my fingers on my jeans, I answer.

"You okay?" she asks.

"I'm fine. Why? What's up?"

"Nothing," she answers after a pause. "I mean, nothing's wrong."

"Then why are you calling?"

Silence.

"I didn't mean it like that," I say.

"You got quiet earlier. I thought you were mad at me or something."

"I'm not mad at you. I'm not mad."

"Then what?"

I stare at the TV and the make-believe people imitating real life. It's funny. Not the show or anything about this day, but everything that's supposed to appear one way but instead is the other. I'm supposed to feel sad because everyone in this screwed up town is sad. Or maybe I'm supposed to laugh because of my stupid bell-curve shaped life, my average apartment and my meaningless job.

"Tony?" she asks from across the line.

"It's nothing," I answer.

She's quiet, and I can hear her thinking from five miles away. I know her. She conjures a hundred different choose-your-own-adventures at once, and then she gets flustered when she doesn't know which door to open. Suddenly it'll be all about me and what I'm thinking even when I haven't said a word.

"You're going to leave, aren't you?"

I shrug before remembering that we're talking on the phone. "Eventually."

Silence.

I might be the world's biggest moron. The girl of my dreams is within reach, and I'm once again holding her at arm's length. I let her go once before, and now I'm doing it all over again. And why? So I can go back to my cocoon life in the big city.

"We'll talk about it tomorrow," I say. "I need tonight off. My head's all messed up. I need some time to process."

"Guys don't process."

"We process."

"Guys aren't built to process."

"Then maybe I'll ruminate."

She's quiet a few moments. "And tomorrow?"

I stare across the room at the TV where people are pretending to be alive. For some reason, to the rest of the world, that's funny. "Pick me up in the morning." I do the math in my head. "Around ten."

"Where are we going?"

"I want to show you something."

"Show me what?"

I stare out my window while smelling the pizza in my lap. "You'll see." Thunder rumbles beyond the window and the audience cracks up from the television. Watching the idiots hopping around onscreen, I feel like my life is a script pinned together by mediocre actors and sub-par jokes like a sitcom with no punch line. Yet everyone's laughing while I feel like crying. "You'll see," I repeat, hoping she'll finally give up then hang up.

"I'm going to lie awake all night wondering what."

"You won't."

"I'll just lie here."

"You're exaggerating."

"...naked."

I pause. "You're not naked."

"And if I am?"

I exhale, holding the phone away. If she is? Then I'm the biggest moron ever. But what if she isn't? What if it's a ploy? That would be typical. It would be just like her. It would be just like my ex-wife too. Heather pulled that shit and got another 15%.

"I need to go," I say. "Dinner's here."

"What's on the menu?"

"Dominos."

132

"Dominos? You flew halfway across the country, and you're having fast food at a Days Inn?"

"I'm an unoriginal bastard."

Long pause. "Want company?"

My choices are to wallow in self-pity or get laid, and I haven't been laid in nearly a year. I *think* the last time was with Stephanie, not that I remember what Stephanie looked like or if that was even her name. Regardless, the experience wasn't all that memorable. Neither was she.

"I'd love company," I answer. "But not tonight. Like I said, I've got a lot to process."

"Guys don't—"

"Or ruminate over," I snap, looking toward the window where lightning flashes, lighting up the curtains. "I just need to be alone for awhile."

She's quiet.

Commercial. The TV stops laughing.

"I gotta go," I murmur. "Pick me up at ten."

Thunder.

"Sure," and she hangs up without saying goodbye. She's probably mad, and if not mad, she's at least disappointed. She's processing. I'm ruminating. We're connected, yet we couldn't be further apart.

I dig into my dinner and enjoy burning the roof of my mouth. I'm sitting Indian style on my frumpy hotel bed, watching bad TV and realizing that I've not only been lying to her, but I've also been lying to myself. I've been lying because I *do* remember what happened twenty years ago. I remember what happened with Joanne and Kristie and even Ritchie.

Thunder.

I *remember*.

I sit there, an idiot sitting in the middle of a stained bed, a steaming pizza in my lap, fingers greasy, a terrible comedy reminding me why real life is so much better than what we spend our time watching. It almost feels like a vacation. After all, this is what people do when they run away. Though it doesn't feel like I ran away. It feels like I ran home. Not that I feel at home either. I feel like an idiot eating a pizza from the middle of frumpy bed tucked inside a shitty hotel room.

# Sixteen

## *Yesterday*

"Anywhere," she answers dreamily while staring up at the sky. "Anywhere in the world." Kristie waves her hands as though floating in a dream. "Anywhere at all."

I frown as I think. It's another one of her questions that would sound lame had it been anyone else asking, but since it's her, then by default, it's not lame. We're lying on our backs on a soft bedding of pine needles beneath our favorite tree, head-to-head with our arms and legs splayed outward. We're a Hallmark card, and it's a perfect afternoon. I've almost even forgotten how the party ended two days ago. Almost.

*I saw it, and I saw you seeing me see it...*

I've avoided bringing up the conversation between me and Ritchie with Kristie. There's no reason to tell her. Besides, Kristie doesn't like him any more than Joanne does, so she'd likely be in favor of a fight that leaves me and him at odds.

"Bermuda," I say aloud.

"Why Bermuda?"

"Why not Bermuda?"

She shrugs. "I don't know. It's not that it's a bad choice. It's just seems so...it seems like an easy answer."

"Would Iraq be more romantic?"

"Yeah, that'd be great."

"Implied sarcasm noted."

"I'm not implying anything." She giggles. "I'm *inferring*."

"Is this your fantasy or mine? You asked me, and I'm answering."

She's quiet for a second. "You okay?"

"I've heard really good things about Bermuda."

"I'm not talking about Bermuda. I'm asking you. You seem on edge."

So much for the Hallmark moment. Now it's Psych 101. She seems innocent enough as she lures me along with a sweet smile and pretty eyes, but at that perfect moment when I start to relax, that's when she strikes, digging her talons in just like a woman does.

"I didn't mean anything by it," Kristie whispers.

"You didn't do anything," I lie. Frustrated, I peel a blade of grass into pieces and flick them away.

"Then what's going on?" she asks.

"Nothing." I scooch into a sitting position and lean back against the old tree.

She rolls onto her stomach and rests her chin on the backs of her folded hands. "I know when something's bothering you. Is it that you're moving to Atlanta?"

"I'm just in one of those moods."

"Are you scared to go?"

"No, I'm not scared."

"Do you want to go?"

I don't answer.

"Then what?"

"I'm just in one of those moods."

"Is it Ritchie?"

"What about him?"

She shrugs. "You tell me. You were both acting weird last night."

"You always watch our moves this closely?"

"Again, I'm not implying anything. I'm just saying."

She's not wrong. Ritchie's a loose cannon, probably off somewhere stabbing a Voodoo doll with my likeness. He's my best friend in the whole world, but that doesn't mean I'm somehow exempt. "We had an argument."

"Over Joanne?"

"What is this, the third degree?"

"You like her?"

"Yes, I like her. But not like that, and that's not it. Ritchie's my friend, and Joanne's my friend. Ritchie likes Joanne, but Joanne doesn't like him back."

"I'm not…" She shakes her head. "I'm not accusing you of anything."

"Of course not." I shake my head and draw my knees, blocking my view of her, or rather blocking her view of me. "You're just *inferring*."

"I wish he'd leave her alone," she says softly. "I don't like the way he looks at her."

"You like the way I look at you."

"I think Joanne has a crush on you."

I frown.

"The way she talks about you."

"I thought this was about Ritchie."

"It's about both of them. I don't know. I just…" She sits up and wipes off a few pine needles still sticking to her shirt. "Something's happening."

"Nothing's happening."

She drops her eyes. "Can you feel it? It's in the air. Like electricity."

I can't say that I don't know what she means. I felt it the other day when we were lying together in her hammock, and I feel it again now. Apparently, she does too. "You wanna get out of here?"

"Like out of this town?"

"Actually, I meant out of the park."

She smiles, considers and finally shakes her head. "Nah. I'm happy just to be here with you."

Two kids in love. It's shouldn't be anymore complicated than that. The problem is Ritchie. He's ruining everything, and I take my frustration out on another unwilling blade of grass.

Kristie pushes herself up and crawls my way on her hands and knees, a curious little smile on her face, a twinkle in her eye. She stops with her face inches from mine before closing her perfect eyes and tilting her perfect head as she leans in. Her lips brush mine.

"My parents won't be home until late," Kristie whispers, her breath smelling like peppermint. I smile back, and in a moment we're on our feet, hand in hand, heading out of the park. It's a long walk back to the Beaver, and it's a bit of a trek back home from there. All the while she's rattling on about things that have little relevance in the grand scheme of things, and I'm doing my best to listen while trying not to notice how her hair cascades over her shoulders, or how her hand feels in mine. She's adorable, so by default, her meandering questions are adorable too, and when she asks me again where I'd like to travel if I could pick anywhere—anywhere in the world, well as far as I'm concerned, anywhere with her is just fine with me.

## *Part II*

Monday night. Two days from graduation. Five days from leaving. It's been a long week already with finals and Ritchie's shit and stuff at work. The week's only getting started, but I've got about a billion loose ends to tie up before taking off, yet all I want to do is say fuck it and relax down by the Beaver. Originally, it was only supposed to be a few of us, but word spread, and now there's a whole group of us hanging out under the shade of the tall oak. Greg has brought a few of his friends from last Friday's party, and they've brought their girlfriends. Then there's this guy no one seems to know, and he's brought his own entourage, though they seem to be doing their own thing and talking mostly amongst themselves.

Kristie is late.

I talked to her on the phone just this morning, and she said she'd be here by seven, but here it is already after eight. Everyone else seems to have made it, so I put on a good show of appearing relaxed. In truth, I'm a bit worried. Kristie is never late. She's the 'always reliable, always dependable' one while her sister's the exact opposite. Jo's the brains of the two, but clocks and calendars are as foreign to her as another language.

Everyone's laughing, having a good time, kicking back in the comfort of a summer breeze. I keep an eye out for my girlfriend as I sit up slightly at the sight of someone approaching from the other side of the creek. Almost immediately I know it's not her. The form is too big. Way too big. And I recognize the swagger even before I see his face. Ritchie's carrying a twelve-pack of cheap beer and smoking a cigar even though he doesn't smoke. The stogie is fat, and it's been smoked down to the nub. He's been chewing on the butt for some time so that it sits comfortably pinched between yellow teeth. He's wearing shades and a cutoff T-shirt, and he looks intimidating as hell.

"Ladies and lug nuts," he says as he grins through the cigar smoke, "the party can now begin."

"Ritchie!" several voices cheer.

He looks my way, and I nod his as he pulls one of the cans from the plastic ring and pops the top—all with one hand. He doesn't smile, at least not with his mouth, and I can't see his eyes behind the shades. Ritchie makes his rounds, stepping over legs or clumsily slithering between folding chairs. He pats his friends on the back and taps beverages with the girls until he reaches my side where he sits down in the chair I've saved for Kristie, kicks back, crosses his ankles and exhales a plum of gray smoke in three consecutive O's.

"How are ya?" I ask with feigned enthusiasm.

"Where you been?"

I shrug. "Right here. Where you been?"

"Want a stogie?"

"New habit?"

"My cousin Joey had a baby boy last night. It's tradition."

"Joey who?"

"My cousin."

"By blood?"

"More than you."

I bite my tongue.

Ritchie burps, takes a hit from the cigar and raises his beer in a toast. I hesitate then clink cans.

"What are you drinking?" He asks. "Pepsi?"

"What's wrong with Pepsi?"

"Kristie got your balls in her purse too?"

"Jesus, Rich."

He clams up and glares at me, his lips pinched tightly.

"Don't give me that look," I murmur. "I really don't care if you approve of my choice of profane words or not."

"Big man."

"And I'm tired of worrying about what offends you and what doesn't."

He drags on his cigar, the tip brightening to an orange tip. He blows smoke-rings in three perfect circles before winking at me. "Missed ya."

I nod toward the group. "I prefer blondes."

He chuckles. "Speaking of which…"

"Don't start." I knew he'd get right to the point. He didn't come here to hang out with me. He came here to see Joanne. I'm just the conduit.

*You think you got what it takes, small time…*

I look around. Everyone's congregating in small groups of two and three. Ritchie strikes a conversation with a girl I don't know. I suspect she came with the guy on her right, but she's being friendly and acting interested even though it's obvious that she isn't. The sad reality is I know Ritchie and the way he thinks. He doesn't want her. He wants Joanne. He'd hit on someone else's girl just to get Joanne's attention, and Joanne's not even here.

Yet there are two figures approaching from along the game trail. Same height, same build, same hair, same walk. Twins. If Joanne's never on time, then the fact that they came together explains why they're late. Right away I feel defensive, unconsciously crossing my arms and glaring as them as they step around the fire and stop directly in front of me. They're dressed the same. Exactly the same even though they *never* dress the same. Kristie likes the attention, while Joanne is conservative. Tonight they're both dolled up. Same eye-shadow, hair free-flowing, sharp dresses—great legs. They look exactly the same. Like it's some kind of a game. Until one of them speaks, I'd never know the difference.

"So, who's who?" Greg asks.

Both offer a smile, but neither speak, which only confirms my suspicion that this is a game. They're not speaking because speaking would give away who's who. Kristie and her sweet voice. Joanne and her slurred accent. It's a game. A game that has nothing to do with either the party or Ritchie. It's a game intended for me, and I have to play.

Now I'm pissed.

They stand there unmoving, eyeing me, waiting for me to somehow magically determine who's who just because I 'love' one more than the other. The guys are whistling, the girls frowning with jealousy. The twins have their hands on hips, eyes on me, waiting for me to choose. Instead, I stand up. Taking a long swallow, I finish my Pepsi, burp and toss the empty can into the fire. Ritchie is silent. I think even he knows when to shut up. And I think the twins suddenly know it too.

"Good one," I snap at the both of them, walking away.

"Tony?" Kristie calls.

I ignore her. The hell with her. And her sister. I keep going.

"Tony!"

I don't want to, but I stop. Then I turn. Neither of them say anything, so I still can't tell which is which. Real funny.

"Don't be mad," Kristie says. Apparently, she's the one on the left.

I want to say something, but I'm afraid of how it'll come off, pain in my chest and my eyes, which are stinging with tears I swore would never fall.

"It was a stupid trick," she says. "I'm sorry."

"You think I love you just because of how you look?" I ask.

"Please don't be angry."

"Believe me, you've already crossed that line, princess."

Now she's crying, and I hate it when girls cry. The eyes of the group are all trained on me. Everyone's looking. No one's talking.

"Don't do this," I mutter. "Don't guilt-trip me into apologizing."

"I'm sorry," she whispers.

"Tony…" Joanne says in that awkward accent of hers.

"Yo, Triple A," Ritchie says. "Don't be a dick. It was a joke. Lighten up."

As if I needed Ritchie's input. But I finally step forward anyway and wrap my arms around Kristie. She clings to me.

"You two good?" Ritchie asks.

I have no idea if we're good or not. It feels weird. Me and her. We're standing in a circle with everyone staring. She's my girlfriend, but she hurt me. And I didn't do anything to deserve it.

Ritchie watches quietly from a few feet away. He and I haven't exactly made up, but apparently this is his way of moving on.

"We're good," I say, and the tension around the circle seems to ease. Kristie smiles, sniffs and wipes her eyes. Then she leans on her toes and kisses my cheek.

"You owe me about a hundred thousand of those," I say gruffly.

"That many?"

"Give or take."

She smiles. "I'll be in your debt for the rest of my life."

"And then some."

"So you're going to make me your slave?"

"My apology wench."

She laughs out loud, then covers her mouth, and for a moment we just stand there, holding one another, all alone while surrounded by people. It's relatively serene, only soft voices, quiet laughter and the sounds of nature around us—a bird singing in the tree, the Old Beaver gurgling a few feet away. It's when I notice how serene it is that I get nervous. After all, Ritchie's here, and he's not a serene kind of guy. He's more of an in-your-face kind of guy, and if he's not in my face, then he's looking to get in someone else's.

I look around only to find him staring across the circle. Following his gaze, I find Joanne sitting in the lap of someone I've never seen before. She's swinging her legs, and acting all giggly the way girls do when they're trying to be cute. Girls only try to be cute when they want the guy they're with to think they're cute, which means…

"Who's that?" I ask Kristie.

"She met him on Saturday. At the party. Travis."

I wait for more, and when it doesn't come, I get impatient. "So, who's Travis?"

She shrugs. "I dunno. He showed right before the party wound down after you and Ritchie had already taken off. I guess they stayed up the whole night talking."

"Why you didn't tell me?"

"Tell you what?"

I just shake my head.

"Is this about Ritchie?" She asks. "You worried he'll do something?"

"Well, he certainly doesn't look all that thrilled."

To be more accurate, he looks to be in shock. I can see it in his eyes. He's just staring, that half empty beer squeezed between white-knuckled fingers. Eventually, he'll crack. Then he'll react. Even now I can see the color draining from his face, his mouth hanging slightly open. A gun could go off, and I doubt he'd notice. He's fixated, and I expect Joanne knows it. I expect she's doing this on purpose, though her performance is worthy of an Oscar judging by how well she's ignoring him.

"He looks…" Kristie starts.

"Pissed," I finish.

In a way I feel sorry for him, and in a way I'm glad. It doesn't matter how many times I tell him Joanne's not interested. It doesn't matter how much Joanne's blows him off. In his mind, they're meant to be. Maybe this will be the wakeup call he needs. Then again, I'm not so sure Payton County is prepared for a Ritchie Hudson wakeup call.

Ritchie stands, and I'm expecting him to charge Travis, but all he does is turn and walk away without so much as a word. He hurtles his can of beer into the Beaver and storms toward Payton, his huge hulk of a frame slowly being absorbed by the setting afternoon sun.

Kristie smiles. "That wasn't so bad."

I continue to watch after my fleeing friend. That was too clean. No words, no insults, no punches thrown. I know him too well. This isn't over. This is just starting.

Joanne and Travis are oblivious, making out and laughing and all those things that come in the first stages of any new relationship. She deserves this. At the same time, something feels out of place—like a missing ingredient to the perfect recipe or the missing piece to one of those replica toy models they sell as numbered plastic pieces in a cardboard box. I'm not happy about any of it, and I'm wondering if Kristie might have been onto something earlier when she said something's happening—something's in the air. Four days ago Ritchie was my best friend, yet now I feel like we're just pretending. Kristie and I were in love, yet a part of me wonders if I'm also pretending about that too. I'm at a party where *everyone* is pretending to be happy, but nobody's saying anything. Ritchie's gone, and now Joanne's staring after him, this ugly look on her face, almost like she did it on purpose.

"Don't think about them," Kristie says, turning my head back so my eyes meet hers. She's smiling the way only she can. "It'll be okay."

I smile and try. I honestly try. I want to think that Ritchie finally got the hint and he'll just let things go. After all, there are plenty of women in Payton that adore him. He's a superstar in a small town, and maybe this will be all the encouragement he needs.

He's gone, having disappeared over the hill leading back into Payton. I should be feeling better. Instead, I feel anxious as though there's a spider on my back that I can't quite reach. Eight clammy feet slowly crawling along my spine, its touch ticklish— just enough to know it's there.

"It'll be okay," she repeats in a whisper, but I'm not so sure.

# Seventeen

## *Today*

The rain hasn't stopped. It hasn't even slowed. It's been raining like this for hours on end, feeling like it's been raining since I got here. Maybe the rain will never stop. It'll just fall forever.

Change the channel.

Another realty TV show. This one is all about a hoarder's lifestyle. It makes me reflect on what a complex organ the human brain is, and how ostensively unique people are as a result. I normally don't feel bad for people who suffer as a consequence of their own decisions, but I find myself feeling worse and worse, slipping into a pit of black depression as I finish my dinner.

Change the channel.

Another shampoo commercial. This time of day it's either diapers, shampoo or some kind common cure for erectile dysfunction. It's advertising for the unhappy housewife as if they're the only sad souls watching this channel at this time.

I wash my hands, brush my teeth, peel back the curtain and check to see what's going on outside. It's still raining.

Change the channel.

An infomercial on the world's most prolific vacuum cleaner. It's the biggest sucker of them all.

I hate this. I hate television, and moreover I hate commercials. To top off my list of hates, I especially hate sitting still. It's still raining, but I need to do something before I put my fist through a wall. However, having learned my lesson the hard way, I first peer through the peephole to make sure there are no bitter childhood friends lurking on the other side of the door. The coast is clear, so I open up, step outside and stand beneath the overhang while water cascades in front of me like a waterfall. The sky is muddy and foreboding, but it's also silent in its own way. There is no thunder or lightning. Just rain. The air smells clean, the silence of the small town familiar.

I start walking. I don't have a raincoat or an umbrella, but it's just water, and in a childish way, it's nice just to feel something clean. It's a warm rain, quickly plastering my shirt to my skin, flattening my hair to my head, and it's a beautiful moment, a moment I'll cherish. It's a moment I can't—

"Hey, buttface."

My golden moment ends with cartoonish drivel, that swirling sound that goes lower and lower until there's a 'ploop,' signifying the end.

"What do you want?" I ask without turning.

"I told you to leave. Why you still here?"

I won't turn around. I won't let him see my fear. I've been through hell over the past few days, and the last thing I need is another scar to compliment the other myriad of scars I've earned since showing my face in town.

"My car got wrecked," I say slowly.

"Yeah, I saw that."

"So, I guess I'm stuck here until the pencil pushers sort it out."

"That ain't it," Ritchie returns. "You got money, and you're a hotshot working for some shithead somewhere. You got means."

"Are you planning on giving me a lift?"

"Are you man enough to face me?"

"What do you want?" I ask, turning around.

"I want you out of my town," he says. The rain is coursing through what little hair he has left. Ritchie has three chins now instead of one, and while he still boasts the broad shoulders of a one-time athlete, he exemplifies the complacent couch-potato who hasn't pushed himself in more than a decade.

"Why are you doing this?" I ask. "I never did anything to you."

"You know why."

"That was twenty years ago. No one even remembers what happened here."

"I remember. And so do you. That's why you came back."

"I came back because Kristie called me."

"Oh, come on. You ain't given two thoughts to that bitch since you left. Are you really that hard up?"

"You're impossible."

"I make the impossible possible, shit dick."

"Always with the colorful language."

Ritchie grins, one tooth cracked in half, and for a moment I see my former friend. "You think you got what it takes?" he asks, that smile tipping the corners of his mouth, that smile I remember from so long ago when we'd toss around the football or play video games or just hang out for no reason. I remember him smiling like this when we'd talk about girls or motorcycles or sports. It's a big grin with lots of teeth and cheeks, yet it's a façade, because I can tell there's no life behind those dark eyes of his. There's no empathy. Whatever we once had is long gone.

"We got a rich history," he continues. "We go way back. I love you like a brother, but I told you to stay away. And you shoulda." Ritchie glares at me, but I swear there's a gleam in there someone. Maybe he's proud of me. Or maybe he found his excuse to unleash Hell. "Did you really come back for her?" he asks. "Just to dredge up old memories? See an old piece of pussy?" He shakes his head while pacing in front of me. "No one wants you here no more."

I have to blink the rain from my eyes. "Kristie wants me here."

"Kristie's using you. If you don't see it, then yer blind. She suspects you, and if she don't, then she will."

I stare at him for a long moment, rainwater dripping along my face. "I'm responsible."

He eyes me through the rain. "Thought you didn't remember nothin'?"

"I believe you said I remember enough."

Ritchie frowns. "You got a smart mouth too. You keep stickin' yer nose where it don't belong and diggin' up old ghosts, and yer gonna find yerself in a word of hurt."

"I'm not here to dig up old ghosts." The distance between us is wide, the rain coming down in torrents, flooding the streets, the water winding in currents toward the drains that thunder from underfoot. I wipe the rain from my eyes and stare back. "I'm here to bury them."

Ritchie eyes me for a long moment, and I can feel his gaze digging into my soul. Finally, he offers a doubtful grin. "To bury 'em, huh?" He chuckles and begins pacing again. "And just what the hell do you plan on buryin'?"

I stare at him a long moment before leaning back on my heels. "I haven't decided yet," I answer. "Maybe this whole goddamn town."

Ritchie scowls. "You know how much I hate that language."

"At this point, do you really think I care what you like?"

Ritchie glares at me through the rain. "Despite what you might wanna think, that little whore don't want you no more. She didn't bring you back here to pick up where you left off. She brought you back to remember why she forgot about you in the first place."

I step forward with every intention of walking past him, but he holds up a hand and gently pushes me back. Apparently, this conversation isn't over.

"You don't want to do this, Rich," I say, but even I can hear the crack in my voice. "There are important people who will come looking for me."

"Do what? This ain't nothin'. This is just a warning shot. A shot across the brow."

"Bow, you dumb shit." I'm scared. As much as he was my protector when we were friends, he also scared the crap out of me with that smothering way of his.

"This ain't your home no more," he grumbles.

But it *is* my home, and I'm strangely aware that I've felt more alive in these last few days than I've felt in the past several years. I've begun to *feel* again, and it's been ripe and painful and scary and beautiful. Old feelings are resurfacing, causing my heart to leap—some of it good and some of it bad. Good or bad, beautiful or terrible, it's *something*, and something is better than nothing.

"Go home, Rich."

"I ain't goin' home."

144

"Then what are you going to do? Kill me right here? Right out in the open where the whole town can see? Is that going to fix things?"

"It might."

"Go home, Rich." I turn away and make my way back toward the hotel. Worst case scenario has him chasing me down, bashing my head into the cement until things go dark. Best case scenario has him leaving me alone so I can return to my mundane life back in Atlanta. I'd go back to InteGREAT Inc. and my 8th floor perch where I'll stare longingly out the window down into our inglorious parking lot before noticing a scuff on my loafer and licking a Kleenex to use as wax to rub it out. Best case scenario has me dying one day at a time instead of all at once. And one's got to ask one's self; what's the point in that?

"Boogieman is watchin'," Ritchie calls. He's been following from several paces back. I want to stop in my tracks, whirl and scream in his face that I'm not afraid, but I am so I don't. The best I can do is duck my head and walk away.

And that's the best case scenario.

## Part II

I'm happy to shut the hotel door behind me, draw the chain and turn the deadbolt. Water drips from my hair, my clothes soaked. I'm shivering with cold even though it's warm in here. I slump against the door, feeling terribly small. The lamp is warm and bright, the TV cheery, a group of whoever busting out in laughter.

—at my expense no doubt.

## Part III

I change my clothes and dry my hair, and within ten minutes I'm exactly where I was a half-hour ago—sitting on the edge of my bed while flipping through the channels. My presence here is pointless. I'm not accomplishing anything. I'm a distraction—a speed bump. I know what it is I *should* do, but I don't know that I *can* do it. I figured everything would just kind of work itself out when I came back. Somehow Kristie and I would stumble from one clue to the next until we were led by the hand exactly where we needed to go. But none of that has happened. There aren't a lot of clues. There never were. There was a letter and hearing aid and a missing person. That's it, and that's what made the mystery of Joanne's disappearance such a mystery. She was just gone.

Then again, maybe my return home has nothing to do with Joanne. Maybe it has something to do with Payton County, reconnecting with Kristie, reconciling with Ritchie and getting square with all the guilt I left behind years ago.

Guilt.

Because there *is* guilt now that I remember. There *is* guilt, because I remember more than just bits and pieces, and I remember enough to know that I did something wrong, but I can't quite…

And yet I can.

There are the things that I *do* remember. Things we said. Something we hid. Something I've never talked about. Not to anyone. This alone brings about a stab of guilt—like a hot flash reminding me what I have to do, not because I want to, but because it's time. Kristie has a right to know, so I'll take her there tomorrow. It'll lead to anger and tears and regrets for pretending the things that happened never did.

If I just up and left town the way Ritchie wants me to, then I could deny everything. I could avoid the grief by returning to my life in the big city. Tomorrow is Monday where things return to normal. Same city, same traffic lights, same streets, same buildings, same elevators, same desk, same coffee, same notes—same shit. I'm expected to show up for staff meetings, status meetings, change control meetings, quarterly earnings meetings and my one-on-one with the bossman himself. I'm supposed to be in his office at 9:30 sharp, and I'm already trying to think of what I'll say when he calls wondering why I'm not there.

Pacing.

I can't leave, because now there's guilt. I can't leave, and I'm afraid to stay. Tomorrow is it. No more secrets. No more lies. Tomorrow is only a few hours away, and it's coming whether I want it to or not.

7:22 p.m.

Now that I've conceded, I just want it to be over. I want to give myself up, throw up my hands and walk into the Payton Police Department begging for forgiveness. And even as I pinch my eyes like a kid wishing on birthday candles, I'm still not sure I remember everything that happened the way it happened. I remember how it ended, but the things in between are fuzzy, like frosty glass. It'll come back. Once we're there. Tomorrow morning the rest will come back. That much I'm sure of. Once we're there, I'll remember. The big question is whether or not I *want* to remember.

And then what? What will happen? To me? To Kristie? Will I be left at the side of the road thumbing my way back to the airport while the rain continues to fall?

I flip through the channels one last time, and this time there's a ballgame on. Baseball. The crowds, the field, the hopes and dreams of an entire city hinging on a 3:2 pitch with two outs and two on. Something's got to give, and I'm reminded of the fourth row and the fourth seat of an event in my life a million and a half hours ago.

I settle back against the headboard and cross my ankles, folding my hands behind my head. The pitcher adjusts his cap, a single bead of sweat rolling from his sideburn to his chin. It's only the first inning, yet he's 32 pitches in, the bases are loaded, and he's already feeling the pressure. Reminds me of Ritchie in a weird way. Ritchie sweats in the middle of winter even when he's sitting still, but on the mound he was a god. He lived for this kind of pressure. He would rather have three men on than have the bases empty. He was the rock the team relied upon, and it wasn't until 'that' night, that he finally cracked.

That night.

I turn out the light but leave the T.V. on. I'm left to dwell within my own conclusions while the game plays out somewhat differently.

## Part IV

9:37 p.m. Night is falling, but daylight hasn't given up yet. Summer in Michigan seems to last forever. The game is only in the sixth, but the score indicates the game ended a long time ago. The news is nothing new, and the Sunday night movie of the week wasn't all that good even when I saw it in the theater some six years ago.

I feel antsy, like a caged animal set to be fed to the predators waiting outside, but I can't just sit around twiddling my thumbs. I need to clear my head even if that means getting wet or risking another encounter with Ritchie, so I undo the deadbolt and pull the chain. The air is fresh and familiar—the smell of Payton County after a summer rain. Not all of the memories flooding back are good, but they do remind me of a time that *felt* simpler even if in reality it wasn't.

Wandering the streets for awhile, probably looking like I'm lost, I decide to pick up a six-pack to pass the time. There's a Gas 'n' Go kitty-corner from the hotel, so I turn back. The bell over the door announces me, and I offer the pimply kid behind the register a nod. He does not return the gesture. He just stares at me, a not-too-bright look on his face.

There's nothing good in the cooler, so I grab something domestic and plop it on the counter so Mr. Pimples can ring me up. He doesn't even ask if there'll be anything else, so I just pay and leave before stealing my way back to my room where I'm careful to pull the chain and turn the deadbolt. I kick off my shoes, crawl onto the bed and plop the six-pack between my legs.

Time for some liquid relaxation.

There's still nothing good on TV. I flip through the channels thinking something should have ended and something else should have started by now, but it all looks the same. It's as if the FCC is conspiring against the consumer. Then again, maybe bad beer makes for better TV. To test this hypothesis, I decide my entertainment barometer will be gauged by the decibel level of my laughter based on bad jokes an hour from now once I've polished off a few cold ones.

Shake, pop, fizz, and I slurp the suds.

I'm not ready for tomorrow, and I can't help but hope that if I'm careless enough, tomorrow won't come, though even if it does, then maybe she won't show. I stop surfing channels, having settled on one of those crime dramas that are meant to look like a movie but can't hide the fact that it was produced on a small budget. I haven't seen this episode, but the answer to the riddle of whodunit seems obvious. It's clearly the husband. They're trying to make it look otherwise, but I've seen evil before—real evil—so there's not much they can do on TV to convince me that the best-of-intentions can be hidden behind bad dialogue, spooky music and poor foreshadowing.

Shake, pop, fizz, and I slurp the suds.

I feel nothing other than boredom, so I start pacing, irritated that the TV has nothing better to offer than a crime saga, three dumb sitcoms and a bad infomercial on best practices for a green lawn. I don't even own a lawn, which leaves me here wasting away while waiting.

Empty again.

I count them up to find I've already blown through three beers. Pulling number four, I pace through the cramped room. I'm not ready for tomorrow any more than I was ready for today. Tomorrow will be worse. Tomorrow I'll break her heart. Again. Almost twenty years worth of poetic justice is about to be served up in a 24-hour window. Now that my memory is drifting back, I know I am where I am, because this is where I'm supposed to be, and I know *who* I am because of what happened.

Shake, pop, fizz, and I slurp the suds.

Now I'm watching an advertisement for high-speed internet, which happens to be offering the deal of the century, but only if I call now. It's feeling warm in my room, so I open the door to let some cool air in. Then I crank up the tube and start rockin' out to one of those commercials featuring a Foreigner song as a backdrop. There are only two other cars parked on the lot, so I can't imagine there will be too many complaints. I'm all alone, my door wide open, the night looking in.

The alcohol is finally kicking in, and it's about time. Sure enough, these sitcoms are suddenly hilarious, my comedy barometer spiking. The beer catches up fast, my mood changing like the weather, and soon I'm wondering if it was fear that brought me home instead of courage. I'm certainly no hero, and I'm not here to put the wrong things right. I'm here to cover up what was botched years ago.

11:37.

It's only been two hours since I decided to go out, and now that the alcohol has blocked my ability to care, I'd just as soon get tomorrow over with. Either that or just leave. I'd skip town if there was a Taxi service, or a bus route, but there isn't, so I can't. This place really is at the end of the earth. You don't just move here. You die here too.

I wince as I chug again, this time too much. Number five is gone, so I start wondering how much attention I'll attract if I stumble into the same Gas n' Go to buy another six. Of course the commercials aren't helping. They're encouraging me to keep going. In fact, there's one on right now telling me it's okay to drink so long as I drink responsibly, and since I don't have car, I guess I'm being responsible enough.

It's just after midnight, and for the past twenty minutes, I've been reciting what I plan to say to Kristie tomorrow. My words have to be chosen carefully or she'll freak out, and what I have to say has to be said just right or she'll miss the point. After five and a half beers, it's sounding somewhat poetic, which makes sense, because I'm a poetic bastard when I'm drunk. Of course, it's not quite as poetic when I scamper into the bathroom, put the seat, settle on my knees and puke my guts out. Foul beer runs in streams from my nose, and it feels like my eyes are going to pop straight out of my skull. My stomach lurches, forcing warm beer and stomach acid up my throat, filling the toilet with the red mess I had intentionally swallowed. One more gag, and I think the worst has passed.

Flush.

Standing, the reflection in the mirror reveals a face covered with beer and snot. I didn't think I'd get this drunk, but then again, I haven't binged like this in a single sitting since college.

12:13.

The world is spinning. I crank open the tap and drink cool water from my palms before bathing my face and washing off the sticky, smelly mess. I look old. I look tired, and now that my drunken stupor has taken a turn, I'm regretting everything from the moment I decided to come back to Payton to the last few hours of this night. This is not how I envisioned things would go. I expected a red carpet and a trip down memory lane. Maybe I'd even score with an old flame. This was supposed to be therapeutic. Even fun.

I shut out the bathroom light and cross the room where I collapse into bed. Then I reach over and shut out the light hanging over the bed, pull the covers up to my neck and proceed to sweat to death despite the sound of the AC grumbling in the corner.

# Eighteen

## *Yesterday*

"Ritchie, what's the matter with you?" I shout, hands up. But he's a maniac, like the Tasmanian Devil—that whirling and spinning dog-wolf thing that slobbers all over itself, engorged in rage and consumed with hate. Ritchie charges me, holds up, backs off, charges again and stops just short, his face flushed.

"You shut up!" he shouts. "You shut the *fuck* up! You started this!"

My hands are still raised, my heart pounding with fear. "Started what? What did I do? I didn't do anything!"

Ritchie stands there, his shirt soaked with sweat while looking like he'll charge again. I think he wants to, but he's conflicted. Something's holding him back, and finally, he turns away, his fists coming unclenched. He looks winded but calmer. "She was supposed to be mine…"

"You're scaring the shit out of me."

"She was supposed to be mine…"

"Is that what this is about? You and Joanne?"

"No. I mean, yes, she's a part of it, but no, that's not what this is about. It's about me and you. We were supposed to be neighbors. The backyard barbecues, the wives, kids—maybe a dog. The whole deal."

"You nearly gave me a heart attack."

"But yer leavin'," he says. "You don't care about friendship or nothin' else. You're just willing to up and go. This Saturday and you're all the way gone."

"Ritchie, look at yourself. Is this healthy?" I shake my head. "Things change, man. People change. People grow up, and sometimes they move away. Sometimes—"

"I don't want things to change! That's my point! What's so great about OGA or OGU or wherever the fuck it is you're goin'?"

"UGA, and the answer is I don't know. I have no clue what to expect. What I'm doing is giving it a shot. Am I scared? Hell yes, I'm scared. I'm moving away from my home. I'm moving away from my best friend, and that's killing me. I'm moving away from my girlfriend, the town I grew up in…everything. And I'm doing it because things change. But I'm giving it a shot, because I want something more than to just scrape by for the rest of my life, and if I stayed here working for scraps, then that's exactly what I'd be doing."

"But Saturday? Why you gotta go so soon? What's so special about that job you're takin' down there?"

"Nothing. It's a job. It'll help with tuition."

"So, why can't you work here over the summer?"

"Because there might not be a job waiting for me in the fall."

"You're leavin' Kristie behind."

"It's not like it's permanent. I'm coming back for her."

"Yeah, you say that now. Then you'll forget all about her. And me."

"This isn't easy for me, Rich. Life is tough. For everyone. It's full of hard decisions that come with big consequences. High risk, high reward. But you gotta try, or what's the point?"

He frowns. I can almost see him sorting things out, yet the pieces fail to click.

"Look," I say, my tone calm. "You've got the whole world in the palm of your hand. You have the potential to be a Major League ballplayer. You have the potential to be a multi-millionaire. You could play for the Braves, and we'd still be able to hang out. We'll even paint my name on the fourth row, fourth seat up in the stands. It'll be just like here, only better. And once that happens, you'll have girls sending their underwear to you in the mail."

"I can't."

"You can. But *you* have to take that first step."

"I can't."

"You want Joanne? Then you got to make her *want* you back."

He looks up at me, something sinister instead. "Yeah, I'll make her *want* me."

"That's not what I meant."

"She'll want me."

"Ritchie, I swear to God you are going down a path I can't follow."

"God? You swear to God? What the fuck do you know about God?" Ritchie asks. "You met Him?" His eyes penetrate my soul. "No? Then shut the *fuck* up." He paces, his eyes red, but he stops suddenly, closing one eye while thumping his temple with the palm of his hand. "God talks to me," he says finally. "Tells me what's what."

My heart is racing in my chest. "He talks to you?"

"He talks to me."

"How are the headaches?"

"She was supposed to be my girl," Ritchie grumbles, ignoring me. "What's she doing with that guy? No one even knows who he is."

"It doesn't matter who he is."

"But she's supposed to be mine…"

"She likes him more than you," I say. "That's all that matters. Bottom line. End of story."

He starts pacing the way he sometimes does. "I can't…"

151

"Breathe, Rich."

He looks really, really angry. "What if Kristie did it to you? What if she just up and left you for another guy? Would you be like, 'oh, well. Maybe next time?'"

I shake my head. "No."

"And now yer just gonna leave her behind?"

"I'm not leaving her behind. I'm not leaving anyone behind."

"Everything's fallin' apart."

"Quit whining, and get your goddamn game face on, will ya?"

Ritchie clams up, his eyes narrowing.

"Sorry," I murmur. "I didn't mean it like that."

He just glares.

"Trust me," I continue. "You'll be glad to be rid of me and my dirty mouth."

"God loves you," he mutters, ignoring my attempt at humor. "Whether you love Him or not."

"I have no qualms with God."

Ritchie is about to say something when he suddenly cringes, his face scrunching into a painful grimace. Something else takes over—something ugly and dark. He bows his head, cocking it to the side, wincing and closing one eye tightly while grinding his teeth. His fingers curl into balled fists at his sides, and he trembles for a few seconds before relaxing. Slightly. When he looks up again, some of the anger has returned. "All I ask is you don't disrespect Him."

"You really need to get those headaches checked out. It could be serious."

"Don't change the subject."

"I'm not changing the subject. But I *am* concerned."

"It goes away."

"That doesn't mean it's gone. You should see a doctor."

"My parents won't pay for no doctor visits to treat a stupid headache. Besides, you already said you don't give a shit, so why should I?"

"You're right. That's exactly what I said."

"Whatever."

"Do what you want, Rich. I'll visit you at the loony asylum." I've had enough arguing with him, so I walk away while knowing full well the conversation isn't over. Arguing with Ritchie is like arguing with a fart. It's going to happen, and it smells like shit, and sure enough, after a few moments, I hear his shoes shuffling across the pavement as he scrambles after me.

"Just have some reversion," he says glumly.

"Reverence," I say softly. "And I don't want to talk about it anymore."

"Would you just hold up?"

"I'm not holding up."

"But Joanne's gonna—"

"Fuck Joanne!" I shout, whirling. "I'm sick of hearing about her! This conversation is over! It is what it is. She's *not* your girlfriend. She doesn't want you. She doesn't *like* you. Get *over* it!"

Ritchie stands there like the big oaf that he is, hands at his sides, feet spread duck-like, sweat raining down his face. He looks like a child. A scared child.

"I need to go," I murmur, turning away.

"Everything's ruined," I hear him murmur.

I stop and put my hands on hips. For a long moment, I just stand there, my back to him before I finally turn around. I've put a good twenty yards between us. "Ritchie," I say softly. "It'll all work out. Trust me. Have some faith."

He's got something of a superfluous frown on his face. "Have faith?" He waves his arms before letting them slap his sides. "Faith in what? We're graduating tomorrow, and then yer leavin.'" He waves me off, his shoulders sagging as he turns away. "It's over." He shakes his head. "It's over."

"Where are you going?" I call.

"Piss off. I need to get ready for the game."

I curse under my breath. I even use one of Ritchie's bad words while knowing full well I can't leave things like this. Groaning, I catch up. To the casual observer watching from their rear-view window, we must look like a pair of idiots, chasing one another up and down the road. I even feel like an idiot.

"You okay?" I ask.

"I'm fine."

"You sure?"

"If I ain't, you plannin' on fuckin' my ass to make it all better?"

I snort. "Not a chance."

"Then it don't matter, does it?"

"It matters." I pause. "You matter."

"What's that? Some kind of quote of the week?"

"It matters, Rich."

He settles back, his eyes locked me. "You for real?"

"You've known me for ten years. What do you think?"

He stares at me, then just like that, a smile starts to win the edges of his mouth. He doesn't want to smile, but he can't hide it. He's a big lug who just wants things to stay like they are. "Stop bein' my girlfriend," he says.

"It's game day," I say enthusiastically, slugging him playfully in the arm.

Ritchie looks at me with those big eyes and flushed cheeks. "Why'd you do it?" he asks, his tone soft.

"Do what?"

"Dance with Joanne."

I draw a breath and exhale. "Are you really still bent about that?"

Silence.

153

"Look," I say. "You have to believe me when I say that it meant nothing. It was a dance. It was *not* a romantic dance. She's my friend, and she was upset. I was just trying to be there for her. Nothing more. I swear it. On blood."

"Blood?"

"Blood."

He keeps walking. "You're my best friend," he says, clearly trying to find words to articulate what he's thinking. "But you hurt me pretty bad."

"You're acting like I betrayed you," I say. "I didn't. I promise. I'm in love with Kristie, and believe me, there's a *big* difference between being friends with Joanne and what Kristie and I have."

He seems to think for a minute. "I can't do it without you."

"Do what?"

"You know."

"Actually, I'm drawing a blank."

"Forty-four."

"What about it?"

"Fourth row, fourth seat."

Fourth row, fourth seat. My place in Ritchie's little world. I've been sitting in lucky #44 for the last four years. It's the same worn spot on the same old bleachers. From his tunnel-vision perspective, Ritchie is days away from completing his masterpiece. Tonight's the last regular season game. Then there's the playoffs. And after that? After that there's nothing. It's win it all or lose everything. If he wins, he gets a front page article, a signed game jersey on the wall of the local sports bar and maybe a deal down at the used car lot if he's willing to hang around and sign a few autographs.

If he loses, he loses everything. Everyone forgets. And then he slips into obscurity. The Pirates are one loss away from ending Ritchie's career. They're one loss away from ending his legacy. Everything he is hinges on these last few days as the Ritchie-Hudson-sandglass drains away while leading up to nothing.

"I don't need Joanne," Ritchie mumbles.

"You're godda—" I cut myself off mid-word. "You're *darn* right you don't need her. Her or anyone else. You're a one-man rockin' machine."

"I ain't," Ritchie says, shivering. He's actually shaking, and it's not because he's cold. "It takes two."

"Nothing you do out there has anything to do with me. You're the one out there on an island throwing mad heat. I'm just a guy in the bleachers."

He nods, but he's not looking at me. He's staring off into the distance, hands on hips, the edges of his mouth curved downward. "We do this together," he says finally. "One last time."

I hold out my hand. "One last time."

He locks grip, and it's my big lug of a friend who thinks in whole numbers and comes up with remainders who looks back.

"Let's go," I say. There's a moment of repose before Ritchie rotates a finger in three concentric circles over his head before pointing in the general direction of the stadium. Now that we seem to have finally settled on a destination, we begin walking again, this time without changing direction or chasing the other down. We're side-by-side—best buds—and for the moment, the storm has subsided. It's a hot afternoon. Summer is coming early this year.

## Part II

"You're in my seat," I say to the man sitting on 44. He's a big guy—older than me, and he might have lost his hair, but he's well-proportioned and outweighs me two to one. And there's not a lot of fat making up the difference.

"Excuse me?" he says, his wife looking at me with the same shocked expression.

"Fourth row, fourth seat," I answer. "It's reserved." Then I smile. "For me."

"Hon," Kristie says softly from behind me, but I shake her off.

"Your seat?" the big guy says with an arrogant smile. "I don't see your name on it."

"Then lift your hairy ass and take a closer look, because it's there."

He frowns, stands and turns around.

"Triple A," I say, filling in the blanks. "Stands for Anthony Alexander Abbott. That's me. You're in my seat."

The big guy isn't intimidated. "Then maybe you should have gotten here sooner. It's my seat now."

Normally, I'm a patient guy. Normally, I'd be just as content to let him and his flock stay put, but it's been a weird day, and I'm in a weird mood. I've lost any patience I had, and given the state of things between me and Ritchie, me and Joanne, Joanne and Ritchie, me and Kristie, and pretty much everyone else in this rinky dink town for that matter, I'm either in the mood to pick a fight or I'm in the mood to lose one.

"You don't want to do this," I say, baiting the hook.

"Do what?"

I smile. "Last chance."

We lock eyes, and in those angry browns, I can still see a hint of hesitation. He knows he outweighs me, but that's why there's doubt. He's got to be wondering why I'm so confident if I can't beat him in a fight. "Are you threatening me?" he asks.

I smile. "No." Then I whistle sharp and shrill, and a few faces poke out from the dugout below. Within moments, the entire team emerges. Ritchie leads the way, his eyes fixed on the hairy goon who took my seat. "But *they* might," I finish with a grin.

The big man takes a cautious step back, tripping against the bleacher seat.

"What's goin' on, Triple A?" Ritchie asks, reaching my side.

"It seems someone sold my seat."

155

Ritchie looks at the big man, then the man's wife, then the man's daughter. "You guys can't scooch down far enough to make room for my two best friends?"

The man looks at the bleacher row. "It's pretty full."

Ritchie sizes the situation, then nods, his face contorted in thought. "You're right. I guess that means you and your brood will have to move."

"Excuse me?" the man asks.

"We're moving," the man's wife says, motioning for her daughter to get up and head for the exit. Suddenly I feel bad. The girl looks to be about eight years old. She came to watch a baseball game, not see her parents get bullied. This will be one of the moments she'll remember for the rest of her life. She won't remember who wins the game or what I look like, but she'll remember me, she'll remember this, and she'll remember that her dad isn't invincible the way she thought. But it's too late to take it back. They're already wading through a sea of knees to get to the stairs on the other side. I look down at #44, and I realize in a moment of absolute clarity how much I hate it and what it represents. Or maybe I hate myself and what I've become.

The moment will pass. It always does. Kristie and I will sit down, and the game will start, and we'll get caught up in the drama, and we'll be treated like royalty. Popcorn will be on the house, and everyone will ask me about Ritchie—how he's feeling, how his shoulder is, how he does what he does. Then the game will start, and the attention will turn to the big man on the mound.

The team returns to the dugout while Kristie and I take our seats. On impulse, she leans over and kisses me on the cheek. "I love you."

We rise for the National Anthem. Every baseball cap around the park comes off. Every voice goes silent. A little girl, announced as Rhiannon Greene from Miss Garcia's fourth grade class is standing on home plate, holding a microphone disproportionly large, her voice disproportionly modulated as she belts out a painful rendition of our nation's anthem. As bad as it is, once she hits the high notes, the crowd starts cheering anyway, and they keep right on cheering until the anthem ends and the little girl takes a bow. Then they quiet down. There are a few flashes, a few murmurs, but mostly silence. We sit, waiting, looking around as though we're waiting for Jesus Christ himself to suddenly appear.

"And now," the PA announcer calls out, his voice rocketing through the park, "the electrical union #491 and the city council of Payton County are pleased to bring you the starting lineup of *your* Payton Pirates!"

The local faithful clap, but it's more of a polite applause. It's not the response I'm sure the PA guy was expecting. We're sitting, waiting, engaged in conversation, spilling drinks, looking for cameras. We're holding back—waiting.

For him.

The PA guy calls out the scorecard, name, number, position, and the player being announced walks out from the dugout, tips his hat and waves to the crowd. There a few claps, a few whistles, a few laughs. We're holding back—waiting.

For him.

Then the music kicks in.

It's a low rumble at first, kind of a preamble just so everyone knows that the time has finally come. Butts come off the bleachers, and everyone stands. Then the lights start spinning, followed by the ear-piercing opening chords to *Welcome to the Jungle*. It's loud, it's in your face, and I swear the bleachers are rocking. All the lights, the blistering noise, the music, the fans. I don't know much about what happens outside of Payton, but what happens on this field is something special, and it all has to do with the big guy who's just now emerging from the dugout and beginning the slow walk toward the mound, his head bowed, his ball cap hiding his eyes. The place goes ballistic, a slew of fireworks lighting the evening sky.

"Starting at pitcher," the PA blares, his voice drowning beneath the cheers. "Number 44…" The crowd has become so loud that I have to cover my ears. "Your very own…Ritchieeeeeeee Hudsooooooooooooooooooon!"

I look over at the visiting dugout, and in a way, I sort of feel bad for them. After all it's a bit unfair. Playtime is over. Ritchie's on the mound.

This is Pirate country.

Welcome to the jungle, bitches.


## *Part III*


Ritchie doesn't acknowledge the crowd. He just settles into his warm-ups, the music deafening as Guns 'n' Roses bleeds over the loudspeakers, energizing the crowd. There isn't a single soul sitting. We're all standing, clapping, stomping, cheering. The Rockford Rams (or the 'Rockford Retards' as we like to call them) swept us in a double-header a few weeks back. Ritchie had just pitched the night before, and despite begging and pleading with the skipper, he was ordered to sit. Ritchie can't remember his multiplication tables, but he remembers losing two in a row, so tonight is important to him. Fuck the playoffs. Tonight is personal.

"Here we goooooooooooooooo!" the PA hollers, and it's stomping feet, pumping fists and Styrofoam fingers waving in chaos. It's cheers and screams. It's flashing lights and loud music, and even though this isn't a big-league ballpark, the local townsfolk have done their best to make it look like one. Everyone is here. Everyone.

First pitch; right down the middle for strike-one, and while there are likely 200 more pitches to go before all is said and done, it sounds as though we just scored the winning touchdown in the Super Bowl. I can't help but admire my friend. His is so cool.

Ritchie reaches back and hurls another bullet.

"Steeeeeeeeeeeeeeeeeerike!" the ump shouts, pointing.

So cool. My friend. My best friend.

## *Part IV*

1-2-3. Rockford goes down, and Ritchie receives a standing ovation as he approaches the dugout. He never looks up. He just stares at the ground, those familiar stains spreading under his arms. I keep wishing he'd look up, scan the crowd until he finds the fourth row, fourth seat. He'd smile and nod my way the way he does when things are going okay. But he doesn't, so maybe they're not. It makes me wonder if he's still angry or if he's just so locked in that he can't think of anything other than getting back out there. Then he's gone, having disappeared into the dugout and out of view until the top of the next inning.

And now Joanne and Travis are making their way through the lineup of knees toward us. Joanne's grinning as she waves with one hand, the other hand locked in *his*. Kristie stands and the two embrace as though they haven't seen each other in years. Jo sits next to Kristie, and Travis sits at the end. Personally, I have nothing against him. He seems a decent enough guy—a guy's guy, but he's not thinking. Neither is Joanne. This is a bad move. I nudge Kristie, lean in and whisper. "It's probably not a great idea that she sits here."

"She's my sister."

"I get that, but—"

"Are you jealous?"

"No."

"Then what's the problem?'

"There's no problem. And I'm not arguing," I say it only loud enough for her to hear. "But still, Ritchie will eventually notice."

"We're not talking about this again."

"I'm not—"

"The hell with Ritchie. She's *my* sister. I don't care who he is. He could be…Joe Montana for all I care."

"Wrong sport."

"The only reason *any* of us even tolerate him is because he's *your* friend. That's *it*."

"I get that, but—"

"That's *it!*" Kristie shouts.

I sit back and fold my arms. I hate it when she does that. That stubbornness. She gets on her soapbox and starts talking about Ritchie as though I keep his company out of pity. He's my best friend. And he's earned it. She doesn't know half the shit he's done for me. Angrily, I return my attention to the game. Screw her. Her and Joanne and Truman or Travis or whatever his name is. I know what's coming even if they don't.

Our guys out on the field can't muster any offense, and just like that Ritchie is back on the field. He throws seven pitches, and just like that he's back off again— much to the hysterical delight of the sold-out crowd.

Seven pitches.

"Let's get something going!" Travis says, clapping enthusiastically, which is ironic considering he's from Lawton.

"Like what?" I ask, sarcasm lining my tone. "The wave?"

"Yeah!" he shouts. "Let's do the wave!"

"We don't do the wave in this ballpark," I grumble.

Kristie frowns at me.

Maybe Travis is a fan. Or maybe he's afraid. Maybe he's oblivious. After all, anyone who wants to do the wave is a tourist. This isn't his town. This isn't his team. And she's not his girl. And if he's not careful, he's going to screw with Ritchie's mojo.

Even so, Travis gives the wave the ol' heave-ho, rising to his feet and throwing his hands up before sitting back down, rising up and doing it all over again. But no one follows his lead. It's not because we don't like him. We don't, but that's not the point. The point is we don't do the wave here. The wave is for amateurs, and this is *Pirate* baseball.

Out on the field, a walk, a pop-out, a base-hit and a double, and the crowd is cheering an early 2-0 lead. Under normal circumstances, a two run lead would be tenuous, but with Hudson on the mound, the hometown crowd is actually hoping the scoring will stop so they can see Ritchie shut them down. And just like that, the Pirates hit into an inning-ending double-play, and just like that, we're heading to the third.

Another standing ovation as Ritchie takes the field. He keeps his head dipped the way he does when he's in the zone. I know him. I know the way he thinks. He couldn't care less if he's winning or losing. There's only one thing on his mind, and it's the guy at the plate. He stretches, rotating his arms, loosening up. He cracks his neck and finally turns to face the batter.

The crowd rises, clapping frenetically.

Ritchie kicks dirt from the plate, settles into his wind, rears back and hurls eight pitches. Eight. That's all it takes until we're on our way to the bottom of the third. No hits, no walks and definitely no runs. Ritchie has a perfect game through three. That's the way he throws. He'll do this for four or five innings until he tires. Then he'll dig down and find something else.

"He's good," Kristie says, and it's the first time she's ever complimented him. Of course, if Ritchie was merely 'good,' this stadium would be half empty, there wouldn't be any music, and no one would really care. It would just be another baseball game where a few parents show up to see their kid play. Ritchie isn't 'good.' Ritchie's *special*, and everyone knows it. Everyone knows the game ended when our first run crossed home plate, so now that it's 2-0, they're just sticking around to see how good Ritchie can be.

They cheer him on with a standing ovation as he plods off the field, another inning in the bag. Now that Joanne and Travis are here, I'm glad he's not looking up and searching me out. He knows I'm here, and that should be enough. As long as he knows I'm here, he'll be fine.

Fast forward to the top of the sixth. We're up 4-0. Four more runs and the umps will enforce the mercy rule. Something tells me that would actually disappoint the hometown faithful. I think they'd like the game to go on forever. They stopped rooting for us to score a long time ago. They want to see all seven innings, and given how we've run the base pads the previous two innings, I'm not so sure even the ballplayers don't feel the same. So long as Ritchie is at the plate, people want more. More groundouts, more pop outs, more strikeouts. More.

And the crowd gets more, because our offense dies in our half of the sixth. Heading into the seventh, I've never seen him throw like this before. Through six complete, he's thrown only 62 pitches, 41 for strikes. No walks and only one hit. One lousy hit. The crowd is energized and focused. Even Kristie is caught up in the magic. She's clapping with the music, a cute little smile on her cute little face. It flees quickly when she looks over and sees me sweating. I'm just praying to get through the last inning without Ritchie looking over. The last thing in the world I want—the very last thing—is for him to see Joanne and Travis wrapped around each other like a pretzel.

"You okay?" Kristie asks.

"Fine."

"You don't look fine. What's wrong?"

"He's going to see."

She looks over at her sister before turning back to me. "So what?"

I watch the field. "Never mind."

"It's not like he's going to do anything."

"You're probably right."

She doesn't reply, but she gives me a look as if to say that if something *does* happen then it's my fault for not preventing it. Then she turns back to the game.

Three more outs is all we need, and the crowd will light this place up. Ritchie's already tossed six complete. By now the skipper should have called on the bullpen. Ritchie's pitch count is still low, but with the score out of hand, they should be saving his arm. My guess is they talked about pulling him. They probably even asked him how he felt, and if I were a betting man, the outcome of that conversation was one-sided. Ritchie doesn't sit. Period.

Three more outs.

Another standing ovation as my best friend takes the field. It's so loud that my ears feel like they're going to pop. I'm caught up in the frenzy as much as anyone, but these people are nuts. They're waving fists, waving sparklers, waving lighters. They're stomping their feet, clapping their hands, screaming at the top of their lungs.

Ritchie finishes his warm ups and settles in. Strike one is followed by strike two. He's throwing bullets, though the second pitch did look suspiciously inside.

"Steeeeeerike!" the ump shouts, and the crowd explodes as the beleaguered batter hurtles his bat toward the enemy bullpen and walks away. Ritchie kicks away the loose dust on the pitcher's plate before turning his back.

Flashbulbs.

One out.

Two to go.

Three quick balls, and the crowd is stunned at the idea of a one-out walk, but Ritchie rebounds with a curveball the batter chases in the dirt. Then he follows it up with a heater that hits the catcher's glove before the batter has a chance to blink. At three and two, Ritchie's a pitch away from a second out. The crowd stands and begins clapping—making noise. Ritchie lifts his hat to wipe his forehead with his sleeve, kicks the dirt from the mound and licks his fingers before going into his wind.

Strike three.

Ritchie pays no notice to the cheering crowd as he turns his back and bows his head. He cracks his neck and loosens up before exhaling and turning back to the action. He again kicks away the loose dirt and prepares to face the last batter. By this point, it's pretty obvious that the crowd isn't here to see the Pirates. They're not even here to see the Pirates defeat the Rams. They're here to see Ritchie.

Strike one.

An enthusiastic cheer backs him up. It's been an amazing performance. Ritchie missed out on a perfect game, but maybe that's fate. Had he pitched a no-no, he'd make headlines, and headlines would give him a way out of Payton. A one-hitter means no one outside of our close-knit community will ever know what happened. A one-hitter only solidifies his permanent place on a small plaque in a small town that will someday forget his name.

Strike two.

The crowd is on its feet—clapping, chanting and hollering. The stands are shaking beneath stomping feet. The entire city of Payton is here. We're all watching. All of us. He's one strike away from a complete-game shutout. He's one pitch from ending the game.

And then it happens.

Winded, gasping, tired but focused, he looks up. Then he looks over. Maybe he's looking for an encouraging nod from me, but he instead finds Joanne draped all over Travis, her head on his shoulder, her hand under his shirt.

Ritchie's shoulder's slump.

He turns back to the mound, but I can immediately sense that something's wrong—something's off. He kicks at the dust on the plate the way he normally does but misses and kicks dirt instead. Stumbling, he rights himself and turns his back on home plate. I can see him drawing one deep breath after another.

"Uh oh," I hear Kristie murmur.

"Yeah, uh oh," I mutter with sarcasm.

Ritchie turns back to the game, and his eyes are blazing. For a moment I'm assured that this renewed energy will play in his favor, but his pitch is so far outside that not even the catcher can react fast enough, and the ball sails over his head and strikes the backstop with fury. The crowd cheers—not at the wild pitch but at the ferocity in which it strikes the fence. However, when the second pitch sails over the batter's head and into the crowd, there are some concerned mumbles. Ritchie shakes his head and accepts a new ball. He goes into his wind and hurtles a strike, which brings the crowd to an enthusiastic cheer. It's when ball three and ball four sail wildly to the backstop that they go quiet and sit down.

The bullpen begins to warm, but they're five minutes away from being ready. It's Ritchie's game. For better or for worse, it ends here. There's only one out left. One out. If he can dig deep enough, the maybe...

The first pitch settles softly over home plate, and the batter smacks it to left field moving runners to first and second.

Of course, even if one or two runs cross, it's not the end of the world. It's just that the crowd wants to see a shutout. They want a shutout even when at end of the day, the win is the all that really matters. Two pitches later and the bases are loaded. Ritchie is looking discouraged more than he's looking tired, and he keeps looking Joanne's way.

"What's happening?" Kristie whispers.

"He can't process it," I answer.

"Process what?"

Ritchie hurtles another ball all the way to the backstop, and the runners advance—the first Ram crossing home plate.

"This," I answer.

The bullpen still isn't ready, and Ritchie is gassed. Another batter, and the first pitch is sent to outer space with a bases-clearing three-run homer, tying the game at four. It's only the second homerun Ritchie's given all season. He yanks his hat down and spits before turning his back and pounding the inside of his glove. The hometown loyal are quiet.

The pitching coach emerges from the dugout, but Ritchie flips him off, sending him back. For some reason, this reinvigorates the crowd, and they jump back on the Ritchie Hudson bandwagon. Meanwhile, Ritchie looks exhausted. More than that, he looks angry. Even more than that, he looks heartbroken. He shakes his head and digs in. Wiping his face, I think I see tears mixing with the sweat.

I stand, but no one sees.

Ritchie settles into his wind and hurls every last bit of junk he has saved, the velocity somewhere near 100 mph. If the pitch is on point, the batter won't have a chance. As it turns out, the batter doesn't have a chance anyhow, but for different reasons. The ball strikes the poor kid in the face, and he goes down—out cold. Then the benches clear. Most pitchers would recoil or show some kind of regret, but Ritchie

162

just smiles, lowering himself and bracing for impact. The first player he encounters is wasted with one punch. After that, it's like that old saying; *I went to a hockey fight, and a baseball game broke out.* The umps have lost control, and as far as the crowd is concerned, that's okay. They're here to see Ritchie. They don't care if he's pitching or just beating the shit out of someone.

I leap forward, racing down the steps toward the field. Kristie is screaming my name, but her voice is drowned under as I maneuver the bleachers, hurdle the railing and race onto the field. Ritchie's holding his own. I expected him to, but he's not only beating back his opponents, he's destroying them. Referees are blowing whistles, the PA is screaming for calm, and players are fueling an all-out brawl—all of it backed by the frenzied Payton faithful who are rushing the field—me leading the charge.

Ritchie's being pummeled. He's bleeding yet he's shrieking with rage, and he's fighting back. I figure every person he faces is named 'Travis', and every blow he lands is meant to avenge the only girl he'll ever allow himself to love. The fireworks have started, but the skies are dark. I know I need to get to my friend, but someone must've seen me coming, because someone lands a blow, and I see white. I hit the dirt, and while everything is foggy and painful, I realize that I'm lying face down in the sweet smell of the grass and dirt of a small-town baseball field. Less privileged kids never see this much green. And here I am, bleeding all over myself while soaking it all in as people race in chaos overhead.

# Nineteen

## Today

Screaming, I sit straight up, my room drenched in shadows. I'm covered in sweat, my sheets soaked. Feels like I'm lying in a puddle, so I tear away the covers and swing my legs over the edge of the bed, my head in my hands as I gasp for air.

It was just a dream. It didn't—*couldn't* have actually happened. The television is still on, but the game is over, and it's now late-night TV with cheap commercials and over-modulated sound.

It's too loud.

I use the remote to turn the sound down, the volume level on the screen counting backwards like a time bomb ticking down. The LED clock beside the bed has stopped, hanging on 2:13 forever, the woman on the TV fossilized with fear while the audience jeers and heckles. Apparently, they hate her the way I hate myself.

I need a drink of water.

Crossing the small room toward the bathroom, the carpet is crusty from soap and shampoo and God knows what else, and the bathroom tile is still sticky from whatever the previous tenant left behind. Rinsing my face, I drink from my cupped hands before shutting the water off and drying my face with a damp towel. Returning to bed, the sheets are clammy and wet. Frustrated, I consider my options before shoving the bedspread aside and taking a seat in one of those useless chairs they keep in the corner.

It's 3:02 in the morning. My mind is on fire with thoughts and memories, and I figure I'll never fall asleep again. And maybe I don't want to. After all, the dream wasn't about him. It was about the other one.

## Part II

The hangover isn't as bad as I thought it would be. I think vomiting up the final two or three beers minimized the damage and prevented what would have been bad from becoming *really* bad. I don't bother to shower. Or shave. The five o'clock shadow adds color to my face, and I'm hoping she'll notice the stubble before she notices how red my eyes are.

It's 9:09 on Monday morning, which means she'll be here shortly. It'll also means I am now officially late for work, so I dig out my phone and flip through my contacts before selecting 'Phillip Beltran' and pressing *send*. Knowing Phil the way I do, he wandered in through the security doors five minutes ago, crossed through the lobby with that smug look of self-importance on his acne-pocked face while en route to his office. By 9:10 he'll be booting his computer, and by 9:13 he'll have already checked his email. Two minutes later, he'll be wondering how he can ruin the rest of the day for guys like me.

Ring number one.

Phil never picks up on the first ring. God forbid executive management connects the dots and draws a natural conclusion that Phillip K. Beltran has idle time. Beltran is a corporate stooge. He even has a brass plaque hanging on his wall that reads; *Project an image of success at all times.* It's one of four things you see upon entering his office, the first being a very bold nameplate announcing *Phillip K. Beltran, Senior Vice President.* The second is that big gaudy metal desk, the third is a five foot plastic ficus tree, and the fourth is that ridiculous plaque.

Ring number two.

Beltran makes an art form out of appearing distracted. After all, it's an honor to solicit the wisdom of a Senior Vice Douchebag, and since the phones at InteGREAT Inc. only ring three times before going to voicemail, it's always in the middle of the third ring that he'll answer. When he picks up today, it's with that same irritated yet professional "Philip Beltran" that I've come to loathe.

My mouth is sticky, and my breath stinks, reminding me to brush my teeth before Kristie shows. "Phil, it's Tony."

"Tony," Beltran says, his voice managerial. "I stopped by your cube a few minutes ago."

"I'm not there."

"But you're weren't in," he finishes.

"I was in a car accident," I say. "I'm still in Payton." I leave it at that. Let him draw his own conclusions. If the man has a heart, which he doesn't, the first words out of his mouth should be *are you okay?* But knowing him the way I do, he'll be less interested in me and more concerned with the work stacking up on my desk.

"We've got Crimson nTernal coming onsite this week," Beltran says. "You're my lead. I need you here."

"Yeah, I know. If you've got any suggestions, I'm all ears, but I'm kind of stuck in a holding pattern until Allstate figures out what to do."

"So, you're not coming in." It's a statement. Not a question.

"It shouldn't be more than a few days."

"So, you're not coming in."

I bite my tongue. "The airport is eighty miles away, Phil. And there's no taxi service in or out. Like I said, I'm open to suggestions."

"And you said you're where?"

"Payton County. It's in Michigan. My hometown."

"What are you doing there?"

"I'm fine, by the way," I sneer. "Thanks for asking."

"You know how important this week is."

"Which is why I'm calling."

A heavy sigh. "This is disappointing."

"I'm glad you pointed that out, because whatever it is you're not implying is coming off loud and clear."

"So, what do we do?"

"The insurance company is working as fast as they can."

"I need you onsite by Thursday morning. Do whatever you have to do, but be here by Thursday."

"I'll call as soon as I know more."

Phil is quiet for a moment, and I wonder if I lost the signal even though the phone shows we're still connected. "Dustin can fill in through Wednesday," he mumbles over the line. "But I need you here by Thursday. Wednesday if possible. Thursday at the latest."

"I'll call you."

A second audible sigh. Phillip Beltran doesn't like to be 'told' anything. He does the telling. "Let me know if you need anything. I can be somewhat persuasive when push comes to shove."

"Thanks," I answer. "I'll call."

"Keep me posted."

Beltran can't let go, but I hang up anyway. I don't even say goodbye, and despite our awkward banter, I figure the exchange went better than expected. Part of me was thinking I'd be unemployed by now, and part of me is disappointed that I'm not.

Checking my watch, I still have a few minutes before Kristie shows, and once she's here, it'll be too late to turn back. Then we'll go to a place no one's been in twenty years, and we'll see things no one's ever seen. Those things will rewind the clock and reopen old wounds. They'll include me, her, Joanne, Ritchie—all of it and all of us. It makes me wonder if she'll be able to handle the deluge of memories. I still don't remember all of the details, but I remember enough to know where we're going and why. I remember enough to know I'm responsible for Joanne's death, and I know enough to remember how Kristie will react.

She's not ready.

I'm not either.

Joanne didn't just hitchhike out of town. I remembered this tiny little tidbit of relevant information at some point yesterday. I remembered enough to know that Jo never even left. She's still here just like her sister suspected when she found Joanne's

166

hearing aid rotting in that old barn. Joanne's still here, Kristie's still here, Ritchie's still here, and now I'm here. I'm back. The sad thing is I know this, and all the aspirin in the world won't change it even though I take four anyway.

For the headache, of course.

# Twenty

## *Yesterday*

Graduation day. The whole town has turned out for the big event. It's not quite like one of Ritchie's games, but it's standing room only, and they're all standing and they're all clapping, cheering us on. We're dressed in our best, behaving better than our parents up in the stands who are doing their best to embarrass us. As we file in as pairs—a sea of black robes and flat caps—we're talking in calm voices about how this summer is going to be "off the hook," and how we can't wait to get out of this one horse town. We talk about next steps as if we're planning our next trip to Chuck E. Cheese while quietly, we all have that look of terror, we're all hoping we're not the only one, and we all smile when we're told to.

I take my seat in one of those plastic cafeteria chairs with one of those awful backrests. Our tassels are on the left, and we're waiting to swing them to the right, thereby symbolically releasing us from our childhood prison and opening the door into the great unknown. Principal Price is up there talking about responsibility and reverence and leadership, his face a river of smiles while we're down here, silently wishing we could rewind time to when we were only seniors and all underclassmen looked at us like gods. Principal Price is saying a lot of nice things, and he's smiling, and we're smiling, and the crowd out there is smiling, but I'm dying inside. Today is supposed to be beautiful, but instead it feels empty. I'm sitting among 156 of my peers, when I know I should be sitting among 157.

My best friend isn't here.

"Franklin Roosevelt said it right," Price continues as he looks around, hands planted firmly on the podium. "As you have viewed this world of which you are about to become a more active part, I have no doubt that you have been impressed by its chaos." The crowd laughs, but he's stolid. "FDR was referring to the growing pains we all experience as we go from boy to man or from girl to woman. It's a scary world out there, and this is just a first step. A high school diploma will only open so many doors. You have to shoot for the moon, be willing to risk everything, be all in or be nothing at all."

The student body falls silent. Masking our fear is suddenly not as easy as it was only a few minutes ago.

"Shoot for the moon," Price repeats. "It's within your grasp. Believe me, it's there for the taking, but *you* have to reach out and take it. No one will hand it to you. You have to take that first step. And then you'll have to take that second and third step too. Never give up. Never settle for average. Shoot for the moon, and I promise that even if you don't make it, you'll be among the stars."

The crowd erupts. We erupt. We're a bunch of zombies going with the flow and doing what we told. We're told to smile. We're told to clap. We're told to cheer. Principal Price stands at the podium, the sweat raining like beads over his face, his hands out, his grin toothy. It's supposed to be our big day, a day every one of us seniors will remember for the rest of our lives. But someone is missing, and as a result, I can't relax. My best friend isn't here. I'm set to leave home in three days, but given the number of loose ends that I don't know how to tie off, everything feels like it's falling apart.

Ritchie's not here.

But it's not because his alarm didn't go off or because he's staging a coup, or even because his dad beat the hell out of him. Ritchie's not here because he wasn't invited.

# Twenty One

## *Today*

I'm sitting beneath the overhang of the Days Inn, my knees up—my back against the paint-flaking wall when she turns into the parking lot. She pulls right up to my room before shutting off the engine. She stares at me through the windshield and from behind the dark shades hiding her eyes before opening her door, snaking out a well-manicured foot in a flip-flop and climbing out. The door to my hotel room is wide open, but I'm not inside. I'm out here, my head resting against the paint-flaking wall. Just as I suspected, she's early. Nine minutes.

"What are you doing out here?" she asks, removing her sunglasses.

My clothes are wrinkled, my hair a mess. Two days of stubble complete the picture of a hapless and perhaps even hopeless train wreck of a man. The aspirin are helping with the pain, but not the dread. "I forgot what mornings smell like here."

She sniffs, looking around. "I don't smell anything."

I close my eyes and draw in a deep breath. "If I concentrate, I think I can even smell the Beaver." I look up at her. "I think I'd like to see it again before I leave."

"You're not leaving."

I frown.

She smiles. "Not if I have anything to say about it, anyway."

I get to my feet, wiping my jeans. I don't feel humorous, and in a little while she'll know why.

"You haven't showered," she says, looking me up and down.

"I had a long night."

"Have you been drinking?"

"Some."

"Are you still drunk?"

"I don't think so."

"You're not sure?"

"I'm not driving, so what's the difference?" I answer as I walk around the car to the passenger side. "Let's go."

"Where are we going?"

The door is locked, so I knock on the roof of the car. "It's locked."

"Tony?" Kristie persists. "Where are we going?"

I look at her. I hate doing this. I can still see the girl I once loved, and I know how much this is going to hurt. All that pain she's tucked behind a single thread of hope is about to come undone. I'm about to make her world that much smaller.

"You okay?" she asks.

"Fine."

"Then where are we going?"

"It's just this place…" I manage, my voice locked in phlegm at the back of my throat. "Hidden away." I look away. I don't want her to see my eyes. I don't want her to read my thoughts. She deserves closure, but I'm worried there can't be closure in a situation like this, because even if there is an answer, there won't be an end.

Nothing ends.

Not here. Not in Payton. I knew that the moment I came back. The moment I arrived I felt that I'd never leave again. Somehow, without even trying to, I've become one of the townsfolk. I'm one of 'those guys' who used to make cracks about Route 89, but it won't be long before I'm regaling stories of what it's like on the outside with neighbors or co-workers or friends. Only over time, those stories will become embellished, watered down—incomplete. Over time, I'll forget I ever left, and I'll be here, just like everyone else, until the day I finally get out by being buried six feet down.

"Come on," I say, tapping the car again. The sun slips behind some clouds, and when I look up, the sky is hinting at rain again. I draw a breath and look her in the eye. "I'll take you to see your sister."

The color drains from her face. So does any trace of good humor. Her eyes get dark, the distance between us not enough to hide what she's suddenly feeling. "What did you just say?"

"Unlock the door," I answer. I have a bad headache, and if we're going to do this, then I'd just as soon get it over with.

She holds out her remote key, presses a button, and something behind the passenger door clicks, allowing me entry. She returns to the car and takes the wheel, but she doesn't start the engine right away. She just sits there, still for a moment, gathering her thoughts.

"That way," I say, pointing forward.

Kristie glares at me. "Are you telling me you know where she is?" she asks. "You've known all along?"

"No." I shake my head. "Like I said before, it's been coming back in bits and pieces."

"But now you suddenly, *conveniently,* remember?"

"There's nothing convenient about it."

"But now you know?"

"Yes."

"You son of a bitch."

"I'm sorry."

"Did you kill my sister?"

I consider going into detail, but there aren't many details to draw from that are relevant. The puzzle pieces are all there, but the picture image just won't focus.

"Did you kill my sister?"

"Start the engine, Kristine."

She stares at me for a long moment before turning the key, throwing into reverse and peeling out. "Where are we going?"

"You'll see."

"I can't read your mind. You tell me to drive, but you—"

"Turn left."

And just like that, we're on our way, heading straight into the worst day of the rest of my life.

# Twenty Two

## *Yesterday*

Ritchie is sitting on the top of someone's car, whittling a stick, sharpening its tip. From his vantage point, he has a good view of Payton High and particularly the baseball field. Today isn't a game day, but even if it was, he wouldn't be pitching anyway. Not now. Not ever again. Ritchie's done with Payton High. Actually, Payton High is done with Ritchie. He was expelled for fighting, and without a scholarship, his grades aren't good enough for a community college let alone a university. He'll never get accepted anywhere, not even a school with a baseball program. Just like that, Ritchie Hudson has gone from someone to no one.

Our friendship is a mess, but knowing him the way I do, he's either forgotten about our little argument and moved on, or he's waiting for the right moment to knock my lights out. I can't just pretend I didn't see him, because if I walk by without stopping, he'll draw new conclusions regardless of what they had been only twenty seconds earlier. Then he'll come after me.

I at least have to say goodbye.

I cross the lot and stop beside the car he's perched atop. He keeps right on whittling while I try to come up with something casual to say. Nothing comes to mind, so I hop up on the car beside him. It's been four days since the brawl at Pirate Stadium. His face is still bruised, but his eyes are sharp.

"You okay?" I ask.

"I shouldna lost my temper," he mumbles.

"No, you shouldn't have. It was a game, Rich. You lost your cool over a stupid game. You were one lousy out away from something really special, but you had to go all psycho and flip out. And for what? For a girl?"

"It wasn't her. It was *him*."

"I'm telling you, you need to let that go."

"I wanted to kill him," he mutters.

"Yeah, I know you wanted to kill him. I also know that you've been saying things like that an awful lot lately."

"Things like what?"

"Like how you want to kill him or your dad…or *me*."

Ritchie just frowns as he whittles with more urgency. "They kicked me outta school."

Expelled is more like it.

"I heard."

"How was graduation?" he asks.

I shrug. "Like you'd expect. You didn't miss much. It was actually kind of lame."

He nods, still whittling, large chunks breaking from the stick and sliding down the windshield of the car we're sitting on. "No more baseball," he mutters. "Didn't even get to finish out the season. That means it's over. No colleges will look at me now. My life's ruined. All cuzza him."

"He didn't even do anything."

He glares at me.

"You know what?" I say, hopping down off the car. "I stopped to say goodbye, but it's still just the same ol' shit with you, isn't it? You are *obsessed* with her, and it's gotten to the point of disturbing. But you go ahead and make excuses for why you're not going to be playing ball somewhere next spring. I got better things to do with my time. I gotta go. See ya."

"Where you goin'?"

"Piss off."

I hear him jump off the car and land clumsily before his footsteps loom up behind me. I fully expect him to sock me in the back, but instead, he only smacks me upside the head. "What do you mean you stopped to say goodbye?"

"It means I'm leaving."

"Where you goin'?"

"I'm on the midnight express out of town. We talked about this."

"That's tonight?"

"For the umpteenth time, yes, that's tonight."

"Well, that ain't much of a goodbye. Is that how you say goodbye to your best friend?"

"You didn't give me much of a choice."

"So, where you goin' now?"

"To say goodbye to my girlfriend."

Ritchie stops, and when I turn to him, he looks like a wet puppy. "You're really goin'?"

I put my hands on hips, wondering how to navigate this situation without making things worse.

"Fine," he says. "Then go. See if I care."

"Look, Kristie and I already have plans for tonight. It's my last night, and I need to spend what little time I have left with her. I have to. She's a chick, and she's totally PMSing over this."

Ritchie just stands there, and for a big guy, he looks awfully small.

174

"Tell you what," I say. "I'm planning to leave her place at around ten, grab my shit back at the house and head for the bus station. You want to meet me?"

"You want me to walk you to the bus station? Like a little girl?"

"I'm doing my best, Rich. My mom's car won't start, and she can't walk that far, so I'm saying goodbye to her at the house. And Kristie won't go with me. She refuses to."

He kicks at a stone. "So, you want me to walk you to the bus station…"

"What better send off than one last midnight walk downtown with my best buddy?"

"You're just demon…demonstrating me…"

"It's dismissing, stupid, and no I'm not. You've been my best friend since we were eight years old."

"Best friends don't abandon one another." The fire is gone from his eyes, and that youthful, curiously innocent young man looks older. He's stopped walking, and I think he's waiting for me to continue on so he can turn his back.

"Well," I say, sounding almost apologetic. "You know where I'll be, and I'd like you to be there too. But it's your call."

Ritchie's says nothing. He just stands there.

"Are you game?" I ask.

Nothing. He looks right through me like I mean nothing to him.

"I'll see you then," I say, though I doubt I'll see him at all. I turn away, my heart thundering in my chest, afraid he'll sense the lie I just told. Now that I'm going, and given what's happened, I'd just as soon slip out of Payton unnoticed—a Spielberg ending to a small town drama. It's time to go, and the sooner the better. Better to go now than wait for the pieces to fall and bury me beneath the weight of my own guilt.


## Part II

I make my way through town, through the fields and over the Beaver toward Lawton. I'm all torn up inside, skittish—jumping at every little sound. Paranoia has me second guessing how I handled things with Ritchie. Paranoia has me wondering if he's following. Paranoia also has me wondering what he'll do if he is. That sense of something 'bad' feels like a storm settling right over the top of Payton and threatening to rip us to pieces before scattering us to the wind like leaves. But the sun is out. There is no storm. And there's Kristie. She's greeting me with a big warm smile and open arms, and instantly I forget all about Ritchie.

"You okay?" she asks.

"I'm fine."

"Thinking about tonight?"

"Are you?"

175

She bites her lip, looks away and lets go of me, turning for the stairs leaving up to the porch. "Come on. We're all inside."

"We?"

"Travis and Joanne."

I hesitate, quietly disappointed that it's not going to be just the two of us like we'd planned, but I cover well, don a phony smile and follow her up the steps, through the screen door and into the living room where Joanne and Travis are seated on the couch. Kristie curls up in the big chair, taking the whole thing by tucking her feet up under her. I stand there feeling like a lump. There's another chair, but it's on the other side of the end table, and that kind of defeats the point. It also means she's doing this on purpose—creating a barrier so as to make me feel guilty.

"Is there room for me?" I ask, but she says nothing. No one says anything. They won't even look at me. "Or should I just go?"

This time Kristie does lift her eyes before sighing heavily and swinging her legs out to make room for two. I sit down and wrap my arm around her. I even kiss the back of her neck, but she's rigid—cold. Pretending not to notice, I look around at what everyone's up to. By the looks of things, Joanne's trying to teach Travis sign-language.

"Cute," I murmur.

"What?" she asks.

I shrug. "I don't know. It just seems a little soon for learning Sign is all."

Kristie frowns. "Are you jealous?"

"Don't you take that tone with me, young lady," I murmur, nudging her playfully. She smirks, elbows me right back before getting up and heading into the kitchen.

Joanne looks great—too good for Travis anyway. No, I'm not jealous, but I am a bit curious what makes him so damn special. His hand is on her thigh, and while I barely know him, I know enough to know I'm starting to understand what's been eating at Ritchie, and there's a piece of me that agrees. Travis doesn't care about learning sign language. He wants to get laid. He's acting innocently stupid—intentionally messing up—so she'll grant him a pity fuck. Of course, his ignorance has limits. Just when she shows even the slightest bit of impatience, he signs the word 'beautiful' before pointing at her. She settles down, gets all gooey and snuggles up to him.

Kristie reemerges from the kitchen, a glass of ice water in each hand. She hands me one. "Let's help," she says before sitting in that empty chair on the other side of the end table. She'd didn't sit with me. She chose the empty chair.

"This'll be fun," she says.

Fun.

I know her well enough to know she used the glass of water as an excuse to get up, and now she's sitting in another chair just to make a point. She's pissed. She's a good liar though, because she's acting relaxed, and she's smiling, and she's giggling as Joanne signs something she finds particularly funny.

176

Travis looks at me with a frown. "Any idea what's she saying?"

I do, though I know enough to realize that I shouldn't say so. I know my place, and my place is to shrug and play dumb, but I can't. I'm irritated by Kristie's attitude, and I'm disgusted with Travis. Maybe it's because I don't trust him, and my lack of trust seems the easiest way to expose him as a fraud even if it embarrasses the girls. Besides, I'm on my way out of town anyway, so what difference does it make?

"She said she thinks you're cute," I grumble.

Joanne's mouth drops open in horror.

Kristie shoots me an angry glare before reaching across the end table between us and smacking my arm with the back of her hand. "Why'd you do that?"

"Because he asked."

"Since when did you get good at Sign?"

"I know more than I let on."

"So, you're some kind of sign language prodigy?"

"Not really." I lock eyes with Travis and smile. "It means I'm a guy. It means I learned how to sign the important words so I can use them at times like this."

Travis stares back.

"It also means if we play our cards right," I continue, "we might get a hand job, but if we're good enough liars, we might even get laid."

He glares at me, and I can tell he wants to fight. We face off, separated by a coffee table littered with a number of Country Living magazines, but neither of us move.

"For the record," he says, keeping his tone light. "I'm okay with being cute. I'd rather be handsome, but I'll take cute."

The two girls giggle, and Travis is all grins, because he's Mr. Perfect. He even smiles at me, but his eyes give him away. He's not happy with me. In fact, I think I just made an enemy. But fuck him and everything he stands for. I'm sure he's super-duper and all that, and all I have to do is keep my mouth shut and we'll be friends, but I don't want to be friends. I don't like him, and I don't want to like him. He's pretending to be interested in a deaf girl when it's obvious that scoring is his only goal.

"Focus," Joanne says as she casts a stern look my way. "You're not paying attention."

"What?" I ask.

Everyone laughs. Apparently, I made an ironic funny.

"Now, tell me what color my hair is."

"Blond," I answer.

"In Sign, you dummy," she smirks.

I know the answer. I can actually do this, but it seems like we're all lying, so I keep it going by putting on my own show of *innocent* and *cute*. I look to Travis for help, but he just shrugs. He's the best actor of the bunch, so I pick up a yellow pillow and point at it. "Blond."

Kristie sneers. "Cheater."

177

"But am I wrong?"

"No, you're an idiot," Kristie says.

"I resemble that remark," I grin. "Go ahead. Challenge me."

"Fine," Joanne answers, looking me in the eye, "But this one's gonna hurt."

"Ooooh," I say, rubbing my hands together. "Naughty."

Once again, Kristie reaches across the vast divide between us, nearly topples, and slugs me.

"You really think you can stump me?" I ask.

"I don't think it," Joanne answers in that weird accent of hers. "I know it."

"Give it your best shot, sweetheart," I say with a growl. "I'm ready."

Travis smiles.

Joanne squints.

It's another one of those good old-fashioned Mexican standoffs—sans pan flute and tumbleweed, of course, and I can't help but marvel how much she looks like Kristie when she's not speaking. "Tell me what the weather's like," she says before wagging a warning finger. "Without cheating."

I sit back, trying for a debonair look as if I know what debonair is supposed to look like. Finally, I get creative, hold up my arms and make a large circle over my head.

"What is that supposed to mean?" Kristie asks with a laugh.

"The sun," I answer. "It's sunny outside, right? I was making a sun."

"That's not sign-language. That's the stupidest thing I've ever seen."

I look to Travis for help. "What do you think?"

He busts up laughing. "I gotta be honest, I thought it was some kind of weird Celtic dance."

"Okay, genius, then you tell them in sign-language what the weather's like," I snap, but he's already laughing, and so are they. Hook, line and sinker. Once again, I'm the funny guy. Funnier than *him* anyway, and that's what matters as far as I'm concerned. "I'm glad you're all enjoying yourselves at my expense," I mumble, though this time it's an act.

"You're so adorable when you're frustrated," Kristie murmurs, getting out of her chair and coming over to sit with me.

"I'll take cute over adorable any day," Travis says.

"Yeah, well 'adorable' got me a girl in my lap. How's 'cute' working out for ya?"

Joanne snuggles up to her 'man' and makes a spectacle out of it.

"Game on," he says with a sinister smile.

Everyone else finds this particularly hilarious, and they're suddenly howling with laughter. Kristie is having a good ol' time, and Joanne is laughing in a way I rarely see. She looks truly happy for once. As much as that douchebag makes me squirm, I do my best to pretend everything's okay. I even smile, but I don't mean it. This is supposed to be one of those good moments between young couples feeling each other out, but I don't trust him.

Slowly, the forced smile slips from my lips, and I'm on the verge of saying something I probably shouldn't when I feel something press up against my shoulder. I turn to find Kristie snuggling up to me, her hair brushing my neck and cascading over my shoulder, and it makes me wonder why I'm pissed at Travis. I shouldn't care who she dates. I've got Kristie.

"Well," Travis says, standing.

And just like that...

"I'm late as it is." He nods my way. "Tony, we'll need to continue this at Christmas when you're back in town, and we're both learned men."

"Where are you going?" Kristie asks.

"He has to work," Joanne answers, disappointment in her voice.

Travis shrugs before opening his arms to her. They embrace and kiss quickly before he nods my way and smiles at Kristie. Then he's gone, and it's just us three.

"I thought he had tonight off," Kristie says.

"He did," Joanne answers as she goes to the door and watches him off. "Someone called in sick."

"Who gets sick in the middle of summer?"

"What's it matter? He's gone."

The thing is, she doesn't look all that upset. Or maybe I'm not reading her right.

"Let's go outside," Kristie suggests. "At least there's a breeze."

I look beyond the screen door at the trees that stand listlessly—motionless.

## Part III

We migrate to the backyard where there's a hammock and some shade and absolutely no breeze to speak of. We try to fit three into the hammock by sitting on it like a porch swing, but it sags, smooshing us together and bringing about a lot of laughs. At first, I'm okay with the close proximity of two gorgeous girls pressing up against me until I realize I'm pinched between two gorgeous girls pressing up against me—one of which is my girlfriend and the other is my girlfriend's sister. This reminds me of the stunt they pulled down by the Old Beaver, and suddenly our arrangement on the hammock feels awkward.

"Why do you have to go?" Kristie asks suddenly. She's referring to Georgia, of course. She brings it up every time she starts feeling insecure, and since tonight is the big night, she must be feeling awfully insecure. She doesn't want me to go away to a big school. She wants me to stay in Michigan, go to school here and get a safe little job working a desk at the bank. Nothing too extravagant, but nice enough to afford a three-bedroom rancher, a couple of kids, a family dog and a nice little life for 'us'. She doesn't want me to leave, because she knows she can't. Her grades have been 'intimidating,' meaning community college is her only option. If I'm at UGA, and if she's here, then there's 900 miles between us, and there's 900 other girls vying for my attention.

"I told you," I say. "I'm coming back."

"Well, call me crazy, but I think you're running away."

"I'm running away?"

"You could get your associates here and save a ton of money, but you're so eager to get out of town and get away from *me*, that you're jumping on the first bus out."

"It's not you, and you know that."

"You don't even know what you want to do. You haven't even picked a major."

"Please don't make me feel even more guilty than I already am. UGA is a huge opportunity. It's a big time school with endless potential. If I don't jump on it now, it might not be there in two years."

"If you got a four-point over at Lawton Community, you might have a shot at something even bigger."

"Is that where you're planning on getting your masters?" Joanne smirks.

"You shut up," Kristie warns.

"You shut up."

"Both of you shut up," I snap.

"He's never coming back," Joanne sneers.

"Enough," I interrupt before turning to Kristie. "I love you. And I *will* be back. I promise."

"He's never coming back," Joanne repeats.

"I'm coming back," I snap. "Jesus, what is with you two today?"

"You're coming back?" Kristie asks. "As what? A high-powered executive? A VIP? Shiny shoes and pressed slacks? You're leaving, Tony. Jo's right. I have no idea who's coming back."

"This is entirely unfair," I say. "I thought you'd be supportive. This is a big deal—for both of us. It'll open doors."

"Fuck doors. God opens windows."

"You don't even go to church."

"I call it like I see it."

"I invited you to come with me."

Joanne snorts. "She doesn't exactly have the grades."

"I'm not talking about school. I just said she could come with me."

"Lucky me," Kristie pouts. "I get to *tag along*. I can wring my hands with worry while my big man is away at school getting an education so he can provide for his stupid little wifey who's back home scrubbing the toilet."

"That's not what I meant."

Joanne giggles again.

"This isn't funny!" Kristie shouts. "God…"

180

"She's kidding," I say softly as I wrap my arm over Kristie' shoulder and pull her close. The thing is, it doesn't feel natural. It feels like we're playing a role, so I kiss her forehead and stand up before taking a few steps away.

"I don't want you to go," Kristie says.

"I'm coming back. I promise."

"That's not it. Something's wrong. I can feel it. Something's off, like it's—"

"I'm not sure Travis is right for me," Joanne interrupts suddenly, and Kristie and I are quickly reminded someone else is here too. When we turn around, Joanne looks somewhat pitiful sitting on the edge of the hammock, the hammock wrapped up around her, squeezing her in.

"What do you mean?" Kristie asks. "He adores you."

She shrugs. "There just isn't much chemistry. I mean, I like him, but I don't know that it's going anywhere. You know, like with you and Tony."

"Oh, my god, in the last five minutes, what kind of chemistry have you been smoking, because I want some."

"At least you're fighting because you're afraid of losing each other."

"Is this what you want? To be fighting with your boyfriend in the last few hours before he *abandons* you?"

"I'm not abandoning anyone."

"You and Travis have been together for a week," Kristie continues. "You don't know anything after one week."

"Almost two," she counters.

"You know what I mean."

"Yeah, but shouldn't there be some kind of…spark or something?"

"No yeah-buts," Kristie snaps. "I don't want to hear it. You've been waiting for a good guy, and Travis is a *good* guy. At least give him a chance before you throw him back and whine about how the only guy that's willing to put up with your retarded stutter is Ritchie Hudson."

"She's not retarded," I murmur.

"And it's not a stutter," Joanne quips.

"Whatever." Kristie says, raising her hands. "It's not a stutter, and you're not retarded."

"I'm out of here," I murmur.

"Tony…" Kristie gripes.

"Tony…" Joanne begs.

I stop walking, but I'm not ready to turn back yet. "This is not how I wanted my last day here to go."

"She's right," Joanne says.

"I am?" Kristie asks.

"Which part?" I ask.

"The part where Ritchie is the only guy willing to put up with my retarded stutter."

"Accent," I correct.

181

Joanne shakes her head. "Travis hates it. It's obvious."

"He doesn't hate it," Kristie argues.

"Like you know. You don't know what it's like to be looked at like the town clown. You're Miss Perfect."

This is a fun conversation. I'm glad I stuck around...

"Besides," Joanne continues. "I'm tired of him. He bores me."

Kristie stands. "How could he bore you? You just met."

"It means I'm bored," Joanne returns. She's angry, shifting back and forth from her spot on the hammock.

"Maybe I should just go," I say.

Kristie holds up a finger. "I've got you for the next five hours, so you're not going anywhere." She turns back to her sister. "And you're never happy unless you have something to bitch about."

Joanne frowns. "Says the princess with everything."

"It's really hot out here," I murmur.

"I have *everything*?" Kristie says all shrilly. It's not a pleasant sound. "You think I have everything? You're GPA is over a full point higher than mine. You think I'm not jealous of how easily trigonometry comes to you?"

"I think I'm going to go," I suggest.

"You're going to stay put," Kristie snaps.

"I really don't want to be a part of this."

"Travis is a good guy," Kristie says to Joanne, ignoring me. "He's sweet, good looking, smart and aside from your paranoid allusions that he's merely putting up with your slur, he seems okay with you just the way you are."

"Delusions," Joanne corrects.

"Huh?"

"Paranoid *delusions*."

"It's really hot out here," I complain.

Both girls stop talking and turn on me. Kristie looks pissed. "Would you like cheese with your whine?"

"Maybe I should just go."

"You're not going. This is the last time I get to see you until Christmas, so you're staying."

"I'm really thirsty."

"Then I'll get you a *fucking* glass of water!" She storms toward the house leaving me feeling like a heel.

I turn to Joanne. "That went well."

She giggles and pats the hammock beside her.

"I think I've had enough of the hammock for one day."

"Hammock or Kristie?"

I frown. "What's that supposed to mean?"

"Do you love her?"

182

I think a second before nodding. "Well, I...sure."

She shrugs. "I'm convinced." She gets up off the hammock and stands, stretching. She's showing off her body, or if she isn't, then that's how I'm perceiving it. She has a sultry walk that doesn't look all that natural, but it's sexy anyway *because* it doesn't look all that natural. And she's using that unnatural sultry walk as she steps closer, her eyes locked on mine. I frown. Again. I'm doing a lot of frowning, because I'm pretty confused.

"Why Kristie?" she asks as she reaches my side.

"Why Kristie what?"

"Instead of me? You and me have more in common than you and her."

"What?" I ask.

"Why her?"

"I'm sorry, what I meant to say was *what?*"

She doesn't bite at my poor attempt at humor. Instead, she takes another half step closer. Now we're practically touching. We're so close that I can smell her perfume. It's the same stuff her sister wears, which only heightens my confusion. They're the same. The two of them are exactly the same, except for the mere fact that they're not. Joanne and I actually do have more in common than Kristie and me.

"When you look at me," she says, "what do you see?"

"Is this a trick question?"

"No. I'm being serious. What do you see?"

"My friend. You."

She says nothing.

I say nothing though I get what she's driving at. I can't say it, but I get it. I see a pretty girl. A gorgeous girl. I see someone I've known since grade school but never looked at in *that* way. Not until now. Now I suddenly see her as the perfect girl. The girl who would support my choice to go away to school instead of fighting it. Hell, she'd go with me. We'd both excel, and we'd both wind up with MBAs, high-paying jobs, a fancy house on some cul-de-sac and two BMWs parking in our three-stall garage. She's every bit as pretty as Kristie, and I just realized that her goofy slur, while annoying at times, is kind of cute in its own right. She's smiling as though reading my mind, and I can't help but feel that this guttural, knee-jerk, nose-pinching, breath-holding moment is nothing more than teenage hormones screwing with my head. Joanne tries to wrap her arms around me, but I back off—holding her at arm's length. "What are you doing?"

"One kiss," she pleads.

"I can't..."

"If it's awkward, then at least we'll know. We won't have to wonder all the time."

"But I'm with Kristie."

"You two are entirely incompatible, and what's more is you know it. You're dating her because she's pretty and she showed you attention. It's convenient."

"I love her."

"You love the idea of her. One kiss. If it's horrible, we'll laugh about it later, and I'll never bother you again." She just stands there looking exactly like Kristie. The same pale skin—smooth and soft. The same pretty blue eyes, the same dirty blonde hair. She presses up against me. She's shorter than me, so it's her lower belly that presses against my mid-section, but there's a flicker of knowing light in her eyes, and this has officially gone from weird to wrong. As conflicted as I feel emotionally, logically I already know—

"Jo, I can't do this."

There's disappointment in her eyes, but I think she understands. Unfortunately, it's at that moment when I start to think that while I've demonstrated loyalty to Kristie and saved face with Joanne that I hear the sound of glass shattering on pavement followed by something even worse.

"Joanne?" Kristie shrieks. She's standing at the top of the steps. The drinks she had carried out are lying in pieces on the sidewalk below, two puddles running in streams toward the grass.

## Part IV

Kristie hesitates for only a moment at the top of the stairs before she comes running. She doesn't look surprised, anxious or even concerned. She looks pissed. Doing what I tend to do be doing a lot of lately, I shove Joanne behind me, thereby placing myself in the middle of exactly what I had tried to stay out of in the first place.

"Nothing happened," I try, but Kristie will have none of it. Her hand comes out of nowhere and slashes me across my neck with four fingernails that feel like razorblades. I cringe as she goes right around me and pounces on her sister.

I touch my hand against my flaming neck and feel the broken skin beneath the tips of my fingers. Kristie and Joanne are rolling around on the ground and shrieking, and while this scene might be humorous if set to Benny Hill music, now I'm angry too. I jump in, wrap my hands under Kristie's stomach and pull. The two separate, though they continue to swing and kick. I struggle to control Kristie, but she's a fireball, screaming at me and her sister. Her arms and legs are flailing like a wriggling fish, but I wrap her up and hold on until she tires. She's still mad, still crying, but at least she stops fighting.

"Nothing happened," I say softly. "Nothing." I can feel her heart thundering in her chest. "We were just talking."

"Talking," Kristie says, her voice breaking with sobs. "You were talking."

"Talking," I repeat.

Joanne is on her feet, her face covered with tear-streaked dirt. There is real rage boiling in her eyes. "Another two minutes," she hisses, "and I'd have had him on his back. I'd have been riding him like a rodeo cowgirl."

184

"You're not helping," I murmur.

"I'll kill you."

"I hate you."

"Enough!" I shout.

"The feeling's mutual, bitch," Kristie hisses.

Joanne is in tears. She looks one more time my way before turning her back and storming off. "I'm out of here," she calls. "For good! *For good!*"

I want to go after her, but Kristie pulls me back. "Let her go," she whispers.

Turning to Kristie, my heart is racing. "I swear nothing happened. I swear it. I didn't do anything."

"No, you didn't," she answers coldly. "But she did." She wraps her arms around me and holds on desperately. "And I saw it."

"Nothing happened," I whisper, so afraid of losing Kristie that I'm relieved she's holding onto me so tightly. Now she's crying, and if there's one sound I can't stand, it's the sound of a girl crying. I look after Joanne, but she's already almost out of sight. She'll be back. This was just a fight among sisters, but she'll be back, because they're family and they love each other. She'll be back, they'll make up, and everything will be okay.

Kristie finally starts to settle down, but it's been ten minutes—maybe longer, and Joanne has disappeared over the hilltop. Payton isn't all that big, so it's not that I'm concerned about her safety, but I've never seen her that broken up before, and I certainly don't pretend to understand the 'logic' of a female. Everyone has a breaking point, and given how freaked out she was, I wonder if she's passed hers.

"Let's go inside," I say softly. Kristie agrees, though I think she'd agree to pretty much anything. She's not altogether with it, so I lead her back to the house, up the porch steps and into the living room where we sit on the couch. Just a little while ago, we were all in here, playing a game and having fun. Now the mood has turned sour, and the room feels oddly empty.

"Please don't do this to me," she whispers. "Please don't go."

"I have to," I answer. "I mean…everything's been arranged. I *have* to go."

"You don't *have* to do anything. You could stay if you wanted to, but maybe you don't want to."

"You want to know the truth?" I ask. "I actually don't want to *go*. I actually want to stay. I'm scared shitless, and I don't want to leave you. I want to bail on this whole stupid idea more than I can even put into words. But you know what? I have to do this. I have to do this for us. I'm leaving tonight because this is something I *have* to try. And as shitty as that might sound, there's a silver lining, because I *will* be back, and I'll be back for you."

"I hate you," she whispers.

"You don't hate me."

She's crying again. "Yes I do." Then, using the soft tips of her fingers, she brushes the cuts she raked across my neck.

185

"Does it look as bad as it feels?"

"She likes you," Kristie whispers, ignoring my question as another tear rolls down her cheek before she presses her face against my chest. "I've felt it ever since you and I started going out."

"She just wants what we have. It's not me. She just wants someone."

"You heard her today," Kristie murmurs. "She's not even all that into Trevor."

"Travis," I correct.

"She likes you. I know it. I *saw* it."

There's nothing I can say to convince her otherwise, and there's nothing I can do other than hold on and hope the storm passes. I want to leave, but there's no manual that says when it's okay to. Joanne's out there, and it's not like her to go off on her own like this. With Ritchie going postal, Joanne taking off, Kristie flipping out, and the clock counting backwards until I'm supposed to leave with all these things unresolved, it feels like my world is falling apart.

"I have to go," I say.

"Go where?"

"I have to go," I repeat as I gently separate myself from her.

"Why?"

Why? Because I have to fix it, and if I can't fix it, then I at least have to try. Not that I know how to say it in a way that'll make sense to an emotional teenage girl, so I lie, because truth is elusive, my world is fucked, and I can only work on one problem at a time. "I promised Ritchie I'd meet him," I say. "Maybe shoot some hoops or something."

"I thought you two weren't getting along."

"We're not, but he's still my friend, and I need to patch things up before I leave."

"You promised me until ten."

"I'm trying," I say. "I swear to God, Kris, I'm trying. I'm trying to do everything and be all things to everybody. And I'm failing miserably."

She just stares at me, forcing me to commit to a decision.

"I have to go," I repeat.

"Fine. Then go. If you're so eager to go, then go. Have a nice life."

I bite my tongue. "It's not like that."

"Of course not." She's wrapping herself into a ball upon the couch. "It never is."

"I'll call you."

She nods, but she won't look at me, and she's wiping fresh tears from her cheeks.

"I love you."

Still nothing.

Dating sucks, which means dating really sucks. I'm not trying to hurt her. I'm not trying to hurt anyone. I'm trying to do the right thing, and right now Joanne needs me more than Kristie does. I have to go. I *have* to.

Retreating from the house, I trot down the steps, follow the sidewalk and step onto the road leading toward the edge of town. I have no idea which way to go, but I have

186

to try. I have to look. I try to put myself in Joanne's shoes and wonder what I'd be thinking if it had been me. In a small town with eyes and ears everywhere with nowhere to hide, where would I go?

And just like that, I think I've figured it out. I'll need my bike to get there, but I haven't ridden that damn thing in years. It's under the porch, a big conglomeration of rust and sprockets. I have no idea if it's even roadworthy, but I'm about to find out, because I'll need it for where I'm going—all the way to the edge of the earth and beyond.

# Twenty Three

## *Today*

"Tony," she says softly. "You're scaring me." But she's not scared. There might be some anger and confusion and sadness, but she's not scared. I'm the one who's scared, because I know where we're going, and I know what's waiting for us once we get there. If she was scared, she wouldn't have gotten in the car, she wouldn't have started the engine, and she wouldn't be following my instructions. But here we are, almost out of town where Lincoln Street turns into Route 89.

Thump-thump, thump-thump.

"Where are we going?" Kristie asks, but I don't need to answer. I suspect she already knows where we're going. There's not a lot on this road. Trees, road, more trees and more road. Other than the old Johnson farm, there's a lot of nothing, which is why I suspect she knows where we're going.

Thump-thump, thump-thump.

"Did you kill her?" Kristie asks again in a sheepish whisper.

I don't answer. It's not that I'm ignoring her. I'm trying to remember what actually happened. There's still so much that doesn't make sense.

Payton fades in our mirrors, leaving a rolling landscape of green. It would have been a long walk back then, but when you're too young to drive, five miles each way is a good way to kill a Saturday afternoon. The old Johnson farm stood like a lighthouse at the edge of the county line—a beacon signifying the point of no return. It was also the one place accessible to teenagers where parents wouldn't think to follow and cops wouldn't bother to patrol. Everyone would rather turn a blind eye and let boys be boys than worry about what goes on out at an abandoned farmhouse. Break a window, build a fort, whatever. It's kids being kids. No harm, no foul.

"Why are we here again?" Kristie says as we draw closer. "We were just here yesterday."

"We missed something."

She turns and looks at me. "Like what? My sister?"

I don't answer.

"Did you send the letter?" Kristie continues. She shakes her head and drives. "I swear to God if you did, I'll kill you. I swear it."

I remain stoic. "I didn't send the letter. I had no idea there even was a letter."
"Then who did?"

"Turn here," I answer, though Kristie probably doesn't need to be told. We've
reached the farm, and she's already pulling into the overgrown driveway. Just like
yesterday, we drives as far inland as we can get. Overhead, the sky is ugly, bloated
and uneasy. There's even a rumble of thunder in the distance. There's going to be a
storm for sure. Not like the spring rains we've seen these last few days. A real storm.
The kind that buries things—things that need to be buried. The kind that drowns the
world.

"You ready?" I ask.

She turns to me. "Why? Are you going to kill me too?"

"Nobody's dying."

"Did you kill her?"

I shift anxiously. "Come on. It's going to rain." I open the door and climb out as
lightning flashes overhead. As if on cue, fat raindrops begin to splatter like broken
eggs. It's slow at first—mini grenades—nature's way of saying that we have less than
thirty seconds until all hell breaks loose. I trot to the porch and jump the steps two at a
time before turning. She's still in the car, eyeing me from behind the rain-splattered
windshield. I wave her in, and when she doesn't move, I point up at the sky. Finally,
her door opens, and she steps out. She doesn't run. She just walks, and she's about
twenty feet from the porch when the skies open up. She continues to stare at me
through the rain, her eyes fixed as she walks through the tall grass to the rotting porch.
Her hair is plastered to her neck, her skirt glued to her legs by the time she climbs the
steps.

"What happened here, Tony?" she asks harshly as she climbs the rickety steps.
"You owe me that much."

"As naïve as it might sound, trust me when I say we're both about to find out."
Thunder. "Come on," I say, motioning her inside.

Kristie stalls. "I found the headband in the barn, not the house." She blinks away
raindrops.

"It's not in the barn," I answer.

"It?" she asks. "Or *her*?"

A jagged bolt of lightning creases the sky and the whole house shudders.

"It," I answer. "The answer you've been waiting twenty years for." I turn away and
step into the house. "Come on. You're getting soaked."

Even though we're inside, nothing is dry. Half the roof rotted away years ago, and
the rain is already making its way through the ceiling overhead and onto the kitchen
table. Water streams along the inside of the intact windows—inside out—before
running along the kitchen counter like a snaking river toward the edge where it spills
over the edge onto the floor. Water runs in bubbles under the old wallpaper and soaks
what's left of the chewed up carpeting. Drips bounce off the silent grandfather's
clock, ticking against the old brass pendulum.

Opening the basement door, I hesitate, making sure she'll follow. Part of me wants her to run. Part of me wants it to end, and the only way it can end is down where it started, so I take the first step. The stairs are wet, rainwater dripping from one step to the next like a slow Slinky. I don't turn to see if she's following, but I can hear her footfalls behind me.

"Why are you bringing me here?" she asks, her voice shaking. "What is it you didn't show me yesterday?"

"I didn't remember."

"And now you do?"

"Some of it."

Thunder cracks, the entire house shuddering. The basement is damp and dark, the old bricks wet with moisture and moss. It even smells wet down here. There are spider-webs stretched among the joists, soulless corpses trapped in the stringy goo, and had we not been down here just twenty-four hours earlier, I'd swear nobody had for years. Instead of heading toward the canning room, I step into the coal room where the floor, still covered beneath a small pile of dusty coal, reveals nothing. The door had been removed a long time ago. It's leaning up against the wall, and other than a small pile of coal, an old pair of rubber boots and a shovel in the corner, there's nothing in here.

Kristie hesitates just outside. "Why did you bring me here?"

Instead of answering, I look down at the floor and kick away a few bricks of coal. Then I pick up the old shovel and begin shoveling away the dusty chunks, revealing a sandy floor.

"I don't understand," Kristie answers.

I look at her, lightning flashing through the tiny basement window over my shoulder.

# Twenty Four

## Yesterday

I try to convince myself that I have no idea which way Joanne went, but I do. When someone threatens to leave town, there's only one way out: Route 89. Of course, along that desolate road running along the edge of town, there's only one place to stop and rest. The last outpost—the point of no return. Battered, weathered, and scorned, the old Johnson farm, as mysterious as it is charismatic, marks the end of the line.

My bike is a piece of shit. I bought it at a garage sale for ten bucks a few years back, and it was bad then. It's worse now. I've invested exactly zero dollars into its maintenance, and after a few years of neglect beneath our less-than-weatherproof porch, its condition hasn't exactly improved. The chain is rusty, the spokes worn, the tires half inflated, the paint rusting away. It still rides, but it certainly won't win any beauty contests. Or races. But I pedal my ass off anyway.

Squeak, squeak, squeak, squeak.

I zip through town, across the football field, shortcut around a scattering of cars in the school parking lot, and through three backyards. I pedal until my calves feel like bursting and the houses begin to thin. Then I pedal some more. Eventually, the houses disappear altogether, leaving nothing but pines and maples on either side of the two-lane road. There's hardly any traffic once I make it past the city limits. Of course, it wouldn't matter what time of day, what day of the week or what the weather is like, because there's hardly ever any traffic on Route 89. Certainly no big rigs, no buses and no cabs. It's just a lonely highway stretching toward the horizon. Once I crest the hill, I'll see the old farm on the other side.

I keep pedaling, pumping my legs, sweat raining down my face. The old bitch is squeaking and whining, and I swear she's going to fall apart at any second. Ironically, it's at that perfect moment when I'm cresting the top of the hill that she finally does. The chain breaks, leaping from the sprocket and whipping me sharply across the leg before getting tangled in the spokes of the front tire. Logically, this seems impossible, but I only have a few tenths of a second to ponder physics while considering what I'm going to do once I'm propelled over the handlebars. Sadly, once the tire locks up, the bike stopping on a dime, I realize I'm not going fast enough to clear the bike altogether. Instead, I slide over the handlebars like I'm wave surfing. The bike follows suit, the front tire skidding, the back tire more than eager to keep going. We both go head over heels, and I land hard—skidding across the cracked asphalt. For the briefest of moments I'm convinced that I landed gracefully. Then I'm pretty sure I didn't. First the pain is limited to the palms of my hands which were shredded when I used them as landing pads. Then the side of my face starts to burn. I can already feel blood running along my cheek. I'm sprawled on my back in the middle of the road, but I can't feel much of anything else aside from searing pain.

I hear someone shouting, and the voice is drawing nearer, but I can't breathe very well given my state of shock. Breathing hurts, and that seems more important than listening. Besides, all I can do is lay quivering in the middle of the road while hoping I'll either die or the pain will go away.

## *Part II*

I open my eyes to see Kristie hovering over me, tears racing down her cheeks. She's shouting my name, asking me what I was thinking, calling me a stupid ass while wondering if I'm okay. Her voice sounds funny. She has a slur—as if she's got a fat tongue. Which means...

"I'm fine," I croak. I need to get off the road and into the shade or something.

"What happened?" Joanne asks.

"Help me up," I say, not that I know if I can actually stand or not.

"You're bleeding everywhere," she cries. "Oh my god, your hands!"

"Help me up," I repeat. Maybe she didn't hear me. She just keeps panicking, so I roll onto my stomach and push myself up, my hands raw, the blood hissing on the burning pavement.

Standing feels no better than baking on the blacktop, but at least I'm up, and she's wrapping my arm over her shoulder and helping me limp down the hill toward the Johnson farm. We manage our way through the tall grass and up the steps of the rotting porch leading into the open door where she leads me to the old couch still sitting in the living room beside the silent grandfather clock.

"I'll find some water to clean it," she says with motherly care. "Don't you dare move."

Then she's gone, and I have a moment to study the damage. The skin is broken, and tiny stones are imbedded within the meat of my palms. My hands look like cotto salami. I expected worse, probably because of her reaction, but I remind myself that she's never been a boy, so she doesn't understand that bad injuries as a consequence of stupid stunts is what we excel at. Especially when it comes to impressing girls. I'm only hoping my face isn't as bad. I don't want her to think I'm hideous, because if I'm—

It suddenly occurs to me that I'm worrying whether or not Joanne finds me attractive. Joanne. Not Kristine.

She smiles as she returns with a wet rag. "Rain water." She shrugs. "Should be clean…ish."

"Your confidence is overwhelming," I answer.

"Don't move." Gingerly, she taps the wet rag against the side of my burning face. Each time she does, I wince, and she winces empathetically before giggling. At this point I'm pretty sure she has a crush on me, and she's probably had a crush on me for some time. I never saw it. Not until now. What's worse is I think I have a crush on her too, which makes me feel dirty and disloyal and sad. I think I want her more than I want Kristie. I think I want her so bad that I'm willing to do anything for her, and it's at this vulnerable moment of narcissistic clarity devoid of altruistic intention that our eyes suddenly meet, and she stops dabbing at my face. She's not Kristie, but in a way she is. She's just as beautiful, twice as smart, and more romantic. I tell myself this is wrong, but in a way, nothing has ever felt more right. I have genuine feelings for Kristie, but there's always been this…*thing*, or at least there's always been *some*thing. Joanne was right. She and I have more in common, and we can relate on levels Kristie and I never could. We can talk about science and math or English or politics. I can't do any of that with Kristie. Not that Kristie's stupid. She just has different interests.

Joanne's giving me that look. It's the same look her sister gives me when she wants me to kiss her. Lips slightly open, eyes dancing up and down, her breaths coming quickly. "You came for me," she whispers.

"I don't like to see you and Kristie fight."

She rolls her eyes. "Can we not talk about my sister for once?"

"I just hate to see you two like this."

"Well, I'm angry with her," Joanne says. "Sister's fight, Tony."

"I know. I get it."

"Do you?" She slides her hair behind her ears. "You're an only child. You don't have any siblings."

"I still don't like seeing you fight. You both mean a lot to me."

"Which one means more?"

"You don't honestly expect me to answer that, do you?"

"She stole you from me."

"What?"

"She knew I had a crush on you. She didn't even like you at first. I did. And since she thought I always got all the attention due to my hearing problems, she was jealous. Once she found out I liked you, she swooped in like it was a competition." Tears spring to her eyes. "I didn't know what to say. I couldn't talk to you. I couldn't talk. I have this fucking slur, and she has a cute voice, and none of it had anything to do about love with her. She just had to have something I wanted."

I feel the air leaving my lungs, the hairs on my arms standing up, and an overwhelming squeeze on my heart. "I…"

193

She takes that as an invitation and leans in, her lips touching mine, her arms suddenly wrapped around me and pulling me to her. If it didn't feel so good, I would push her away, but it feels just right, and she's so soft and alive—so hungry for *me*. I'm always fighting for Kristie, but Joanne isn't making me fight. She's throwing herself at me. Right here. Right now. So, I kiss her back, the excitement intoxicating. I'm scared, but at the same time, I feel more alive than I've ever felt. Something inside me has switched on, and I knew it the moment she tried to kiss me back at the house. I think I've always wanted Joanne, but it was Kristie who showed me attention, so I convinced myself that she was the right one—the *only* one.

It's perfectly silent around us save that of the rusty springs of the ancient couch as we hungrily—urgently—consume one another. The old couch squeaks, she giggles, and I realize how much I like her sound, not because it's perfect, because it's not. That slur is flawed, her voice far from cute the way her sister's is, but I love it anyway because it is uniquely hers. She and I are so desperately into each other that the sounds of summer outside are lost, and the discomfort of our perch is forgotten. Maybe I didn't ride all the way out here to save the relationship between her and her sister. I think maybe I came out here for me. I came here for her.

In my mind I suddenly see Kristie, and I see her eyes welling with anguish at my betrayal. All of our conversations, all of our promises—and every time she cries from this moment forward, my heart is going to break knowing I did this to her.

"I can't do this," I whisper, breaking away.

"What's wrong?" Joanne asks. There's panic in her voice. "Is it me? What did I do?"

"It's not you. You didn't—"

But she's cut off mid-sentence by another voice, a menacing growl that carries throughout the room, startling us from our secret little world.

"What the *fuck*?"

Ritchie's massive frame fills the doorway, his face flaming red—his fists clenched at his sides. His eyes are bloodshot with rage, his chest heaving. He must have followed me. Joanne instinctively rolls away and sits calmly with her hands in her lap, but it's too late. He's already seen us together, and I've already seen that look on his face. He's not here to sort it out. It's sorted. He's here to make things right—according to him.

Standing, I take a step toward him, my hands up defensively. "It's not what it looks like," I say calmly. "I don't want to fight."

"One ain't enough, is it? You gotta have 'em both."

"It's not like that, Rich" I answer, but even I realize it is.

"No?" he storms. "What do you think Kristie would say if she saw you like this?"

"Did you follow us here?" I ask.

"Would she turn the other cheek?" Ritchie continues. "Look the other way?"

"Did you follow us here?"

"One whore ain't enough?"

194

"Don't go there," I snap.

"You gonna make me, Triple A?" he growls, and it may be a million degrees outside, but the blood in my veins just froze.

"Ritchie," Joanne says, standing behind me. "This was our choice, not Kristie's."

His eyes go from me to her—slits glinting in the light. He looks powerful, like a full grown man instead of the boy I feel like. All of that nervous tongue-tied energy he struggles with every time he's around her has been replaced by hatred. He's cool—calm. Too calm. "This ain't your house, bitch," he growls.

"Ritchie!" I shout.

He turns back. "What's she gonna do when she finds out?" He shakes his head, tears spilling down his cheeks. "Will she get angry?" I've never seen him cry before, and I think that scares me more than anything else. "Or is she gonna cry?" he asks, his voice growing deeper. "What's she gonna do?"

"Ritchie," I say softly as I try to conceal the fact that my hands are beginning to shake.

"I wanna know."

"It's not—"

"I WANNA KNOW!"

"You're freakin' out, man. Relax. Let's talk this through. No one needs to get hurt."

"Oh, I guarantee you someone's about to get hurt," he grumbles, the blood returning to his face. "You were supposed to be with Kristie. I was supposed to be with Joanne. That's the way things work between *best* friends, asshole!"

Joanne begins to whimper. Ritchie's on the brink. For him, fighting is an outlet. It's a game. But not today. Today he's not playing.

"That fuckin' whore's mine," Ritchie growls as he faces her.

Joanne looks paralyzed with fear. She's standing beside the rotting couch, under a sagging roof, scared stiff. Even I'm terrified as I turn back to Ritchie. "Don't do it."

"Yeah?" Ritchie answers, a small smile curving his lower lip upward. "What you gonna do? You think you got what it takes, small time?"

The time for diplomacy is over. Ritchie doesn't negotiate. Not with his enemies, and apparently not with his friends. Something in him has snapped. Snapped like a rubber band, and now that it's broken, he doesn't have the pressure of considering options. Whatever he and I ever were—the very best of friends—is long gone. All I am now is the last obstacle standing between him and redemption.

Ritchie smiles.

"Run," I whisper.

"What?" Joanne asks, frantic.

"Run," I repeat.

In circles.

# Twenty Five

## *Today*

Kristie drags her heel through the sand, drawing a crooked line. She studies the line a moment before backing up, taking a timid step back. "It's only sand," she says. She slides her foot side to side, pushing sand back and forth. "Didn't they have cement floors back then?"

"Sometimes," I answer. "Not always. Back then, they didn't always pour a basement floor. They were usually sand. Or dirt."

She looks around, but eventually, her eyes settle on me. "Why did you bring me down here?"

"It's complicated."

"There is no *it*, Tony."

Instead of answering, I return to my shovel, shifting it to the other hand and starting to dig, feeling numb. This is it. There's no going back. No matter what, this is where it ends.

"Talk to me."

I keep digging, feeling queasy. First I move the coal, tossing it to the side. Then I start on the sand. One shovelful of decrepit earth after another, I build a hill of dirty sand. Finally, after a few minutes, the shovel hits something solid, and I stop.

"Oh my god," Kristie whispers. "Oh my god."

Rain water is running in thin streams along the walls, turning to puddles pooling on the sandy floor. I shovel away the remainder of the heavy soil before crouching down and wiping the loose sand from the remnants of a rug wrapped around the form of what appears to be a body. When I look up, she's still standing, but she looks wobbly in her stance as though she might topple.

"That's not her," she whispers. "That's not her."

I gently pull the rug from the loose sand and carefully set it down—half in and half out of the hole.

"That's not her," Kristie repeats. "Please, Tony, please don't let that be her."

I begin to unravel the rug. I'm scared. It's been so long—I was so young. Everything was so different then than it is now. I take hold of the top corner and pull it gently downward to reveal the gray bone of a human skull and what remains of the blond hairs still clinging to it.

Kristie breaks down, her entire body wracked with sobs. For years her family believed Joanne had simply hitch-hiked her way out of town and disappeared. It was easier to believe she just wanted to start over. After 'the letter,' they even convinced themselves she was living happily in California, biding her time until the time was right to come home. Nobody wanted to believe she had been killed. More than that, nobody believed she might still be here.

Kristie is wailing, her voice filling the room, her pain amplified. She slides against the wall to the ground, but when she lifts her eyes to me, they're red with hatred. She blames me, and maybe she should. After all, I'm responsible.

I cover Joanne's skull with the rug and sit down on the floor, my back to her. "I don't know what happened that day," I whisper.

Kristie sneers. "What do you mean you don't know? You knew! You knew all along!"

"You and Joanne had a fight."

"Yes, we had a fight," Kristie snaps. "Over you! You were leaving town, and you said you wanted to patch things up with Ritchie before you went."

I nod, my back still turned.

"But that's not where you went, was it?"

"No."

"And why not? Did you want to *fuck* my sister? Did you want to fuck her right before you killed her?"

This time I turn to her. "That's not what happened."

"I thought you couldn't remember what happened?"

"I remember enough. I remember enough to know that I went looking for her."

She just sits there, tear-stained cheeks.

"I wrecked my bike," I continue. "I got hurt pretty bad trying to find her, but she found me first. That's how we wound up here."

Kristie smiles through her tears. "And why not? Route 89 is the only way out of town. Isn't that what you and Ritchie always said?"

"That's what the whole town used to say."

"So, how'd you do it? Strangle her? Maybe hit her over the head with a shovel?"

"That's not what happened."

"How did you kill my sister?" she asks.

"I didn't kill your sister."

"How did you kill my sister!?"

I stare at the soiled floor. "I didn't kill your sister."

"You said you were responsible. How can you be responsible and not—"

"Ritchie showed up."

Instantly, her sobs subside.

"He found out," I whisper.

197

"Found out?" she asks, doubt drifting into the room. Things quiet down. I can hear the rain outside, and I can hear the water trickling into the house, pooling in the dirt. The sounds are peaceful. Even the smells are natural and serene, but we're sitting in an abandoned basement with the corpse of a seventeen year-old girl. Kristie sniffs, wipes her nose on her sleeve and then wipes her eyes with her fingers before looking at me. "Found out what?"

# Twenty Six

## *Yesterday*

Joanne leaps through the broken window, taking the last shards of broken glass with her. I turn back to Ritchie, and his eyes are on her, not me. I know him. He'll go after her if I don't do something. He loves her, but it's not real love. It's possession, and if he feels he's lost her, he'll hurt her. It won't even occur to him what he's done until it's too late.

Ritchie takes a step forward, but I block his path. He's twice my size, but I have to do something. I at least have to try. My face is still bleeding, my hands hamburger, but I know that look in his eyes. He's not about to just let this go.

"She's gone," I say. "It's over."

"Nothin's over," he grumbles.

"Let it go, man."

"You don't tell me what to do," he thunders. "You don't tell me nothin'! You don't—"

"Goddamn it, Ritchie! NO!"

Ritchie looks like he wants to say something, but he stops. His eyes shrink to slits. His body recoils a bit, and he grinds his teeth, one of his eyes unwillingly twitching. "You always gotta—"

"Fuck you!" I shout, the words like sand between my teeth. "Let me ask you something. You think you got what it takes, big guy?"

"You just tryin' to irrigate me?"

"The word you're looking for is 'irritate,' you stupid moron."

He frowns. "I'm just…"

"Well, I'm not, and if you want her, you gotta go through me first."

Ritchie scrunches up his face. "Don't think I won't."

"I love you like a brother, Rich, but this ain't happenin'."

Ritchie wavers, hovering. His eyes are dark, his lips pinched so tightly it's like they're not even there.

"Ritchie?"

And just like that, he responds. His fist comes out of nowhere, cracking me across the jaw and knocking me flat. I hit the floor hard, dizziness consuming me along with enough pain to make me forget about my raw hands. I expect him to start kicking me next, but he's gone, retreating through the foyer and out the front door. He's already trotting down the steps and heading into the knee-deep grass leading toward the barn. There's blood seeping into my mouth, and my jaw feels broken, but Joanne's in trouble, and I'm all she has left.

Ritchie's lost it. His mental capacity for deciphering between reality and fantasy has been deteriorating for some time, but I ignored the signs. I sensed it that day when he took on those guys in the Walmart parking lot and again that day in his bedroom with his dad. He's been slowly slipping away, consumed with the arrogance of his own invincibility, but I figured he'd just implode—maybe mentally breakdown. I figured he'd meltdown and go catatonic. But he didn't. He's become *this*. Joanne has metamorphosed from his crush into his opponent. She's the devil taunting him—punishing him. I doubt if he even sees her as human anymore. I've seen schizophrenia, but this isn't schizophrenia or bipolar disorder or borderline personality. This is something else. When he started that brawl on the baseball field, I saw it plainly in his eyes. It's not giddiness or glee. It's pain.

I start crawling toward the door. There's blood on my tongue, and I feel like crying or sleeping or pretty much anything other than chasing after him, but if I don't do something, Joanne will die. The best I can do is crawl through the room before using a chair to hoist myself to my feet. I make it only a few steps into the kitchen before collapsing with dizziness.

"Come on," I whisper, forcing myself to keep going, forcing myself up again. I'm wavy on my feet, but I manage to stumble from the house while bracing myself with the assistance of the handrail as I make my way down the steps into the tall grass. Suddenly without support, I go tumbling, rolling like a wrecking ball. Gasping, I pick myself up and crawl toward the screams coming from the barn. My arms feel like dead-weights. Everything is running in tear-colored streams. I fumble face first into the dirt, but I pick myself up again and continue forward. A few more feet, and I right myself into a standing position. My legs are rubbery, but they'll hold. They have to hold.

The barn.

I stumble inside, greeted instantly with a scene my mind can't quite wrap itself around. Ritchie has Joanne bent over a bale of hay. He's got one of her arms pinned behind her back, and with his free hand, he's yanking on her belt, trying to get her pants down.

"Get out!" he shouts.

She's sobbing—screaming. Instead of getting out, I stumble his way, scooping a pitchfork from the hay. I know I can't beat him, but I have to try.

I have to.

He lets go and steps toward me, his eyes wild. "What you got? You gonna fight me? You gonna fight Ritchie? You gonna fight Ritchie Hudson?"

Fight him? Not hardly. Using his own words, I'm gonna kill him, skin him, filet him and fuckin' eat him. I level the pitch fork, an overwhelming feeling of hatred filling me like a heavy chill. He was supposed to be in love with her. He was supposed to protect her. But this isn't love. This is possession.

"Come on, Triple A," Ritchie growls as he crouches down. It's the same stance he took when the benches cleared the other night, and that glint in his eye is the same too. "Show me what you got," he hisses.

I swing, but he slaps the pitchfork aside, steps in and swings a sharp fist that brings searing pain and unwanted tears. I fall backward, the pitchfork flying from my grip. I hit the sand and recoil into a defensive position, but Ritchie is already on top of me, kneeing me sharply in the ribs. Again, and again and again until I can't breathe. One more kick to the face, and I see a flash of white, the stench of dirt and dust and decay oddly visceral. I roll over to shield myself, but he's gone, his footsteps falling away. I'm alone. He's gone.

He's gone after her.

The barn door squeaks on its dry hinges, a soft summer breeze drifting into the quiet barn where I'm left lying on the floor. Lifting my face from the dirt, the sun is bleeding through the cracks with sharp beams, dust particles floating listlessly in the thin shafts of light. It's quiet in here—peaceful. Too peaceful. It should be a lazy afternoon, but he's still out there, and so is she.

I get to my feet and make a mad, stumbling dash for the door before tumbling face first into the dirt. I use my arms to swim for the door, spitting sand and blood and hay from my mouth. I use the swinging door to pull myself up, but I only make it a few steps before sinking to my knees, gasping for air. The farmhouse is to my right, the tall grass swaying as if dancing, the sun burning the world around me.

Squinting, I collect myself and again struggle to my feet. I stumble through the tall grass, crawling at times, muddling my way toward the house where I trip on the steps. I crawl along the wooden planks into the living room. Then I crawl to the couch, hoisting myself up, wiping my ruined face on the sleeve of my ruined shirt. It's the same couch she and I made out on. The same couch. That was minutes ago, but it feels like another lifetime.

Joanne.

I can't hear her. I can't hear anything other than the sound of insects outside. I spit another wad of blood and use the couch as balance to get to my feet. Drifting along the wall, I make my way into the kitchen. The cellar door is wide open, and even though it seems quiet down there, there's something evil drifting upward that greets me like a breath of cold air. So, I start down, wobbly on my feet as I brace myself against the loose railing.

Reaching the basement floor, I look around. The door into the coal room is open, and Ritchie's inside, standing still, head bowed, his back to me. And he's not alone. He's hovering over a body. A body that isn't moving. Joanne. She's lying still, her head cocked sharply to the side and a stream of blood running from both her nose and mouth.

"Ritchie," I whisper. "What happened?"

He sniffles, draws a few sharp breaths and clenches his fists. "I was her last love," he mumbles. "Not you." He wipes his eyes. "I loved her last."

"What did you do?" I choke. I can barely stand. "Did you kill her?"

He doesn't answer. He doesn't even turn. He just stands there, a hulk of a man.

"Jesus Christ, Ritchie, you killed her. You fucking killed her?"

Now he turns, his eyes flashing. "And you're going to bury her."

I shake my head, taking a step back. "No way, man. I won't do it."

"You already done it," he says. "You're responsible." Tears are rolling over his cheeks, but he doesn't look sad. He looks angry. He tosses me the shovel, and I react defensively by curling into a ball. The shovel bounces off my shoulder and settles in the sand. I look at the shovel and then the body of the girl lying dead on the floor.

It's happening. It's real.

Just a little while ago I was laughing with Kristie and Joanne and Travis. Two hours later, I was making out with Joanne here in this house. Ten minutes after that and she's dead. She's dead, and my life is ruined.

Ritchie nods toward the shovel lying at my feet. "You bury her," he says gruffly. "That's how we stay brothers."

# Twenty Seven

## Today

Kristie's still crying, but there's not much I can do. It's not like there's anything I can say that will be of any consolation, and there's nothing I can say to make any of it any better. It's a shitty end to a terrible nightmare that I spent twenty years trying to forget, and it was one lousy phone call five days ago that started the bleeding all over again. All those years of counseling, all those years of running—all those years trying to convince myself that I'm not a bad person, and all I can do is sit and stare at the rag-wrapped body that has been rotting in this basement for two decades.

"How could you!" she cries.

I just sit there.

"How could you…"

I don't have answer.

"How did it happen?" Kristie asks. "How did your little party with your good buddy Ritchie go down?"

"I kissed her," I say. "That's all."

"Oh, so you…" Kristie snarls with sarcasm until she suddenly stops and looks up. "What? You did what?"

I shift nervously. "I kissed her."

"You kissed her? Why?"

"I think I might have been in love with her. I don't know. I mean, we had a…we had this moment."

"You think you might have been in love with her?"

"Maybe. I'm not sure. I don't know. I might have been. But when Ritchie saw—"

"I thought you loved me?"

"I was just a kid. I didn't know what I was doing, or what I was feeling."

"And Ritchie saw you?"

"He saw *us*."

Kristie tries to regroup, but I can tell she's struggling.

"Joanne tried to…*pretend* that nothing had happened."

Kristie wipes her eyes and gets to her feet. Makeup streaks her face, smeared like hell. She looks awful, and I feel awful. Coming clean is supposed to be liberating, but it feels sciatic. "Did you kill my sister, Tony?"

I stand up and turn my back. "It doesn't matter anymore."

"It matters to me."

"I buried her."

"Did you kill her?"

"What difference does it make? I'm responsible!"

"How are you responsible? Did you kill my sister?"

"I was responsible."

"Did you kill my sister!?"

"No!" I shout. "I didn't kill your sister. But I *am* responsible."

The room falls silent as we square off, standing opposed, the fight fleeing my body, the tears welling in my eyes. It's not just me, the tears are slipping over her cheeks too. We're both in pretty deep, and it feels awful.

"And then you left town?"

I nod.

"Why? Why didn't you say something? Why didn't you stay?"

"You don't know him. And by that time, I didn't either. Besides, I was already set to go. My bags were packed. I had a ticket and an alibi. It was the perfect murder, and I was the perfect witness."

"Why didn't you say anything?"

"Because he told me to leave town and never come back."

"Or what?"

"Or he'd bury me right there with her."

I can hear her step closer, but she pauses. Then she takes another hesitant step before pausing again.

"Don't forgive me," I say, tears welling in my eyes.

"But…"

"What I did is unforgivable. This whole thing is my fault."

"Even if you didn't kill her?"

"I didn't kill her, but I couldn't stop him either. And I never told anyone, and your sister's been down here for twenty years, because I was too big of a coward to say anything. I buried her, and then I left her here, and I swear to God I forgot about her and you and everything else."

"But you didn't kill her," she whispers, and I guess this is some kind of precious moment where we're supposed to bond as the floodgates of truth open up and embrace us within the arms of angels. But it's not precious. It's prickly and painful, and I hate myself. I did this. Her sister is wrapped in rags, having spent two decades in a basement because of my cowardice.

"You didn't kill her," Kristie repeats.

"If I hadn't kissed her," I say defiantly. I shake my head. "If I had just let her go..."

Jonathan Korbecki

Kristie wraps her arms around me from behind despite my opposition. "You said you loved her."

I shrug. "I was a kid."

"Did you love her more than me?"

"What difference does it make? Really?"

"It matters, because no one else loved her."

"Oh, come on. You loved her."

"Sure, I loved her, but my Dad looked at her like she was defective, and my mom always wanted boys. And all the kids at school made fun of her." She looks at me. "I treated her awful, because I was jealous. She was so much smarter than me. But, yes, I loved her, because she was my sister."

"She knew you loved her."

"She knew I loved her, and I knew she loved you, and that's why I went after you."

I clam up. Joanne had mentioned something just like that, but to hear Kristie say it...

"If you loved her," Kristie continues, "and if she knew it, then at least she had that. At least once. At least for a little while."

"Ritchie loved her."

"Ritchie possessed her."

I turn to her. "He also killed her."

Kristie's face wrinkles, and she starts crying again.

"I'm sorry," I say. "I didn't mean for it to come off so harsh like that."

"I knew she was dead. I knew it from the very first moment. She had taken off, and you followed her." She smiles. "You said you were going to see Ritchie, but I *knew*, and I was confused and frantic, and it was something like two hours later when this weird wave of calm settled over me. And I *knew*." She sniffs. "I just *knew*. I knew she was gone. I couldn't feel her anymore. I couldn't...it's like she wasn't there..."

"I'm so sorry."

"I want him to burn for this."

"He will. I promise."

"You could go to prison."

"I'm every bit as guilty as he is."

She steps up, burying her face against my chest and begins to sob. Again. I wrap my arms around her, rocking her ever so gently, my nose buried in her hair, her breath hot against my neck. When I open my eyes and look up, I suppose I should be surprised by what I see hulking in the shadows blocking the stairs going up, but given my luck over the last week or so, I figure it's just par for the course.

"Why did you come back?" she asks through her tears, her face pressed against my shirt. "I mean, you didn't have to come. You could have said no. And you didn't have to bring me back here." She's sniffing and ruining my shirt. "So, why'd you do it?"

But I'm not really paying attention. Instead, I'm staring destiny in the eye, and destiny's staring back, filling the doorway with that massive frame of his.

205

"To finish it," I answer.

Kristie looks up, but I'm not looking at her. I'm looking over her shoulder into the eyes of the devil himself. He's covered in shadow, but his features are distinct. I'd know that form anywhere. The broad shoulders, the lazy gut, the fists clenched at his side.

She turns, sees him, and backs away. Twenty years later, and it's a big ol' class reunion. The four of us are in the same room for the first time in nearly two decades. For better or for worse, the loose ends of the perfect homicide will be buried where it began, all the pieces quickly falling into place. This is the showdown I was terrified of, but now that it's here, I feel surprisingly little. I should be terrified. I think Ritchie could kill both me and her without losing sleep. The thing is, at this point I think I could do the same to him.

# Twenty Eight

## *Yesterday*

Ritchie looks at me the way I expect he would look at a little brother. His eyes offer comfort and protection along with a careful warning. Everything will be okay so long as I do what I'm told, and so far I've done what I've been told. "You done good," he says in that way he often does when he's feeling proud. It's almost like we're friends again even though I hate him more than I have ever hated anyone ever before.

I look down at the sandy floor. It's hard to tell anyone's buried here. Jo's gone. She's gone unless anyone ever suspects a reason to dig, and there's no reason to suspect anyone ever will, so she's gone.

"Now we can be friends again," Ritchie continues. "You wanna go for ice cream?"

"Ice cream. You want to go for ice cream? Seriously?"

"When it comes to ice cream, I'm always serious." He grins. "I got me a hankering for moose tracks."

"You're unbelievable."

"Think of it as a celebratory parting gift now that you're leavin' town and all."

"I'm not going to squeal."

"Oh, I know you ain't gonna squeal," he answers with a smile. "Turns out that you leavin' town tonight is a lucky coincidence, 'cause the only thing savin' yer skinny ass is the fact that you're already packed and ready to go."

"Are you threatening me?"

"Depends. I was plannin' to—" but he locks up, suddenly pinching one eye shut. He leans over and repeatedly smacks the side of his head with the palm of his hand before crouching down, grinding his teeth.

"How are the headaches, Rich?"

He slaps at his head, a bit of spittle dripping from his lower lip.

"Does it hurt?" I ask. "How's it feel? Does it feel like it's ripping your fucking head apart?"

"It's…fine…" he manages.

"It's fine? That feels good? You mean you're not worried?"

He slaps at the side of his head, over and over, crouching over, spit running from his mouth. Settling down on one knee, he continues to rap the side of his head.

"It's gonna kill you," I sneer.

"I'll kill you first."

"You're not going to kill me," I murmur.

"You don't think so?" he asks through gritted teeth, looking up.

"I *know* so."

"And what makes you so sure?"

"Because I'm the only friend you've got."

He stares at me for a long moment, and I can see the conflict between the left and right hemispheres battling each other, both winning and both losing. One of his eyes even twitches. He clears his throat, hacks up a loogie and spits. "You killed her," he murmurs. "I seen you do it."

"Keep telling yourself that."

"I'll tell whoever I gotta tell if you don't shut your pie hole and leave the way yer supposed to." He winces once or twice, the seizure or headache nearly gone.

"I still have to stop by the house." I say, stalling.

"What for?"

"To pick up my stuff."

"You want cash? I got cash. I got enough cash so you can buy a whole new wardrobe. You don't need to stop by the house."

"It's not about cash. You want my mom asking questions?"

He wavers.

"Because she will. She's expecting me before I go."

He huffs and he puffs, but he finally frowns and agrees with a half-hearted nod.

"Why are you doing this?" I ask.

"Doin' what? I ain't doin' nothin'."

"What about Joanne?"

He grins, and it's that simple, stupid, toothless grin that I learned to trust and later learned to hate. He's grinning at me as if this is just a conversation like any other—maybe an argument over baseball cards. "Joanne's dead," he says. "And if you ever talk, I'll bury Kristie too."

I could say something in retort, but that's Ritchie. He's already said his peace. His mind is made up. He's black and white—like a cartoon robber. There is no in between. Love him or hate him, Ritchie is Ritchie. For better or worse.

Mostly worse.

## *Part II*

Ritchie follows me home, trailing a few paces behind so we won't have to talk. But he's still back there. He's got those awkward, familiar steps. His left leg is a half-inch short, which makes him drag the right foot, leaving a scraping sound like fingernails on a chalkboard. I keep hoping he'll eventually get bored and wander off, but the closer we get to my house, the closer those dragging steps creep. He wants me gone, and he's going to see it through.

We reach my house, and I leave Ritchie standing in the driveway as I crawl through my bedroom window like it's any other night. Mom's left my window open a crack the way she always does so I can sneak in one last time. She's waiting for me out in the living room, her feet in her bunny-slippers, her tattered nightgown. I know this because I can hear the TV laughing like this is funny. She knows tonight is the night I'm leaving, and she's playing 'mom' one last time, pretending I'm not actually going—pretending her 'baby boy' hasn't grown up and isn't flying the coop.

I wash the blood from my face, not that it helps much. I still look a mess. I also look scared, and I feel sick to my stomach. Joanne is dead. She's really dead, and I really buried her, and now I'm really going to leave town without saying goodbye.

I dry off my face and turn out the light.

This is it.


## *Part III*

Almost made it. Almost. I was hoping I'd be able to play it out as I'd originally planned. A suitcase, a hug, a few tears and a heartfelt goodbye with a promise to call. I almost made it, but I guess Ritchie doesn't trust me, because the doorbell rings, which is followed by the sound of her recliner snapping shut and our squeaky front door opening up. Then I hear his voice and his charm followed by Mom's laughter.

"Tony?" she calls. "Ritchie's here!"

I bite my tongue, wishing I was stronger than I feel. "I'll be right there," I answer while camouflaging my voice behind good humor. Not that it matters much. She's not even listening to me. She's talking to *him*.

"I can't believe he's leaving," Ritchie says politely. "He's actually leavin'."

Our walls are paper thin.

"I'm proud of him," she says, and I hear her broken recliner squeak as she sits back down. "You should be too. He's worked awfully hard to get where he is. He's earned it."

"Oh, he done good all right. It just hurts to let him go," Ritchie says, "He's my best friend."

"You're such a sweetheart."

"Yeah, he's a real peach," I mutter under my breath as I close the suitcase and turn out the light in my bedroom. The room goes dark, and I stand there like a lump, looking around for what will likely be the last time. Finally, I turn my back, make my way along the narrow hall and cross through the living room.

"What happened to your face?" Mom snaps, sitting up.

"Don't worry about it," I say. "It was a scrimmage."

"A scrimmage? What's that mean, a scrimmage?"

"It means don't worry about it."

"It means he saved *my* butt for once," Ritchie says with a smile.

"It means I have to go," I say. "The bus is thirty minutes out."

She cranks down the recliner again and stands up in her bunny slippers and worn nightgown. She extends her arms, two tears slipping from her eyes over her cheeks. "I can't believe my baby boy is already moving out."

"It's not like I won't be back, ma."

"It'll be so lonely here without you."

"You'll still have your friends."

She waves me off. "My friends."

"I'll stop by," Ritchie says. "If you need anything, I'll be you surrnigate son."

"Surrogate," I mutter under my breath.

Mom smiles. "I'd like that. Thank you, Ritchie."

Ritchie smiles that broken-tooth smile. "My pleasure."

Mom holds her arms out to me, the folds hanging like swinging water balloons. "You'll call me?" she asks.

"Every week."

She kisses my neck and pats me on the back before pulling away and wiping her eyes. My mom. I didn't think letting go was going to be so hard. She and I have had only each other for so long that I barely remember my life when Dad was a part of it. I'm going to miss her. I'm going to miss this house. I'm going to miss the things I've taken for granted for so long. Her, Kristie, my school—all of it.

Except Ritchie.

Ritchie stands at my side with that dumb grin on his face. By now he's probably convinced himself that I did it. He's probably convinced that he's innocent. After all, he loved Joanne, and I took her from him. He's probably itching to finish me off too as if to avenge the hole in his heart, and yet I have to stand at his side, my own stupid smile on my own stupid face while I tearlessly say goodbye to my mother.

"Call me when you get there," she finally says with a smile.

"I will."

"Let's go," Ritchie says, slapping me on the back. "It's a long walk."

I stop in the doorway and turn back. "Lock the door after us," I say. "And don't stay up too late."

She waves me off. "You're always worryin' after you're old ma. I'll be fine."

She's tearing up, and as a consequence, I'm tearing up too. I'm going to miss her—her and her weird, overburdening, overly concerned, overly messy, overly motherly ways. I want to say something, maybe drop some kind of subtle hint that would break things open and expose what happened, but I don't, because that would put her in danger too, and I already have enough to worry about. After all, if Ritchie is willing to kill me, then he won't stop until he feels threat-free.

"I'll call," I say with a smile.

"I love you."

I swear she's said it a million times, but this is the first time I think I've ever actually heard it. My eyes well as Mom heads back to her chair where she'll kick back, pull the footrest and go back to watching her program. I wonder how long it'll take before she begins to worry. Tomorrow? The next day? Certainly once the news starts reporting on the disappearance of the twin sister of the girlfriend I'm leaving behind.

I say nothing. I just stand there looking at her, wanting to scream.

"We gotta go," Ritchie says, patting me on the back.

Instead of screaming, I pick up my suitcase and head out the door. Ritchie follows, pulling the door shut behind him.

"We'd better get movin'," he murmurs, jarring me from my nostalgic little moment. "Missing that bus would be a bad idea." I don't answer, and we don't talk as we walk through town—so-called best friends. Once we arrive at the bus station, he hangs around, apparently determined to see me off. We don't have much to say, so we just stand there like two strangers, wishing we could get on with it already. Eventually, the headlights of the Greyhound appear over the top of the hill as it heads toward town.

"I'm gonna miss you, bud," Ritchie says, actual sadness in his voice.

"Fuck you, Ritchie."

"It's a nice offer, but I prefer chicks."

"Do I look like I'm joking?" I snap.

"No. But you do look scared."

Ignoring him, I take a step closer, lowering my voice. "I'll keep my end of the bargain. I'll stay away, and I won't talk."

"Good. That'll make things easy for both of us."

"But I swear to God, if you so much as touch Kristie…"

He snickers. "You'll what?"

I stare at him a long moment. "Not even you can dodge bullets."

Ritchie smiles. "Now yer talkin'. My little buddy is finally becoming a man."

"That's a promise."

"Relax. You ain't got nothin' to worry about. I'll keep my word. After all, a man's only as good as his word." He cocks his head. "You believe that, right?"

The bus pulls up, and I look at my 'friend' for the last time. "God saw you do it," I say as the doors open, inviting me to board. "And He's got a long memory. Your day *will* come."

He smiles. "You tryin' to scare me with religion?"

"You're the one always getting on my case for my language."

"Yeah, well, I say a lot of things," Ritchie says. "I talk a lot of shit, but this is still Payton County. It ain't a church. Here I don't gotta be afraid of nothin'."

"How do you figure?"

"Look around. It's my town. *My* town. Here I *am* God."

I say nothing. All I can do is glare at him while wishing the bus would suddenly explode, killing us both.

"I know you hate me," he says. "But I don't hate you, and despite all this, I think I'm actually gonna miss you."

Turning my back, I climb aboard the bus, make my way down the aisle and choose a seat near the back. As the finality sets in, I've never felt so scared and so alone in my whole life. This is it. This is how it ends. I'm actually leaving. With everything that's happened, I'm tucking tail and leaving it all behind. The bus moves forward, and outside, Ritchie lifts his middle finger, that big dumb grin of his on his puffy face.

I just look away.

## Part IV

"Are we there?" a man asks from three seats ahead of mine. "I thought I felt us stop." I can see the back of his bald head turning as he looks as his wife.

"Go back to sleep," she answers. "We've got a long way to go."

A long way to go.

Damn right. Route 89 runs forever. It leads all the way to the edge of the earth and beyond. At least that's what we used to say. The last outpost the Greyhound will pass by on the way out of Payton is the old Johnson farm, and as I look out my window, the old farm is coming up on the right now. There are no lights inside. The house is quiet and dark—blending with the shadows while secrets lie inside. A casual observer would disregard the place as just an abandoned farm, and one might wonder why it hasn't been torn down. Not that any of the other passengers seem all that interested, and not that there are a lot of other passengers. I count five. And none of them are familiar. They're tourists along for the ride, passing through a small town on the brink of extinction, yet they're witnesses to the demise of a few hundred ordinary lives.

Now the farm is directly out my window, and I feel like crying. Joanne's in there. She's cold and alone. It was only hours ago that she was alive and eager—excited. It was such a beautiful day, a happy day, and this is how it ends.

Thump, thump, thump, thump.

I lean my head against the cool glass of the bus window. The cracks in the road beneath the tires sing a song I know all too well, and it's the familiarity that I find soothing. I shift to get comfortable and wrap myself within my own warmth.

Thump, thump, thump, thump.

The voices around me aren't friendly. They sound bored and uncomfortable. The people are making conversation if only to pass the time. We're trapped together on a steel arc while counting down the moments until we can go our separate ways. Closing my eyes, I filter the strangers out, replacing the monotone chatter with voices from my past. *You be careful*, Mom warns from the back of my mind. *I love you*, Kristie giggles. *Kiss my grits*, Ritchie laughs.

Recoiling, I dissolve into my mind until there's nothing but a shell occupying space on this ripped seat. The Johnson farm passes by, its broken windows looking like dark eyes, the front door wide open just like a mouth.

# Twenty Nine

## Today

Kristie is crying again, but this time there's fear in her sound. I guess I should be scared too, but something in me snapped the moment I looked up and found Ritchie hulking in the doorway. I should have seen this coming. I should also be afraid, but I'm not.

"You really are stupid," Ritchie growls. "This is how you tell her? You bring her here and show her? You dig up the body of her dead sister and show it to her?" He chuckles. "Great plan, genius. I remember you bein' smarter'n that." Stepping into the light, his face is creased with age, but he has the exact same look he had the last time we were down here in this exact same spot. "Guess what?" he continues. "There's no one around to hear her scream, and there's no one to stop me from doin' what I'm about to do."

"Why didn't you just kill me then?" I ask. "If this was your plan all along."

He chuckles. "Like I said, I remember you bein' smarter'n that." He takes another step closer.

"I'm a slow learner."

"You and Joanne disappeared on the same day. That made them go lookin' for you. They thought maybe you'd eloped, or maybe you even had somethin' to do with it. Nobody ever even thought to question me. I just pleaded arrogant while you went off to your big school on your big scholarship, and that was that."

"Ignorant," I mumble.

"I was worried for awhile until I figured out how much you were afraid of me."

"So, now what?" I ask. "Are you're going to kill us?"

He shrugs. "Haven't decided yet, but you gotta admit, it would certainly tie things off neat and clean." He chuckles—mostly to himself. "Of course, what kind of man would that make me? You're my best friend, and you know how much stock I put in friendship."

I just glare.

"I always wanted us to be equals," Ritchie continues. "Neighbors, the backyard barbecues—the whole bit."

My heart seizes. "You wouldn't."

He grins. "I might."

"Ritchie, don't."

"I already killed my girlfriend, and I was thinkin' maybe you might even things up."

"If you touch her, I swear to God I'll—"

"You ain't gonna do nothin', except what I say." He looks around the room. "I told you not to come back, but you did. Then you brung her here, because you can't keep that big fuckin' trap of yours shut."

"Ritchie…please…"

"We can do this the easy way, or we can do it the *real* easy way. All I gotta do is stage a murder-suicide, and they'll think you done it. Both Joanne *and* Kristie. I'll show up at your funeral and say what a great guy you were. I'll even add that I don't think it's fair that they labeled you a killer. After all, it musta been a crime of passion or somethin' like that."

"No one will believe it," I argue.

"You don't think so? I think everyone'll believe it. Think about it. You two disappearing at the same time, then you coming back twenty years later because Kristie started askin' questions? So you killed her too before turning the gun on yourself. It's not even one of them head-scratchers. It's reality TV."

Ritchie seems to have actually thought this through, and apparently, I'm predictable enough to do exactly what he knew I would. Leaning over, I pick up the shovel, take a step back and hand it to Kristie. It's just a shovel, but something is better than nothing, and Ritchie's right; I brought her here. Kristie doesn't deserve this. She didn't deserve to lose her sister, and she doesn't deserve to lose her life in this basement. I'm no hero, and I'm not tough, but I sure as hell won't make it easy for him.

"When he goes after me," I say without taking my eyes from Ritchie, "hit him with the shovel as hard as you can."

"What?" she asks, terrified.

"Then run," I say. "Lock the car doors, floor it, and don't stop until you reach the police station. Drive through the front door if you have to, but don't stop for anything. Red lights or anything."

Ritchie smiles, but there's hesitation in his response. "What you gonna do, Triple A?"

"Whatever I have to."

"She won't make it."

Thunder rumbles somewhere outside.

"She'll make it," I say confidently. "By the time you're done with me, she'll be halfway back to town." I smile. "I'm going to Hell, but you're going to prison."

"We can do this together," Kristie whimpers—her voice shaking.

"We *are* doing this together," I snap. "This is the plan."

Ritchie's eyes are going from me to her—the smile on his face replaced with concern. He's trying to sort things out, planning to charge, but not quite sure how or when. She and I are standing on the opposite side of the hole Joanne's resting in, and he's not nimble enough to jump over it. He doesn't have a straight shot at either of us.

"He's going to kill you," she whimpers.

"I'm responsible for Joanne's death," I say. "This is my chance to make it right."

"Oh, boo hoo," Ritchie growls. "Are you still crying over that dumb whore? I did you both a favor. I caught her and Tony makin' out upstairs the day I done her."

I smile. "You're panicking, Rich. I know that tone. You're panicking because you know you're going to get caught. You know you're going to lose."

Thunder cracks outside. Rain splashes up against the dirty basement window, water running like beads along the inside of the walls down here.

"You dumb fuck!" Ritchie shouts, his voice echoing through the room. "I told you not to come back! No one had to know!"

I'm glaring at him through slits, daring—almost wishing for him to charge me and get it over with. "This has nothing to do with me," I growl. "This is for Joanne."

Ritchie just glares.

"It's over," I grumble.

"I beg to differ," he sneers. "Things are just gettin' interesting." But something's wrong. Suddenly, his left eye twitches, and he closes it tightly, doubling over as he smacks the side of his head.

The headaches.

Kristie takes a step back while I take a hesitant step forward. Suddenly, I understand, and the simplicity of it all is so obvious that I'm surprised I never saw it before. They're not headaches. They're a reaction to conflicting motivations. It's that broken mind of his, wires mixed up and crossing over, the dilemma between right and wrong—kind of like the good bad words and the bad bad words. It's the little boy versus the man he never wanted to grow into that is momentarily paralyzing him and momentarily opening a window for us.

Lightning flashes, lighting the basement as thunder blasts the house. Reacting rather than waiting, I leap the hole. "Now!" I shout as I hit Ritchie head on, the two of us tumbling to the dirt floor. Kristie starts screaming. I start punching, but Ritchie outweighs me two to one, and it doesn't take much of an effort to overpower me.

"Now!" I shout again.

Kristie is still shrieking when she swings the shovel. Her swing is clumsy, and the shovel smashes me in the face, sending white stars to my eyes and bringing more frantic screams of terror.

"Run!" I manage through a stream of blood running from my nose into my mouth. Ritchie reaches out and trips her as she tries to slip past, sending her sprawling. She scrambles to her feet, still moaning with terror, and she's out the door, stumbling up the stairs. Ritchie returns to me and delivers a haymaker that steals my wind before landing another blow that opens a fresh wound on my other cheek. But I'm not done yet, and I swing back, managing to connect with some part of him that feels like bone. I can't tell what I hit since my eyes are filling with blood soaked tears, but I hear him 'ooof', and I feel his body relax. I swing again, this time missing. Something hard strikes me across the chin causing my head to whip painfully to the side. Another sharp crack sends me to a white world where there are no dreams.

## Part II

Kristie can't quite get her footing as she races up the stairs. She's frantic and sloppy— clumsily tripping over her own feet. Tears race along her cheeks, cutting through her makeup. Throwing herself up the last three stairs, she rolls onto the kitchen floor into a pool of rainwater where she's greeted by a bright burst of lightning that causes her to squint. Water is running along the walls in a sheet of clear liquid glass that spreads like tendrils across the floor. She splashes through the puddle as she crawls through the kitchen into the living room.

"Kristie!" Ritchie bellows from below. "Where you at? I'm comin' for ya!"

She tries getting to her feet only to slip on the wet floor and crash forward, the oxygen ripped from her lungs. She can't seem to get enough air as she coughs into the puddle she's laying in.

Pounding footfalls are climbing toward her. "I can hear you, sweetheart!" Ritchie shouts. "Come to Daddy."

She tries to stand but can't, so she scampers on all fours, pushing through the screen door onto the porch. The boards beneath her whine under the strain and threaten to give, but she rolls to the edge where she swings her legs over the side and drops to the ground. No stumbling this time. No falling.

The rain is coming down in torrents, immediately soaking her to the core. It's raining so hard that her car looks a million miles away. She begins stumbling through the tall grass, trips over an old stump and tumbles face first into the mud. Crawling again, hand over hand, she's sobbing, her tears mixing with the rain.

"Kristie!" Ritchie bellows, this time from the front porch. He leaps and hits the ground running. "Where you at?"

Terrified, she scrambles to her feet and races forward, charging head first into the side of her car. The impact brings a flash of white light and sends her tumbling backward, but she's already pushing herself up again and groping for the handle. Pulling the door open, she crawls into the front seat. Ritchie is charging with powerful strides. She reaches out into the rain, fumbling for the door handle, finds it, and yanks, pulling the door shut. Her trembling hand smacks the automatic lock just as Ritchie crashes against the side of the car, the whites of his eyes bloodshot with rage as he pounds on the glass.

Fumbling through her pocket, she finds her keys and promptly drops them on the floor. Ritchie yanks on the handle before balling a fist and striking the window. The glass holds, and he howls in pain. "Open the fuckin' door!"

Kristie reaches between her feet, her fingers searching for the keys. She finds them, her trembling fingers sliding the right one into the ignition, the idiot lights lighting up the inside of the car.

"No!" he shouts. He looks toward his own truck before turning back to her. Snarling one last time, he balls his fist before turning away and breaking into a run for his pickup.

Peering through the water-streaked glass, she casts one last look toward the house. Joanne and Tony are in there, both in the basement, both presumably dead. She turns the key—firing up the engine—drops into reverse and slams on the gas while silently promising that she'll come back.

## Part III

It's quiet down here. Too quiet. The only sound is that of the water trickling along the walls and pooling on the floor. I open my good eye and look around. Joanne's body still rests half in and half out of the hole. There are scattered footprints all over the sandy floor, but there's no sign of either Ritchie or Kristie, which means they're not down here. They're out there.

I warily stumble to my feet and limp through the room to the stairs where I reach out and grab for the hand railing. I yank myself upward, groaning as I go. I limp my way through the kitchen and into the living room where the couch Joanne and I made out twenty years ago rests against the wall. I look beyond the screen door into the yard where Ritchie is racing through the rain toward Kristie's car.

Hopefully, she's locked herself safely inside. Hopefully, she'll be able to get out of the driveway without getting stuck in the mud. Hopefully, she'll get away. But I'm not so naïve as to simply hope for the best, so I limp down the steps into the tall grass, the rain instantly melting my clothing to my body. My legs are rubbery. I can barely stand, and as I weave my way through the wet grass, I realize there's nothing I can do to help her. At least not from here. I have only one play, and it's a gamble at best.

## Part IV

The tires throw mud up on the windows as the car fishtails backward along the overgrown driveway. Kristie turns the wheel, and stomps on the brakes, bringing the car to a stop, the headlights cutting through the downpour where she sits idling in the middle of the road.

Ritchie is climbing into his truck. He pulls the door shut and flips on the blinding head beams, the yellow eyes cutting through the rain. The engine of his big F350 roars to life, and the tires spin, propelling the truck forward. He races through the mud, the fearsome front end a monster bearing down on her.

She throws the car into drive and mashes the gas pedal to the floor. Ritchie's truck careens into the road, managing to clip her rear bumper and send the car skidding slightly to the side. She recovers, points the car toward town and bolts forward into the storm. In her rearview mirror, Ritchie's headlights are already drawing closer. Her car is all over the road, the nearly bald tires threatening to hydroplane.

Lightning flashes overhead as she tears over the hill.

*Don't stop until you reach the police station,* Tony's voice echoes in her mind. *Drive through the front door if you have to, but don't stop for anything. Red lights or anything...*

Her wipers are on high but of hardly any use. She can't see anything. Hydroplaning is a real concern, but more than that, she could drive right off the road without even knowing until it's already too late. It's raining too hard. And once Ritchie catches her, it's over. No more games. No more talk. She has to make it to town. If she can make it to town, maybe he'll back off. Especially if there are other people around. He'd have to kill her in public...

Her car weaves to the side, skating on water, but she's careful not to over-compensate, careful to bring the vehicle back under control. The speedometer inches over seventy, but that's as far as she dares to push it.

Ritchie is drawing closer, his 4x4 plowing through the water. His high beams are cutting through the rain, growing larger and more menacing. He's racing closer as if she's sitting still. Keeping one hand and one eye on the wheel, she reaches across the passenger seat to the glove-box. Ripping it down, she reaches inside and grabs for her phone. She thumbs 9-1-1 and presses 'send' just as her car is struck from behind, lurching forward. Checking her rearview again, Ritchie's truck is closing in for a second strike.

Ring.

She tightens her grip on the wheel, bracing for impact. He rams her sharply, her car threatening to spin out of control. Dropping the phone, she puts both hands on the wheel and straightens out. Ritchie backs off, the yellow eyes of his rig flaring in her rearview mirror. Her hand searches the floor for the phone, fumbling around until she finds it. Thunder rumbles overhead, clouds tumbling over one another. She can barely make out the road through the torrential rain.

"911 emergency," an operator says through the tiny earpiece.

"Hello?"

"911. What's your emergency?"

"Hello? Can you hear me?"

"Yes, ma'am. What's your emergency?"

"There's this guy who's chasing me!" she screams. "He's trying to run me off the road!"

"Can you give me your location? Your name?"

"Kristine Lambert. I'm on Route 89 heading southbound into town. He killed my sister, and now he's after me!"

This time there's urgency in the voice. "Someone's trying to kill you?"

Ritchie's truck smacks her from behind again, but it's a straight-on shot and the blow only propels her forward. Up ahead she can see the dim glow of Payton drawing closer.

"Ma'am?"

"Ritchie Hudson!" she screams. "He's trying to kill me!"

The two vehicles cut through the rain like razors. The headlights in her rearview are drawing closer again, and they're coming on fast.

A stoplight is up ahead, the light turning yellow.

*Don't stop for anything. Red lights or anything...*

"Oh, my god!" Kristie shouts into the phone. "I'm going through!"

"Ma'am?"

Kristie mashes the gas, pulling ahead of Ritchie's front bumper. The light turns red and cars begin moving forward through the intersection. Screaming, she keeps her foot on the gas, the 911 operator shouting through the phone. The cars are passing back and forth in front of her, entirely oblivious to the approaching vehicles moving too fast to stop.

Barreling through the intersection, horns blare, and cars skid sideways, whipping out of her way. Even so, Kristie feels her bumper clip the rear bumper of one car and the front bumper of another as she sails between them. The impact sends both cars spinning, her own car slowed slightly as she streaks through the intersection, Ritchie close behind.

A bolt of lightning strikes a tree as she races by, the tree bursting into flame—a huge branch collapsing onto a power line and sending a shower of sparks raining down on top of her. The branch bounces in the road behind them both, the power in the homes on the right side of the road blinking out.

"Ma'am?" the operator calls. "Are you there?" Her voice sounds far away.

"I'm heading toward the police station!" she shouts.

A sharp corner is coming up, but she can't slow down or he'll punch her backend and send her spinning. The turn is sharp. Too sharp. She won't make it. She's going to—

"Help me!" she screams.

"Ma'am? Where are you?"

Kristie tosses the phone into the seat beside her and takes hold of the wheel with both hands, her foot poised over the brake pedal.

*This is it. This is it. This is it.*

The curb races at her.
*Three...*
The turn looks too sharp. Way too sharp.
*Two...*
She'll never make it. She's going over. She's—
*One...*
Biting down, she stomps the brake and jerks the wheel to the left. The car goes sideways, the headlights of Ritchie's truck bearing down on her. Her foot goes from the brake to the gas and the car finds purchase, yanking her forward. Ritchie's truck lurches as he tries the sharp turn, the Ford tilting to the side, running off the road where the tires spin in the wet grass. The engine growls, the tires chewing up the manicured lawn and spitting it out as he charges forward.

The police station is close. She can see the lights. She can make it. She *has* to make it. Checking her mirrors, the truck has found its four feet and is quickly closing the distance. Ritchie must know that this is it. He must. But he's not giving up. He just keeps coming.

Kristie is sobbing as she pushes the pedal to the floor. Forty, fifty, sixty miles per hour. The truck is still closing in, the headlights blinding in her mirror. There's another sharp turn coming up, but she has no intention of trying to navigate it. The police station is straight ahead. Across the parking lot, over the grass and up the front steps. She'll drive right through the front door if she has to. Just like Tony said.

She floors it, leaping the curb, bending the front axle, the car bouncing uncontrollably as she barrels through the parking lot, narrowly missing some of the parked cars, skidding against the sides of others. She's screaming as her car hurdles another curb, the front wheels twisting inward, the nose of the Grand Am digging into the lawn, the car's back end whipping around. The big eyes of Ritchie's truck race at her, and she shrieks, bracing for impact. When it happens, she's thrown against the seatbelt, the side of her car caving in—pinching her against the center consol. Ritchie continues to push her forward, the grill of his truck growling and hissing just inches from her face through the blown-out driver's side window. His truck pushes her car sideways over the lawn and then over the edge of the next curb, up the front steps and—

*Drive through the front door if you have to, but don't stop for anything...*

—through the front door, glass exploding around her. People leap from their desks, her broken car sliding over marble flooring under fluorescent lights. Desks splinter into jagged pieces, her car turned sideways as the truck pushes her deeper into the building. The fluorescents explode overhead, showering the two vehicles in sparks. Three tons of metal slide into the police station on a demonic path.

Then everything stops.

Everything goes quiet.

Both vehicles come to a rest, both engines dead. Emergency lights are swinging from the ceiling, blinking on and off, casting shadows around the destroyed room.

She's covered in blood, frozen in shock. Outside, it's still storming, the rain cascading off the roof and running into the building through the gaping hole her car had made.

## Part V

Soaking wet, bruised and bleeding, I open my eyes. Everything's gone silent. Even the rain has stopped. Then I look around and realize that it actually hasn't. We're just not outside anymore. There's a roof overhead, lights swinging back and forth, casting broken light across the interior of what looks something like a police station. Slowly pushing myself into a sitting position, the pain is like spikes being driven through my left leg. Grimacing, I pause to catch my breath, surprised that I survived.

It's eerily quiet. So quiet that I can hear the rainwater dripping from my hair and the sounds of someone softly sobbing not far away. There's a squeak followed by a metallic groan as the truck's cabin door swings open. Then his huge frame climbs out, his back to me.

This isn't over.

I look around, searching for a weapon—a shovel, a rake, a club, anything. Then my eyes stop. There's a rusty old 12 gauge double barrel lying in a pool of bloody rainwater right here with me in the bed of Ritchie's truck.

## Part VI

Kristie wriggles from where she's pinned under her steering wheel, the driver's side door crushed up against her. She's bleeding. She can taste it, and something feels terribly wrong.

It's quiet now.

A woman approaches, her heels clicking on the marble floor. She's not a cop. At least she's not dressed like one. She's wearing office attire, a runner in her pantyhose. She peers through the cracked windshield of Kristie's car. "Ma'am? Are you okay?"

"He's trying…" she gasps, unable to draw enough air. "…trying to kill me."

Ritchie kicks open his door, his leg snaking out. Shards of glass crunch beneath his weight as he stands. He looks pissed. A deep-seated frown ruins his face as he straightens before hobbling a step closer, a handgun in his hand trembling at his side.

"He's trying to kill me," Kristie repeats, her voice weak.

The woman turns, sees Ritchie and shrieks, stumbling backward before tripping—tumbling to the floor. She starts kicking, trying to back away, her heels useless on the waxed floors. Yet she keeps kicking, her hands opening up and leaving two trails of red behind her as she fishes through the sea of glass.

"Hands up, Hudson!" someone shouts—an officer. He's on one knee, a bad gash on his forehead spilling blood into one eye.

Ritchie limps forward. The lights overhead continue to swing back and forth, blinking and casting shadows.

"Oh, my god…" Kristie wheezes. "Help me…"

"Drop it!" the officer yells. "Now!"

"She killed her sister!" Ritchie thunders. "She killed Joanne Lambert! Her and Tony Abbott. They both done her together!"

"Put the weapon down!" the bloody officer shouts.

"Shoot him…" Kristie manages. "Shoot him…"

Ritchie limps her way, the pistol hanging at his side. "But I brung her to you. I brung you the killer."

"Drop it!" another officer shouts.

Ritchie looks up, his eyes crazed. He's panting, his hand twitching at his side. "She killed her sister!" he growls. His eyes go from the officers to Kristie. There's nothing inside. No feeling or sympathy. Only entitlement. He *expects* to be exonerated for everything that's happened. Not because he's innocent, but because he's Ritchie Hudson—the hometown hero that everyone loves. He doesn't realize that it's over. He doesn't realize that it's *been* over. To him it's like high school never ended, and he's still inches away from completing some kind of masterpiece that will somehow enshrine him. He doesn't understand that his legacy is nothing more than a signed game jersey hanging on the back wall of the only tavern here in town. The days on the pitching mound, the days down by the Beaver, the memories and the cheers are all behind him. All that's left is a half-forgotten ghost of a man, and that ghost is standing in broken glass and clutching a Beretta, a scowl on his face.

"She ruined my life," Ritchie says. He's panting as he looks around. Then he zeroes in, his eyes going from light to dark. "So she dies first." He jerks his wrist, raising the pistol.

There's a thunderous crack as a gun goes off.

## Part VII

"Shoot him…" Kristie manages. "Shoot him…" Her voice is raspy and strained.

Ritchie limps her way, the pistol dangling from his hand at his side. "But I brung her to you. I brung you the killer!"

"Drop it!" another officer shouts.

"She killed her sister!"

223

My shoulder is out of whack, and my left leg feels on fire—my jeans soaked with blood. But I'm still here, and as long as I'm breathing, I will do whatever I can to end this. Clumsily slipping out of the bed of Ritchie's truck, I step gingerly, my bad leg threatening to buckle. Broken glass is sprinkled on the floor like diamonds. There's too much to avoid, so I limp along the best I can while trying to sneak up on the turned back of who was once my best friend.

"She ruined my life," Ritchie says.

I lift the shotgun waist high and lock the hammer.

"So she dies first," he says, jerking his wrist, raising the pistol.

I close my eyes and squeeze the trigger.

## Part VIII

Ritchie stumbles forward like he'd been shoved from behind. Then he squares up, planting his feet solidly on the floor to keep from tumbling. The gun he's holding slips to his waist, his hand swinging loosely back and forth. He starts sucking wind, his chest heaving. He tries to lift the pistol, but it only rises a few inches before settling back at his side. He stumbles forward a few more steps toward her ruined car, and through the cracked glass of her Pontiac, Kristie continues to tug frantically against her seatbelt.

"Drop the gun!" one of the cops shout, but they're not shouting at Ritchie. They're looking at me.

"I'm putting it down," I answer, kneeling down and setting the shotgun on the floor before raising my hands up over my head.

Ritchie is gasping, but he manages to remain on his feet, his massive frame teetering ever so slightly.

Kristie tugs at her seatbelt one last time, and it finally comes free. She lunges at the window, trying to crawl through the broken window, her eyes flashing, but she's still pinched beneath the steering wheel. "He killed my sister," she shrieks, her voice raspy. "He killed her…"

Ritchie is wavering unsteadily on his feet. "Someone shot me," he mumbles. "Who…" He turns around, his eyes dancing. He's looking—searching, a string of blood stretching from his lip to his chin. His face has gone pale, but when he finds me, he relaxes. Then he grins, that stupid ass smile of his spreading across his stupid ass face and into his eyes. Not just any grin, but that famous Ritchie grin of old. I see the man-child I knew as a boy. "Damn, man," he says, spitting a wad of dark red blood. "You do that?"

I say nothing. I just glare at him.

"How'd you get here so fast?"

I just stare.

Ritchie looks around. "What'd you do? Hitch a ride in the back of my truck?"

I continue to glare.

"That had to be one helluva ride." He snorts, and clears his throat, gagging as he hacks up a wad of bloody phlegm before spitting. "Shot me in the back."

"Put the gun down, Hudson!" one the officers shout.

Ritchie winces, gritting his teeth. "I can't believe you…I can't believe you really done it." He winces again and drops the gun. It clatters uselessly on the tile floor. He crouches down, shuffling into a sitting position. The pistol is inches from his hand, but he's not interested in it anymore. Instead, he's looking at the shotgun I'd set on the floor. "Is that my dad's gun?"

I say nothing.

"That damn thing…" He just stares at it, his face wrinkling slightly as if he'd tasted something sour. "The fucker keeled over," he mutters, clearing his throat. He snorts, hacks up, and spits another wad of thick blood that slaps the floor. "'Bout ten years back." He licks his lips. "I remember when me and him would go hunting," he whispers, grimacing. He breathes heavily for a few seconds, his eyes tired. "I'm glad…" he says softly, blood dipping from his mouth onto shirt. "I'm glad it was you that done it, and not one of them…"

Now I feel something. Anger. Anger at him for ruining what had been the perfect friendship. Anger at him for ruining what should have been the perfect childhood. Anger at him for ruining my life and ending Joanne's. After everything that's happened, how dare he make me feel something? For him or anyone else. How dare he…

He looks at his bloody palms before lifting his eyes to me. Then he grins again, which is irritating enough until I realize why he's doing it. This is his moment—one last time in the spotlight. He'll make the local headlines tomorrow morning, thereby inscribing himself in the history pages of a small town teetering on the brink of extinction.

"You're going to jail, Rich," I say, but tears are welling in my eyes anyway. I can't tell if they're tears of pain, relief or anger. "For the murder of Joanne Lambert."

He chuckles. "The hell I am." He sucks in a deep breath before settling onto his back, his chest heaving as he struggles to draw air. "Kiss my grits, Triple A." He clenches his hands into fists, grinding his teeth, groaning softly. "You don't tell me nothin'."

Presently, his fists open up, his fingers relax, and his breathing stops.

Kristie looks at me through the spider web windshield before burying her face against the steering wheel. The lights overhead continue to swing lazily back and forth, and outside lightning continues to flash as the rain continues to fall. There are cops everywhere. One is kneeling. Two are standing. All are holding guns, and all guns are trained on the deceased body of Ritchie Hudson.

225

## *Part IX*

I continue to kneel, my hands locked behind my head. Around me, some are standing, some are kneeling, some are crying. Guns remain pointed, people whispering, people sobbing. The rain continues to fall beyond the gaping hole over my shoulder, thunder rumbling from far away like a distant warning.

I wonder what she's thinking. Will she ever be able to forgive me? I wonder who she loves, or if she loves anyone at all. After everything that's happened, and after all we've both lost, I figure she probably feels more hate than love, though even now as she sits pinched behind the steering wheel of her ruined car, blood running from her nose, her hair plastered to her forehead, she's suddenly the most beautiful thing I have ever seen.

It's over. The tears run over my cheeks. I smile, but it's not for her. It's for me.

The weird thing is, she's smiling back.

## Payton Hidden Away

S amuel and Ken keep kicking. I do all I can to defend myself, but there's two of them, and they're both bigger than me. I'm breathing dirt in through my nose and mouth, and it's caking the back of my throat like mud, so I curl up and close my eyes, wishing they'd just leave me alone. I didn't do anything. Not to them anyway. Mrs. Clymer gave us all the same assignment. I just did what she told us to. I must've gotten all the answers right, and they must've gotten 'em all wrong, 'cuz otherwise they wouldn't be so mad.

I retreat to my safe place—that quiet space I think about at night when I hide from the monsters that lurk in the shadows. In my safe place, I'm beside a brook, and all the trees are green, and the stream is cold and clear like glass with little minnows hovering over colored pebbles hiding in the sand. But the kicking and the laughing doesn't stop, and it hurts, and I can't stay in my safe place. I don't want to cry, but I'm scared, and they're bigger than me, and—

Then the kicking stops.

The laughing stops.

The hurting stops too.

I look up to see Samuel and Ken fighting this other kid. The other kid's all red-faced and chubby, but he's big too, and eventually he hits Samuel smack dab in the face, and Samuel stumbles backward. He even starts to cry when blood starts spurting from his nose. And then the red-faced kid looks at Ken, and Ken freaks out and runs away. Samuel gets up and runs away too. The red-faced kid glares after them for awhile, his fists balled at his sides, before he turns to me, this big angry frown on his face. "You okay?" he asks.

I'm still crying.

"Are you crying?"

I shake my head.

"What are you, a big baby or somethin'?"

I shake my head again. I don't want him to think I'm a crybaby. I want him to think I'm cool. I want him to like me. He just beat up two other kids, which makes him the toughest kid ever.

"Come on," he says, offering his hand. "Get up."

I reach out, and he pulls me to my feet. I wipe my eyes on my sleeve.

"Who were those guys?"

I shrug.

"They're assholes," he says all tough like, and I realize that this kid must be cool. He swears, and kids that swear aren't afraid of anything. "What's yer name?" he asks.

"Anthony," I answer.

"Anthony? You go by Anthony?"

"Yeah."

"Anthony what?"

"Anthony Alexander Abbott."

The kid scrunches his face. "All your names start with 'A.'"

"I guess so."

"You like baseball?"

I shrug. "It's okay."

"I'm gonna play in the pros one day."

"That's cool," I say even though I kinda doubt he'll make it. He's too fat. He's studying me. "You got a best friend?"

I shake my head.

"You wanna be my best friend?"

I shrug. "I don't know. I mean it doesn't really work like that."

"Why not?"

I think about it for a second, but I can't come up with a good answer. Maybe there aren't any rules that determine how one goes about getting a best friend. "I don't even know your name."

"Ritchie."

I just stand there.

"So?" Ritchie asks.

"So what?"

"So, you wanna be my best friend?"

"I guess."

"Cool. So, why were those kids picking on you?"

I shrug. "Maybe 'cuz I get good grades."

"You know what you say to assholes like that?" He grins, and it's a big, weird, toothless grin. "You say 'kiss my grits.'"

I frown. "What's that mean?"

He shrugs. "I dunno. My dad taught me." Ritchie turns away, steps up on the curb and starts tight roping the razor's edge, his arms out to balance him like wings. The sun is over his shoulder, making him look just like an angel. He walks along the curb, the sunlight bleeding through the trees and sprinkling him a weird halo-like glow. He continues to walk the line, one foot after the other, his arms outstretched to keep him from tumbling.

"Your dad?" I ask.

"Yeah." Ritchie nods as he goes. "He's the best dad in the whole world."